FEMI KAYODE grew up in Lagos, Nigeria. He studied Clinical Psychology at the University of Ibadan and has worked in advertising over the last two decades. He was a Packard Fellow in Film and Media at the University of Southern California and a Gates-Packard Fellow in International Health at the University of Washington, Seattle. His writing credits include several award winning work for the stage and screen. He has an MA in Creative Writing – Crime Fiction at the University of East Anglia, where *Lightseekers* won the Little, Brown/UEA Crime Fiction Award. He lives in Namibia with his family.

LIGHT SEEKERS

FEMI KAYODE

RAVEN BOOKS
LONDON • OXFORD • NEW YORK • NEW DELHI • SYDNEY

RAVEN BOOKS
Bloomsbury Publishing Plc
50 Bedford Square, London, WC1B 3DP, UK
29 Earlsfort Terrace, Dublin 2, Ireland

BLOOMSBURY, RAVEN BOOKS and the Raven Books logo are
trademarks of Bloomsbury Publishing Plc

First published in Great Britain 2021
This edition published 2022

A catalogue record for this book is available from the British Library

ISBN: HB: 978-1-5266-1759-0; TPB: 978-1-5266-1760-6;
PB: 978-1-5266-1757-6; Waterstones Exclusive edition 978-1-5266-5771-8;
eBook: 978-1-5266-1756-9; ePDF: 978-1-5266-4310-0

2 4 6 8 10 9 7 5 3 1

Typeset by Integra Software Services Pvt. Ltd.
Printed and bound in Great Britain by CPI Group (UK) Ltd, Croydon CR0 4YY

To find out more about our authors and books visit www.bloomsbury.com
and sign up for our newsletters

For my family
and
the friends who became a part of it

SOURCE

The October sun is as hot as the blood of the angry mob.

John Paul follows the crowd as they chant and push the three young men. They've been stripped naked, their scrotums shrunken from fear as the beatings result in wounds that will never become scars. Sticks. Stones. Bricks. Iron. Bones break, blood flows. Tearing flesh draws short-lived screams from tired lungs. The men fall but are swiftly pulled up and dragged through the streets, towards a place no one picked out, but everyone seems to know.

It rained the day before, making the red earth muddy in several places. When the young men fall here, they're kicked further into the ground; their blood mixing with sludge. By the time tyres are thrown over their heads like oversized necklaces, and the smell of petrol wafts so strong that some in the crowd cover their noses, madness has staked its claim on what is left of the day.

The strike of a match births flame as a brick crushes the skull of one of the men, leaking brain matter and life, so he doesn't howl and writhe like the other two, when fire starts to lick their skin and hair.

The phone thrums in John Paul's hand. The battery indicator flashes red. He lowers the smartphone and looks around. He's not the only one bearing digital witness to the execution in progress. He considers using the cell phone he had taken off one of the burning men before the mob

1

pounced, but the irony wouldn't be worth it. It's over anyway. Time to go.

As John Paul walks away, I follow him in the shadows, unable to unsee the nightmare he created behind us.

And because he doesn't look back, neither can I.

ACT ONE

*light reflects in several directions when
it bounces off a rough barrier*

THE WHY, NOT THE WHAT

Unless I'm mistaken, a riot is about to break out in the departure lounge of the Lagos Domestic Airport.

'Someone should at least tell us what's going on!' an irate passenger barks into the face of an unruffled airline staff member, spraying her with spit.

Good luck with that, I think from where I sit with my meat pie and Coca-Cola. I'm at a table in the Mr Biggs's restaurant opposite the 9ja Air check-in counter, a position I carefully chose so I won't be left behind when the delayed airplane finally decides to fly to Port Harcourt.

'Sir, the flight is delayed,' the staff person repeats. 'I've told you –'

'What's delaying it?'

'I can't answer that, sir. If you'll be patient –'

'For how long?' This question is from another sweaty passenger who has no right to be this frustrated, considering I saw her come through the entrance less than thirty minutes before the flight was supposed to have departed. 'We've been waiting for ...'

Three hours, seventeen minutes. But if you count how long since the Uber dropped me at the airport, it would be five hours plus. I suppose the other passengers weren't running away from their homes to avoid a confrontation with their cheating spouse. Okay. *Likely* cheating spouse. Truth is, the hurried way I packed my bags and left home in the early hours of this morning had little to do with punctuality and everything to do with my unwillingness to ask my wife the question that was uppermost in my mind.

Are you having an affair?

It had taken a lot of willpower to tamp down that question this morning, as Folake stood in her light cotton housecoat, arms akimbo. Her long locks were pulled back from her face, so there was no masking her disapproval as she watched me pack.

'You're really doing this?'

'Yes,' I grunted and made a show of counting some underpants.

'And it doesn't matter that I think it's a bad idea?'

I placed boxers in my suitcase and responded in what I hoped was a well-crafted, neutral voice. 'We've been through this, Folake.'

'You're not a detective, Philip.' She stressed my name in the way she does when she's trying, unsuccessfully, to hold on to her patience.

'Your faith inspires and motivates,' I replied ruefully.

'Don't play that card! No one has shown more faith in you than me.'

'You reckon now's the time to stop?'

'You can't go off to some village to solve a case that's been cold for more than a year and expect me to throw a send-off party.'

I faced her, finally making eye contact.

'I'm not solving anything. I'm investigating why what happened, happened.'

'How's that not solving a case? Surely you can't understand why something happened without knowing *what* happened?'

Had I gone into an explanation of my work as an investigative psychologist, I wouldn't be here waiting on a delayed flight. Despite supporting each other through our respective PhDs, my wife pretends to misunderstand my work when it suits her.

'Folake, this is an opportunity to put my skills to use in the real world –'

'A real and dangerous world,' she cut in sharply.

No doubt travelling to Okriki might be considered dangerous for someone like me, who until eight months ago had spent the better part of his adult life in the States, but it would've been nice if my wife had said instead: 'Go, Sweets. If anyone can find out what led to the mobbing and burning to death of three undergraduates, you're the one. You've got this.'

'It's a foolhardy scheme, and you know it! I don't know what you're trying to prove.'

'That I'm more than a two-bit academic without tenure,' I shot back, restraining myself from shouting.

'Leaving your family to go investigate multiple murders isn't going to get you tenure,' she said, no less strident.

But it'll take my mind off the sad possibility you're cheating on me.

Of course, I didn't say this out loud. I hate fighting, especially when it involves raised voices. Moreover, there aren't a lot of people who can hold their own in a war of words with Professor Afolake Taiwo, the youngest Professor of Law at the University of Lagos. In almost seventeen years of marriage, I've rarely won an argument with my wife.

'Okay, Philip. Let's say you get there and you find out what really happened, or why it happened. What then? What do you want to do? Write a book?'

'This is Nigeria, Folake,' I scoffed. 'You don't chase down the details of a mob action in the hopes of writing a best-seller.'

'Then in the name of everything holy, tell me what you're hoping for?'

'I told you the father of one of victims hired me to –'

'Yes, yes, I know.' She threw her hands in the air and rolled her eyes. 'He wants you to write some report because he doesn't believe his son was a thief, even though it's all there on social media.'

'Have you seen the video?'

Folake shuddered.

'I've watched it a hundred times at least,' I continued, to stop her from recounting what she must have seen on any of the several sites where the deaths of the Okriki Three were posted. 'And you know what? Every time the same thought goes through my mind – people can't be so crazy as to burn three boys in broad daylight just because they are caught stealing.'

Folake sat on the bed, shoulders slumped, and I wasn't sure if it was from our argument or my reference to the distressing video.

'Nothing makes sense in this country,' she said, shaking her head.

'Everything makes sense when you know why people do what they do.'

'Psychobabble nonsense,' she snapped and her hand rose quickly to her mouth as if to take back her words. She'd crossed a line and she knew it.

I made a production of zipping my suitcase till I was sure I could keep my face impassive. When I looked at her, my voice was as neutral as when we started the conversation.

'Thank you. Now I'll go apply my psychobabble on a matter for which I'm going to be well rewarded. Excuse me.'

I lifted the suitcase and walked out quickly before she gathered her wits.

Another passenger's angry voice breaks through my reverie.

'This is unacceptable! Only in Nigeria is this kind of –'

I give it another hour or so before irate passengers and rude airline ground crew exchange blows. For now, I turn my attention to the one thing I am trained to understand.

A crime scene.

CHECK

Crime scenes can range from orderly to maddeningly chaotic.

I try to drown out the noise of the airport and reflect on the words of my old teacher and mentor, Professor Albert Cook.

'Death is messy, Philip, but dying is a shithouse.'

Prof, as I still fondly call him, never subscribed to the idea that a crime scene could fit into a given set of typologies. He used to say: 'People fuck up, and therein lies the clue to what really happened.'

Prof was my PhD thesis supervisor at the University of Southern California, my first boss and the person who introduced me to the then evolving field of investigative psychology. Although retired now, Prof remains active by 'butting into other people's shithouses', as he calls it. Perhaps I should send him the YouTube link to the Okriki Three's execution. It would be interesting to hear the old man's thoughts on this particular shithouse.

I look at my notes. Under the section where I had written: *Organised crime scene*, I draw a large question mark.

When one considers how the mob's rage seemed so focused on the three young men they were killing – murdering – at least some of the conditions of a staged crime scene could apply. Take the aggression directed at the victims before they were burnt. Classic premeditation. And the tyres. Surely they couldn't have just appeared. Someone, or some people, had to have gone out of their way to bring them to the crime scene, which for this exercise I should limit to where the boys were finally killed.

Personalisation of victim(s). Theoretically, it's safe to assume a mob killing is not personal and would, therefore, present the characteristics of a disorganised crime scene. Practically, given the intensity with which the Okriki Three were killed, a collective displacement can't be ruled out. If the young men were suspected thieves, a significant number of their attackers may have been victims of past robberies that went unpunished. But is that argument tenable for almost a hundred angry people?

I place several question marks against 'personalisation' and write: *Get data on the rate of robberies in the neighbourhood before or during the month of the killing.*

There are other indications of an organised crime scene; the demand for the victims to be submissive and the use of restraints at some point during the whole heart-breaking exercise are classic indicators. But this is where the staged crime scene typology ends.

I look up to see whether any of the frustrated passengers has resorted to violence. Not yet. Then, back to my notes where I had listed the characteristics of a disorganised crime scene.

Bodies left at the scene of the crime. Check.
Bodies left in full view for anyone to see. Check.
Depersonalisation of victims. Check.

11

I doodle around this. Can one be sure? Is it possible that no one knew the boys? What about the person who claimed he was being robbed?

I write: *Interview alarm raiser.*

Minimal conversation. Mobs don't engage in discussions or negotiations with their victims. So, Check.

Spontaneity –

Apparently, the mob had descended on the boys after an alarm was raised that they were robbing another student off campus. Since there was no way a hundred angry people were lying in wait to be summoned to participate in a neck-lace killing, this is also a check.

Indeed, dying *is* a shithouse. The mix of typologies in this crime scene is infuriating but can present unique possibili-ties for the task at hand. I must remember to keep an open mind until I get more data beyond the still images grabbed off YouTube videos and interviews with the victims' parents.

I write: *A singular motive masked by a collective purpose or bias?* This might explain the mixed typology, the most telling characteristic of a disorganised crime scene.

Unexpected and sudden violence against victims. Check. I pause here. How unexpected and sudden was the violence, though? The human stories about a crime are as important as the crime scene itself. The motivations of the narrator – perpetrator, victim or witness – can shed consid-erable light on what really happened.

I flip my notes to where I wrote: *Emeka Nwamadi.*

FIRST CONTACT

'Chiemeka Nwamadi,' he said as he shook my hand.

'Good to meet you, Mr Nwamadi.'

'Emeka, please. Let's not stand on formalities.'

'Let's not stand at all,' said Abubakar Tukur, who'd have been my boss if my contract at the Police College was permanent rather than that of a guest lecturer whose services are procured strictly upon the availability of a budget. He ushered – more like ordered – us to sit on the front row of chairs that faced the desk from where I'd just delivered a lecture on crowd control. Abubakar is old school; the 32nd Commandant of the Police College who still harbours illusions of restoring the glory days of the Nigerian Police Force.

As we made ourselves comfortable on the sturdy chairs, I couldn't shake the feeling that the name 'Nwamadi' was familiar.

'Emeka is the MD of National Bank,' Abubakar said, and it clicked. The man is the head of the country's third-largest commercial bank. As soon as that registered, another hazy detail hovered on the fringes of my mind and, again, Abubakar came to the rescue.

'I'm not sure if you know of the Okriki Three case …' he began.

Shock was my first reaction, then compassion. Three weeks into my first lecture series on crowd psychology at the college, I had asked the cadets to present case studies of crimes committed by crowds. More than half of the papers were about an incident in the south-eastern part of the country, which the media had dubbed the 'Okriki Three'. Since most of the papers were disjointed – as most student presentations tend to be – I had taken the time to read up on the case in the media. That's how I knew Emeka Nwamadi was the father of one of the three undergraduate boys beaten and burnt to death over a year ago in the university town of Okriki. His fight, along with the other parents, to bring the people who killed their sons to some kind of justice had been the stuff of headlines months before I left the States to follow my wife on her sabbatical at the University of Lagos.

What does one say to a parent who lost a child in such an unspeakably cruel manner?

'I'm so sorry, sir,' I offered awkwardly.

Emeka Nwamadi nodded, his face unreadable.

'This is why we're here, Philip. Everyone knows what ha*ff*ened.' When Abubakar is excited, his Hausa heritage betrays him. His *p*'s turn to *f*'s and *r*'s roll into *l*'s.

Actually, I didn't know enough. Not then. After reading enough to get context for grading the cadets' papers, I tried to shut it all out of my mind. My twin sons have just turned sixteen and it's not hard to picture them at university, away from home and finding themselves in the wrong place at the wrong time. Self-preservation prevented me

14

from researching about the Okriki Three or even watching the video on YouTube.

'I'm not sure where I come in, sir?' I responded.

'Tell him.' Abubakar nodded at Emeka.

Emeka didn't speak. Instead, he reached into his leather briefcase and brought out two bound documents. He placed them on the table between us, and I immediately knew what they were. The first was my masters' thesis, poetically titled: 'Strange Fruit: Understanding the Psychology of Lynch Mobs in the South'. The second was my PhD thesis, a continuation of sorts: 'Strange Harvest: How Crowds Get Away with Murder'. Both printouts must have been downloaded from the online library of the university where I had researched and written them. I had also presented them as part of my résumé when I applied to the Police College.

I looked at Abubakar, but it was Emeka who spoke.

'There are a lot of stories about what happened the day my son was killed. I don't believe any of them, so I'm here to ask you to help me find out what *really* happened.'

I was no stranger to these sorts of requests, and I had my standard response. 'You mustn't mistake me for a detective, Mr Nwamadi. I'm a psychologist with expertise in studying the motives behind crimes and how they are committed. Most of my investigations are purely exercises in academic exploration.'

It was a speech well rehearsed from years of explaining the limits of my expertise to my ex-colleagues at the San Francisco Police Department.

'I read these books,' Emeka said, pointing at them.

'They're academic papers.'

'Brilliant in my opinion. I've never read anything like your analysis of crowd behaviour.'

'They're post-event observations. Hardly forensic.' I tried to sound dismissive but I was pleased at the compliment.

'Insightful nonetheless,' Emeka insisted.

'I told you he's humble,' Abubakar said to Emeka, then turned to me. 'Phi*rif*,' his Hausa police-boss mode was in full bloom, 'you're the only one that can *feece* together what ha*ff*ened. These *feefu*l need your *herf*. As the only investigative psychologist in this country –'

'That you know of.'

Abubakar waved his hand like he was warding off a ludicrous proposition. 'I*p* I don't know them, they don't exist. You, I know.'

If there was anything I had learnt from eight-and-a-half soul-numbing years of 'piecing together' the motives and modus operandi of some of the most heinous crimes known to man at the SFPD, it was that there are no winners in any crime involving the loss of life. I was quite happy being a lecturer. I was ready to voice a more determined refusal.

'Have you watched the video, Dr Taiwo?' Emeka asked.

'Please, call me Philip.'

'Philip,' he conceded without missing a beat. 'Have you watched the video?'

I shook my head and Emeka reached for his smartphone, tapped the screen twice and handed it to me, a challenge in his eyes. Seconds later, the last minutes of Kevin Nwamadi's life played out in my palm.

For quite a while after Abubakar and Emeka left me in that classroom, the horror of what I saw stayed with me. After over a decade and a half of studying human transgressions, I have *almost* mastered the necessary art of detachment. But this is the first time I am witnessing a crime in progress, yet paralysed by the fact that it had already happened and could not be stopped.

I couldn't shake the images of the three young men as they were beaten, broken and burnt alive. It was difficult to fathom the pain Emeka Nwamadi and the other parents must feel. The loss of a child is unbearable enough, but to have that painful death – that *dying* – playing out in a continuous digital loop on the World Wide Web must be the most terrible of existences.

There were many reasons why taking the assignment appealed to the researcher in me. One of them was the opportunity to localise some of my hypotheses on crowd psychology to the Nigerian context. It also would not hurt my chances of getting a more permanent consultancy at the Police College or an equally reputable institution. However, it was the father in me that made me want to help Emeka Nwamadi find the closure he so clearly needed.

I left work earlier than planned that day, and drove to Folake's office, eager to share my initial impressions of the case. But I never did.

In fact, it ended up being a complicated day; distressing and depressing in equal measure because it was from the parking lot that I looked up and saw my wife in the embrace of another man.

THE SINS OF FATHERS

For days, Abubakar followed up, trying to convince me to take the assignment, but I couldn't tell him that the Okriki Three was the last thing on my mind. I ignored Emeka Nwamadi's text messages and refused to take his calls. I wasn't being difficult. I just wasn't functioning well enough to commit to anything.

Until the day my father summoned me.

You could tell the gravity of a situation in the Taiwo clan by the time of day my parents chose to discuss it.

Family discussions ranging from scolding for subpar academic performances to grave infractions against the family name were late at night, when there was no danger of interruption by visitors. These days, serious conversations, which my dad called 'strategic meetings', are reserved for dawn. This is when career paths are discussed, worry is shared regarding the behaviour of any of my three siblings or the size of our financial contribution to a number of the family projects my father has committed his children to, usually without our permission.

When I got the text message summoning me to our family home on Lagos Island at the crack of dawn, I wondered if Folake had confessed her indiscretion to him and asked his intervention in asking for my forgiveness, but I quickly dismissed the thought. My dad is Folake's godfather and they have been close since her childhood. There are few things I have done in my life to impress my dad, but marrying his god-daughter must rank as what my twin brother calls the 'checkmate of sibling rivalry'. Folake wouldn't risk tainting the image he had of her, except as a last resort.

Dad was waiting for me when I arrived. My mom was still in bed. Ever since she retired from being the chief nurse at my father's practice, she insisted on sleeping in; recovering, she claimed, from raising two sets of twins and managing a workaholic husband. When asked why my parents did not have more kids, my dad always joked that he was afraid the next set of children would be sextuplets! In his late seventies, he still works at his practice not too far from home, where I knew he would be heading as soon as our meeting was over.

'Kehinde!' he exclaimed, as he pulled me into an embrace and ushered me through the large living room into his study.

My father never calls me 'Philip'. He insists 'Kehinde' was the name I was born with and Philip was my mom's idea at my baptism. I was worried that he didn't call me by his nickname for me – Kenny Boy – which he coined to differentiate me from one of the younger twins, another Kehinde. She is 'Kenny Girl'. While I'm more forgiving of the old man's moniker for me, my sister baulks at being called a 'girl' at forty-four.

'I spoke to the boys last week,' my father said, as I settled into the well-worn leather sofa across from the shelves that held his admirable collection of books.

I breathed in and waited for the old man to finish his favourite topic: his grandchildren's educational achievements or lack thereof. He lamented their handwriting which he described as 'spidery'. Ironic, coming from a medical doctor. He informed me he just finished reading the Harry Potter novel my daughter gave him – 'Witches and wizards! Is this what these children are learning nowadays?' He talked of my mother's recently acquired habit of removing gluten from their diet, 'I am seventy-eight! What is her point?'

When he finally paused for breath, I rose, heading towards the Nespresso machine in the corner of the room, before venturing to ask why he had summoned me.

'Sit,' Dad ordered.

I did, abandoning my plans for coffee, still clueless and nervous. He sat too and his expression became sombre, which heightened my unease.

'A good friend of mine says you're avoiding him,' he said finally.

'Pardon?'

'Emeka Nwamadi.'

'You know him?' I shouldn't be surprised. My father's network of friends and patients reads like a *Who's Who* of the Lagos elite.

'Yes. He and I play golf at the country club.'

'He failed to mention that when we met. He was introduced to me by the Commandant at the Police College.'

'I know. I think he didn't want to put undue influence on you.'

'Hmm, I wonder what changed,' I said wryly, settling again into the sofa, more relaxed now that I had an idea where this was going.

'It's really sad what happened to his son and those other boys, don't you think?'

'Terrible,' I said tentatively, not sure where my dad was going with the conversation.

'I think you should consider taking the case.' He held my gaze as he said this, his tone steely.

'But, Dad, I don't know what I can do. All the reports –'

'– are speculation, rumours and conjecture. We need to get to the truth.'

'We?'

My father gave a deep sigh, stood and padded to his bookshelf, where he retrieved a battered manila file. He took an old photograph from it and handed it to me.

I recognised a younger version of my dad – my twin sons bear an uncanny resemblance to him, and I could have been looking at any of them in the picture – surrounded by five other young men of about the same age.

'Your university days, huh?' I thought I recognised at least two young men in the picture. They were familiar faces from the alumni gatherings my father had hosted many times at the house.

'My fraternity at University of Ibadan.' My father's tone was softened by nostalgia. 'We were inseparable. Live together as brothers or perish as fools. That was our motto.'

My eyes registered the red bandana around all of the young men's heads and it hit me. 'Dad, were you a cult member?'

'Don't say that,' he retorted sharply. 'Never ever call us that –'

'Fraternity, cult … What difference does it make?'

He bristled. 'We were distinguished gentlemen.' His voice was imperious and brooked no argument. 'We were nothing like these university boys now. We were brothers; politically aware, academically excellent and, above all, gentlemen.'

I looked at the picture and my hand shook slightly at the realisation that I had to revise the image I had of my dad, no matter what he said.

'I am still that person,' he said as if he could read my mind. He sat down next to me and took the picture. His voice softened as he looked at it. 'And so are all the men in this picture.'

'This,' he pointed, 'is Dr Chukwuji Nwamadi. He was one of the pioneering lecturers at the University of Nigeria, in Nsukka, and we lost him during the bombing of that campus during the war. The rest of us have pitched in to look after his family ever since. His wife, his children –' He looked pointedly at me, 'especially his eldest son, Emeka.'

'And that's why you want me to take the case? Because you knew Emeka's father?'

'I feel a sense of responsibility towards him. All of us in that picture feel the same. His father was blood. But this goes beyond that. These children today, running around with weapons and killing each other; they've tarnished our legacy. The laws we fought to get passed, the awareness we raised about injustice, our protest against the civil war, all of that gone because when people think about university fraternities now, all they see is mayhem.' He shuddered, shaking his head sadly. 'And when something occurs that's as violent as what happened to those boys, one can't but wonder what role we had in all this and if all the bloodshed could have been avoided. This wasn't the plan. Our vision was heroic in the beginning.' He let out a deflated sigh.

'Does Emeka know this about you? You know, with the … er, fraternity.'

My father nodded. 'Everyone in that picture pitched in to send him to university here and to the US for his MBA. He knows.'

'Do you think his son was killed because he was in a cult?'

'What do you think?'

I shrugged. 'I don't know enough to think anything of consequence.'

My father nodded again. 'There's so much that's unknown. But maybe, just maybe, if the facts came out, the unfortunate events that led to the death of Kevin and those boys would never be repeated.'

I stood up to create some distance between us. 'You want me to prove the killings were not gang-related, so you and your friends can sleep better at night?'

'I want you to help a grieving father, to give him some closure. I want you to find out the truth, and if the truth is one more thing on my conscience, then so be it.'

Gone was the jovial doctor, the affectionate father, the affable grandfather and loving husband.

'I still can't picture you …' I shook my head. 'The things I've heard about what these gangs get up to on campus.' My eyes widened as a memory came to me. 'I remember you calling Taiye and me when we were thinking of studying here. You told us, no, you warned us not to even think of joining a cult.'

Dad wagged a finger at me. 'I never used that word "cult", when I spoke to you and your brother. I said gang.'

I snorted. 'Is that not what your fraternities have become? Violent gangs that you warned your own children about joining?'

My father shook his head, but could not give me an answer that cleared my confusion.

'We've tried, Kehinde. All of us, alumni of different fraternities in different campuses all over the country. We have tried to end this violence. We've consulted with university authorities, served on advisory boards and even helped to formulate laws to control what everyone calls "secret cults". But nothing has worked.'

'Why didn't you say something? Even when you were warning Taiye and me, why didn't you tell us you were in a fraternity yourself?'

'If you saw the way you're looking at me now, you'd know why.'

I left my childhood home that morning with a heavy heart. In less than a week, the two people closest to me had shattered some of my core beliefs. My wife made me question my faith in our union, while my father planted doubt about what I knew of him for the past forty-six years.

While I wasn't ready to deal with Folake, I had the skills and training to take on the Okriki Three case. I needed the distraction. So, the day after my meeting with my dad, I called Emeka Nwamadi and agreed to take the assignment.

I didn't mention my father, but I knew he knew. We were bound together.

24

RED-HOT ARRIVAL

Ladies and gentlemen, welcome to Flight NJ2406 going to Port Harcourt. We apologise for the delay of this –

One would think the delay was an hour at most. And I had been right in my reading of the crowd at the counter. Only the announcement that the plane would in fact fly just two hours ago had prevented the pummelling of airline staff. Total waiting time: five hours, twenty-eight minutes. That's almost eight hours of me sitting in Mr Biggs, periodically buying snacks in lieu of rental space.

Captain Duke and the crew will do our best to arrive in Port Harcourt quickly, with your safety and comfort as our primary goals. Please take your seat as the plane refuels and we will be on our way.

Logic dictates that aviation fuel is not the same as the one that goes into my four-year-old Prado, but announcing a refuelling after all that delay doesn't allay my scepticism that this plane will actually get to Port Harcourt.

Although the flight should be no more than an hour, the long delay makes me wonder again why Emeka had not agreed to my suggestion of making the trip by road. I've never been to the south-eastern part of the country, and I'd hoped the drive, which GPS informed me takes about ten hours and fifteen minutes, would enrich my assimilation. But Emeka and Abubakar had insisted that, apart from the bad roads, it was safer to travel by air. The road-trip-loving American in me had hoped to wrap up the assignment quickly and drive towards the border shared with Cameroun, but Abubakar had sputtered into his drink when I suggested this. When I asked for an explanation, he had cryptically asked me to trust him when he said flying was best. In hindsight, I recall neither Emeka nor Abubakar had said it was *faster*.

The passenger in the adjacent seat arrives. One look at her and I immediately forget my anxiety about another possible delay. Her face is so perfectly made-up that I'm certain it couldn't have been applied by hand. Her waist is squeezed into a form-fitting dress that accentuates her full figure as she reaches up to put away several bags in the overhead compartment. Her leather laptop bag won't go in, so she puts it under the seat in front of her and turns to me with a thousand-megawatt smile.

'Hi,' she says.

I find my voice a second too late. 'Hello.'

'I was afraid I'd be late.' She smooths her dress and settles back in her seat.

'The flight was delayed.'

'My queue boy told me, but the traffic getting here was manic.'

'Queue boy?'

She raises an expertly pencilled eyebrow. 'Someone you hire to stand in the queue for you. These flights are always late. So, you pay someone to stand in the queue and check you in. They call you as soon as boarding starts.'

I can't hide my bafflement. 'But the traffic … Surely there's no way you can make it between the call and boarding?'

She laughs; a rich, bubbly laugh that calls attention to itself. If any of the women on board had Folake's number, her phone would be ringing this second. *You leave your husband to travel alone to Port Harcourt? Are you crazy? Get here now and come save him from witchcraft parading in Chanel No. 5!* Meanwhile, a middle-aged man sitting across the aisle from us looks like he would trade places with me in a Lagos bus-stop minute.

'Which is why I'm the last to get on the flight.'

It's my turn to laugh. I hold out my hand, 'Philip Taiwo. Pleasure to meet you.'

She holds out ringed fingers. 'Salome Briggs. Likewise.'

I'm careful not to let the handshake linger. 'So, Port Harcourt. Business or pleasure?'

'In PH, it has to be both. I live there. Lagos for me is always business. You?'

'Definitely business.'

Her eyes rest on my wedding band. 'Madam is here in Lagos?'

'Yes. She's a lecturer at Unilag.' I resent that the note of pride in my voice is unaffected by my sense of betrayal at Folake's possible infidelity.

'Ah, the brains in the family,' Salome says. 'Which would make you the money, I assume.'

'Alas, not so. I'm working on it, though. Hence, the business in Port Harcourt.'

'I take it you're not a regular visitor to this side of the country.'

'What gave me away?'

'Saying "Port Harcourt" where "PH" will do.'

'Guilty as charged.'

She chuckles. 'So, what's happening in PH?'

I'm not sure the killing of the Okriki Three is the kind of conversation anyone signs up for on a flight like this. But here I am, going to a place I've never been, and this friendly passenger lives near there.

'I'm writing a report on an event that happened there a couple of years back. Well, not there exactly but in one of the outlying towns.'

'I'm generally a good judge of character, and I can bet my iPhone you're not a journalist.' She leans close to me in a conspiratorial whisper. 'My whole life is on my iPhone.'

I can't help but laugh. Salome Briggs seems to do everything for effect, from her make-up to her clothes to the way she speaks.

'I'm an investigative psychologist.'

'A shrink?'

'No, no …' I laugh again at the way her kohled eyes widen like I just confessed to harbouring Tupac Shakur at my house. 'I study crimes and determine why and how they occurred.'

She snorts as only a Nigerian woman can. A dismissive grunt accompanied by multiple facial movements that simultaneously include eyes rolling, brows raising and a downward curve to the lips. 'What's the point? It has happened *abi*?'

'When we understand how a particular crime occurred and can identify the motivations that led to it, the chance of preventing it from happening again is much higher.'

'Hmm. That's what they told you when you were filling in your admission forms for whatever fancy American university you went to, right?'

I should take offence, but I can't. 'Am I that obvious?'

'Don't worry. I won't tell your alumni group. Now this event. You're going to write a report on it so it doesn't happen again?'

'It's more complicated than that –'

Ladies and gentlemen, please turn off your electronic devices and fasten your seat belts as we begin our preflight –

I reach for my cell phone and see two messages from Folake. I switch it off without reading them. Salome does the same to her rose-gold iPhone, and to another, less flashy not-an-iPhone. She puts them and her iPad in the side pocket of the laptop bag and pushes it under her seat just as the plane starts to move. She sits back, turns to me and flashes that smile again.

'Define complicated.'

'Huh?' I try to shake off my guilt for not reading my wife's messages.

'You said this event you're investigating is complicated.'

'The media called it the Okriki Three. It's a tragic inci—'

My voice trails off as Salome turns away and makes a show of adjusting the bag under her seat as the plane taxies down the runway.

'Good luck with that,' she says without her earlier warmth.

THE WELCOME PARTY

As soon as the seat-belt sign goes off, Salome retrieves her iPad, plugs her ears with headphones and proceeds to act like we didn't just introduce ourselves. Through the catering service offer of a pitiful sandwich wrapped in cellophane with juice and/or water – a no-thank-you from both of us – she ignores me, and I pretend to go back to my notes.

We've been up in the air for more than thirty minutes when I decide to grab the tusks of the elephant on the plane. I nudge her by the elbow. Gently, but firmly enough to demand attention. Salome arcs an eyebrow but doesn't take off her headphones. I gesture towards her ears. She sighs and reluctantly takes the left ear off.

'I thought we had a thing going there –'

The second the words leave my lips, I realise they are the wrong ones. Her eyebrow rises even higher, and the crease on her forehead betrays her irritation.

'I didn't mean it that way –' I begin.

'How did you mean it? Because I smiled at you and was polite when we met, you think we have a thing?'

'I'm sorry. I meant … well, I thought we were having an interesting conversation, but you shut me out as soon as I shared my reason for going to Port Harcourt.'

'One. The issue of how interesting our conversation was is a matter of opinion. You're entitled to yours. Two. As I said, I was simply making polite conversation with a fellow passenger and –'

'I'm sorry if I said anything wrong, or did anything to make you angry.'

She is silent. Apologising for doing nothing wrong is a tactic I learned over seventeen years of marriage.

'There's nothing to apologise for,' Salome replies grudgingly.

'There is. I miss my friend of thirty minutes ago.'

'You make friends easily.'

'Only if they're worth it. I'm a gut-feel kinda guy.'

'Then you'll be hurt easily.' She says this like a warning, and I wonder if she's talking about my intuition or something else.

'I'll live,' I respond rather glibly, trying to quell the unease I feel at her words.

She holds my gaze briefly and laughs, again drawing curious stares from the other passengers. She puts away her headphones and iPad, then turns back to me with her dazzling smile.

'Okay, Dr Taiwo, let's start again …'

'Philip. And life's too short. I prefer to move on. You closed off when I told you the reason for my trip. Why?'

She is silent for a beat, perhaps gauging my determination to get an answer. 'Because you're pulling at a tiger's tail.'

'It's a cold case, Salome. I'm just going to write a report –'

'I know the story, Philip. Those boys were killed in my mother's village.'

Later I will reflect on how close the degrees of separation in this assignment were already becoming. For now, all I can think to say is, 'I'm sorry.'

'Don't be. But I can assure you there won't be welcoming arms in Okriki, eager to tell you what happened. Or to quote you – why and how it occurred.'

'So, I might as well go back to Lagos before I even get to Okriki?'

'You might as well.'

'And if I don't?'

'I'll pray for you. Now, can we change the subject?'

Her eyes dare me to continue on a path that will most likely lead to the retrieval of her headphones.

'Of course we can.'

We talk about my work as a part-time lecturer at the Police College. She tells me she's a lawyer specialising in the oil and gas sector and I smile inwardly. It seems I have a type.

Ladies and gentlemen, we will begin our descent shortly. Please ensure that your tray table is –

We touch down without drama and when we're told it's okay to switch on our cell phones, Salome and I exchange contact details. She stands to take her bags from the overhead compartment.

'If all this is your hand luggage, I dread to see the number of bags you checked in.'

She shakes her head in mock pity. 'As soon as that door opens, you'll see why I never check in my luggage on any flight to PH.'

Even the blast of hot, humid air and her words couldn't have prepared anyone for the chaos that awaits me after the short walk from the plane to the arrivals area. My shock must be evident because Salome is laughing.

'Welcome to PH, Dr Taiwo,' she says. 'Keep in touch.'

She waves daintily and is gone.

I look around me, feeling lost. On top of a dilapidated building is a huge sign – Port Harcourt International Airport – that towers over a structure someone must have had the intention of completing but didn't get around to. Behind me, people are still disembarking, but I feel like rushing back into the plane and commandeering it back to my life in Lagos.

'Dr Taiwo? Dr Philip Taiwo?'

The gruff voice belongs to a dark-skinned man who must be in his early thirties but looks older in his rumpled shirt and tie. There are patches of sweat around his armpits, but one can see he has made an effort to look presentable and even professional. He's holding a piece of A4 paper with my name on it and a picture that could only have been printed off the faculty page of the Police College website. This must be the chaperone Emeka promised me.

'Yes, I'm Philip Taiwo. Are you Chika?'

He smiles and reveals perfect white teeth. 'Yes, sir. Chika Makuochi.'

We manage a handshake as he puts aside the rudimentary sign and we are jostled by the mass of people around us on the tarmac.

'Come with me, please.'

I follow him into a canvas tent labelled 'Arrivals' and find more chaos.

Suitcases, Ghana-must-go jute bags, boxes and more are spread on the ground. Men dressed in overalls bring yet more luggage into the tent, dumping them with the ones already there. Now, I see Salome's point.

'Which one is yours?'

I look at Chika in a daze.

'Your luggage, sir. Point at yours, and I'll get it.'

For a moment, I can't remember the colour of the suitcase I checked in. What if I point at luggage that's not mine but looks like mine? What if I take one that has contraband and I am arrested?

'Don't worry. Just point, and we'll confirm it's yours before we leave,' Chika says reassuringly.

I really have to do something about my poker face.

I point at the Samsonite suitcase that looks closest to what I had placed my belongings in over ten hours ago. Chika retrieves it, turns it this way and that, and we see the name tag didn't survive the rough handling.

'I think it's mine.' I bend to run the combination on the lock. *2302*. Day and month of my birth. The lock opens.

Chika carries the luggage. 'Follow me, sir.'

He speaks rapid pidgin to the security men we meet. He gestures towards me as the traveller, but I sense this is a formality since he is quick to remind one that he has 'settled' with everyone before they let him meet me on the tarmac. Another recognises him, and after more exchanges of pidgin and laughter, they let us through to the outside.

By the time we get to a Land Cruiser in the parking lot, I'm drained and sweaty. Chika holds the rear passenger door of the 4x4 open, but I shake my head and indicate that I'd rather sit in front. Before I get in, I look around to be sure I didn't imagine the past fifteen minutes.

'It can be a bit overwhelming,' Chika says. 'The airport has been like this for over a decade. Doesn't stop the government from allocating millions for its completion every year. Let's go, sir.'

He turns on the engine and a blast of cold air from the AC hits me.

'Welcome to PH,' Chika says as he reverses, and expertly turns the car in the direction of the exit sign.

ENTER THE DARKNESS

'How long is it to Okriki?' I ask Chika as he turns off the airport road on to one that has a stop–start relationship with tar.

'About an hour, sir. Today's a Sunday, so traffic is light.'

I look around. Even by Lagos standards, the neglect of such a major road can't be good for any kind of traffic. I suspect many flights have been missed while stuck in Port Harcourt's version of 'light traffic'.

'We're heading to Okriki now, PH is that way,' Chika explains.

'We're not in Port Harcourt?'

'Not really. The airport's technically in Omagwa, which is on the outskirts of PH. That road,' he indicates behind us, 'is to Port Harcourt, but you'll still pass other towns like Rukpokwu, Elele, Isiokpo.'

I only partly listen as I take in my first view of Port Harcourt, the capital of Rivers State; a city once deemed so beautiful that it was declared the 'Garden City'. Today everywhere is hot and dusty and I'm not feeling charitable enough to call what I see a garden of any sort.

'Okriki is in the opposite direction of PH,' Chika is saying, 'but maybe sometime, I'll take you there to show you around.'

Just then, he slows the Land Cruiser down. Ahead of us is a long line of cars approaching what appears to be a police barricade.

'Police?' I ask.

'Military police.'

I consider using the pass Abubakar gave me before I left Lagos. It is a bona fide police badge that he insisted would reduce a lot of the hassle on this assignment. But even I know when it comes to the military police – basically, army officers with the dubious mandate to terrorise civilians in the absence of war – presenting an honorary police badge can be counterproductive.

'The trick is not to argue, sir,' Chika says, as he weaves from one lane to another. 'Give them something as quickly as possible and move on.'

We make a snail-paced approach towards the heavily armed men. A seamless operation is in progress. The officer standing on the driver's side bends slightly to reach into the car. He collects cash that he deftly puts in the front pocket of his bulletproof vest, then nods to the officer standing further down the road to open the barricade.

When it's our turn, I stare straight ahead. Chika hands over the cash, and we are cleared to move on. I look back at the officer as he waves us off. Implacable, with no indication he just broke the very law he is sworn to keep.

'They're here every day?'

'And night. Those barricades cause the go-slow just as much as the bad roads.'

'It's the same in Lagos, but it's usually regular police.'

'The militants and gang-related kidnappings have put this part of the country in an undeclared state of emergency.'

'The situation is still as dire as one hears?'

Chika shrugs. 'It's a bit better, but still quite tense. It might seem strange but the presence of the military police really makes a big difference. The violence is now more sporadic and focused around the oil rigs.'

I wish I could curb my dismay at how we've all learnt to live with this paradox. So much so that no one questions military personnel when they collect bribes in broad daylight because they protect us from the violence fuelled by the inequitable access to the country's most precious resource: crude oil. The whole situation fills me with the same helpless rage I have when mall security in the States follows me around because of my skin colour. At least I could leave the US, but here my frustration is worse because this is home.

It's getting dark and the only illumination is from the headlights of other cars. I decide not to ask Chika more questions since he'll need all his wits to navigate the road.

I close my eyes for what seems like a minute.

'We're here,' Chika announces.

I jerk awake. It's pitch black with flickers of light here and there. The sound of generators follows our journey through the town. In Lagos, this is a regular soundtrack to the hustle and bustle of life. In Okriki, far away from city noise, it sounds like the continuous rumbling of heavy machines on a construction site.

'The electricity situation is better here than in PH normally,' Chika is saying as I look around. 'I'm sure it won't be long before they bring light.'

Nigerians are perennial optimists especially when it comes to electricity. Since I returned, I've accepted the possibility of constant 'light' is as distant as Abubakar's desire to bring back the glory days of the Nigerian Police Force.

'I checked in for you earlier today, so the manager is expecting us.'

I see some people sitting outside their houses. There are clusters of men in front of bungalows, drinking and playing board games, their faces illuminated by kerosene lamps. Children are running and laughing, playing in the darkness. There's singing in the distance. Clapping too. A church. Churches actually, as the singing seems to come from different directions.

'There are lots of churches around here?' I ask, not really surprised but inwardly groaning. Living in the staff quarters of the university insulates us from the multitude of churches and mosques on every corner of most Lagos streets, with their megaphones and singing.

Chika pulls up in front of gates with a 'Hotel Royale' sign affixed to them.

'There's a service every day in any given church,' Chika answers as he honks. 'Sunday services last the whole day.'

The gates are opened by a security guard who yawns widely, as he waves us towards what looks closer to a guest house than a hotel.

Chika drives into the compound of well-tended lawns, illuminated by bulbs attached to the two-storey rectangular building at different angles. The generator, a white beast on the far side of the building, is the less noisy type more upmarket hotels use. I mentally thank the heavens for this and hope the place has stocked up on enough diesel for the duration of my stay.

A scene of fading glory meets us as soon as we enter the reception area. Two huge TVs are on in a lounge littered with an assortment of chairs, sofas and tables. The same rugby game plays loudly on both screens, and I imagine this must be the reason why the reception area, which looks like it doubles as a viewing centre, is empty.

At the front desk, we are greeted by loud snores coming from underneath a head of poorly executed braids. Chika raps his knuckle on the desk and a sleepy face rises, hands our room keys to Chika without any greeting and goes back to sleep. Chika gives me an apologetic smile, before carrying my luggage up a short flight of stairs to a door marked Room 7.

'I'm in 11 over there.' He indicates the rooms further down the hallway. 'I checked all the rooms and selected this one for you. It's the best of all of them.'

It's a rather big room. The sheets of the king-sized bed are clean and smooth. There's a table with a chair and a small sitting area that has a pretty-worn leather sofa facing a flat-screen TV. The air conditioning is on full blast, but I know I'll be turning it off soon since the noise it makes nullifies the relative silence of the generator.

'Thank you, Chika,' I say as I look around.

'You're welcome, sir. The list of the places you're going to tomorrow are in that file.'

I go to the desk and open the file. I look at Chika. 'You did this?'

He nods. I am impressed as I riffle through the well-categorised notes, names and locations.

'So, you know why I'm here.'

'Yes, sir.'

'Who briefed you?'

'The big boss. The MD. Mr Nwamadi.'

'You work at the bank?'

'I'm the driver and PA for the Branch Manager in PH.'

'Forgive me, Chika, but you don't seem like a driver ...'

Chika smiles ruefully. 'I studied Computer Science at the university here. Graduated six years ago.'

'And you're working as a driver?'

He shrugs. 'And PA, sir,' he says and walks to the door. 'I'll be ready for you from seven-thirty. Your first meeting is at nine.'

I express my appreciation for all his work again and then he's gone.

I undress and switch on my phone. There are voicemail notifications and text messages from Folake and the kids. In my hurry to leave home, a kiss to my still sleepy thirteen-year-old daughter and quick shout-outs to the twin boys, who grunted their responses from under the covers of their beds, was all I had time for.

I'm nervous about reading my wife's messages. Folake's frank nature might prompt her to come clean about her affair and, while I'm relatively sure she's not the sort to do this via text, her messages may be invitations to 'talk'. Given that similar fears where my dad was concerned were unfounded though, I know I am just being a coward.

But I'm missing home already so I dial Tai, my elder son, who'll most likely be playing games on his phone while his twin brother has headphones on to allow the music of Kendrick Lamar to lull him to sleep.

'Hey, Dad!' Tai says as soon as he picks up.

'You shouldn't sound so awake when you know you should be in bed.'

'I *am* in bed.'

'You know what I mean ...'

'Yes, Dad, but I was staying awake to hear from you.'

'Yeah, right!'

We both laugh, and soon I'm telling him about the long wait at the airport and my first impressions of Port Harcourt and Okriki. Tai then puts me on speakerphone after ordering his brother to pull off his headphones so he can join the conversation.

As they tell me about their day and performance on the basketball court, I can't help but think how blessed I am. Three beautiful kids and a marriage that has been relatively happy for almost seventeen years. Is it possible that I might lose it all?

'Dad, you should call Mom,' Kay says.

'Is she okay?'

'Not sure,' Tai answers.

'She was quite testy today.'

'And she kept looking at her phone all day,' Kay adds. 'Maybe she's worried about you?'

'I'll call her as soon as you guys promise you're going to sleep.'

They both lie, but I let them be and hang up.

Folake's texts are really just a series of *'have you landed?'* messages that appear to have been resent repeatedly over the past six hours. But I promised the boys, so I type: *'Arrived safe. All good'*, then hit send.

There's a message from my dad, too. *'Heard you left. Thank you. Be safe.'* I choose not to respond.

I walk into the shower and stay under the cold water for a long time. When I finally get to bed, I see Folake didn't respond although I can sense she's awake. Just as I'm about to put the phone away, it vibrates in my hand. I open the message.

'*All settled in, Americana?*' Salome Briggs.

I smile at the memory of our encounter earlier today and respond, '*Big room. Big bed. Generator at full blast with rumbling A/C.*'

'*Ah. 5 Star welcome. Enjoy*', beeps back.

I resist the temptation of late-night banter with an attractive woman while I'm feeling vulnerable about my marriage.

I put the phone away, and although I'm tired, sleep only comes after I wilfully replace the image of my wife in another man's arms with memories of her kissing my forehead after a long day and whispering: 'Sleep now, my sweet.'

A PAST COMES CALLING

Sundays are the busiest days of the week at the Monastery of The Anargyroi Order of St Cosmas and Damian, which is why I am expected to come and help at the dispensary. It is the day when the monks, whose vocation is to provide free spiritual and medical care to those who cannot afford to pay, work the hardest.

Today is no different and I am so tired by the time the last patient leaves that I consider spending the night in my old room instead of going back to campus.

Father Ambrose comes in as I am packing away the generic drugs and taking stock of the medicines that need replenishing.

'The Abbot wants to see you,' Father Ambrose says.

I leave what I am doing and walk to the office. As soon as I enter the austere space, crammed with books and several versions of the Bible, I start to feel suffocated. This is the place I hate the most of all in the monastery, second only to the old monk who had summoned me here.

'John Paul,' he says, calling me by the name they gave me as a sign of my new life at the monastery. The same one I appropriated when it was time to give my affliction a name.

'You're doing well at the dispensary.'

'Thank you, Father,' I say respectfully, having perfected the art of hiding my abhorrence of him over the years.

He looks up at me, his fading eyes struggling to focus over his pince-nez. 'Your school reports are also good.'

I'd say better than good, but I keep quiet lest my response is read as prideful.

The old monk pushes a folder of rubber-banded envelopes towards me. 'We decided that you're ready to have these.'

I reach for the folder and my hands start to shake when I open it.

'Those are from your mother. She has written to you frequently over the past eleven years.'

I flip through the envelopes, all addressed to me and none appear opened.

'We all felt it was better not to give them to you right away.'

Better for who? I want to scream, but I can't trust myself to speak. The rage inside me threatens to call John Paul to the light. I put the envelopes back in the folder, close it and force myself to look at Father Olayiwola.

'Her letters would only have been reminders of your sin, for which you were still making penance.'

'I understand, Father. But why give them to me now?'

The old monk reclines on the wooden chair. 'You're a man now. We've done our part. Your whole life is ahead of you, and the past shouldn't dictate how you go into your future.'

The self-righteous way he speaks infuriates me. How dare he? How dare they all think they can decide for me?

'Thank you, Father,' I say instead.

'That's not all.'

I wait. Nothing can be worse than the first seven years of living at the monastery. Even the unopened letters only prove this.

45

'Those letters used to come regularly,' the Abbot continues. 'Sometimes every three months. Then they stopped. Because I knew the day would come when we would have to hand over these letters to you, I requested the parish in Port Harcourt to look for your mother.'

I keep silent even as my heart beats fast. The urge to choke the life out of this man is strong. I resist it because to give in would mean calling John Paul into the light. But, not now. Not yet.

'I'm afraid she's very sick and has been for some time. That's why the letters stopped coming.'

Still, I say nothing and can see Father Olayiwola is becoming disconcerted.

'We think you should go and see her.'

'Why?' I can feel the knocking at the back of my head. That precursor to John Paul stepping out of the shadows. I find my voice to stem the rage that threatens to swallow me.

'Because she's your mother.'

'She abandoned me.'

'She saved you.'

I don't trust myself to respond to this. I start putting the envelopes back in the folder. When Father Olayiwola's wrinkled hand touches mine across the desk, I try not to flinch.

'We believe your penance will be complete if you visit her at the hospital. God has forgiven you both. But it's time you forgive yourselves and each other.'

I make a quick sign of the cross, bow and force myself not to run. From here, him and everything that's kept the contents in the folder from me all these years.

'… your penance will be complete.'

The Abbot's words reverberate in my head all through the taxi ride back to campus. So, what have I been doing in all these years? How many beatings, enforced self-flagellation to the point of irreversible scarring would it take? Who decides what makes penance complete?

'Not them. Certainly not them,' John Paul says from the shadows and I know he is eager as I am to complete The Final Plan. To wipe away the past, with everything and everyone in it. To start afresh, sinless and without a need for penance.

Soon, but not now.

The folder of unopened letters weighs me down as I walk from the taxi stop to the residential hall. Though deep down, I know I cannot wait to read each of them, through the night if need be.

My hurried steps slow as I make my way past the other rooms towards mine. My door is ajar. I can sense Amaso Dabara is waiting for me inside.

I take a deep breath and give John Paul the light before walking in.

POOR, UNFORTUNATE SOULS

On my first night in Okriki, I dream that I'm locked in a burning Land Cruiser. My fists pound the windows and pull at unyielding locks as Folake walks away from my sound-less screaming.

I wake up sweating and remember I had switched off the noisy air conditioner. I turn it back on, the ensuing sound guaranteeing that it'll be a while before I go back to sleep. I check the time. 3:14 a.m. Might as well get some work done.

In Chika's file, the list of potential interviewees and the places to visit mirrors the one I made in Lagos, although there's more detail here. While I referred to witnesses by their position or role in the killing, Chika's notes have names, addresses and brief information about who they are. I cross out some names on both lists and place question marks next to a few.

One name I put a question mark against is Stella Aligbe, the mother of one of the boys, Bonaventure. She lives in the east and had not been part of the interview session Emeka had organised for me in his office boardroom with the parents of the third victim.

I open my laptop and click on the folder containing my concise but detailed bios on the victims.

Winston Babajide Coker.

Third-year sociology student at the State University. Middle child and five months shy of turning twenty-two when he was killed. His mother, a well-preserved diminutive woman in her late fifties, dressed elegantly, but without any jewellery or make-up. She had been stoic as she sat there and told me God was going to rain hailstones of wrath on the town of Okriki. She had spoken like someone who had no more tears to cry, her voice cold and detached as she informed me that her son may have been many things, but he was not a thief.

'What do you mean?' I had asked tentatively, since this was not a typical summation of a child by a grieving parent.

'He lied. He was a bully and always fought authority,' Mrs Coker had answered matter-of-factly.

'He was just young,' her husband had interjected. He was a very slim and tall man, who anyone could see had decided to take the back seat in their marriage.

'He needed Jesus,' Mrs Coker had insisted, and her eyes dared her husband to contradict her. He didn't.

'There's talk that these boys were in some kind of a gang,' I had ventured to ask.

'Secret cult,' Mrs Coker had hissed. 'That evil spirit that has taken over all the universities.'

'Yes,' I had agreed, quickly pushing thoughts of my dad away. 'You think it's true?'

'How would we know when it's supposed to be a secret?' she had scoffed. 'All I can tell you is that Winston was far away in that school, and we didn't know what he was up to because we're here in Lagos.'

'But you don't believe he was trying to rob anyone even if he might have been part of a cult or gang?'

'Absolutely not!' Mr Coker had stated vehemently. 'Why would he steal? He was well taken care of, with access to the best life could offer. Why would he steal?'

'Even if he was stealing,' Mrs Coker had added, 'no one deserves to be killed that way. Why didn't they just hand them over to the authorities? Why kill our child like that?'

She had started to rock in her seat and pray softly in a strange language. Definitely a Pentecostal. I had wondered then if the conversion was before or after her son was killed. I turned to the husband.

'So, you think people are lying about your son?'

'To be honest, I really don't care about their reasons,' Mr Coker had answered unconvincingly. 'Only God will judge.'

The interview hadn't revealed much more after that. The Cokers only reiterated how much effort they had put into ensuring the legal system brought the people of Okriki to justice. Their son was dead and they could do nothing to bring him back.

'Vengeance is the Lord's. I've forgiven them,' Mrs Coker had concluded fervently. She was even less convincing than her husband.

I click on the second file in the victims' folder.

Bonaventure 'Bona' Cosmos Aligbe.

Last born son of a single mother of five children, with a reputation for being a hellraiser. From the pictures I had downloaded off the Internet, it's easy to see why he'd been considered a ladies' man. At twenty-four, the oldest of the Okriki Three, Bonaventure's most flattering descriptions came from several girls on campus, while the boys told stories of wild parties, boozing and skipping classes. In a written statement, his mother had described him as a good boy who sometimes 'forgot the son of whom he was'. Another grieving parent using religion as a balm of comfort.

Last, not least: *Kevin Chinedu Nwamadi.*

I remain shaken by my introduction to Emeka's son from when his father showed me the video.

'I'm sorry,' Emeka had said after we watched it together, 'for showing you like that.'

'But it was necessa*l*y,' Abubakar had interjected.

'I remember reading that they were planning to rob someone.' I had delicately put forward a piece of information I recalled from my students' presentations.

Emeka had waved his hand dismissively, his irritation evident. 'Look at me, Philip. I'm the Managing Director of a major commercial bank. Do you think my only son would be so deprived that he would leave his campus and go to some village to steal cell phones and laptops?'

'Were any arrests made?' I had asked.

'Eighteen months ago!' Emeka had shot back harshly. 'Only seven people are standing trial. Seven! Did you see all those people in the video? Did that look like seven killers? But that doesn't bother me as much as the lies and the sheer apathy of the police in investigating the allegations made against my son.'

'What are they claiming?' I had asked.

'Exactly what the media also claimed. That my son was part of a secret cult. That he and his friends were robbing another student. No one bothered to investigate when the student in question clearly gave testimony that he didn't know Kevin. No one wanted to hear us when both my wife and I said we could prove that Kevin was not even friends with the other two boys.'

'This is where you come in, Philip,' Abubakar then had said, more to calm Emeka down than anything else.

'The conclusions drawn from that video imply that my son was a criminal and deserved to die the way he did. I won't have that.' Emeka's had eyes burned with anger, as he leaned towards me, with an intensity that brooked no argument. 'Something happened, a mistaken identity at best, or a planned attack at worst. The fact is we don't know, which is worse than the fact that I buried my son in a closed casket because it would be too cruel to allow his mother see what was left of his body.'

'But this happened in the east. For me to recreate the crime, I would have to go there, talk to people, do some crime scene analysis –'

'– and for this, I'm willing to reward you handsomely,' Emeka had interrupted but then changed his tone when he saw me flinch at his insinuation that my decision could be bought. 'Please, Dr Taiwo. Philip. All I want is a report. I want your expertise in recreating crime scenes so I can make some sense of the senseless murder of my son. Please, if only for the fact that you're a father too.'

There had been silence for a beat. Then Emeka had reached for his iPhone again, and handed it to me.

'Don't worry. It's not the video.'

I had looked at the screen and the picture nearly broke my heart. Kevin was good looking and there was a wholesomeness and kindness in the broad smile he flashed at the camera that made me feel rage on Emeka's behalf.

'That's my boy,' Emeka had said with a sad smile. 'Kevin Chinedu Nwamadi. Third-year law student. He was twenty and the baby of the family. His sisters and mother doted on him. He was a good boy. Top of his class. Best son a father could ask for.'

That was when the dam broke, and in that classroom at the Police College in Lagos, Emeka Nwamadi, the Managing Director of the third largest bank in Nigeria, had heaved, shuddered and finally, cried.

POLICE IS YOUR FRIEND

'You called Tai and Kay!' my daughter snaps as soon as I pick up her call. It's 7:18 and I know they'll be ready for school and most likely, the boys had bragged about our late-night conversation.

'You were sleeping, moppet,' I say.

Lara lowers her voice dramatically. 'I wasn't. I was waiting for your call.'

'Your mom is there, right?'

'Don't change the subject, Dad.'

'Okay, okay. I'm sorry. I just thought you'd be sleeping. Won't happen again.'

'I googled that airport, Dad. You know it's been voted the worst airport in the world more than three times? Like in the whole wide world!'

'It wasn't that bad.'

I spend some time downplaying my experience at the airport, but when Lara asks if I have pictures, I realise how disoriented I was yesterday. I tend to take photographs on my trips and send them to her for her scrapbook.

'Mom's ready. Gotta go. Wanna speak with her?'

'I'll call her later. Don't keep her waiting.'

'Okay. Chat later?'

'Mos def, moppet.'

I hang up and check the time. I rush into the shower, dress at record speed and I'm ready when Chika knocks on my door.

We decide to skip the complimentary breakfast of eggs swimming in oil, and a butchered loaf passing for sliced bread. The coffee is lukewarm and tastes horrible. We both push our mugs aside and decide it's best to start the day with an empty stomach.

We set out to the police station, and I get to see the town in daylight. Several rows of bungalows line the uneven untarred road. I now appreciate why Emeka gave Chika a 4x4. It is a bumpy ride.

Rust-spotted roofing sheets come in and out of view as we drive through the town. People on bicycles, motorcycles, and in cars weave past and around us. It is a bit disconcerting to see people looking up from whatever they are doing to stare at us. A small town's fascination with strangers or something more? I test this theory quickly as I wave at three boys who should be in school, but instead are kicking a dirty soccer ball on the side of the road. They wave back. I relax. It is a small-town thing.

Soon, we're in front of an unpainted bungalow. The red rust here has dripped down the walls to create strips of brown that almost seem intentional. A hand-painted sign says where we are, but I still look at Chika askance. Surely it can't be –

'We're here,' Chika says as he parks the car.

The police station. We've driven past bungalows this morning that are more impressive in size and level of maintenance.

'I will wait here, sir,' Chika says.

'Nonsense,' I protest immediately. 'You can come with me.'

'But sir, I'm not sure –'

'Come,' I insist.

He smiles mischievously. 'Sir, it's the police station. Nothing like the airport yesterday, I assure you.'

The mention of the airport reminds me of my out-of-depthness, and I make a mental note to call Emeka. The efficient way Chika navigated me out of there, not to mention the careful and orderly compilation of the case notes, convinces me that he could be much more than a driver on this assignment.

'Chika,' I say in a voice I hope puts paid to any argument, 'it's either you come in with me or you'll have to call Emeka to explain why you're driving me straight back to the airport.'

I mean it as a joke of course, but Chika seems to take me seriously. He turns off the engine and we head in. The open-plan reception – technically, the living room of the bungalow – is furnished with desks held upright by broken pieces of other furniture. It's early, but there are already a few people in the station. One man is speaking agitatedly to an officer who is writing morosely. Two men sit on a bench staring straight ahead; both are sweaty, breathing heavily and, on closer observation, I notice they're holding on to the waistband of one another's trousers, apparently from a scuffle they refuse to resolve without the intervention of the law.

An officer sitting on the other side of another precariously positioned desk beckons us over. I can see he's a rookie from how clean and new his uniform is. Behind him, a poster with a fresh-faced male model in police uniform proclaims: 'Police is your friend. Help Police.'

The rookie tries to sound imperious. 'What do you want?'

'We're here to see Inspector Omereji,' Chika answers.

'In connection with?'

I proffer the envelope with the seal of the Commandant of Police College, Lagos. The rookie turns the package over in his hands with ill-concealed curiosity.

'Wait here,' he orders and leaves us.

The two men gripping each other's clothes have started arguing, using their free hands to make fists.

The bored statement-taking officer raises his voice. 'Hey! Hey! This is not a beer parlour! Keep quiet, or I'll lock both of you up!'

The men shut up almost instantly, but neither releases the other.

'They don't speak Igbo here?' I whisper to Chika.

'No. They speak Ikwerre,' he whispers back.

'I thought all easterners speak Igbo.'

'Don't let them hear you say that here, sir.'

I want to ask why, but the rookie is back and motions for us to follow him.

We walk down a hall with files and paperwork arranged on the floor in haphazard piles and quickly past what appears to be a holding cell with about half a dozen men playing cards and smoking. I catch a glimpse of beer bottles on the floor. Clearly, the inmates know how to get what they want.

We enter an office that's large enough to have been the master bedroom of the bungalow-turned-police-station, and the officer I assume to be Inspector Michael Omereji stands to greet us. He is a tall man, light-skinned with a moustache so well trimmed it suggests a streak of vanity. He's good looking and he knows it.

'Thanks for seeing us, Inspector,' I say, as I shake his proffered hand.

'Mike, please,' he answers graciously, as he motions towards the chairs in front of his desk. 'Have a seat.'

'Thank you,' I reply as I take the seat across from him. I notice Chika is not sitting and I motion for him to take the chair next to mine. He shakes his head almost imperceptibly.

I turn back to the inspector. 'The Commandant sends his regards.'

'Sadly, I've never met him. The Commandant is quite legendary.'

Some chit-chat about how well the Police College is doing since Abubakar took over trails into an awkward silence. I quickly introduce Chika as my research assistant and ignore his raised brow at this dubious promotion. The Inspector barely nods at my 'assistant' and does not offer Chika a handshake.

'Regarding the case I am writing the report on,' I begin.

'Yes, yes,' the Inspector cuts in. 'I read the Commandant's letter, but I can't help you.'

'All I need is the case file.'

'The investigations are over, and all the files have been handed over to the Prosecutor General's office.'

'Surely there must be copies?'

'Look around you, Dr Taiwo. Do you think we have space to keep months-old files, let alone the ones for a closed case?'

'Closed?'

'I'm sure you follow the news. The sad incident was investigated. Twenty-three people were arrested and I believe seven of them are on trial now. The case is in court. Justice is being carried out, and our job is done. Hence, the case is closed.' He pauses to look down on Abubakar's letter, which he pushes back to me with a shrug. I don't reach for it, my gaze fixed on him.

If the Inspector is fazed, he doesn't show it. 'Right now,' he continues, 'seven people have been charged with the killing of the three boys, and they're facing trial in the State High Court in PH. The case file is there. I'm sorry, there's nothing here for you.'

'That makes sense,' I say.

The Inspector seems encouraged by my acquiescence because he stands. 'If the Commandant had sent an email in advance, it would've saved you much trouble.'

I don't rise. 'May I speak to some of the investigating officers?'

'Why?'

'As the letter states, I'm compiling case studies of forensic precedents across the country. We're looking for interesting cases that support our curriculum at the Police College. The Okriki Three case is one such. I'm sure the investigating officers will be able to provide information that'll enrich the text even if the case is ... closed.'

Inspector Omereji looks at me, his watch, then back at me.

'It's rather early to pull hard-working officers off duty to come for interviews they're not prepared for.'

'We can come back. Just give me a time.'

'That'll be best.' He raises his voice, 'Constable Doubra!'
The rookie appears instantly.

'Please take Dr Taiwo's details. Remind me to tell the team that worked on the Okriki Three to make time to speak to Dr Taiwo and his ... colleague.'

'Yes, sir.' The rookie salutes and turns to me. 'This way, sir.'

I stand, shake Inspector Omereji's hand and walk out with the rookie Doubra, right behind Chika, who again isn't offered a handshake.

'He's lying, sir,' Chika says, as soon as we're in the car.

'I know, but there's nothing we can do. If the matter has been handed over to the Prosecutor General –'

'Yes, but why is he lying about the officers being busy? This is Okriki, not the underbelly of Aba market. How busy can they be?'

'Maybe he's buying time.'

'To prep the officers?'

I like Chika's street-smart distrust, which I've come to associate with people operating at a lower level than their qualifications. Survival forces insight, I guess.

'Back to the hotel, sir?' he asks as he starts the car.

'No. The crime scene.'

GHOST ROAD

If I were in the States, visiting the site of a cold case could still yield previously unknown information years after an incident. Investigators would check whether there were previously unnoticed security cameras on the streets. They would look for buildings around the scene that had windows facing where the crime took place. They will then go into those buildings and speak to possible witnesses, even those that have already given their testimonies when the case was live.

However, this is Okriki. The crime scene is a small clearing off to the side of a gravel road, less than twelve minutes' bumpy drive from the police station. There are no houses around. Or street lights. No cameras. Nothing really.

I look around and take pictures of angles that I hope to match to the video clips of the lynching later tonight. I quickly check the setting of my old crime scene companion: my Nikon 500. It's on automatic, and I switch to manual to control the precision of the images against the harsh sun.

'Where does this road lead?' I ask Chika.

'To Ochuko. We will pass the university's main campus before we get to the town proper.'

'So, it's like a major road?'

'Sort of. You can also take the road leading from our hotel around the town towards the main campus. It's a better road but takes longer.' He gesticulates northwards. 'This one takes you through to the campus directly, the other one from our hotel will take you through several villages before getting to the university.'

'Can we assume that this is the road most people would take if they're driving directly to the campus?' I ask, frowning. There is something strange about this road, deserted and neglected, despite the fact that it is the shortest and most direct route to the State University's main campus.

'I guess so,' Chika says but I can sense he is trying to understand my line of questioning. 'I would have said no, because of its current state, but then most roads in these parts are like this.'

A battered Volvo drives by. Its occupants look at us, curious until they are out of sight. A Toyota loaded with heaps of unripe plantain follows soon after.

'If this is the road that's the fastest to the campus, it doesn't make sense that it's so deserted. Come.'

We walk back to the 4x4. Chika starts the car so that the AC can be turned on, and we can close the doors and escape from the heat and dust. I bring out my iPhone and open one of the videos of the lynching, which I had saved. As it starts to play, Chika takes in a deep breath.

'You don't have to –' I start to say.

'It's okay, sir. I've seen it before.'

'It doesn't get easier ...'

'It *shouldn't* get easier.' Chika bends to peer at the small screen. 'What are you looking for, sir?'

I press pause. 'If you can take your eyes away from the boys, just study the road.' I press fast forward and continue speaking, 'We know they were brought here from that side. See?'

I raise the phone and look in the direction we came from.

'Can you see that?' I pause the video. 'See that tree? That tall one. Is that not the same one in the distance …?'

I point at the unusually tall palm tree in the distance that matches the one that stands out in the video where, at this point, the Okriki Three are still being paraded down the road like Christ on the Via Dolorosa.

'I see it,' Chika says, squinting in concentration as I enlarge the scene on the screen.

'If they were coming via this road, there's no way they wouldn't have passed the police station.'

Chika hisses in anger, 'The police must have seen the mob.'

'Exactly. Perhaps that's why Inspector Omereji needed to prep them for our questions. Look –'

I rewind and press play again, and it is almost surreal the way the journey of the doomed boys matches our drive from the police station. But now, there are no makeshift shops, stalls and kiosks like on the video. I see the edge of a table stacked with homemade gin; another seems to have battered bottles of engine oil and lubricants. If it's anything like Lagos, there should also be gallons of petrol and kerosene for sale, bread sellers ready to smear margarine on your purchase, water peddled in plastic bags and a myriad of food stalls lining the side of a significant road like this.

I freeze the image where this particular recording follows the Okriki Three as they fall down. There they are: stacks of old tyres with a vulcanising machine next to what seems to be the long, dirty tube of a pump. The mystery of the origin of the tyres thrown over the victims is explained. Albeit partially.

'Let's drive back to the police station.'

Chika turns the car around.

'Slowly,' I say, as we begin to drive back, my eyes darting from the iPhone screen to the road and back again.

Chika goes slowly. I pause the video intermittently. I focus on the surroundings and not the dying boys, and I switch programmes quickly, taking pictures of scenes that match what I see in the video.

When we get to the police station for the second time today, I ask Chika to turn the car round again.

'To the scene again?'

'Yes. And even slower this time.'

We must be coming off as very strange to those passing by. But I know I'm on to something here, although it's far from a breakthrough.

The second time we get to where the Okriki Three met their tragic end, I pause the video and look at Chika.

'The road was cleared,' I declare.

'Cleared, sir?' Chika looks at me briefly, then back to the road.

'There were shops here … Stop here! See?' I gesture to the frozen video, then outside. 'See the similarities in the vegetation? Look at that power line. And the transformer in the bush there? You see? We're at the same place and yet, in the video, there were shops and makeshift stalls, but now, there's nothing. The road is not deserted. It was cleared.'

'Maybe the people were traumatised and didn't want to remember?

I shake my head. 'It's possible but not plausible. All of them can't be affected to the same degree that they would all clear their wares off the most potentially profitable route to the university.'

'You think they cleared the route of the witnesses who saw what happened?'

'Or were even part of the lynching.'

'But there is proof on the video.'

'Yes. But look.' I press play again, and inch the iPhone towards Chika on the driver's side. 'Remember that Omereji said twenty-three people were arrested, but even if we can't see the faces, there are much more than that here ...'

I stop the video, look around and back at Chika.

'I need to go to where it all started.'

MADAM LANDLADY

The compound where the undergraduate named Godwin Emefele had lived is like most of the houses on the street; separated from the next one by trees and a patch of vegetables, maize and yams. In the large yard stands a double-storey building that appears to have been recently painted a bright yellow with dark brown highlights around the window ledges.

Chika and I are parked at the corner of the road, measuring the distance between the nearby market where we were told most of the mob came from and the police station that lies in the opposite direction.

'It's quiet for such a large compound,' I say, trying to picture a crowd entering the yard, apprehending the alleged thieves and dragging them all the way past the police station, to where they were finally killed. 'No tenants? Kids of families living here?'

'It was built for students.' Chika says, pointing. 'See? The big windows are the rooms themselves and the smaller ones are the bathrooms and toilets.'

I nod and try to count the number of large windows from where we are standing, while discreetly taking pictures with my phone. Six large windows downstairs on the side we are facing, so I assume the same will be on the other side. Give or take. Fewer upstairs because it has a large balcony at the front, so I would say eight or ten rooms on the top floor.

'If the townspeople say no one knew the boys were students, and yet the house is mainly occupied by undergrads –'

'I read that the townspeople said they've always been terrorised by students coming in from campus to steal their belongings.' Chika squints against the glare of the sun. 'The fact that they're students might have even aggravated the violence.'

'And there weren't other students around to disprove this Godwin's accusation?'

'You think the Godwin boy may have lied, sir?'

'We'll know soon enough,' I answer, recalling my interviewee list where Godwin is at the top.

I look back at the compound, standing forlorn and empty in such a big yard. Goats and chickens walk around, stopping to peck food off the unpaved ground. There are several other buildings of similar size down the road that leads to the market and the bus stop.

'If a lot of the houses are built to accommodate students, where are they all?' I wonder aloud.

'After the killing of the boys, most of them ran back to campus. The university warned them there'd be no protection for any student who lived off campus, especially during the early days afterwards. Most of them never came back.'

'The school created accommodation for them?'

Chika snorts. 'If there was, the students would not be living off campus in the first place. No, most of the students stayed with friends and sympathetic classmates. The squatter population swelled in most of the residential halls. Some students even dropped out of school because of the living conditions.'

I can imagine the scenario Chika describes. A tragedy like what happened to the Okriki Three would have induced mass hysteria amongst the student population, placing immense pressures on the university's resources. The outcome for the town can be likened to the aftermath of a natural disaster, and having volunteered in various shelters after terrible fires in California, I can understand why this part of Okriki looks so empty.

I want to say the town deserved whatever repercussions came from its tragic vigilante justice, but the silence around me strikes a sad note. I am about to say this when a young girl, no more than twelve, emerges from behind the house. Chika looks at me, seeking my permission. I nod and Chika calls out.

The girl stops but does not come to us, so we hurry away from the car.

'You wan rent?' the girl asks when we get to her.

'Yes,' Chika answers smoothly.

Darn, Chika is quick. I see the girl visibly relax and point back at the house. 'Madam Landlady dey for backyard.'

'You fit take us go meet am?'

The girl nods, and as I look around, we follow her into the compound. Definitely newly renovated, but as I peek into some of the rooms through the windows, almost entirely empty. I count five big windows on the side we walk on, noting that the sixth window is for a communal kitchen of sorts, so definitely ten rooms on the first floor and eight on top to accommodate the balcony.

At the back of the house, a massive woman with broad shoulders is bent over a spread of drying cassava. By the time we reach her, she has risen to an impressive height and crossed her arms over her ample bosom, much like a body-guard at the doorway of a nightclub.

'Mama Landlady, dem wan rent house.' The girl points at us excitedly.

'You be agent? Go where I send you now or na your head I go rent out!'

The girl scampers away and the landlady turns to us. Her suspicious stance doesn't change even when she switches to proper English. 'Who's renting?'

Chika smiles charmingly and answers, 'My friend here. Are you the landlady?'

'It is my property.'

I try to be as charming as Chika and proffer my hand. She eyes it as one would a buzzing mosquito courting swift death. I let my hand drop but keep the smile. 'Dr Taiwo. Philip Taiwo.'

'Doctor? And you want to rent here?'

Chika takes a deferential step forward while I move back. I'm not sure I can successfully pretend that I want to live under this woman's roof.

'Yes,' Chika again answers smoothly. 'The Doctor just got an appointment at the university, but they've not sorted out his staff quarters. We hear you just renovated and I must say, you've done a really nice job.'

The woman smiles and reveals a gap tooth. The ogre is gone, replaced by quite a personable human.

'The deposit is six months in advance.'

I don't bat an eyelid. Landlords being paid months, and even years in advance is common practice.

'It's not a problem, madam,' I say. 'Can you show me around?'

Madam Landlady immediately herds us into the house, briefly disappears to get a large bunch of keys and starts leading us from one room to another.

'I used to stay not too far from here and rented this place out,' she says as she opens a room and parlour with an en-suite bathroom and a not-too-shabby kitchen. 'This is one of my big ones. I stay in a similar one upstairs. You have a family?'

'Err, yes. My sabbatical is just for a year so they may come for a visit, but they won't be joining me.' I'm impressed by how easily the lie rolls off my tongue.

'Then this is a good place for you,' the landlady declares like I have little choice in the matter. 'There's a two-bedroom at the back too, but usually, the students prefer that one because they can share.'

'Are there many students renting?'

'Not like before. Now I have mostly temporary university staff like yourself.'

People without prior knowledge of the infamous compound's history, I bet.

'I like it,' I nod approvingly, and the landlady beams. 'May I ask where all the tenants are?'

'Why?' the landlady snaps. Attack and defence in one question, her smile gone.

'I just want to know how noisy it gets during the weekend when other tenants are home.'

'There're no tenants right now.'

'They left because of the renovations?' Chika asks.

'Yes!' She smiles with relief at Chika. I can imagine she's now found a new narrative for other prospective tenants. 'But many of them are coming back. I have an agent marketing the property at the university.'

I frown as if thinking hard about something, walk towards the window and look out into the compound yard. 'Isn't this the house …? The one those boys tried to rob and the people came to his rescue?'

Madam Landlady's smile disappears again, but there's no hostility when she answers guardedly, 'That was a long time ago.'

'Yes, but this is the house?'

'Yes.'

'Great!' I exclaim enthusiastically. 'I love a neighbourhood that looks out for each other.'

'Wonderful.' Madam Landlady claps with glee and relief. 'It's so nice to finally have reasonable people around. People have been so nasty to us.'

'It must have been hard for the whole town,' Chika proffers sympathetically.

'You can't imagine. I used to be a teacher in the primary school. My husband, God give him eternal rest, was the headmaster. We used all our savings to build this house so we could provide accommodation for those children at the university. We treated them like our own. Then, when everything happened, everyone started telling stories, saying how wicked we were! Some even said we used the boys for juju!'

'How silly,' I scoff. 'A whole town ganged up on young boys to use them for juju?'

'Search me, my brother,' Madam Landlady says.

'Were you here?' Chika asks, with just the right amount of curiosity.

'I wasn't. I told you I used to live on the other side of town. But when all the tenants moved out, I couldn't afford to keep two homes, so I moved back here.'

'No one remembers the good deeds of people when something like that happens,' Chika adds sympathetically.

Madam Landlady laps up our understanding. 'Common criminals, that's what those boys were!'

I look around like I can already see myself living here. 'Where was the boy staying?'

'Which boy?'

'The one they tried to rob.' I turn to the landlady. 'Was it this apartment?'

'You mean Godwin! His was down the corridor. Poor boy. I don't know what I would have done if someone came to my house with a gun. Come, let me show you.'

We follow the landlady, who I am confident could disarm anyone trying to rob her with or without a gun. She points down the corridor, towards the front entrance of the building.

'Over there, see?' she says. 'That one facing the road.'

'So, that's why it was so easy for people to hear when he cried for help,' Chika says, as if he now understands a significant part of a mystery that keeps him awake at night.

'And the other students?' I frown, measuring the proximity of Godwin's former room to the road. 'Why didn't they come out to help?'

'Many of them were in school and the other people staying here were at work. The ones at home said when they

72

heard the gunshots, they were too scared to come out and only did when the crowd came.'

'So, this Godwin was practically alone when the robbers pounced.' Chika has raised his voice in anger on behalf of the victim.

'Imagine! And everyone is calling our people wicked. How is it wicked to run to the aid of another human being?'

'And from what I read, they were quick,' I say.

'It was the gunshots that got everyone's attention,' the landlady explains.

'Gunshots? You mean it was more than one shot?' Chika inches closer to Madam Landlady like her words could change the course of history.

'Several! In fact, the whole town thought they were being attacked by an army!' Given that all reports had agreed that three, at most, four gunshots were heard, I can now add exaggeration to the landlady's skill set.

'So, they came from the shops on the road?' I ask.

'From everywhere. Those students had been robbing the town blind in the past, and we couldn't do anything because they're the lifeblood of our businesses. But when guns became involved, people just got tired.'

By now we are at the end of the corridor that leads outside. A gunshot from inside would be easily heard if the windows were open. I've seen enough.

'Thank you, madam. I'll definitely consider your lovely house.' My conscience won't allow me to commit beyond this. 'Please let me have your phone number.'

She calls out a series of numbers, which I save on my phone. Who knows when I might need to speak to her again, with or without a rental agreement in place.

As we drive away, Madam Landlady waves cheerily, happy at the possibility that her house, with a fresh coat of paint, may finally overcome its tarnished reputation.

Her joy makes me inordinately sad.

SMALL TOWN, FAST NEWS

Back in the Land Cruiser, I compliment Chika on his quick thinking and sense that he's not as uncomfortable as he was earlier about his promotion to my unofficial assistant.

Our self-congratulation regarding our acting skills dissipates when we notice the stares of some of the people passing by. It has a different quality from what I had earlier put down to small town curiosity.

I picture the rookie at the police station making calls to his girlfriend, who then calls her best friend, who in turn calls her mother. I recall Salome's ominous words.

As soon as we get to Hotel Royale, a rotund and balding man hurriedly comes to meet us.

'Hello, hello,' the man says with a fake smile. 'I was not here to welcome you last night. So sorry. I'm Oroma Atoka, the manager.'

I stretch out my hand to shake his, but I see a slight hesitation. He looks around quickly. The coast seems clear, so he takes my hand.

'Dr Taiwo?'

'Yes. And this is Chika, my assistant.'

Atoka nods towards Chika. 'We met when he came to book the rooms. He paid for two weeks, but we have a problem.'

'A problem?' I ask with a studied polite concern.

'Yes.' The manager's head bounces in pretend apology, then he turns to Chika. 'You see when I spoke with you, Mr Chika, I didn't know my girl in reception had already booked a party of people coming for a wedding. All the way from Lagos and even some from Abuja. The wedding is next week, and I'm afraid I'll not be able to accommodate you longer than one week.'

'But we paid in advance,' Chika protests, annoyed.

'I'll return your money,' the manager offers too quickly, 'and even see whether you can get accommodation in another guest house. There are nicer ones in Aluu, and even in Obio Akpor. I assure you, our small town has little to offer compared to those two.'

'You must be joking.' Chika's tone is derisive and irritated all at once. 'When I came, I explained to you that we might even extend our stay, and you assured me you'd have rooms for us for as long as we're here.'

'It's fine,' I quickly intervene, sensing Chika is not beyond a fist fight at this point. 'Look, Mr Atoka, let's talk about it in a week when the wedding is closer. I'm sure we can arrange something before then.'

The manager appears thrown by my compliance. He stutters a bit as he answers.

'It may even be less than a week. We have to prepare the rooms for the guests –'

'A week and we talk, okay?' I say in a voice that indicates the matter is closed and walk past him. Chika follows.

When we get to my room, Chika is a ball of rage.

'Somebody got to him!'

'We shouldn't jump to conclusions.'

'Sir, did you see the way people were looking at us when we were driving back?'

I nod, reluctant to verbalise assumptions without more facts.

'I'm telling you, sir, someone told him to get rid of us!'

'And there's nothing we can do about that,' I say to stop him pacing around the room like a restless bull. 'We can only plan around it. Are there any other guest houses or hotels around?'

'There's quite a number but none as nice as this one.'

I look around at my room. As far as rooms go in a town like this, it's okay. But I consider the ache in my shoulder blades from the lumpy mattress, the horrible breakfast, and shudder to think about the state of the other guest houses in town.

'Besides,' Chika continues, 'if someone wants the manager to get rid of us, I'm sure the same instruction has been given to all the other hotels in town. If we leave here, sir, I'm very sure we won't get accommodation anywhere else.'

'We can move to another town,' I suggest, although I would hate to lose out on the benefits of staying in Okriki itself.

'Most are not so close. The ones closer to the university are just as bad and not worth their room rate.' He shakes his head, and I get a glimpse of how stubborn he can be. 'No. We must stay here.'

I check my watch. Time is going. 'We still have a week to sort it out. For now, come and help me with something.'

I connect my phone to my laptop. 'If you can compare the pictures we took this morning with the video footage of the lynching, I'd appreciate it. Make notes of anything that catches your attention. But concentrate on the scenery. Nothing else.'

I am hoping doing this will keep Chika occupied while I figure out our next steps. If the file he prepared for me yesterday is anything to go by, I suspect Chika will deliver on the task.

I open the video in another window, while the pictures download on to my hard drive. Chika sighs as soon as the infamous opening frames begin.

'I know it's not pleasant,' I say apologetically, 'but we need screenshots of the scenes that match the ones we drove by today.'

The download done, I disconnect my phone from the MacBook as Chika sits at the desk and pulls the laptop closer to him.

I then dial Abubakar Tukur's number.

A SON OF THE SOIL

'Dr Taiwo!' Inspector Omereji exclaims as soon as Chika and I enter his office. 'We called PH, and as luck would have it, they happened to have made copies of the files we sent to the Prosecutor General's office. As soon as they told me the copies were available, I immediately sent someone to get them.'

He waves his hand at the boxes on his desk like a magician revealing a previously chopped-up assistant now hale and hearty. Given the traffic I experienced from the airport yesterday, only a helicopter could have brought the files so quickly from Port Harcourt to the Okriki Police Station.

'Will I be able to speak with the investigating officers?' I make my tone hopeful and respectful.

'That still needs to be arranged. The men are busy, Doctor.'

'I can also speak with you,' I venture to test the waters.

'You don't know?' he asks, eyebrows arched. 'I was posted back here about six months after the unfortunate event.'

I take note of his deliberately proper pattern of speech. Like he doesn't want to say the wrong thing. I sometimes forget Abubakar is more than just the Commandant of the

Police College but also part of the Hausa oligarchy, with strong political connections. If Abubakar pulled all the strings I know him to be capable of, there's no doubt the previously arrogant Inspector is in the hot seat. I wouldn't be surprised if he is recording this conversation.

'Where were you before, if you don't mind my asking?' My tone is as formal as his, infused with the mildest of curiosity.

'Of course not. It's public knowledge. I was posted from Kano.'

'Coming back to Okriki must be a far cry from a big city like Kano,' I say, trying to see behind his blank smile.

'It's home. I'm from here. I even went to TSU.'

'I also went to TSU. What year?' Chika asks.

'I graduated in 2011.' If there's a softening of attitude towards Chika because they're alumni of the same university, I can't see it. 'Sociology. You?'

'Two thousand twelve,' says Chika. 'Computer science.'

Omereji frowns at Chika but says nothing. There's an awkward silence that begs to be broken.

'So, you're a son of the soil,' I interject with contrived joviality.

But Omereji doesn't respond in kind. The blank smile comes back, but his gaze on Chika doesn't waver. It's Chika who breaks the tension by walking to Inspector Omereji's desk and picking up two of the boxes.

'I'll come back for that one,' he says as he passes by the Inspector and me.

I start to protest. 'I can bring –'

'I'll come back, sir,' Chika insists as he leaves, and I'm now left with Inspector Omereji, whose face threatens to crack under the strain of fake conviviality. I try to help him out of his misery.

'You know the officers well?'

'Pardon?'

'The team who investigated the case. They're still at this station, I presume.'

'Only two are. The other was transferred out of here, but I heard he left the force.'

I bite my tongue from commenting on the expedience of such a development. I look at the remaining box on the desk. 'That's a lot of paperwork to be generated by three investigating officers.'

'Look around you, Dr Taiwo. This is hardly the kind and size of station that attracts the best of the best.'

'And yet, you're here,' I retort before I can stop myself.

'Since I had little choice in the matter, I'll take that as a compliment,' the Inspector says with a rueful smile.

It's time for my own fake smile, then a studied frown. 'Given the magnitude of the case, and the media interest, I'd have thought the force would have deployed extra hands?'

'No one wanted to touch it. And can you blame them?'

'But you came.'

'To clean up the mess and control the damage to the force and the town. There were too many ugly stories spreading about this town.'

The switch is quick. Standing before me is an angry man, unpleased by my presence.

My tone is more sympathetic when I say, 'You didn't have to come.'

'My people needed me.'

'It's that bad?'

'You can't imagine. But it's over now, thank God. The media is gone. The students are coming back little by little. There is some peace between the university and the town. People's businesses are picking up. The trial is far away in PH. Slowly, things are getting back to normal.'

'You'll transfer back to Kano?'

'I'll transfer to wherever I can pursue my career in a more, well, dynamic space.'

I acknowledge the diplomatic sound bite with a nod just as Chika returns, picks up the remaining box and leaves.

I stretch out my hand. 'I'm sure the people of Okriki appreciate your sacrifice. Not many people would care enough to come back and help rebuild a town tainted by the kind of horror that happened here.'

'It's my responsibility,' Omereji says as he takes my hand.

'Nonetheless, I applaud you. And when the investigating officers have the time, you'll tell them to give me a call, right?'

The fake smile again. 'Of course. I have your number.'

'Good. Thank you for the files.'

I turn to leave.

'Dr Taiwo …?'

I stop and turn around.

'Try not to open old wounds.'

'If there are still wounds after all this time, maybe they need cleaning and dressing to heal properly.'

I know I'm making light of a serious request, given what I now know of the Inspector's origins, but it's the only way I can deal with the intensity of his gaze.

'This town was on edge for almost two years –'

'And three young men were murdered in broad daylight.'
I instantly regret the sharpness of my tone.

'I thought you were compiling a case study, not investigating what happened?'

'Maybe there's no difference.'

Omereji returns to his desk and starts to shuffle some papers. I take it I am dismissed.

I look at his bowed head. Perhaps he is a genuinely decent officer forced to truncate his ambitions to protect his town and people.

But from what? I wonder as I leave the office.

BOXFULS OF NOTHING

'This is ridiculous!' Chika exclaims and only just stops short of flinging the papers in the air.

I had asked Chika to help me sort out the contents of the boxes, which are proving to reveal nothing worthwhile. It is mostly photocopies of eyewitness accounts, badly written and poorly spelt. On several, one can barely make out the names of the person giving the testimony. There are missing words erased by poor-quality ink toner or cut off by lousy placement on the copy machine, and in most, the grammar is so bad that whole statements make no sense. The police reports are even more pathetic. My thirteen-year-old daughter can construct sentences with greater clarity.

'They did nothing!' Chika waves paper, irritated.

'Or didn't want to do anything,' I say as I stretch awkwardly from the lotus position I had assumed for almost an hour.

'But, sir, they could've at least pretended to do some police work. Look at this.' Chika reads aloud; 'My name is Mr Peter A. Ofunsi. I was there when they catch thieves, but not see them burn. Signed on this Lord's day of October two eight.' He throws the sheets of paper on the floor,

84

already strewn with many of a similar fate. 'How is this even a statement?'

I am looking at a large piece of paper I had to unfold several times while Chika spoke. It appears to be a building floor plan.

'This might be useful.' I stand and stick the architectural drawing on the wall facing my bed.

'Is that –?'

'The layout of Madam Landlady's house,' I announce.

Chika joins me and waves his hand dismissively after peering at the document. 'There's nothing here.'

'Look closely. Each of the rooms have the names of the people that stayed there.'

'Most are initials, sir. It will take a while to figure out who is who. And even if this layout shows the names of the legal tenants, it won't have the names of squatters sharing space with fellow students.'

I shrug. I don't tell Chika that it's this kind of detailed work that excites me. It wouldn't be any sort of investigation if everything is obvious. Besides, the floor plan tells me that the police knew how to put together the basics of an evidentiary trail and what to look for in a crime scene. Which makes the lack of detail in the files even more disturbing.

'But it's a good place to start,' I say. 'We have affidavits with names, we can match them to the ones on this floor plan, and if we hit a jam, we can approach the landlady for –'

I am about to jokingly add that I wouldn't mind signing a rental agreement when I see Chika shaking his head. 'The word on the streets of Okriki about your presence must have reached her by now. I don't think she'll be renting you her house for anything.'

I nod, but I am undaunted. This floor plan has data that I can use. How? I don't know, but I'm pretty sure it will come in handy at some point. It's an intuition I've honed with experience.

Chika walks back to the papers and starts packing them into the boxes. To his credit, he is arranging the papers with more reverence than his opinion of their contents warrants, but his irritation is evident.

I understand Chika's frustration, but I had come prepared. The day after I finally agreed to take on the assignment, Abubakar had called me into his office and warned me not to expect much cooperation from the local police.

'They want this to go away quickly,' he had said as he dragged on a cigarette, still the only officer who dared to smoke in his office.

'Can't they see Emeka won't let it go?' I had said, praying for my lungs.

'Yes, but it's been more than a year of nothing. *Feeful* are *p*orgetting, testimonies are becoming blurred, and the *f*rosecution cannot build a case due to lack of credible evidence.'

'So, I'm going in blind?'

'Not really.' Abubakar had pulled open a drawer and brought out a flash drive, which he placed on the desk.

'What's that?' I had asked.

'Some reports from the independent investigation Emeka has conducted over the last year and a half.'

'Why's he not giving it to me himself?'

'Because I asked him not to.'

I had frowned at this bluntness. 'Why?'

'For one,' Abubakar had puffed and continued, 'because I wanted to spare Emeka the agony of walking you through it, and second, because a lot of the in*por*mation is biased towards Emeka's theories and I wanted us to separate the *p*orest from the t*l*ees.'

After two hours of Abubakar blowing smoke in my face and talking me through several of the documents, I could see why I needed the guidance. Newspaper articles, pictures of the victims alive and post-mortem, court hearings, Internet downloads and videos of the killings in different formats filled several folders. I was impressed with the detail and how much information a private individual could garner independently and had said as much to Abubakar.

'Emeka is a very driven man,' Abubakar had replied.

'Some would say obsessed, but I don't blame him. If either of my sons …' An involuntary shudder had stopped me. While I couldn't tell Abubakar about my conversation with my dad, I was genuinely curious about this case. The sadness in Emeka's eyes and the unimaginable thought of losing any of my children in such a horrible manner would have been enough to make me commit to the assignment if I wasn't already dealing with Folake's betrayal.

'You have to understand that the police force in Okriki is full of locals. They were *f*rejudiced from the get-go, and it didn't make it easier when one of them was seen with the mob.'

'You think they closed ranks to protect him?'

'Maybe at the beginning but soon it became to *f*rotect the whole town.' He had ejected the flash drive and handed it to me. 'Study it. I know you won't get much from the police reports.'

'I still need to see the reports.'

'But I just told you what's on this drive is much more com*f*rehensive.'

'I want to see the leads the police didn't follow or refused to.'

It was Abubakar's turn to frown. 'Why?'

'Because if they didn't follow up on a lead, then maybe that's where I should be looking.'

'I knew you were the right man for the job,' Abubakar had said as I stood, shook his hand and made a quick getaway with the flash drive in hand. My discomfort with second-hand smoke outweighed the boost to my ego.

'It's not as useless as you might think,' I say to Chika now, surrounded by police reports that confirm the wisdom of Abubakar's words.

'But, sir, there's nothing here that's not in the public record,' Chika says.

I wave him over as I click open the folder containing the material from Emeka on my laptop. 'I'll read out a piece of evidence off the screen and you look for corroborating or contradictory evidence amongst the pile of police reports, okay?'

'Okay, sir.'

We work late into the night and try to match accounts of what we know happened with what's included in the police reports. Most of them cover the basics: when Winston, Bona and Kevin left the campus, the time locals claimed to have seen the three come into the town, and the the number of gunshots that were heard from Godwin's compound.

We have a breakthrough in matching some of the names on the affidavits with the initials of residents listed on the floor plan. Unfortunately, all claimed to be at school when the incident happened.

We also single out information that contradicts Emeka's independent report. For instance, many of the witnesses in the police reports claimed to have seen the three boys come into town together, yet some were clear that Winston was with Bona, and Kevin only joined them later.

The testimony of Kevin's girlfriend, Mercy, is particularly relevant since she claimed that Kevin had been at her parents' house to visit her and couldn't have come into town with Winston and Bona. Yet there's no record of Mercy's testimony in the police reports. Even more curious, Godwin's written testimony claimed that he didn't know how Kevin became part of the Okriki Three.

'There are enough contradictions for them to have investigated further,' I say, bending my neck left and right to relieve stiffness. It's been a long night.

'Perhaps they believed there was no point since the boys were dead anyway?' Chika posits unconvincingly.

'Maybe, but it's still not an excuse.' I open my list of interviewees in another folder. 'We must follow the evidence of divergence in the reports to identify the right people to interview. They will be the clue to the missing parts.'

Chika frowns. 'Like finding answers in the things *not* in police files?'

'Bingo.'

THE POWER OF ONE

My room is a mess. Papers are strewn everywhere. Sticky notes are tacked on every inch of wall not covered by curtains or cheap print artwork in even cheaper frames. It is late, I'm exhausted, and Chika has retired for the night.

I pour myself a tall glass of beer from the bottle I ordered from the bar downstairs. It is now quite warm, but I am fine with that. The warmer the beer, the faster it'll knock me out and grant me momentary reprieve from my turbulent thoughts.

I take a deep breath, annoyed at how my fingers hover over the call prompt beneath Folake's number on my phone screen. Just as I'm about to hit the call button, I get a text message:

'I hear you caused a stir in town today, Americana.'

How did Salome know? News may travel fast in Okriki, but all the way to Port Harcourt? I remember she said her mother hails from here, but it does seem like she has a more active connection to this town than she's let on. Is the text message a friendly enquiry about my welfare or a continuation of her warning on the plane? *Chill, Philip.*

'Your sources exaggerate. Perhaps we meet, and I can tell you the facts?'

As soon as I press send, I regret what may be miscon-strued as a request for a date. My panic propels me to call my wife.

'Well, you took your time.' Trust Folake not to beat around the bush.

'It's been hectic,' I say guardedly.

'I'm sure.' She doesn't bother to mask her irritation.

There's an uncomfortable silence.

'I'm sorry,' I say and, even to my ears, it sounds feeble.

She exhales down the line. 'It's okay. The kids miss you.'

Do you miss me?

'I spoke to the boys and Lara. I called them before school −'

And so goes the classic tension-breaker in any trou-bled marriage: deflection. We talk about our children, sharing known information as if it's news: the twins in the middle of their mock tests to prepare them for their final year of high school, Lara playing Juliet in the school play.

'Aren't they too young for such a play?' I wonder.

'She's thirteen, Sweets.'

I can hear the chuckle in her voice and the way she says 'Sweets' sets me at ease enough to share some details of my time in Okriki.

I tell her about Chika, the townspeople and my impres-sions of Inspector Omereji and the local police force. We hang up around midnight, and there's a warmth in my belly that has nothing to do with beer. Once again, for the umpteenth time in twelve days, I wish there was another way to explain what I saw through her office window, but I can't let myself think about that now.

I down the last of my beer and look at the colour-coded Post-its Chika and I have put up on the wall encircling the floor plan of Madam Landlady's house.

Blue for facts: the number of victims, their gender, their ages, et cetera.

Red for information that raises red flags with more questions than answers: the police reluctance to cooperate falls in this category, as does our guest house's sudden need to be rid of us.

Yellow for names of people initially arrested for the crime. We've highlighted the ones later released.

Green for witnesses and their location on that tragic day.

Orange for things we don't know yet.

The wall of my room looks like a Montessori classroom.

Prof always said that the more you understand the living, the easier it is to understand death. I wonder now about the limits of that assertion with at least a hundred suspects who might have just as many motivations for attacking the Okriki Three.

The Wi-Fi in the hotel is passable, but maybe because of the late hour, the Internet responds relatively fast when I search 'robberies in Okriki town'.

Several of the news items are from the local paper, *Okriki Express*. After scrolling past innumerable mentions and articles on the Okriki Three, a trend of regular clashes between the students and the indigenes of town emerges. Fights have broken out in marketplaces, bars and local concerts. Landlords assert there have been damages arising from violent clashes between students supposedly in rival cults. Market women accuse young people they claim must be from TSU of taking their wares and refusing to pay. The list of incidents is long and confirms that the town has a very uneasy relationship with the university students.

I summarise these in my notebook, on the page I had written: *Get data on the rate of robberies in the neighbourhood before or during the month of the killing.*

I look at the wall again. I have drawn lines across the Post-it notes to link one possibility to the next, and it now resembles an admittedly confusing web.

I flip the notebook to the page where I'd written: *A singular motive masked by a collective purpose or bias?*

I need to simplify, to think of all these as *one*.

My study of the lynchings in the south of the US, had showed that most, if not all, were caused by some innocuous event – Emmett Till, for instance, had reportedly whistled at a white woman. The mobs were always determined to make the lynching as public as possible, ostensibly to serve as a deterrent to other black people who might have thought about overstepping their boundaries. However, the public nature of lynching served a purpose beyond perpetuating the notion of white superiority and the subjugation of black people. It made so many people complicit in the crime that prosecution was almost impossible. Each 'strange fruit' that hung off a tree was both a symbol of racial terrorism and connivance. A unified force rallying behind a crime initiated by *one*, covered by *all*.

I look back at the wall. Many hands had struck the Okriki Three, but if there was someone in that crowd acting with a different motive from the rest of the mob, I had to find out who he or she is.

There's no more logical place to start than with the young man who raised an alarm and set into motion the string of events that ended with the lynching.

THE NARRATIVE

I'm roused from my sleep by my phone ringing. It's my father.

'I didn't get a response to my text, so I thought to check on you.' The admonition is clear in his tone.

'I am sorry, sir. I got in late and things got hectic almost immediately.'

'But you're okay?'

'I am. Emeka did know that I arrived safely. The chaperone he provided has been excellent.'

'I am pleased you're not doing this alone.' My father isn't taking the bait. If he is in constant talks with Emeka, he is not letting on. 'I can't help but worry that I persuaded you to take a job that might put you in harm's way.'

Now I feel bad for avoiding him since our talk in his study almost a week ago.

'Nothing has happened to suggest I am in any kind of danger, Dad. You can relax.'

'Okay. I also wanted to know if you told Folake what I shared with you ...' His voice trails off.

'I didn't tell her anything, sir.'

'Thank you.' His relief is unmistakable, even over the phone. 'I'd like to be the one to tell her if it becomes necessary.'

His point is clear: if he is going to be outed to his daughter-in-law, it must be on his terms. I can't contest this given my current situation with Folake, so I am quiet.

'Anyway, take care of yourself. Let me know if you need anything.'

'I will, sir.'

'Okay. Your mom sends her regards.'

'Give her mine.'

He doesn't hang up, so I hold the line as the silence stretches. This is unusual territory for us.

'Kenny Boy,' he says finally, 'I just want you to know how much I appreciate you doing this. For Emeka and, you know, all of us.'

'I have to go now, sir,' I say but wait till he hangs up.

I take a shower and I'm almost fully dressed when breakfast is brought to my room by the receptionist, who is now looking decidedly less dour, trailing behind Chika. She places the serving tray on the only available space on my desk, collects some cash from him and leaves.

'I took matters into my own hands,' Chika says, pointing at the tray with flourish.

'You cooked this?' A perfectly fried omelette, with three neatly cut slices of boiled yam. There's a bottle of cold water on the side and a tall glass of juice. I'm not big on eating this early, but my stomach rumbles at the sight of the food.

'I might as well have,' Chika answers, as he unwraps the cutlery from paper napkins and hands it to me. 'I gave the cook step-by-step instructions, and then rewarded her with two hundred naira after she was done.'

'Best two hundred you ever spent, I bet.' I cut into the eggs and yam. Delicious.

'Where's yours?' I ask Chika through a mouthful.

'In my room –'

'Go get it. Let's eat together. We have a lot to talk about.'

I can sense Chika's hesitation. Playing my assistant is one thing but eating within the informal setting of my hotel room might be a bit too much for him.

My phone beeps just as Chika leaves. It's a message from Salome: *'My sources are solid, but I won't pass up the opportunity of free drinks. Let me know when you're free.'*

I am relieved that she didn't read more into my text yesterday, but it is to Emeka I send a quick message.

'Good morning,' I type quickly. *'V. impressed with Chika. Can do more than just driving. Ok to ask?'*

The response is almost instant. *'Pls go ahead.'*

When Chika comes back with his tray, we clear the desk of papers, the laptop, Post-it notes, and then settle down to eat while attempting to formulate a coherent chain of events.

Godwin Emefele, a student of the State University, who resided off campus in Okriki, had been visited by three fellow students: Winston, Bona and Kevin. A fight had ensued because, according to Godwin, the students attempted to extort money from him.

Godwin had raised an alarm when one of his three alleged assailants pulled a gun on him. The sound of gunfire convinced the townsfolk that a robbery was in progress. A crowd descended on the three young men, setting off a tragic chain of events that led to the 'necklace killings'.

Twenty-three people were charged, including a police officer identified at the scene from the videos uploaded on social media. The officer, a Sergeant James Johnson – an ethnically amorphous name that gives as little information as his written account – was released because he claimed he was there to stop the mob. Since no one disputed his testimony, he was discharged and immediately transferred to another state. Only seven remain in custody, with the charges against the others having been dropped or dismissed. The fate of the seven is yet to be determined by the courts.

'Nothing new,' Chika says, scraping up the last of his omelette.

'But that's not exactly true,' I muse aloud, struck by a realisation. I push my food aside and reach for my notebook on the bed.

'All the reports say there were gunshots, but there's no gun on the list of evidence.' I flip through my notes quickly and look at Chika. 'If the gun's not with the police, where is it?'

'Maybe someone stole it?' Chika proffers.

'Unlikely, although not impossible.'

'Nothing of the boys' belongings were found,' Chika countered. 'No cell phones, no wallets, no wristwatches, no belts, no shoes, no clothes.'

'So, you think someone in the mob could have taken the gun?'

'Chances are.' Chika shrugs.

'That would mean the gun – if there was a gun – is still around somewhere in Okriki?'

Chika snickers before he can catch himself.

'What's funny?' I ask, confused.

'It's you, sir … I mean, sorry. I don't mean you're funny, but if you don't mind my asking, when did you come back to Nigeria?'

'Eight months now, give or take. Why?'

'It's your questions. I'm sorry, it's like you know nothing of the situation in these parts.'

I'm slightly miffed by this, but if there's something he thinks I am missing, I'd like to hear it.

'Go on, I'm listening.'

'This part of the country is very troubled. There's always conflict, with the government, oil companies, between communities. What with the militancy, people here are always fighting for something.'

'The We-Dey boys, right? I read a little about them before coming here.'

'They believe themselves to be freedom fighters, politicians and economic emancipators all rolled into one,' Chika continues, and I get the sense he's not a fan. 'Some people see them as heroes of sorts, Robin Hood types.'

'Ah!' I finally get the picture. 'If there was a gun, it's probably been passed on to militants.'

'I'm afraid so. Chances are the gun is pointing at a hostage right now in the bush somewhere.'

I can't let Chika see how unnerved I am by his statement. I have never, in the course of work, felt myself to be in mortal danger. I've largely worked in offices, from the safety of my desk. Fieldwork was interviewing suspects, witnesses and investigating officers.

I try not to dwell too much on my sudden unease. 'We should still look into the gun, though,' I say, keeping my voice level with some effort.

'Why is this gun so important, sir?'

'The gunshots were what motivated the crowd, and yet the gun's not in the evidence chain and no one tried to find it. I understand you're making a calculated assumption in thinking it was stolen, and maybe it was, but there's something here.'

I walk to the wall of Post-it notes and frown at the maze. 'Everyone agrees that there were gunshots, but only one person actually saw the gun or who used it.'

I reach for a marker and draw a circle around Godwin Emefele's name and write 'gun?' next to it.

MOMMY DEAREST

Amaso Dabara's visit was no surprise. I knew he would come as soon as he found out I am weeks away from graduation. After rejecting his request that I fail my exams so I could stay at TSU for one more year, he has become more demanding. Breaking into my room at odd hours with his goons is the latest of his escalating intimidation tactics.

To take my mind off Amaso, I returned to the letters from my mother. And though John Paul left me to read each one, I could hear his derisive laughter from the shadows.

It was clear to me by the time I had gone through those letters that I couldn't live with not knowing, without seeing my mother again. I have no idea how this will affect The Final Plan, but I must see Mama.

But first, I have to do my rounds of the cybercafes at the Students' Village to check on the online progress of The Final Plan for John Paul.

All on track.

I log on to Pastor Oriakpu's online sermons and find inspiration for my next series of posts. The reactions are immediate and expected. Soon, the anger will boil over.

I log off the different accounts and leave the Students' Village as quickly as I can.

I don't think I'll ever be able to get over the fear that comes over me any time I have to manage The Final Plan as me. I know how careful we have been, but it doesn't stop me from constantly looking over my shoulder to be sure some nosy student is not reading the posts as I type at the cybercafe.

There have been times when I walked out of the cafe, absolutely sure everyone on campus knows. Those were terrible moments of searching every face, wondering which one has called the authorities on me, while John Paul hid in the shadows.

The fear and John Paul's mocking laughter make me walk fast, my head low and my shoulders hunched. I avoid eye contact, counting the steps that will get me to the taxi park, and then counting backwards when I hit every hundred. I try not to say the numbers out loud, so people don't think I am talking to myself. It also helps to hear my own voice in my head. That way, I can pretend not to hear John Paul.

It is midday and off-peak; traffic is not so bad. In less than an hour, I am in the reception of the teaching hospital in Port Harcourt, staring at a huge signboard. I see that the ward number Father Olayiwola gave me is on the oncology floor and my heart sinks.

There's a small crowd of people waiting for the elevator, so I take the stairs instead.

When I get to the oncology floor, the nurse at the duty station points me to my mother's ward.

There are five other women in the room, all of them sleeping, all attached to multiple intravenous drips and beeping machines. I would have missed my own mother were it not for a name-board over her bed.

She has grown old. The lines on her face are relaxed in sleep, but there is no doubt that the past eleven years have not been kind.

I feel as though I am in a trance as I walk towards her, my progress slowed by memories, hope and, yes, fear.

As though sensing my presence, my mother opens her eyes, stares straight at me and smiles.

My knees wobble as I get to her bedside and lay my head on her chest.

'You're here.'

I burst into sobs at the sound of her voice. It's weaker now, but still the same.

'No tears,' she says softly. 'You're a man now. No tears.'

Despite her jutting collarbones, her close-cropped grey hair and her skin that's brittle from medication, my mother is still beautiful.

'Mama,' I say over and over. Like a prayer.

'I am not dreaming?'

I shake my head, laughing through a sob. 'No, you're not dreaming.'

'Sometimes I see things that aren't there.'

'I am here, Mama.'

'I ask after you a lot. Do they tell you?'

'Yes, Mama. They tell me.' The anger rises inside me. The fate planned for the monks cannot come soon enough. I will cheer John Paul from the shadows as they all burn.

'You look very handsome. Like your father,' she says and reaches to touch my face. Her hand trembles against my cheek. I gently lay it back on the bed, careful not to upset the attached IV line because I can see that finding a vein will be difficult.

I read the medicines listed on the label of the bag of IV: Cisplatin and paclitaxel. Standard combination chemotherapy for cancer, with hydromorphone for pain management.

I know this from years of working at the monastery's dispensary. I read the dosages of the medicines. Not good.

'You look great, Mama,' I say.

'You lie,' she says. 'But I forgive you.'

She laughs feebly and I join in.

We're together again. Like in my dreams when I have the light.

AT OWNER'S RISK

In an ideal world, Godwin Emefele should have graduated. When the Okriki Three tragedy happened, Godwin was already a third-year political science undergraduate. But since then, the university's academic and non-academic staff have gone on strike a combined total of three times, each lasting at least three months.

In between, there were student riots against rising fuel prices, protests against an increase in registration fees and, most recently, student marches to complain about the water shortage on campus. Almost all the student protests ended in violence, necessitating the closure of the university. It's no surprise that Godwin has only just reached his final year.

Finding him was surprisingly easy. Emeka made a call to the university registrar who scheduled an appointment with us and promised to make Godwin available for an interview.

'I'm surprised by the level of cooperation from the university,' I say to Chika, as we drive towards the TSU campus.

'They've been the most sympathetic to the parents of the three.'

'Probably trying to avoid a lawsuit,' I note.

Chika chuckles. 'Lawsuit? For what? The incident happened off campus. The university didn't sign a contract to protect the students from lynch mobs.'

'That's ridiculous,' I retort, slightly annoyed that he might be right. 'They have a duty of care. There has to be some responsibility.'

Chika pulls into a slot in a row of parking enclosures covered by rusting corrugated iron sheets.

'Look at that sign, sir,' Chika says, pointing. 'See what it says?'

I don't bother to read aloud the 'Cars parked at owner's risk' sign.

'So?' It's hard to mask my impatience at this point.

'It's the same when you send your child to university. When I started here, there were over 6,000 new students across more than fifty departments. Less than 2,000 of the new students had accommodation on campus. The ones that could find a place to squat did, and it wasn't strange to find students living in conditions worse than shanty towns. Many moved off campus, especially the ones who could afford it.'

'So, students preferred to stay off campus?'

'Generally, yes. But often because they had no choice. The university can't accommodate all of them. Where they live and cause problems then becomes the responsibility of towns like Okriki.'

'Regardless, they're students. The school is responsible for them whether they stay on campus or not.'

'In an ideal world, maybe, but here the students come at their own risk. Like the cars.'

I'm irritated by how normal this all sounds to him. To my mind, there is nothing normal about any of this. The Okriki Three tragedy could not have occurred in a saner climate without a slew of lawsuits against the town, the police and the university.

Chika cuts the engine and we get out. He clearly knows his way around. Tall trees line streets with faculty buildings jutting out from all the greenery like trespassers in a jungle. The roads are tarred, and have well-maintained traffic lights. Students walk purposefully amongst staff and visitors. Calm. Peaceful. I'm tempted to like my first impressions of the State University.

We make our way towards an imposing structure bearing the university's coat of arms and marked by stencil as the Senate Building.

Chika slows his pace and turns to me. 'If you don't mind my asking, sir, why did you come back to Nigeria?'

This question comes out of left field and I'm not sure what to make of it. Besides, the 'sir' makes me cautious. I know 'sir' is not necessarily an overt sign of respect or formality around here. I consider it a salutation used to create distance. It says: only this far until you tell me to come closer. Since my reasons for returning to Nigeria are too personal, I'm not willing to share them with Chika. At least, not yet.

'It was time,' I reply noncommittally, an answer that is as cryptic as it is true.

We walk the rest of the way to the registrar's office in silence.

Tom Ikime, the Registrar, is a good-looking man in his early fifties. He is well dressed and sports a tie and blazer that should be above his pay grade, but show me a Nigerian civil servant who lives within his salary, and I'll hand you a live unicorn.

Ikime ushers us into his office once introductions are made. 'I've sent someone to fetch the Godwin boy.'

We settle into plush leather seats that can't be standard university furniture.

'You know Godwin well?' I ask, glad not to pussyfoot around the purpose of our visit.

'Of course, I do. I was closely linked to the investigation after the unfortunate affair, and I headed the panel that the university set up to write a report.'

'I didn't know there was a university report.' This is good news. 'May I see it?'

'Of course. I doubt you'll find anything of note, though. Everything confirms what we already knew. The boys went to Okriki to bully and extort another student. The student cried for help and the town descended on the boys. Sad, but the facts are irrefutable.'

'Mr Nwamadi and the other parents don't agree with those facts.'

'Who can argue with the grief of a parent? Anyone would want to believe the best of their dead child,' Ikime replies levelly.

I detest public officials who peddle platitudes. It's an annoyance I have carried with me since my time standing behind government officials at press conferences in San Francisco, when I had to wear an impassive mask as they put a spin on human tragedies that could've been avoided with better infrastructure in the poorer neighbourhoods of the city.

'I'd like to see that report nonetheless.'

'Sure. It'll be in the public domain soon anyway, available on the university's website once the Vice Chancellor signs off on it.'

'A report like that can be very useful,' I say, holding his gaze. 'I'm sure it has lessons learnt and insights into what the university could have done better –'

'There was nothing the university could have done differently.'

'Oh, but I'm sure there was. And that's the problem, don't you agree?'

Ikime's smile disappears and his eyes become shuttered. An uncomfortable silence follows, but clearly the Registrar is a consummate public servant because his calm voice cuts through it as if the brief tension never occurred.

'You know, when we saw how deeply affected Godwin was by the tragedy and, realising the critical role he would play in the court case, we went to great lengths to support him. We put him in special accommodation where he'd be safe, and we have constantly reminded other students about everything Godwin did to try and avert what happened in Okriki.'

Tom Ikime speaks as though he's reading from a script, perfected by repetition on multiple forums where he's had to defend the university and deny any culpability. Not so different from what would have happened in the States, now that I really think about it.

The Registrar's secretary, a young lady who had ushered us in earlier, knocks softly to inform Ikime of Godwin's arrival.

'Is the boardroom free?' Ikime asks.

'Yes, sir.'

We follow her to the outer office, where a skeletal young man is pacing back and forth. He stops, turns to us and wipes his nose on the sleeve of his jersey, staring at us with belligerence. His gaunt face, bloodshot eyes and crown of unkempt hair tell a story I have seen many times over the years.

There is no doubt in my mind that Godwin Emefele is high.

THE MOST HATED BOY ON CAMPUS

'My dad told me not to talk to anyone without my lawyer,' Godwin states as soon as the registrar leaves us alone in the boardroom.

'We're not the police. We just want to ask you a few questions.' I'm careful to be gentle, considering Godwin's possible altered state of consciousness.

'You don't know how hard this is!' Godwin snaps, startling me. He shakes his head vigorously as though to clear unwanted thoughts. 'Every time I try to forget, someone comes asking the same questions all over again.'

'Who's asking you?' I make the question soft, unthreatening.

'Everyone! If it's not the police or lawyers, it's the other students. Everyone hates me.'

Godwin is getting more agitated, his hands shake, and the cadence of his voice sounds like he's talking to a crowd rather than Chika and me.

'Why would anyone hate you? You did nothing wrong.' I stress the last part to test Godwin's perception of his role in the killing.

Godwin stops and looks at me like he has found a long-lost friend. 'Yes, yes! How was I to know things would end the way they did?'

'Of course, there's no way you could have known,' I say reassuringly.

'Yes!' His voice gets more excited. 'You get it! Even when the crowd came, I tried to tell them it was all a misunderstanding, but no one listened.'

'You must feel really bad.'

Godwin nods vigorously, his eyes threatening to pop out.

'So bad. I don't sleep. I can't eat. I want to run away from here, but I have to stay to help the police and the lawyers and the school. I hate it here. I'm trying to make it right, but no one in the world believes me.'

Is Godwin's magnification of scenarios symptomatic of paranoia brought on by the drugs and/or the consistent exposure to an unsafe space? I need to stop diagnosing Godwin and concentrate on the purpose of the interview.

'Not believing you doesn't mean they hate you –'

'Oh, they do.' He says this with a dry laugh that hints at a sob. 'If they could kill me, they would.'

Drug-induced exaggeration or fact? Being known as the student who caused the lynching of three fellow students cannot be a light burden to carry on a campus.

I pat Godwin briefly on the shoulder and pass him my handkerchief.

'Maybe we can help you. You know, help people understand your side of the story.' My voice is soft, urging.

Godwin looks at me and then at Chika as though he is wondering if the latter can be trusted. I give Chika a slight nod.

'Time has passed, Godwin,' Chika says, taking his cue perfectly; even mimicking my reassuring pat on Godwin's shoulder. 'Maybe now that people have had time to calm down, they'll see you did what they would have done if they were in your place.'

'They won't! Everyone liked those guys. They were the happening guys on campus. No one knew what they were doing to me on the side.'

'What were they doing to you?' I sit up straighter, unable to stop myself from seeking further clarification, despite the risk of breaking Godwin's flow.

Godwin takes a deep breath, closes his eyes like he's steadying his nerves. 'It began in my first year. As soon as I arrived on campus, they were on me. At first, it was little things. They wanted me to buy them food. Sometimes beer and cigarettes. I know it was because I was doing well in my business.'

'You had a business?' Chika asks, emulating the softness of my voice. He catches on fast.

'Yes. I used to travel and buy clothes to sell here. Everyone liked my collections. They said I had taste.' He pauses, looks at me like he's seeking understanding. 'Maybe that's why everyone hates me. They were jealous, you know. My business was doing well. Lots of people owed me money for clothes I sold on credit. Many of them used what happened as an excuse not to pay me.'

'You were travelling a lot? To where?' Chika asks in an admiring tone.

'London. I worked over the summer vacation and used the money to buy stuff to sell here when school resumed. Mostly clothes, shoes, bags for the girls. I got the items on sale and sold them for a good price.'

Godwin must have been born in Europe with a passport that allowed him to travel to the UK or somewhere similar to take up summer jobs without needing a visa.

'Every time it was the same,' Godwin continues. 'As soon as I came back, they were on me, demanding things. And when I said no, they beat me and took my stuff anyway.'

'The same guys who tried to rob you in Okriki?' At this point I needed to be sure we were on the same page.

'Yes. They were everywhere on campus. They and their friends. I was afraid of them all. It was because of them I moved off campus, but they still followed me.'

'You never reported them?'

Even in his apparent manic state, Godwin looks at me the way Chika does when I say something that betrays my returnee status.

'Report cult boys?'

'And you're sure they were part of a cult?' I ask gently, not wanting to overtly challenge him.

'You don't act like that around campus if you don't have some kind of heavy backing. And because they choose their targets carefully and show everyone else their good sides, no one talks about it! They stole from people like me and used what they took to buy nice things for girls and give their friends a good time.'

'So, the bullying started from your first year?'

Chika's tone seems to calm Godwin somewhat.

'Yes. After a while, I came to accept it. They were always obtaining me –'

'Obtaining?' I ask.

'Claiming stuff,' Godwin explains. 'You know, like just taking things without asking.'

Ah. Extortion. I nod that I understand.

'They take anything. Money. Food. Cell phones. Even my clothes if they like them.'

'Even when you were no longer a jambite?' Chika prods, but he shoots me a quick questioning glance.

I reassure him with my eyes that I know 'jambite' is the commonly used word to describe a freshman.

'They never stopped,' Godwin continues, anger seeping into his voice. 'Every year after the long vacation, no matter how many things I gave them, they still wanted more. That's why I moved off campus.'

'But they still came after you.' I am impressed that Chika knows to make this a statement infused with empathy.

'Yes. They sent different guys to harass me, but I knew them all. It was Bona and Winston they sent that day. They wanted me to give them money, and I told them I didn't have any, so they wanted to claim my laptop, TV and cell phone. I said no. They insisted and just walked into my room and started taking stuff. That was when I shouted "thief!" because I thought it would make them stop and we could talk about things and come to an agreement.'

'But people heard you,' I state, like I was with Godwin that day.

'No. It was not the shouting that brought people. It was when Winston shot the gun.'

'Winston was carrying a gun?' I ask as if this is a new piece of information.

'Yes. He brought it out and told me to shut up. It was not the first time they've pulled a gun on me. But this time Winston actually shot it! He said I should stop shouting "thief" and fired it again. I kept screaming, but Bona told me to shut up, and Winston shot into the roof again. There was dust from the holes in the ceiling and smoke everywhere. I ran outside and kept shouting for help.'

'That was when people came?' Chika asks.

Godwin nods. 'They came from everywhere. I recognised a few from the compound, and some from the neighbouring houses, but I think most of them were from the market down the road. They asked me what was going on and I told them I was being robbed. It was true!' He shouts like he expects us to contradict him. 'It was daylight robbery! Armed robbery!'

I nod at him reassuringly. 'If it happened as you tell it, then you were right to ask for help.'

The look of gratitude on Godwin's face makes me sad for him. To have the act of self-preservation end in such tragedy must be hard. I want to ask about his parents, but I worry it might derail the conversation. Maybe another time.

'So, the people came to help you?' I prod gently.

Godwin exhales. 'They called for more people to come. Shouting that the thieves have come again. Then Winston came out and they just went at him. Bona tried to run out through the back of the house, but they caught him too. Before I knew it, they had stripped them and were beating them.'

'Still in the compound?' Chika asks.

'Yes. It was when they started leading them to the road that I saw how bad things were getting.' He bows his head, his chest rising and falling rapidly.

'You didn't follow them out of the compound?' I ask after making sure he is not crying.

'No.' He looks up, but his eyes are darting around, as if he'd rather be anywhere but in this room. 'I ran back to my room and started calling the police, but their emergency number didn't work. I called the school security, but no one took me seriously. When I called my dad, he told me to drive to the police station and tell them what was happening.'

'You have a car?' Chika asks.

'Yes, but not any more.' He shakes his head sadly. 'It was vandalised when I came back to campus after, you know, everything. They stripped everything from it. The stereo. Wheel. Tyres. Seats. Everything. They left an old tyre, a matchbox and a bottle of petrol inside.' He gives a deep, sad sigh. 'Their message was clear.'

So much for the Registrar's claim of supporting the young man.

It's a weird thing about young people in groups, though. They might jostle for relevance and popularity on campus, but on the whole, it's them against the world. I suspect many on campus felt that Godwin overreacted to what was nothing more than a tussle between students. To accuse fellow university students of robbery must have irked many. And studies on the fallout of a mob action have confirmed that stories like the Okriki Three raise people's primal fear of being in the wrong place at the wrong time and becoming victims of vigilante justice themselves.

'You drove to the police station?' Chika now asks.

'Yes,' Godwin answers. 'I got there as fast as I could and told them what was happening. They said an officer had gone to check on the noise, and if he came back to tell them there was a problem, then they'd look into it.'

'Did you tell them that you had cried out only to stop Winston and Bona from claiming your stuff?' Chika asks.

'I did. But the police guy there asked if any of them had fired a gun. When I said yes, he said then they deserved a sound beating for coming into town with a gun.'

Although this isn't new information, I'm disgusted all over again by the role the Okriki policemen had in all this.

'I begged them,' Godwin continued, 'told them that it was all a misunderstanding. But they didn't listen.'

'What did you do next?' I ask.

'I drove to the university. I got the security guys at the gate to come with me, but by the time we got back to Okriki, it was too late.'

At this, Godwin's chest starts to heave. Chika makes to touch the boy's shoulder, but I motion for him not to. Best to stay practical and focused on the matter at hand.

'You did what you could, Godwin,' I say gently. 'If anything, it's the police who didn't do their job.'

'I don't think they thought the boys would be killed.'

It's not the time or place to insist that the police should have been held liable for the deaths. I suspect the redeployment of Inspector Omereji back to Okriki was calculated to deflect such liability. It is also becoming clear to me why the police investigation was filled with inconsistencies. It's conceivable that the police thought the boys were just going to be given a sound beating as punishment for disturbing the peace with a gun, but that was a judgement call that had cost lives and ruined many more. At the very least, it was the responsibility of the police to control the crowd doing damage beyond beating and warning the boys never to come to town with a weapon again.

I sigh as I remember Folake's words on the day I was leaving Lagos for Okriki: *Nothing makes sense in this country.*

Since Godwin has not said anything that's not in his written testimony, I have one last question. 'Godwin, you said

Winston and Bona are the boys that came to your room in the compound. What about the third boy? Kevin.'

'I didn't even know the guy.'

I put the right amount of incredulity in my voice. 'How's that even possible?'

'I didn't. I swear. This Kevin didn't come with Winston and Bona. When I drove to the school security to tell them what was happening, I reported the beating of two university boys, but when they followed me back into town, it was three boys that were burning.'

'How do *you* think Kevin became involved?' I try to sound like this is an answer only he can give.

'I don't know. Some people said he was the lookout guy. The one supposed to warn Winston and Bona if things got nasty.'

'If that were true, why didn't he ... well, look out?'

Godwin shrugs. 'Maybe he left his post for a bit, and by the time he came back, the mob was already beating Winston and Bona. Maybe one of them called out to him, and the crowd realised they were together. Maybe. I don't know. I didn't know the guy.'

I shake my head, making it like I am as unconvinced as I am confused.

'Are you absolutely certain he wasn't somewhere nearby and you were too distressed to notice him?' Chika asks as if imploring him to help clear my confusion.

'He wasn't with Winston and Bona,' Godwin insists.

'Were you high that day, Godwin?' I ask outright, hoping to catch him off guard.

'No!' he answers defensively, and then his eyes widen in outrage as he looks from me to Chika as if we've just betrayed his trust.

'Are you sure?' I ask softly, trying not to sound accusatory.

'I don't get high,' he replies defiantly. 'I don't do drugs, never have.'

I can't hide my deflated sigh. There's no witness more unreliable than a drug user in denial.

'It's okay,' I say finally. 'We believe you.'

ONE PLUS ONE EQUALS THREE

'You think he's lying?' Chika asks as soon as we are in the car.

'A lot of what he said aligns with other witnesses and it is consistent with his own sworn testimony. But it's unclear how much we can trust him.'

'I saw your face when he said he's never touched drugs.'

I smile ruefully. 'Yeah, my poker face needs work.'

We are on the main road to Okriki, but I'm not in the mood to go back there. I check my watch. Quarter past two.

'We should eat something,' I say.

'There's a place down the road, but you might not like it.'

'Why?'

'It's a buka. Like a canteen, you know –'

'I know what a buka is,' I cut in a bit too sharply.

'Goat meat and pounded yam is their specialty.' If Chika caught my shortness, he ignores it.

'You reckon I won't like goat meat soup?'

'Not one served in that kind of place. Very crowded, and hygiene is not a top priority there.'

'Have you eaten there before?'

'Yes.'

'Then it's good enough for me.'

Chika nods, as if to say: I warned you.

When we get to the buka, which has a Coca-Cola endorsed signage that proclaims it to be *Mama Patience Canteen*, it is crowded. There's a queue leading towards a very rotund woman who I assume is Mama Patience. She sits at the centre of a series of large cast-iron pots containing massive pieces of meat protruding out of different soups.

My stomach rumbles. My twin brother and I were regulars at most of the bukas that surrounded our high school. But since I came back from the States, I have yet to check out the haunts of my teen years. Three months into our return, a sense of nostalgia made me want the twins to experience Ghana High, a popular buka around the neighbourhood I grew up in. I made the mistake of suggesting this to Folake and she threatened to sue the buka's management and me if the kids came back with food poisoning. I've yet to summon up the courage to defy her.

Standing in this queue at a buka situated midway between Okriki and the State University, waiting for Mama Patience to dish out a dollop of egusi soup next to my pounded yam, I feel a sense of homecoming I've not had since I arrived from Lagos. The heat and the noisy, crowded canteen combine to rid me momentarily of the horrors I have been reading and analysing in the past week.

'You like it, sir?' Chika asks from behind me.

'You bet,' I answer with unabashed glee.

I can see he's relieved that I'm not as stuck-up as he had me pegged. He laughs as I direct Mama Patience to the exact piece of meat I want – a leg of goat meat with muscle lines so tenderised they pop off the bone. I order a Star beer and prepare myself for a treat.

We are lucky to find seats in a corner where we can talk. Not that anyone would hear us anyway. Everyone is speaking all at once, while different Nollywood movies play loudly on two separate screens.

In between swallowing morsels of pounded yam and wiping the sweat off our foreheads, we discuss our interview with Godwin.

'I still can't wrap my head around how Godwin can't explain how Kevin got involved,' Chika says.

I take a swig from my bottle of beer. 'I guess it makes sense if Kevin *was* the lookout guy. But these cult guys, from what I hear, are gangsters. They had no way of knowing what fate awaited them, so what did they have to fear? Why would Winston and Bona need a lookout guy if they weren't planning to do more than shake Godwin down again?'

Chika nods. 'Bringing a gun means they intended to rough up him big time if he didn't cooperate.'

'But why bring a gun *and* still have a lookout guy? Something seems off.'

'Maybe Godwin owed the guys something,' Chika says. 'There's the drugs. Could be drug money.'

I'm wary about leaning into Godwin's relationship with drugs. It's an unreliable space to extrapolate from, but I'll concede one thing. 'If Godwin was on drugs at the time of the incident, it would be interesting to know where he gets them. On campus? Off campus?'

'What if he's a seller and user?'

I pause at this leap. 'Where is this going?'

'He kept going on about travelling and buying and selling clothes, but I don't really believe that. I'm not saying he was not selling stuff, but too many students do that already for Godwin to be singled out by the cult guys. I think there was something else between them.'

'And you think it's drugs?'

'I mean, what else would it be?'

A boy who denies being on drugs would clearly not admit to selling them. As much as I'd like a key witness who's clean as a flute, Godwin is all I've got; an addict who may tell the absolute truth in every other area of his life but would never volunteer information that might jeopardise his habit.

'What if the guys bought drugs from him and were refusing to pay, or Godwin was buying from them and was refusing to pay?' Chika wonders aloud.

I am not convinced. 'Still doesn't answer how Kevin got involved. Except it was all a mistake in the first place. We know there's no way the people of Okriki would admit that. It's better to lump all of them together and claim they were all armed robbers rather than admit they had killed a potentially innocent bystander.'

'You'd think, even in the crowd frenzy, someone should be able to recall how and why Kevin was included in the beatings,' Chika says as he struggles with his oxtail, careful to avoid splattering both of us with red oil.

I shake my head and resist licking my fingers. 'Crowds don't work like that. Especially violent ones. Many people walk away from such an experience horrified by their role in it. They've been known to repress selected memories or embellish them either to exonerate themselves or justify their role. Point is, you can't trust what anyone who's been part of a mob action says.'

'Perhaps we can ask when you speak to some of the accused already arraigned for trial? After all, they've nothing to lose. They might tell us something that indicates how Kevin became part of this whole thing.'

'Which they'll keep to themselves if they think it might hurt their case even further. Vigilante justice on suspected armed robbers is one thing, and possibly defensible in court. But if an innocent bystander was killed, that's different. Manslaughter can move to first-degree murder in a split second.'

'True,' Chika agrees. 'So, if Godwin could have easily testified that Kevin was with Bona and Winston, but insists otherwise, that means someone else was there.'

'Exactly. And if we find that person, we'll know how Kevin got involved.'

'Involved enough to be called out as thief?'

A sinking feeling hits me. 'Involved enough to have been called out to be *executed*.'

A BREWING STORM

We've almost grown accustomed to the hostile stares, whispering and pointing by the locals whenever we drive through Okriki. Which is why the absence of these signs of unwelcome when we drive into town is so jarring. All the adults we see appear to be heading in one direction, paying us no mind and talking animatedly amongst themselves.

'Something's going on,' Chika says.

'What do you think it is?' The people are walking towards a lone white bungalow down the road.

'That's the community hall,' Chika says. 'Should we follow them?'

He didn't have to ask twice. There was no way I would pass up a chance to see the people of Okriki together and observe their dynamics.

Chika parks across the road from the hall. We approach the side of the building to avoid the people entering via the main doors. An instinctive choice since we both know our presence, if noticed, might elicit a hostile response. We walk stealthily towards the large window, which now frames our view of what appears to be a meeting already in progress inside.

Most of the attendees are men. At this time of day, most of the town's womenfolk are likely at the market or on the farm. The few women I see are older, late fifties and above, clustered at the back of the hall, whispering amongst themselves as the men sit and most stand, closer to the front.

The atmosphere is one of agitation. These people are unhappy about something.

A man in his mid to late seventies, dressed in an all-white caftan and massaging the intricately carved head of his walking stick, sits on a dais. There is something vaguely familiar about him – the way he sits, nods while listening and the commanding manner he raps the stick on the floor when there is too much noise.

'He's the chief of the community,' Chika explains.

'It is time we say enough is enough! This is a free country, and we are tired. Tired of these insults, these abuses. And the disrespect of our faith!' The passionate speaker is dressed in an all-white long *thobe*, with its top part tailored like a shirt, and the bottom flowing loose. He sports a white skullcap on a clean-shaven head framed by a dark beard.

Other similarly dressed men are nodding in agreement and grunting their support, as the speaker declares: 'They are forcing our hand, and one day, monkey go travel go market e no go come back!'

At this last pronouncement, the whole hall erupts into noise, which prompts the Chief to rap his stick on the wooden floor below his makeshift throne.

'Silence!' the Chief bellows, and a near-absolute quiet washes over the crowd. The Chief himself sits at the midpoint of four other men, who look about as old as him but have less authority. They nod in unison to show their support for the Chief's call to order.

'Usman, I was not aware you called us here to make threats,' the Chief says calmly.

'No, your Highness. I apologise if my passionate protest gives the impression of a threat but –'

The Usman guy switches to another language. I look at Chika to decipher.

'I can only pick up a few words here and there,' he says, straining closer, as if this would give him better understanding of the rapid-fire Ikwerre, the local language that I've read has sprinklings of Igbo, Ibibio and Efik.

'It seems there's a fight,' Chika whispers. 'Some church people did or said something, and the Muslims are angry.'

'Close enough,' a familiar voice says from behind us.

We turn around to find Inspector Mike Omereji, staring at us with undisguised hostility.

'This is a meeting of indigenes, and I'm not sure they'd appreciate strangers listening in to what you can see is a closed meeting.'

It strikes me now what I found familiar about the town chief. He and Inspector Omereji bear a striking resemblance, down to the timbre of their voices and the way they speak.

'Hello, Inspector,' I say with contrived cheeriness. 'Chika was showing me the sights of the town.'

There's silence as the Inspector and I stare at each other. The tension makes me feel the burning Okriki sun even more as sweat pours down my back and the noise of angry men in the hall intensifies the antagonism in the air.

'We were leaving anyway,' Chika says. He nudges me and we walk towards Omereji, who holds his position, forcing us to walk around him. We've barely gone three feet when his voice stops us.

'Some Christians are posting social media messages calling for the removal of the mosque.' He speaks like a commentator giving the backstory during the halftime of a soccer match. 'They say this is a Christian town. That it's sacrilege to have a mosque here.' He shrugs. 'Such things happen once in a while in a small town like this.'

'And it never gets violent?' I ask in a tone that I hope does not come across as tongue-in-cheek.

'Contrary to what you might believe, Dr Taiwo, the people of Okriki can resolve their differences with dialogue.'

I look pointedly towards the hall where there's a cacophony of angry voices, again prompting the rapping of the Chief's walking stick to restore order.

Omereji waves a dismissive hand at the noise. 'In the past, tensions between the Muslims and Christians were settled right here by the chief of the community. They would talk and come to agreement, but nowadays every idiot with a smartphone can post rubbish on social media, and it makes dialogue difficult. That's what this meeting is about. Some nonsense on social media that made the Muslims angry.'

He stops and looks at Chika and me as if waiting for questions. I've got a lot, but they have nothing to do with this town hall meeting and everything to do with why the townspeople thought it was okay to beat, torture and burn three young men to death. Where was the dialogue then?

As Chika and I head back to the car, I can't shake the feeling that Inspector Omereji's cold eyes are following us.

MIDNIGHT CALL

Alone in my room, I strip to my boxers and throw myself on the bed. My last thought before drifting off is to stop complaining about the noisy, but functioning AC as it cools my sweaty body.

I wake up a few minutes past 9 p.m. To drown out the rumble of the generator and the air conditioning, I reach for my headphones, and click on my Nina, Ella and Billie playlist.

I prop myself against the headboard on the bed from where I can see the Post-it notes on the wall. I open the folder on my laptop containing the profiles of the three victims.

As an investigation progresses, there is always a need to revise the composite picture of all the actors. In less than forty-eight hours, I think I have enough to revise my initial ideas regarding Winston, Bona and Kevin.

I type quickly, not minding grammar or typos, so as not to lose the flow that sometimes inspires a deeper insight into a person or situation.

Winston. So far, my original summations are supported by the interview I did today. To be fair, apart from his parents, I have not spoken to a friend of his or anyone who might have a contrary opinion. But the reputation of being a hellraiser and something of a party animal appears to have been well earned.

I click on a link I had saved hurriedly the day before I left Lagos. It's Winston's Facebook profile. After scrolling past the several 'never forgottens' and RIPs that were posted on his wall, I find Winston was not much of a Facebook user. Most of his posts were pictures of himself and several people at parties. Almost all have no comments attached to them, but are linked to his Instagram page where he appears to have been more active.

The page itself only confirms a lot of what Godwin said. Winston dressed well in most of the pictures, had multiple girls on his arms and was not camera shy. If there are any indicators in the pictures that he belonged in a secret cult, I can't find them.

Bona. He appears to have been more politically aware than Winston and a great admirer of President Obama since a lot of his posts were quotes from the erstwhile American President. There are also posts around local and international hip hop artists, and a lot of information about concerts on campus or the launch of a new single.

Kevin. I must confess the young man is still an enigma to me. His Facebook page shows that he was a much-loved student and son. The outpouring of grief on his Facebook page is monumental. I scroll past innumerable eulogies that get more verbose and passionate on the one-year anniversary of the Okriki Three killings.

If Bona was politically aware, Kevin seems to have been a bona fide activist. He had an opinion on everything, and backed it up with facts and a lot of legalese. Where Winston showed off his wardrobe on social media, Kevin showed off his intellect. Somehow, I could not picture them being connected in any way.

Several hashtags follow a lot of Kevin's posts. Maybe it's my age and my late introduction to social media, but I do have an aversion to more than two or three hashtags in any given post. I am a little irritated at the almost endless number that Kevin attached to several of his posts. However, the more I scroll the greater the occurrence of one: #justice4momoh.

I follow the links and it becomes clear that Kevin was the one who generated this hashtag in honour of a friend who died in police custody. Hmm. Interesting. I click on another link and everything but my screen goes dark around me.

I take off my headphones, breaking off Ms Simone's 'I Put a Spell on You'.

Everywhere is eerily quiet and the AC has stopped working too. I flip the switch on the bedside lamp and nothing happens. Sighing, I lie in the dark, waiting for the rumble of the generator. It's taking longer than it usually does, so I grope around the bedside table to find my phone.

The kids have sent text messages, and I restrain myself from calling them so late at night. I type *love you, miss you* to each of them with a promise to call in the morning.

There's nothing from Folake, but I don't dwell on this. I have work to do.

It has been two quite revealing days. My encounters with Inspector Omereji, the landlady and the Registrar gave context, while the interview with Godwin raised all the right questions. Recalling his account makes me feel compelled to clarify some things with Emeka.

I check the time. 11:17. It's late, but he did tell me to call him anytime.

'Are you okay?' he asks, answering at the first ring.

'Emeka is a very driven man,' I recall Abubakar saying. Clearly, but does he not sleep?

'I'm fine,' I respond. 'Spoke to the Godwin fellow.'

'Good. The Registrar came through.'

I suspect this is Emeka's way of hinting that he is following my progress as closely as he can from Lagos.

'Yes, he did. Thanks for that.' I pause and try to think how best to pose my questions without sounding insensitive. 'This Godwin boy ... He insists that he was being robbed by cult boys and –'

'Nonsense.' Even over the phone, Emeka's irritation is clear. 'That's what all of them say to justify their criminal acts. While I can't speak for the other boys, I can say with absolute certainty that my son was not a cult member.'

'If he was, would you have known?' I may be pushing a father already on edge, but I have to ask tough questions. 'These cults are secret societies. What makes you so sure you'd have known if Kevin was a member?'

'It's not about whether he'd have told me or not. Kevin would never join a cult. He was not that type of child. Period.'

'Godwin insists Bona and Winston were cult boys. Have you any idea how Kevin could have become lumped in with them?'

'Is this not why I'm so perplexed?' Emeka's voice is close to breaking, and I almost end the conversation, unwilling to take a grieving parent down a painful path. But he continues, his voice strengthened by anger. 'When we pointed out to the police that Godwin's testimony clearly stated that he didn't know how Kevin became involved, you know what they said? That the investigation was into what happened *after* the mob arrived at the scene, and not before. Imagine!'

Even over the phone, Emeka's rage is palpable and I let it run its course.

'I pushed. I used all my connections to ensure that at least that lead – that loophole in the investigation – was looked into and I got nothing. They did nothing because it was easier to believe that my son was part of a cult.'

Emeka's frustration that despite his wealth he was unable to save his son and powerless to force a proper investigation into his death permeates all of my interactions with him. Even now, as in my previous interviews, he laments the assigning of inexperienced investigators on the case. His voice breaks when he talks about how his wife had asked for an audience with the First Lady to seek a federal investigation into the matter.

'You know what she told her?' His voice shakes as he speaks. 'One mother to another, the so-called mother of the nation told my grieving wife that it wouldn't be politically correct to interfere in state matters.'

Abubakar and I had discussed this part of Emeka's independent report. The fact that murder is a capital offence could have easily made this a federal case. The nationwide condemnation of cult activities, militant insurgency in the Niger Delta and an ongoing political feud between the Governor of the state and the President, himself an indigene of the region, meant that forcing a federal investigation into the deaths of the Okriki Three would have escalated an already tense situation. It's a mess indeed. No wonder Abubakar has lost faith in the whole process and wanted me to take the case.

Finally, Emeka seems to calm down and I gently steer him back to my question. 'Are you saying you know all your son's friends?'

'Yes, I am,' he says emphatically. 'Look, Philip, I know most, if not all, my son's friends. He used to invite many of them to Lagos to spend weekends or just stay with us to intern at the bank when the school was closed. Any friends I've not met, I would have heard about from Kevin himself. He never spoke of Winston and Bona.'

'Then how did they end up together?'

'That's what I'm paying you to find out.'

I don't appreciate being spoken to in such a manner, and I let the succeeding silence drag.

'Look, Philip,' Emeka continues, in a less aggressive tone, 'you've spoken to Winston's parents. You know they think their son is capable of being in a cult, of stealing and extorting. If you speak to Bona's mother, I'm sure she'll say the same about her late son.'

'But you don't believe that of Kevin?'

'No, I don't.'

'So, why was Kevin in Okriki in the first place?'

'I told you he was visiting his girlfriend. Her father and mother are teachers at the Grammar School there, so she lives off campus in Okriki.'

While Emeka is talking, I put him on speaker and turn on the iFlashlight app on my phone. I look at my wall of Post-it notes where I had put a question mark against the name: *Mercy*.

'I just can't understand why her testimony is not in any of the witness accounts.'

There's silence on the other side.

'Emeka?'

'I had hoped you could do this without needing to speak to her.'

'Why?'

The heavy sigh on the other end worries me.

'Emeka, are you there?'

'I am.'

'What are you not telling me?'

'Mercy is at the State Psychiatric Hospital in Port Harcourt.'

As if on cue, the generator rumbles to life and the bedside lamp comes on.

ACT TWO

light waves reflecting off a parabolic
barrier will converge at a focal point

A DISTURBING VIEW

The next morning when I walk to Chika's room, the door is ajar, and I can hear him on the phone, his voice raised.

'I told you I'm not into that shit any more!'

Although it's been only three days since we met and I can't claim to know that much about him, I am surprised to hear him so emotional. His voice becomes much lower when he says: 'I know, I know … baby, please. It'll be over soon, and I'll be home.'

Ah. A girlfriend, or even a spouse? I start feeling guilty for my unintentional eavesdropping, so I tap on the door and this causes it to open wider.

'Yes?!' he barks.

I push the door more firmly.

It's the first time I've entered Chika's hotel room, and I've never seen him without a shirt. But here he is, the leanest human machine I've ever seen, the only flaws being hints of scars on his chest and the sides of his ribcage, forcing me to look away lest I crumble to dust in envy.

He turns sharply to pick up a shirt hanging on the chair next to the bed and I catch a glimpse of scars on his back. They are keloidal, mounds of thickened flesh that look like a 3D map. I am even more horrified at the thought of what could have caused such deep, calloused wounds.

My gasp is instinctive and must have been loud because Chika hurriedly pulls on the light blue cotton shirt.

'Good morning, sir! Did you want something?'

'Err … there's a change of plans today …'

As he quickly buttons up the crisp shirt, I pass on what Emeka had told me about Kevin's girlfriend.

'You want to talk to her?'

'I think we should. Emeka's trying to call the parents for permission to visit her, but he says we can go on ahead to Port Harcourt.'

'He thinks the parents will be okay with it?'

'To be honest, he doesn't think they'll be, but he'll try.'

'But if he can't get their permission, won't it be a wasted journey?'

'Even if we don't get to talk to her, I'd like to see her, get a feel for her.'

Chika looks at his watch as he buttons the cuffs of his shirt. 'We should be there in less than an hour.'

'Let's meet up at the restaurant, although I'm guessing today's breakfast won't be as nice as yesterday's.'

Chika laughs but it doesn't reach his eyes. 'Don't worry, sir, the cook is aware of our standards now. I'll be down in five.'

'One more thing,' I say. 'I have been looking through the boys' social media profiles. A particular hashtag kept popping up on Kevin's Facebook profile. Something about justice for a Momoh guy. Some student who died in police custody.'

'Here in Okriki or somewhere else?'

140

'I don't know.'

'You think it might mean something?'

'It's certainly worth exploring. If the boy died in police custody and Kevin was spearheading a campaign to investigate the police, that could explain why they looked the other way when the crowd came.'

Chika nods, his brows furrowed. 'Makes sense, sir. You think the police might be the ones who pointed him out to the crowd?'

'Too early to say that, but I'll like to know what happened to this Momoh and what role Kevin played in the whole thing. You said you studied computer science?'

'Yes, sir.'

'You must have contacts that can get into Kevin's Facebook account.'

'You mean hackers?'

In the States, I wouldn't have bothered having to explain myself to the cybercrime unit of the SFPD, but the way Chika said 'hackers' made me feel like I was asking for something out of the norm.

'Well, yes. But if it's a problem, I don't want you to do anything illegal. I can also ask Emeka for his go ahead, just in case.'

'I'll ask him, sir. I know a guy. Don't worry. Consider it done.'

From the tone of his voice, I get that the conversation is over. I turn to leave, then stop just as he's reaching for his cell phone again.

'Chika?'

He looks at me with an expression I can't read. 'Sir?'

'The scars? I couldn't help but notice ...'

'Oh, those?' He scoffs and shrugs at once. 'A long time ago. A bad car accident. I was lucky to be alive.'

'An accident?' It's hard to reconcile what I saw with the wounds from a car accident, but he doesn't elaborate and I am forced to leave. As I walk down the corridor, I hear the door of his room close. Firmly.

The receptionist cum waiter from yesterday comes to me as soon as I enter the reception/restaurant/viewing room, CNN playing silently on the two TV screens. She tells me rather proudly that breakfast is ready. I offer my thanks, take a seat and ponder on what I saw in Chika's room.

The scars worry me and the athletic physique intrigues me. But it is the lie that alarms me. There is no way those scars were from a car accident, except if scraps of metal from the automobile had been deliberately used to etch deep wounds on his back. But you never know. I would have liked to think that, in the brief time we've known each other, Chika would trust me enough to be honest, and I must admit to being a bit disappointed that this is not the case.

My breakfast arrives just as Chika himself appears and I dig in, famished from being awake most of the night.

'I wish I'd known about this PH trip yesterday,' he says, pulling the chair opposite me, right as the waiter brings his plate of boiled yam and fried eggs. 'If we had left earlier, we would have avoided some of the traffic I'm sure we'll meet now.'

'It's okay. It's not an appointment.'

'Yes. But these things need to be planned. I don't want us to get there and find that we can't see the girl because her father won't let us.'

He avoids my eyes and speaks – no, whines – without the usual 'sir'. What's he nervous about? What I might have heard or what I shouldn't have seen? I weigh the odds and take a gamble.

'So, I couldn't help but overhear you on the phone. Sorry. The door was open.'

He visibly relaxes. Good call, Philip.

'It's okay. Home issues. My wife is pregnant, and I guess she's not coping well with my absence.'

I instantly feel ashamed that I know so little about this man who has been assisting me so well.

'Wow! How far along is she?'

'Seven months.'

'She's due in a couple of months. It can't be easy.'

'I know, but she also knows I need this job. We discussed it and she gave her blessing.'

I smile at him like an elder brother with multiple experiences in the pregnancy space. 'She's expecting and you're not with her. She must be lonely. Is this your first?'

Chika nods. 'Yes, sir. Maybe you're right. It's just that everything was so good when I spoke to her last night. We even discussed names for the baby. Then this morning, bang, it's shouting, blaming and saying how selfish I am for leaving her alone. I just got tired. I guess I could have been nicer.'

The weariness in his voice, and his despondent slouch help me set aside my uneasiness about his lie about the scars. I remember my state of mind when Folake was pregnant with the twins, so I can imagine that right now Chika's preoccupation will be on his recent conversation with his wife.

'From what I heard, I *know* you could've been nicer.'

There's a brief moment when it seems Chika wants to argue and defend his position. Then he seems to think better of it and instead, leans closer to me with a rueful smile.

'What do you think I should do?'

'Give her some time, then call later to apologise,' I declare like the expert I am on these matters.

'For what?' His voice rises with belligerence.

Lawdamercy on amateurs. I sigh and patiently explain why, in a marriage, it's imperative that a husband learns the art of apologising for things he couldn't tell he had done wrong. He appears to listen, and I give more free advice until we finish our breakfast and it's time to set out for Port Harcourt.

MURDER, SHE SAW

The text comes as soon as we arrive at the Psychiatric Hospital. I read it out loud as Chika parks the car.

'Mercy's father says it's not a good idea at this time.'

'I'm not surprised,' Chika says and turns to me, 'but we're here now.'

I think for a beat. I don't know what meeting Mercy will reveal but the question of how Kevin became part of the Okriki Three niggles at me. Since reading Emeka's report and then speaking to Godwin, all I still have are speculations, assumptions and, frankly, confusion. I hate it.

'You did say you might get something from just seeing her,' Chika cuts into my thoughts.

I look around the hospital grounds. It's a well-maintained, large parcel of land that's reminiscent of mental health facilities in several of the places I have worked. Perhaps observing Mercy, even from a distance, can give me something to work with.

'We *are* here,' I say, turning to Chika.

Chika nods and lets himself out of the car. I follow suit, pushing back my misgivings.

Inside, the reception is a picture of peace and serenity. Some nurses, mostly male, pass purposefully around us into the wards. A tall, dark male receptionist stands behind a large desk, rows of filing cabinets framing his thick-set body.

'Let me handle this, sir,' Chika whispers.

I nod and wander through a door with a 'Visiting Room' sign. No one but a grey-haired orderly flipping through a newspaper is there. I catch a glimpse of the sign that states the visiting hours. No wonder. We are here when visitors are not allowed. I am about to head back into reception when Chika comes over to me.

'He says we can speak with her,' he whispers hurriedly. 'But they want to be with us.'

I don't want to think about what Chika may have promised or given to get this concession but if we can see or speak to Mercy under the watchful eyes of hospital staff, surely there can't be any harm? Just a few questions. Nothing heavy.

'Even better if they're with us.'

'Wait here, sir.' Chika goes back to the reception area.

I sit on one of the plastic chairs and bring out my iPhone. Lara sent pictures of some cooking class in school with a '*wish you were here*' and lots of hearts in varying states of GIF animation, while the twins' slew of emojis inspires only incomprehension.

Nothing from Folake.

I scroll to the message from Salome that I hadn't responded to and type quickly.

'*Sorry. Things got hectic. Drinks mos def on the cards. Will let you know.*'

A smiling sunshine emoji comes back immediately. I consider calling to let her know I'm in PH and maybe we can meet.

'We must hurry,' Chika says from behind me, motioning for me to come. 'They're bringing her to the garden at the back.'

I follow him and the receptionist guides us past his desk into the garden area.

The receptionist is eager to please – confirming my suspicions of Chika's method of persuasion – as he ushers us to a bench.

'That's her,' he whispers and points. 'Please be quick.'

Look beyond the hospital overalls, and the lack of make-up or any other adornment, and it is instantly apparent that Kevin Nwamadi had great taste. Mercy Opara looks so slight, and delicate like the child she is, that I can't help but think of my daughter. A part of me regrets doing this, but I'm tired of grasping at straws. I need to form a clearer picture of what happened to Kevin Nwamadi, and Mercy might hold the key to doing that.

'She's having a very good day today, aren't we, Mercy?' the female nurse accompanying her says kindly.

Mercy smiles back and nods. I look for any sign of psychotropic medication; tremors in her extremities, dilated pupils, swollen limbs or dry lips. None.

'I'm Dr Philip Taiwo,' I say and offer a handshake.

'A doctor?' Mercy shakes my hand shyly, but she keeps smiling. 'How nice. Did my dad send you?'

Chika and I exchange quick looks.

'Dr Taiwo is doing some research so he can write a report, and we think you can help us.' Chika gives his name with a reassuring smile and stretches out his hand, which Mercy takes as graciously as she had mine.

Although the receptionist and nurse have retreated to a safe distance, we know they are watching us. Mercy guides us to a bench and as we sit, it strikes me that she's acting as if this is a social visit. So gracious is her attitude that I wouldn't be surprised if she asked us what we would like to drink.

'A report? And you think I can help?' she asks but does not wait for an answer, 'I don't get many visitors. Besides Mom and Dad, and my sisters, of course.'

'Why?' I venture tentatively.

'Sir, this is hardly a hotel.'

The lucidity of the girl makes me wonder what her diagnosis might be. She appears to be very aware of her environment and circumstances. Perhaps it's worth the risk?

'We spoke to Kevin's father –' I start.

Mercy's eyes light up. 'Oh, Mr Nwamadi! How nice. He calls me sometimes.'

'He said Kevin came to see you the day … you know, the day …'

'The day he died?'

This time, her smile is sad. 'You can say it. I know he's gone. It's the memory of how he died that overwhelms me sometimes. I've been in and out of here three times already, but each time is shorter than the last so I think I'm getting better.'

Even if I had received parental consent to speak to her, I had expected to tiptoe around issues. But Mercy is calm, and while she's not eager to share, she's not unwilling. I discreetly bring out my iPhone and start recording.

'Do you mind telling us about Kevin's visit to you that day?' I ask.

'I always wanted him to meet Papa. We'd been going out for two years, since our jambite days. I remember he was nervous about meeting my dad. Papa didn't make things easy, but I know he was happy that I was steady.' Mercy's smile turns melancholy. 'My mom had met Kevin before. I had brought him home one time when Papa travelled. My mom even found out that Kevin's mom was her senior in high school at Umouhia. I was so happy.'

'So, this encouraged you to invite Kevin to meet your dad?' I ask.

'Yes. Actually, it was my mom that invited him. She said he was getting too skinny from campus food.'

She laughs at the memory. Chika and I smile.

'So, your mom invited him that day?' I prod gently.

'Yes. I was at home and we cooked while Papa acted like he was not interested. That man!' Her affection for her father shows in the way her face lights up.

'Kevin came on his own?' I ask gently.

'Yes. He came in the morning. And stayed for the whole day. He and Dad spoke about everything under the sun. We even called Kevin's mom. It was wonderful.'

'When did Kevin leave?' I ask.

She frowns. 'I think about four. We had finished eating, washed the plates and all that. My dad wanted to give him a lift to campus, but Kevin said he had to go somewhere.'

'In Okriki?'

'Yes.'

'You didn't follow him?'

'No!' she exclaims, scandalised. 'That would've been pushing my poor father too far. I bring my boyfriend to visit him for the first time, and then I go away with him?'

She laughs again. But this time, it's a bit shaky. Guarded. Chika and I join in, to make her more at ease.

'So, he left without you?' I ask.

'Yes.'

'When ... when did you learn what happened?'

'Whenever we visited each other on campus, we would call each other afterwards to be sure we got home safe. I waited for about an hour and called him just to be sure he had left Tamuno's place and was on the way back to campus.'

'Tamuno?'

'The student he went to see. He didn't pick up and I called again and again.' Mercy shakes her head sadly. 'But he never did.'

'That's when you became worried?'

'Yes. I called and called, and when it started going to voicemail, I just knew something was wrong.'

'What did you do?' Chika asks. Mercy's smile is becoming less bright, her eyelids have begun twitching slightly, and a vein throbs on her temple.

'But,' Mercy continues, 'my parents had gone to church for evening service. So, I told my sisters where I was going and hailed a bike to take me to Tamuno's place.'

That name again. 'You know this friend Kevin went to see?' I ask.

'Not really. He was classmates with Kevin.'

I want to ask more questions but Mercy is already looking from us again, lost in a terrible recall that I already regret triggering. I have to find a quick way of bringing the interview to a close.

'When I saw them ... the crowd,' Mercy continues. 'I told the bike driver to take another route. But he refused.'

A sheen of sweat is gathering around her forehead. She is blinking rapidly, her words slowing like she is drowsy.

150

'They were chanting. Singing that they've caught the thieves. That they'll make them an example today. I didn't think anything of it. You get used to riots, shouting and stuff like that around here.'

'What did you do?' Chika asks before I can stop him. This girl is on the edge. One wrong word and she'll tip, so it's best to let her lead.

'Nothing,' she says, frowning. 'The bike driver drove straight towards the crowd. And then … that was when … when I saw them.'

Now Mercy is rocking like a child. I look at Chika and shake my head.

'Who?' he asks, ignoring my warning signals.

'The three of them,' Mercy answers in a faraway voice. 'I don't know the other two, but I saw Kevin. I ran towards the crowd and started screaming. I don't even know what I was saying. I just know I was screaming and nobody heard me. Then I started fighting people off, and someone pushed me, and I fell … and when I could stand, the crowd had moved on with them. I called my dad and mom. But they were still in church. So, I called Kevin's dad in Lagos and told him what was happening. He told me to run after them and convince them that Kevin was a relative or something, that he was Ikwerre, and there was no way he could be a thief. He would call the police from Lagos. I ran after them again, begging them to stop. Then someone hit me. Another person said I must be one of the loose girls that encourage the criminals to come to Okriki.'

Mercy's thumb goes to her lips, and she starts to suck on it. Her eyes dart around like a child looking for a comfortable place to lay her head after a long day at the playground.

I can't help but think of my daughter in this moment. This has gone on long enough; I motion to the nurse just as Chika is reaching towards Mercy.

'No! Don't!' I say sharply to him.

But it's too late. Mercy is now fighting off Chika as one would an assailant, crying and trying to ward him off. The receptionist and the nurse get to us at the same time as we hear an imperious voice thunder across the garden.

'What's going on here?'

We turn, except for Mercy who is now sobbing in the arms of the nurse, her thumb in her mouth. An older man stands before us, his anger as clear as his booming voice.

'Papa …' Mercy cries, tears streaming down her face.

Mercy's father! Instinctively, Chika and I move further away from Mercy, while the receptionist disappears and the nurse tries to appear in control.

The older man rushes to his daughter, who collapses into his arms like a doll.

'I'm sorry, sir,' I say rather feebly, even to my ears.

'Get out of here!' Mercy's father thunders over his daughter's head.

Our shame and the rage in the man's eyes prompt us to turn and break into a run.

WETIN YOU CARRY?

'That was a mistake,' I say after we pass the military police barricade and Chika has discreetly passed on a two-hundred naira note. I am still quite annoyed at myself by what I *let* happen at the hospital, so this is the first time I've spoken since we left there.

'I wouldn't say that, sir,' Chika says quietly, his eyes fixed on the road.

'It was,' I insist. 'Given Mercy's state of mind, we can't even rely on her account of events.'

'Why not, sir?'

'Because traumatised people are not reliable witnesses.'

'Even when their version of events matches what we *know* happened?'

'Generally, yes.'

'Is that why the police did not follow up on her story?'

I shake my head. 'No, no. It's only in a court of law that Mercy's testimony can be considered admissible or not. So really, there was no excuse for the police not to follow Mercy's testimony as a line of enquiry.'

'Maybe her being in and out of hospital ever since the tragedy has not helped.'

I know Chika is playing devil's advocate, given what we know about how the police handled the investigation, but I can't help but roll my eyes and kiss my lips loudly. 'Her being in and out of hospital served their purpose. Her version of events does not match theirs, so they disregarded it.'

'So, you don't think she's lying? Or maybe that she's not remembering things as they really happened?'

I look at him, surprised. 'That girl came across as knowing *exactly* what happened. In fact, I suspect the sharpness of her memory must contribute to her current state of mind.'

Chika shrugs. 'Just wanted to be sure, sir, because it seems you're doubting yourself.'

'I am doubting the wisdom of what I did back there.'

'Did it yield something useful?'

'Well, this Tamuno she mentioned ...' I grudgingly concede. I want to go into what I make of it when I see Chika's frown. I follow his gaze and see three armed policemen waving us down.

'What do you think they want?' I ask. This is unusual indeed, especially so close to Okriki. During our drives through the town itself, I don't remember ever seeing a police checkpoint.

'We'll find out,' Chika says as he slowly steers the car to the side of the road. 'You have some cash on you?'

I think of my one-hundred US dollar bill and nod, although this is not the emergency I had in mind when I tucked it into my wallet before leaving home.

One of the policemen walks languidly towards us. Another is on the phone, while the third waves other cars past.

'Good afternoon, sir ...' Chika says respectfully.

'Your particulars,' the policeman asks in a voice that brooks no discussion. I try to gauge whether this is all part of the song and dance before asking for 'something for the boys', but Chika is already rummaging through the glove compartment to locate the documents for the car.

The policeman collects the stapled collection of scanned and photocopied papers, then peers at each one for an inordinate length of time. He looks at Chika several times and back at the documents.

'Come down and open the boot,' he orders, then makes a show of checking the upholstery, and looking under the car seats.

'Officer, is there anything in particular you're looking for?' I ask impatiently.

Chika shoots me a look that tells me to be quiet. 'It's okay, Officer. My friend is just in a hurry.'

The policeman gives me a dirty look and goes back to checking the documents for perhaps the hundredth time.

'Is this your car?' he asks coldly, and I mentally vow not to part with my emergency cash to this unpleasant creature.

'It's not my car, sir,' Chika answers extra-politely. 'I'm the driver. My Oga is in Lagos.'

'He –' the officer points at me, 'is not the owner?'

'No, sir.'

'How will I know if the car is not stolen?'

Seriously? I almost shout out in frustration, but Chika's quick side-eye stops me.

'*Haba*, Officer!' Chika attempts to joke in pidgin English. 'I resemble thief?'

The policeman doesn't laugh but answers in rapid pidgin I can barely follow. Something about armed robbers not tattooing such a vocation on their foreheads. He looks at the papers again and towards the officer on the cell phone a couple of metres away.

'I can call the owner on the phone and let you speak to him?' Chika suggests.

'How will I know if the person on the other side is the real owner –?'

Either I pull out my police pass now or call Abubakar to stop this nonsense. While I am considering which would be the more effective option, the officer on the phone hangs up and walks over to Chika and the obtuse officer, collects the stapled papers from his colleague and hands them over to Chika.

'You can go,' he orders. Just like that.

Chika collects the papers, mumbles thanks and gets into the car.

'What nonsense!' I sputter in anger.

'Please, sir, can we leave here before you say more?' Chika reverses the car, changes gear and drives on to the road.

'If he wanted a bribe, he should have just asked!' I say when the police officers are well behind us. 'Why waste our time unnecessarily?'

'Exactly,' Chika says. 'They didn't ask for anything. They just stopped us …'

'And stopped no other car …' My voice trails off as it hits me. 'Delaying tactics. But for what?'

'I suspect we'll find out soon enough, sir,' Chika answers drily.

I know my being black in America informs my irritation around any random police 'stop and search'. I've been pulled over too many times to accept the same behaviour in my own country. But still.

'I'm sorry, Chika. I should have guessed something was up. I should have trusted you knew what you were doing.'

Chika steals a glance at me, and nods. 'Yes, sir,' he says with a straight face. 'You should have.'

I laugh out loud, and so does he.

'Drop the "sir", man. It's becoming ridiculous.'

Chika considers for a beat, perhaps wondering what this shift would mean, moving forward. I try to make things light by turning up my American accent.

'You gotta admit it's getting really weird every time you insult me and add "sir".'

'Me?' He puts on an outraged face. 'Insult you? Never!'

But he didn't add 'sir', so I just give him a disbelieving side-eye and kiss my teeth just as he turns on to the road that leads to Hotel Royale. The lightness in the air becomes instantly tense as soon as we see the maroon Mercedes Benz CLS Class parked right in front of the entrance to the hotel.

We climb out of the 4x4 and Atoka, the manager, meets us at the reception with a nervous smile. He mutters something about us having visitors, but I barely hear. My eyes are on the carefully staged scene before me. Sitting on one of the chairs facing the TV is the Chief from the town hall meeting yesterday. He doesn't turn around, even though he must have heard the manager announce our presence. He holds his head regally, his back straight while his hand grips the head of his walking stick.

I count five men of varying ages standing silently around the Chief. Like bodyguards. One of them is Inspector Mike Omereji, dressed in civilian clothes and standing closest to the Chief. Their resemblance is even more striking at close range, and I suspect his presence might be the reason for our 'delay'. Enough time to bring the Chief here to wait for us.

Inspector Omereji bends down to the older man. Slowly, the Chief turns and looks at me.

'You're the American,' the old man announces.

'No, sir,' I answer smoothly. 'I'm very Nigerian.'

The Chief smiles and raps his walking stick. As if on cue, Omereji steps back, and two men move to help the Chief stand up although I'm not sure he needs it. I walk over and bow slightly, without being so presumptuous as to offer a handshake.

'Yoruba.' The Chief announces when I give my name. 'They're good people,' he informs the men. 'Apart from that Awolowo, most of them were kind to us during the war.'

The men nod in understanding although, from their ages, I can't see any who could have been born before the end of the Biafran war that I assume the Chief is referring to. Of the famed Finance Minister during the said war – Obafemi Awolowo – I've no clue what the older man is referring to.

'Which part of Yoruba are you?' the Chief asks me.

Nigerians and their tendency to seek precise ethnic identification. This trait is worse in older people, so I try to hide my exasperation.

'I'm from Lagos, sir.'

'Ha!' He waves one hand dismissively. 'Everyone claims Lagos as their own.'

I smile at the truth of this statement. 'My great-great-grandfather came from Dahomey and settled in Lagos long before it became part of Nigeria.'

The old man nods sagely. 'Sometimes when a place becomes as big as Lagos, it is good to remember that people were there before all the tall buildings and foreigners came.'

'I'm sorry, sir, I didn't get your name ...' I let my voice trail off respectfully.

The old man lets out a loud laugh. 'You must think me rude. Chief Kinikanwo Omereji, paramount chief of the Okriki people. Welcome to our town.'

I instinctively look at Mike Omereji's impassive face. Father, grandfather or uncle?

'You have met my son ...' The Chief moves his head towards the Inspector.

Definitely a late child. The Chief looks to be in his seventies and Inspector Omereji, despite his serious demeanour, appears to be on the early side of his thirties.

'We've met, sir,' I announce, 'your son is a fine officer of the law.' I ignore the Inspector's raised eyebrow and turn to introduce the Chief to Chika, but before I can, the man speaks.

'Take a drive with me, Dr Taiwo,' the Chief announces.

'A drive?' I ask, but the Chief is already walking out of the hotel lobby, passing Chika whom he doesn't acknowledge and the hotel manager, to whom he gives a short, imperious wave. His entourage follows, carefully measuring their steps so as not to walk ahead of him and leaving me with Omereji.

I look at Chika, who looks at the Inspector.

'He'll be fine,' Omereji says brusquely and motions for me to follow him.

A MAN OF THE PEOPLE

The Chief gets into the back seat of the Mercedes Benz and one of the men holds open the other rear door for me. I get in beside the Chief, Omereji sits in the front passenger seat, and, after all the doors are closed, the driver reverses out of the compound. I see the other men get into a modest Mazda and follow us.

The Chief turns to me. 'How are you enjoying our town?'

He knows I'm not in Okriki for its tourist attractions, but I play along.

'It's lovely. Very quiet.'

'After Lagos, our town must be heaven,' he says and, without missing a beat, he tells the driver, 'take the road past the market.' He turns back to me. 'I'm told you are here to find out what happened to those hooligans who were terrorising our community.'

I try not to show my surprise at the directness. 'I wouldn't go as far as to call them that, sir. They were students of –'

'I know what they were. Even a thief is someone's child. This community has suffered a lot at the hands of students from that school.'

'So, I hear, sir.' Passive-aggressive might be my best line of defence.

'But you don't believe?'

'No one has really spoken to me since I got here.'

'And no one will if they know why you are here.'

I face him squarely. 'If I may, sir, why do you think I'm here?'

'To find trouble? Divide us with your doubt and make the world hate my people even more.'

'It's a report I am writing, sir. Hardly a judgement.'

'Anything on paper is a judgement of some kind.'

I consider this weird logic and decide the old man might have a point. I change tactics.

'But, Chief,' I say earnestly, 'I'm not here to cause trouble. What I'm doing may even help the community.'

The Chief raises an eyebrow so high it almost reaches his hairline.

'Sir, surely you must want to know why your people would be so cruel.'

'Justice is not cruel, it is the lack of it that breeds cruelty,' the Chief pronounces.

My genuine curiosity forces frankness. 'Does the town really think jungle justice was the best way to have handled the boys even if they were, as you say, hooligans?'

The Chief shrugs. 'Jungle justice is better than no justice.'

'They could've been handed over to the police if –'

'Stop here.'

I stop talking instinctively before I realise that the Chief was speaking to the driver, who's now bringing the car to a slow halt.

'Come,' he says and this time, I think he's talking to me.

The driver comes to help the Chief out of the car. I look at Inspector Omereji in the rear-view mirror askance. He shrugs as if to say, you're on your own. I get out too and stand next to the Chief.

'Can you see that?'

He points at an impressive, rusty old cannon that takes pride of place in the middle of a roundabout. Chika and I had driven past it before, but I'd regarded it with nothing but the mildest curiosity.

'For a very long time, all this –' The old man lifts his cane and uses it to indicate the environs, 'was nothing but bush and wild animals. My people came here many, many years ago. My great-grandfather told stories of the hardships they had, tilling the land, conquering it, but never once doubting their claim to it. Then, the white man came and took everything but the land. They gave us new laws; we obeyed as long as we had the land. They even gave us new names, a new religion, meddled in our language, but they never took the land.'

I look around at the Inspector who has followed us out of the car and is now standing and looking into the distance, his face impassive. The old man himself speaks without a rush, and looks at no one in particular, even though I appear to be his only audience.

'Even when the British brought several tribes together, drew a marker around the Niger and the Benue Rivers and called the funny circle inside Nigeria, our people did not worry. What is in a name? What could be so different after all? Our people had lived in peace with everyone from the west, the north and even amongst the easterners, long before the white man came to call us all by one name.'

The Chief starts walking around the cannon. I follow respectfully. I try to ignore the stares of passers-by, the

162

bodyguards behind us and the cars driving by with their blatantly curious occupants.

The old man moves his hand over the cannon, sighs deeply and says, 'Let us sit here for a bit.'

It takes a while for the old man to ease down on to the concrete platform holding the canon. He looks up at me.

'Am I boring you, Dr Taiwo?'

'Not at all, sir.'

'Gooood,' he drags out the word and takes a moment before he continues. 'My father said most of them came from Enugu – from that direction.' He points his cane towards somewhere in the distance. 'First in ones, then twos, then whole families.'

'The British?' I ask.

The old man looks at me as if surprised that I'm paying enough attention to ask questions and pats the spot for me to sit next to him on the sun-beaten concrete.

'No, the Igbos,' he continues. 'Before then, we were all brothers and sisters. No one had any claim to anything. We shared food, names and several parts of each other's language. But they came with papers claiming the land was theirs because a government we had not chosen told them so. But my people did not fight. We just went further into the bush, conquering other parts, starting all over again.'

He falls silent. He bows his head and shudders as if the burden of remembering overwhelms him.

Inspector Omereji walks over to the old man and places a hand on his shoulder. 'Papa?'

The old man's voice wavers slightly when he lifts his head, 'I am fine.'

'You don't have to do this,' Inspector Omereji says gently.

'He came for answers.'

'You don't have them.'

'But I have our truth.'

Omereji sighs resignedly and steps back while his father looks at me with a tired smile.

'I remember the exact date the war started. The white man had left, but the people he forced to be one no longer wanted to be together. From Omaga to Aluu, the Igbos were going from village to village, asking men to join in the fight to break away and form Biafra. One of their promises was that in Biafra there would be no faceless central government taking our land and giving it away left and right. Those of us who believed joined to fight on the side of the Igbos for Biafra. Those who didn't, stayed. But still, the war came. Forcing those who remained to become soldiers to protect the women, the children and, of course, the land.'

'Did you stay, sir?' I ask to break another long pause.

'Yes. But my father did not. He went to fight because he said no one knew which side would win. He said it was better to go and be part of the negotiations when the fighting is over. I stayed because, to protect my people and our land, someone had to be in charge of this monster.'

He raises his walking stick to rap it against the old cannon. 'For six years, we could hear bombs and explosions as close as Warri. Dying soldiers came. Hungry children and women walked miles to get here. We turned no one back. And for all those years, this was where I, my two younger brothers and three other men slept. We stayed here, ready to fire this beast to protect our people.'

I had read horrible accounts of the Biafran war – perhaps one of the most terrible civil wars in Africa, but I must confess, I've never been so close to anyone who was part of it, as a victim or soldier. I look up at the cannon. It's not hard to imagine young men camping around it, ready to fire it in defence of their lives and belongings.

'When they told us the war was over,' the old man continues, 'we waited to be sure the news was true before we left here. I stayed here until I saw my father limp home with one hand and a leg missing, and he confirmed the war was over. We all went back into the bush and brought out our women and children. And we took back our lands. When some of the Igbos came, we showed them the Land Redistribution Decree that the central government had given us in exchange for renouncing Biafra. The Igbos were not happy. We shouted. We fought. But we were also very tired. After all the killing, no one had the energy to fight longer than necessary. For the Igbos, life had become more important than land. For us, because the land had been taken from us before, there was no life without land.'

'I see,' I say after a while, but only because this time, his silence is longer than usual.

'No, you do not, Dr Taiwo,' he says more forcefully than I expect. 'You came here to look for ways to punish people who were only protecting what is theirs.'

'No, sir. The parents of these boys want closure and –'

'The boys are *dead*, what more closure can there be?'

'But how they died … it haunts the parents.'

'Those boys were robbing us, they've been doing it for years, and no one came to our rescue. And when we said,

165

enough was enough, the whole world is on our doorstep shouting injustice! Murder!'

'If that's true, sir, then I shouldn't have any problem getting the answers I came for.'

'You came for answers that will serve the purpose of the people who sent you,' he says dismissively, and in the manner I am becoming used to, he changes track without warning, 'I shall continue my story.'

He pauses as if daring me to stop him. 'The war was over. We had our land and just as we were getting our lives back, they discovered oil in Bonny and several other towns. We kept hoping they will find some here too, but they didn't. When we saw what the oil was doing to the other communities, we thanked the gods there was no oil in Okriki. But the land was no longer enough. The food from the ground could not feed everyone and still have enough to sell in the market. So, when the government came and very nicely asked for land to build the university, we agreed. And for a time, it was the right decision. People came to our village and made it a town, ate our food, rented our land and brought us a lot of money, but they kept knowledge inside the walls of the university built on our land.'

'I don't understand, sir.'

'Look around my town, Dr Taiwo,' he uses his walking stick to sweep the air in an arc. 'How many youths do you see from here going to that university? How many people from this town have access to the teaching hospital without paying plenty of money? The list goes on. What has that university brought us but discontent?'

'But you said it brought money?'

The Chief breathed deeply. 'Money only breeds a desire for more money. Nothing more.'

'I don't follow how this affects why I'm here –'

'When we gave our land to that university, the people of this town had only one thing to protect, and that was the money they made from its presence in this town. That same money is what those students came to steal.'

'Is that the town's excuse?' I can't keep the disdain from my voice.

'It is our truth, so I repeat, no one will help you find the version you came looking for.'

'Is that a threat, sir?'

'It is a promise.'

I look towards the Inspector and back at the old man whose faded eyes are piercing as they look at me.

I dare to respond, 'Even if it means using your own son to obstruct justice, sir?'

Inspector Omereji steps towards me threateningly but halts as the Chief raises his walking stick.

'Dr Taiwo, go and tell those who sent you that you met the Paramount Chief Kinikanwo Omereji of Okriki. Tell them I will make sure my people are not punished for protecting themselves from those who came to take what does not belong to them. You understand?'

For the life of me, I can do nothing but nod.

BACKTRACK

We say nothing throughout the drive back to the hotel. The driver opens the door for me, and I bid the Chief goodbye. He merely nods, closing his eyes as if I bored him. I don't bother acknowledging the Inspector, expressionless in the front seat.

Chika is waiting for me at the entrance and, after assuring him I am fine, I tell him I'd like to be alone. He understands.

I go to my room, take off my shoes and lie on the bed.

The day has been a string of disasters, first with Mercy and the ethical lines I'd crossed in the bid to get any useful information that could help my investigation. Then, to return from that only to be confronted by the unrepentant arrogance of Chief Omereji was the last straw.

Recalling the look on the father's face as he comforted Mercy fills me with remorse. What separates me from someone like the Chief who would justify murder in the name of protecting his people? Am I becoming Machiavellian, devoid of empathy and entirely focused on my goal?

For the millionth time since I followed my wife back to Nigeria, I curse the circumstances that made that decision for me. Despite the game face I had put on when Folake had presented her arguments for us to come back, I know I still harbour a deep resentment for her insistence.

'Sweet, the boys will turn fifteen this year. I want us to leave before they think they're the colour of their skin.'

She had a point. Social media had democratised information and reports of violence towards people of colour were everywhere. When we were invited to attend a parents–teachers' conference where a whole set of instructions were given to black boys on what to do when stopped by the police, Folake had been livid and disturbed all at once. The disaster in Seattle was the last straw, making her determined to leave the States, with or without me. So, yes, I am a reluctant returnee. And this has clouded my acclimatisation in Nigeria. I've used my *otherness* to look in at my homeland as an outsider. I tell myself that as long as I can rise above the chaos and maintain my separateness, I'll be fine.

Today, my conduct suggests that I may have lost the battle. It seems I have given in to the rush mentality, the tendency to take the shortcut and bypass due process. I have become too involved in a case, setting professional caution aside.

For this, I blame my father. As much as I don't want to make this all about him, his relationship with Emeka matters a lot. His confession about being in a cult – fraternity – on campus shook me since it revealed a side of him that I didn't know existed. Ever since that conversation in his study, I have tried to reconcile my strict but loving father with the violence and mayhem associated with cultism on Nigerian campuses. I don't even know what I hope to find: that the Okriki Three were members of a cult and therefore their violent deaths in the hands of the townsfolk were justified? Or that their deaths had nothing to do with cultism but everything to do with a misguided community set on edge by an insecure environment?

There's a knock on my door. I open it, and Chika stands there with a full bottle of Jameson whiskey and two mismatched glasses.

'Usually, it's when people want to be alone that they really shouldn't be,' he says wryly.

This new-found familiarity is just what I need right now. Chika walks in, places the glasses on the table and starts to open the bottle of whiskey.

'I'm afraid I wasn't the best version of myself today,' I say, as I close the door.

'Neither was I.' He pours the golden liquid into the two glasses and hands me one. 'But it has happened. Can we find something in the whole experience to make it all worthwhile?'

He's right, of course. Perhaps the best way to make my mistake count for some good is to reflect on the information Mercy's interview has yielded.

'Well, for one,' I say, as the whiskey burns down my throat, 'if Kevin came visiting Mercy earlier in the day, then we can confirm that he didn't leave the campus with Bona and Winston.'

'But they could all have met up later in the day.' Chika knocks back his drink and starts to pour another.

'Yes, but if it was a sting, and it was planned carefully enough to select Kevin as a lookout guy –'

'But as you said, if Winston and Bona were cultists, they wouldn't need a lookout guy –'

'Yes, but work with me here ...' I pause as Chika pours more whiskey into my glass. It might be ungracious to tell him that while beer is okay, hard liquor is my real undoing, so I take the glass and hope to nurse it long enough to avert dancing on the ceiling. 'If this was all planned and Kevin was a part of it from the beginning, would he complicate things by visiting his girlfriend, and add the pressure of meeting her father for the first time, on the very day he is planning a robbery?'

'Not a robbery. A shakedown.'

'Whatever. One of them felt the need to bring a gun to the scene. That's a strong indication that whatever was going to happen at Godwin's place was not a courtesy visit.'

'So, you don't think Kevin would visit Mercy on the same day he was planning to shakedown Godwin with his pals?'

'I'm just not sure it's something *anyone* will do.'

I walk to my wall of Post-it notes. I've pasted newspaper clippings of the Okriki Three alongside some of the facts corroborated by the police reports. They're in the 'what we know' section of the wall. Next to the notes are pictures of Winston, Bona and Kevin. Young, handsome and smiling. Under Kevin's picture, there's a lot of information, but I've also put a large question mark against the word 'cultist'.

I stare at the photo for a while. Everyone has described him as wonderful, kind and smart. To be honest, until I met Mercy, I took all these descriptions with a pinch of doubt. Parents especially can be quite biased when describing their kids, generally overselling their skills and attributes. Add the cultural tendency not to speak ill of the dead, and one can see why I tended to avoid basing my composites of the victims on hearsay. But, somehow Mercy's portrait of Kevin resonates. He seemed like a truly well-brought-up boy, kind, respectful and well liked.

I consider Emeka Nwamadi himself. Well educated. A gentleman by all standards and a success story. A conscientious self-made man who has risen to become one of the most respected bankers in the country. It's not hard to picture him raising a son who would have, for all intents and purposes, become an asset to society.

My father's reason for wanting to disprove the idea that Kevin was a cultist comes to mind. Perhaps I have it all wrong, focusing on whether the boys were in a cult or not. So far, the best explanation I have for Kevin being attacked together with Bona and Winston is that they were in a cult, but there's no shred of evidence supporting this theory. Nothing but the words of players whose motives I can't trust. I had hoped to leave this membership theory behind but finding an alternative line of enquiry is proving elusive.

'The Chief insists the boys were killed by his people in self-defence.'

Chika snorts. 'Evil man! You know it's on record that he told his people to hunt and kill any robber? How can he say that, especially if locals who steal are punished with public humiliation at the community hall? It's the strangers they burn alive.' He gives a long hiss. 'Xenophobic bastard!'

'The Chief's not our focus –' I try to remind Chika.

'He should be arrested, nonetheless. He has a big role in this.'

'Chika, focus.'

Chika flashes a rueful smile and lifts his hands up in mock surrender.

'If we can understand the relationship between the three young men,' I continue, 'we might be able to work out how they came to be together in Okriki on that day.'

'Mr Nwamadi is pretty sure his son was not friends with Bona and Winston.'

'Yes. But what about this Tamuno that Mercy says Kevin was going to see? Is he a student too? How close were they? What can he tell us about that day?' I stop walking around the room and look at Chika, watching me from the sofa. 'Remember when we went to the scene of the burning and the compound?'

Chika nods.

'I think we should've backtracked a bit further.'

'To where?' Chika asks with a frown.

'To when the boys left campus … If we want a realistic timeline of what happened that day, we've got to start from the beginning. From *before* they got to Okriki.'

'What will it tell us?' Chika asks, sceptical.

'Well, for one, premeditation. If this was a planned sting, then someone must have known they were planning a visit to Okriki. Who saw them leave the campus? At what time? Did they get a lift or a taxi?'

'I don't know how that will help.' Chika is shaking his head. 'They were here. How they got here or who saw them can't make much of a difference.'

'But we can piece together what their possible intention was, what made this particular shakedown different from the ones Godwin claimed they'd done to him in the past. Did they always have a gun? Had anybody ever seen them with a gun? Had they ever used it before?'

'What if they bought it specifically for the sting?'

'Then it would demonstrate what made *this* sting different!'

'Ah. You want to act on Godwin's testimony. But you said he is unreliable.'

'Yes, he is ... but his testimony that Kevin was not part of the shakedown is corroborated by Mercy's version of events.'

'Another unreliable witness,' Chika says ruefully.

'Two unreliable witnesses who don't know each other having the same version of events certainly makes the story a lot more credible ...'

I walk to the wall again. My eyes are drawn to the layout of Madam Landlady's rooms.

'We need to find this Tamuno individual.'

Chika stands to join me. 'That is a relatively common name in these parts. Even here,' he points at the long list of names of the people interviewed by the police. Three pages of dozens of names. 'There are at least six Tamunos.'

'All students living in the compound?' I squint at the layout of the house, looking for a 'T' in the initials written in the square boxes representing the students' rooms. There are ten Ts.

Chika frowns as he peers at the list. 'There are two students here named Tamuno, but remember this list was compiled by the police. Can we trust it?'

'We can't but two's manageable.' I pick up red and orange blocks of Post-it notes. 'So? Red flag or don't know?'

Chika considers for a beat. 'I'd say red flag but considering it's information from Mercy and the police ...'

I nod. 'Yeah. Let's err on the side of caution.'

I write 'Tamuno' with a question mark on the orange block, tear off the Post-it note and hand it to Chika to stick on the wall. He pours more whiskey for both of us and we continue deliberating into the night.

By the time Chika leaves my room, it's well past midnight. The bottle of Jameson is now half empty, and I suspect Chika's not much more sober than me, since he seemed to have forgotten to take it with him. I crash on the bed, feeling light-headed and rather pleased with myself, considering what a disaster the earlier part of the day had been.

I reach for my phone, preparing my goodnight message to the kids even if it's way past their bedtime. There's a message notification waiting, so I click on it. My heart sinks.

'What did I do so wrong that you'd forget today?'

A BOY IN HAVANA

I am now officially John Paul Afini-Clark.

It had taken thousands of naira, a willing local government clerk in Owerri, patience and a lot of follow-ups to ensure that against my given name the record is marked 'deceased' and new documents have been prepared in the name of John Paul Afini-Clark. I have a birth certificate, signed affidavits that my parents were dead and that other documentation of my identification was lost in a flooding disaster that drowned them and my two siblings a decade and half earlier.

But I didn't plan on being summoned by Amaso on the same day my local government clerk called to say the papers are ready for collection. So, I hire a motorbike from Owerri to PH, and wait around the city centre for the late-night appointment.

Havana is the picture of a once affluent middle-class neighbourhood gone to the dogs. Tell a taxi you're going to Havana, and you will get a double take and double the fare. Hail a motorbike, you will pay through your nose, and the driver will most likely ask to be paid before allowing you on the bike. And when you get to your destination, be ready to get off at the speed of light or you will fall off the bike as the driver speeds away.

The dangers of the neighbourhood do not faze John Paul as he gets off the motorbike and walks towards Amaso

Dabara's house. Five years of being the drug lord's most profitable distributor has its benefits.

'I hope you came with a plan, Aboi,' Amaso says when John Paul stands in front of him, surrounded by groupies and thugs, all high on the drugs Amaso provides to keep them on his leash.

John Paul's face does not betray his hatred of the kingpin's nickname for him. From the beginning of their relationship, Amaso insisted on calling him 'a boy'.

'I have, if you'll go for it.'

The pungent smells of cigarette and marijuana fill the air. Amaso himself is dressed in loose linen trousers and nothing else but a large gold necklace. His jutting ribs look like gnarled fingers gripping the Star of David pendant hanging on his sunken chest.

'Let's hear it,' Amaso says.

John Paul proceeds to outline the plan.

'You trust them?' Amaso asks when John Paul is done talking.

'They've been buying from me for years and as far as I can tell, none of them are users themselves. So, yes, they're reliable.'

'Not like that Godwin boy?'

John Paul tries to keep his voice regretful. We both knew Godwin would come up.

'Godwin was a mistake, but he no longer sells for me. I told you.'

Amaso shakes his head, displacing the cloud of weed smoke around him. 'You should have let me deal with him when he exposed us like that.'

John Paul stays quiet. They've been through this before, and John Paul has learnt not to rise to the bait.

'These buyers,' Amaso breaks the long silence, 'they want to up their game? Become direct suppliers?'

'I've sounded them out but they are scared of you.'

'They should be –' Amaso says arrogantly.

'Which is why you should meet them,' John Paul cuts in. 'Talk to them. Reassure them that you'll take care of them as long as they keep the supply chain going.'

'How can I trust you? You promised to wait another year before graduating –'

'You asked me but I never promised. Besides, how would a first-class student who suddenly fails his finals look?'

'Stop boasting.'

'I'm just stating the facts,' John Paul says without guile.

'I want guarantees before I let you go.'

We anticipated this. 'Like what?'

'Something on these guys to keep them in check.'

John Paul turns to take his backpack off. He bends to open it, aware that the bodyguards are on high alert. Slowly, he brings out the hard drive and hands it to Amaso.

'What's this?'

'Information. Their names. All past transactions. Their full background and how much they each sell on a monthly basis.'

Amaso turns the hard drive this way and that. 'Is it enough?'

'You can be the judge of that.'

'Bring them here.'

'They are too scared. You come to them. Meet them in my room. That will reassure them.'

Amaso has to agree to the plan, but John Paul must not push. Amaso is unpredictable and resents being told what to do.

We wait.

'When?' Amaso eventually asks into a cloud of weed smoke.

THE CULT OF DISTINGUISHED
GENTLEMEN

For the first time in seventeen years, I forgot our wedding anniversary, and the psychologist in me can't help but wonder if there's a Freudian logic to this.

I could make the excuse that yesterday was perhaps the busiest day since I began the investigation. But, if I am being honest, I know my current lack of marital harmony is making me a willing hostage of the Okriki Three's web of intrigue.

To counter my rising guilt, I give in to irritation. She could have called. Or texted a *'happy anniversary!'* No, instead, she waited till the end of the day, well after I lost any chance of redemption, before sending her damning message.

What did I do so wrong ...? I snort. So, she knows she did something wrong? Or was this a lawyer's trick – asking a leading question? No doubt, Folake knows something is wrong, given my behaviour over the past couple of weeks, but I wasn't sure she knew that it was because of her until this text message.

Was there a part of me that wanted her to know that I know? Did I forget yesterday was my anniversary because I didn't *want* to remember?

My thoughts descend to ramblings as I move from tipsy to drunk. The next thing I know, I'm locked in the Land Cruiser. I try to get out, but all the doors are jammed. My knuckles hurt from punching the unyielding glass. I see Folake and Mercy pointing accusing fingers at me. I can't hear them but they're angry at me.

Mercy's father appears with a plastic jerrycan and starts dousing the car. I bang harder on the windows. Folake and Mercy are still shouting words I cannot hear and ignoring my pleas. I see the Chief, Inspector Omereji and several others, including Madam Landlady. They are all raising fists, chanting something that seems to encourage Mercy's father to light a match and throw it towards the car, a malevolent smile on his face. I scream and –

Wake up.

I hold my pounding head, stagger to my suitcase and retrieve a bottle of aspirin. I down three tablets with copious amounts of water, then check the time. Less than two hours before I'm supposed to meet Chika at reception.

I take a long shower and as my headache recedes, I decide to do some research to prepare for the day. I started typing 'cultism' in my search browser and remembered my father's disapproval of the word, so I changed it to 'confraternities in Nigerian universities' and ninety minutes later, I'm as horrified as I am informed.

My shock at knowing my father's involvement in a fraternity during his university days was informed solely by urban legends. These were stories that were shared as whispers amongst Nigerian high school students as they prepared for university. They were like the bogeyman, folklore even, told to young boys to caution them when they became freshmen about the dangers of joining what had descended into being a 'cult'. Factually, I knew very little, and to be honest, based on what I am reading on the Internet, ignorance is indeed bliss.

According to Wikipedia, the first known confraternity was formed at my father's alma mater, the University College, Ibadan, by no less than the Nobel laureate Wole Soyinka with six other students. Their Pyrates Confraternity was initially punted as a fraternity of promising young students that challenged the status quo, and was later registered as The National Association of Seadogs. They had a code of conduct and language that was reminiscent of European pirate-speak, complete with a skull-and-crossbones logo.

More clicks later, and it's unbelievable how something that started out as a fraternity of elite students in the fifties transformed into such a nationwide network of mayhem, which is now popularly referred to as 'cultism'. Every campus in Nigeria seems to have reported some kind of cult violence over the years. From north to south, the confraternities have taken such violent paths that most universities have a zero-tolerance policy against them. This has driven the fraternities underground, making the 'secret' part of their names the norm.

On getting to the tale of a decapitated head impaled on a spike at the entrance gates of the University of Port Harcourt, I decide I've read enough. I check my watch. I still have some time before meeting Chika, so I call my father.

He is already at work, but he takes my call and, after some awkward questions as to my well-being and how the investigation is progressing, I take the plunge.

'Dad, about the cults, sorry, fraternities. Did you … were you ever involved in the kind of violence that I've been reading about?'

I hear a long sigh on the other side of the line. 'Kenny, I told you, in our days it was not a cult.'

'What was it then?'

'We prided ourselves on being a group of distinguished gentlemen, of high moral standards and exemplary academic records.'

'What went wrong? When did it become what it is today?'

Another long silence. I can picture him pulling at his impeccably knotted tie while reclining on the ergonomic leather chair my sister Kenny Girl had presented him for his seventieth.

'When I entered the university, the country was a new nation, and the inequalities in the system were endemic. Most of us were the first in our families to go to university. We had an obligation to change things. Some of us were active in the unions, others took to writing articles, and others, well, we became political activists, effectively becoming an opposition to an authoritarian government.'

'That's not different from how most undergraduates think in any society. They are usually idealists.'

'And we were. But we did *do* things. We created awareness for a lot of what was going on then. I think the problem was that we were too successful.'

'I don't understand.'

'By the time I left med school, the naira was one to the British pound and worth more than the US dollar. The country was rolling in oil money and there was aid from the global community to rebuild the country after the war. I think we all thought our jobs were done and so we did not put in place any structures before handing over the reins of the fraternities to the younger ones. Maybe we thought they would self-organise like we did. Or we just didn't think. The point is, the ones that came after us had no battle to fight, no wrong to right and no responsibility to improve a society that was clearly on the rise.'

'Rebels without a cause?'

'Exactly. At least that's how I see it. Many of us went abroad for further studies, and others were too busy with their new lives in a prosperous nation. By the time we all realised that what we had created in the universities had become this many-headed monster, it was too late.'

'But the country has not always been prosperous, Dad. The naira did plunge and there were several military coups.'

'Which all made the students who came after us lose faith in our generation. We messed up, Kenny. When the fraternities became cults, I think it was almost like the younger generation was giving us the middle finger.'

'What if Kevin was indeed part of a cult?' I ask. 'What if all this happened to Emeka's son because he did indeed do what he was accused of?'

'Son, I didn't persuade you to take this job to find out if that boy was in a cult. I wanted you to find out why the boy was killed because I could see how the tragedy was eating at Emeka, literally killing him before our very eyes.'

'So, this is a mission to save Emeka?'

'You could say that. It's what we've always done ever since his father died.'

While I find this code of looking out for each other quite admirable, I can't shake the feeling that my dad is not telling me everything. I know him too well – when he waxes philosophical, it's usually because he is deflecting. But time is passing and I know Chika will be waiting for me, so I thank my dad and sign off quickly.

We skip breakfast – although I drink a large cup of the bad coffee to ease the light throbbing in my head – and by quarter past eight, we are driving towards TSU.

I bring out my notepad and Chika groans. I look at him with a raised eyebrow.

'When you bring that out, it means you didn't sleep.'

'Well, I didn't ... At least not enough.' I flip through my notes. 'Do we know the number of fraternities that TSU has?'

'Fraternities? Is that what we're calling them now?'

I can't tell him about my dad, and his sensitivities about cults versus fraternities. 'Cult then,' I correct myself, not looking up. 'So, is it possible to know how many there are?'

'There'll be all the ones that have national representations on all campuses ...'

'Like the Pyrates?'

'Yes, the Vikings, Black Axe and Mafia –'

'And there'll be the ones that are specific to TSU?' I interrupt as I look through my notes.

'Chances are.' Chika nods. 'Most cults are formed in retaliation to another one. It's very likely that some disgruntled members of an existing cult decided to form their own and it's yet to have representation in other universities.'

'And all these cults, they're only guys?'

'Female students also have theirs but definitely not as violent as the boys. Usually, it's the girlfriends of the members of one cult that join the female versions,' Chika says, as he makes a turn and the university entrance comes into view.

'If the Okriki Three were part of a cult, any chance we can find out which one?'

'You'll hear rumours.' Chika shrugs as he drives through the massive entrance gates. 'The students will whisper some names.'

'But we won't be able to confirm which one?'

He gives his trademark shrug again. 'It's a secret, after all.'

A TRIBE APART

The Harcourt Whyte Hall of the State University is named after a songwriter who was diagnosed with leprosy and ostracised from his community for over three decades. In that time Harcourt formed a choir with other lepers and created over 600 hymns. Ironically, it was not the disease that killed him, but a car accident in 1977.

This residential hall was where Winston, Bona and Kevin lived at the time of their deaths. Using my interviewee list, selected names from the police case file and information which Tom Ikime had ordered his secretary to give me plus the university's report on the Okriki Three, I was able to deduce that Winston had two official roommates and three squatters at the time of his death. Two of them are currently in their final year, and still reside in the hall. None of Bona's roommates are currently students, but we have the name of one of his course mates who occupied the room next to him. Since Kevin resided in a single room and had no squatter, there is no one to interview.

We park in front of the hall's entrance and I look around while Chika goes to ask the security guard for directions and any information that will jumpstart our interviews.

After a few minutes Chika comes over to where I am standing in the parking lot, smiling, with a piece of rumpled paper in his hands. He tears the paper into two and hands me one half.

'The Security Guard knows the students we want to talk to and most of their room numbers.'

On my half are three names with a set of numbers against two.

'I'm guessing you have no lead on our Tamuno guy.'

Chika sighs. 'I told you it's a common name.'

I look up at the buildings: six blocks of four floors each. 'Which floor is E287?'

Chika points in the direction I should go and we agree to meet back at the Land Cruiser in an hour. If our interviews extend longer, we will call.

The stairs to the second floor of the block are not as arduous as I anticipated, what with my hangover. The door to E287 is ajar, ostensibly to air the room, given the intense heat. There are two young men inside: one lying on an unmade bed, eating a huge chunk of bread as he flips through a textbook, while the other lifts a worn single mattress off the floor and slides it under another bed. A squatter.

'Hello?'

They both look at me.

'I'm looking for ...' I check the piece of paper, 'Sobi Kurubo?'

'Who wants to know?' asks the one moving the mattress.

'Are you Sobi?'

'If I am?' His suspicious tone doesn't faze me. I am sure I look as out of place here as a strip show at the Vatican.

'I'm Dr Philip Taiwo.' I walk into the room and offer my hand. The other roommate perks up at my American accent.

'I just want to ask you a couple of questions for some research I'm doing. Are you Sobi Kurubo?'

A wary pause and then, Sobi takes my hand. 'How can I help you, sir?'

The roommate stands and invites me to sit on the bed. I nod my thanks and accept the offer. He is packing several books, eating and slinging his backpack on his shoulder, all in a series of deft movements. He leaves me with Sobi, who now sits across from me on the other single bed.

'I'd like to talk to you about Winston Babajide Coker.'

There's silence for a beat.

'Are you police or something?'

'No. I'm writing a paper on the whole incident.'

'But, you're not from around here –'

'I'm affiliated with a university in the US.' Since this is not entirely true, I quickly add, 'I am doing a study on mob action and crowd control.'

'Which university?'

'USC.'

'South Carolina or Southern California?'

The boy's knowledge throws me a bit but I recover quickly. 'California.'

'Cool. As soon as I'm out of here, I'll be applying for the summer programme in film production there.'

'Great programme. Why don't I give you my details? I can give you a referral when you're ready …'

Three quarters of an hour later, after answering all my questions and giving me a tour of Harcourt Whyte Hall, including a visit to the room where Winston stayed

– locked, but Winston's picture is posted on the door with 'Never Forgotten' written across it – Sobi informs me that the other interviewee on my list is a 'ghost'.

'He actually graduated last year,' Winston explains, 'but he got a room by paying extra, then rents it out.'

I don't bother expressing any surprise at this bit of information. 'Sobi, you've been such great help, but I wonder if you know a Tamuno, who was Kevin Nwamadi's friend …'

Sobi frowns. 'I'm not sure, but if I remember correctly, the only Tamuno I can associate with Kevin is the one who was in his department.'

'He was supposed to meet a Tamuno on the day he died.'

'Off campus? That would be strange because that Tamuno lives here.'

I am not convinced that we are referring to the same Tamuno, but you never know. 'Maybe he was staying off campus then?'

Sobi shakes his head. 'T-Man – that's what we call him – has always stayed on campus.'

I look at the time and quickly text Chika to give me another half an hour. Then I ask Sobi, 'You think he's around?'

Sobi motions for me to follow him. 'No harm in trying.'

When we stop in front of Room 481, he knocks. No answer.

'It's a busy time. Mock court sessions at the Law Faculty. Especially for final year students.'

I look around. The doors on this floor are fewer. I mention this.

'Single man rooms,' Sobi explains. 'More expensive. You can get one if you apply on time and are willing to grease some palms. T-Man has always lived here.'

It makes no sense that Kevin would go all the way to Okriki to see a student who lived in the same block as him. I am not entirely sure this Tamuno is the same one Mercy was referring to.

I thank Sobi for his time as he walks with me to the parking lot. I can see Chika watching as Sobi saves my number, shakes my hand accompanied with a lot of 'sir's. He heads back towards his block but not before sending a tentative wave and slight frown Chika's way.

'You know he'll certainly call, don't you?' Chika says as soon as the boy is out of earshot.

'I don't mind really. He seems like a bright young man. How did you do?'

'Well, I didn't have an American accent to fall back on but Tochukwu Nwandu happens to come from Enugu, and we found out we come from the same neighbourhood.'

'Are you from Enugu?'

'Owerri. But Tochukwu doesn't know that.'

I chuckle at this, a bit uncomfortable that Chika can read me so well. So well that he could guess how I went about persuading Sobi for an interview.

We get into the car and Chika reverses out of the parking lot. We had booked an appointment with Ikime, but his secretary has yet to confirm. Same with the Dean of the Law Faculty, a Professor Esohe who insists on written approval from the Registrar before he commits to a face-to-face meeting.

'Let's go somewhere we can compare notes while we wait,' I suggest, and Chika turns at a traffic light in the direction given by a sign: 'This way to Students' Village'.

When we get there, the place is bustling with lots of canteens, makeshift second-hand bookshops and several cybercafes. Students mill about, some reading and others already drinking beer even though it's barely noon. There's a youthful carefreeness in the air that makes me feel relaxed.

We find a rather quiet canteen with an outside seating area. There are three students sitting at the table next to us: two guys and a bespectacled girl gathered around a laptop. They're loud but not consistently so. We order some soft drinks and what appears to be the canteen's speciality: plain eggs sealed in toasted bread. When it arrives, it's hot, golden brown and really delicious.

I tell Chika what Sobi said about Tamuno.

'I told you. Could be anyone.'

'This Tamuno is key to knowing what Kevin was doing in that compound that day. But if the one living on campus, who also happens to be his classmate, is not the Tamuno we are looking for ...' I shake my head, already thinking what our options are.

'Let's compare notes first,' Chika interrupts my musing, bringing out his phone and reads off it.

'Tochukwu was Bona's roommate and he recalls being in the room when Winston left that day.'

I check my handwritten notes. 'Could he remember what time?'

'He said it was in the afternoon. Just before four.'

I frown. 'Why is he so sure?'

'He said it's because he was one of the people who gave statements to the police and the university's panel of enquiry.'

I riffle through my notes, 'Sobi says he was also in the room around that time, and Bona was the one that came to pick up Winston.'

'Yes, apparently Bona had told Tochukwu he was going to town with Winston. Tochukwu said he assumed it was a party because Bona was looking really sharp.'

'Same with Sobi. He said Winston had seemed excited and he's sure there were girls involved because when Bona came, there was lots of whistling and laughing between the two guys before they left at around 4 p.m.'

Chika nods. 'Correlates with Tochukwu's timing too.'

'It would've taken them about thirty minutes at least to get to Okriki if they took public transport.'

'That's right. Police reports say that the boys were captured –' Chika puts 'captured' in air quotes and continues, 'around 5:30.'

An involuntary shudder goes through me as I mentally calculate the boys' ordeal. Reports stated that the burning of the three boys had taken place around 7:15 p.m. and the time stamps on some of the videos posted online confirm this. That would imply that the boys had been beaten and tortured for nearly two hours before they were finally killed.

'Sobi said there was no Kevin in the picture. That only Bona had come to the room to meet Winston.'

'Even more,' Chika says, 'Tochukwu said he would have known if Kevin was part of Bona's entourage to Okriki.'

'Why?'

'Because Kevin was his friend. He says one of the things Kevin always asked him was how he could be roommates with someone like Bona.'

'Why would Kevin ask that about Bona?'

'Because of the rumours that Bona was in a cult. Apparently, Bona and Kevin used to be somewhat friends until they had a falling out when Kevin found out that he was in a cult.'

'So,' I quickly cut in, 'Tochukwu can confirm if Bona was in a cult?'

Chika shrugs. 'He insists no one knows for sure. Certainly, Bona was connected and popular, but he was not the violent type. Always well dressed, always managed his image with the girls and definitely a party animal.'

'Sobi says the same about Winston. He said he sometimes thought Winston thrived on the rumours that he was in a cult, and had been known to boast more than once that –' I read from my notes, '"he'll f–up anyone who messes with him because he's a don."'

Chika wipes bread crumbs off his chin and the edge of his lips. 'According to Tochukwu, Bona was known to make threats and boast of his connections, but no one can trace any violence directly to him. But I guess if they were high up in the cult hierarchy, they could be the ones ordering hits without necessarily getting their hands dirty?'

'So why didn't they order their minions to go to Okriki?' I ask.

'Maybe the stakes were higher?'

'Stakes of laptop and cell phones?' I snort. 'The same kinds of items Godwin claims had been extorted from him in the past with minimal violence?'

'You've got a point,' Chika agrees.

I swallow the last of my egg sandwich just as my phone rings. I don't recognise the number but I answer.

'Hello?'

'Dr Taiwo?' I don't know the voice on the other end.

'This is he.'

'I met Sobi on my way from class. He says you're looking for me.'

I try to keep the excitement from my voice. 'And you are?'

'Tamuno.'

BREAKTHROUGH

The young man I assume to be Tamuno enters the canteen. I think it's him because of the way he stops at the entrance, and looks around, his eyes passing over the group of students in a heated discussion then settling on the table where Chika and I are seated.

He is tall, lanky even, with light brown skin covered in a sheen of sweat, perhaps from the exertion of walking from Harcourt Whyte Hall to the Village. He is wearing a slightly rumpled white shirt over well-ironed, dark blue khaki pants.

He walks over to us and looks from Chika to me. 'Dr Taiwo?'

I like that he is not presumptuous. I reach out my hand. 'I am Dr Taiwo. You're Tamuno?'

'Yes, sir. Tamunotonye Princewill. Everyone calls me Tamuno.'

Chika pulls a seat out and the boy sits. 'I am Chika Makuochi.'

'Nice to meet you, sir.'

'Thank you for coming,' I say to help the young man feel comfortable. 'We were close to giving up hope of identifying you. There are a lot of Tamunos in these parts and we didn't have a surname to go with it.'

The boy laughs self-consciously. 'It's a curse and a blessing, sir.'

'Did Sobi tell you why we were looking for you?' I ask, curious about how much he knows.

'He did, sir. That's why I had to meet you.'

The boy's earnestness catches me off guard, and the investigator in me becomes suspicious. Eager witnesses are generally a red flag.

I decide to come clean. 'Truth is, we are writing a report on the Okriki Three, and it's not just a random investigation into mob action as I told Sobi.'

Tamuno's face falls. 'I understand, sir. In fact, I suspected this must be the case, since Sobi said that all your questions were centred around them.'

I nod at Chika to speak, since I can see he is raring to go and I wanted a moment to study the young man.

'We were told Kevin went to the compound in Okriki to see you that day.'

Tamuno looks at Chika with a frown. 'Not really. We agreed to meet there.'

I try to curb my excitement. We *do* have the right Tamuno.

'Why? I ask. 'Both of you lived on campus, didn't you?'

'It's because of our project, sir,' Tamuno answers. 'Well, mine actually. I was writing a paper on the effect of the Anti-Gay laws that were enacted a couple of months before the tragedy.'

Chika looks at me with a slightly raised eyebrow as if to ask what I know of this.

I nod. Folake and I were part of the community of Nigerians in the US who had signed a strongly worded petition to the Consulate in DC to decry the homophobic law that had horrified most of the international community and human rights activists across the globe.

'My paper was investigating the procedural ramifications of prosecuting those accused of engaging in homosexual activities.'

'Kevin was helping you with your project?' Chika asks.

'Not really. He had vested interests. His friend Momoh had been arrested on suspicions of homosexual activity, but he died in custody.'

I put on a frown. 'Momoh?'

'Momoh Kadiri, yes.'

'This Momoh was arrested by the police in Okriki?' Chika asks, taking my cue to act as if this is the first time we've come across the name.

'Yes, but he died in custody. He had an asthma attack and had no access to medical care in jail.'

'And Kevin knew this?' I ask.

'Kevin didn't know anything beyond wanting the police to be held accountable. Momoh was his friend, and he started a movement on campus to demand that the university sue the police. Of course, that didn't happen, but I think the police in Okriki were very aware of Kevin's activities and this was why they didn't step in to help him and the other two when the crowd descended on them.'

'You think the police set them up?' I ask.

'If it were only Kevin, I would have said so, but the involvement of the other two throws my hypothesis into doubt.'

'This Momoh, what was the ruling on his death?' I ask.

'Accidental,' Tamuno says scornfully. 'It was proven that, while Momoh's Ventolin was empty when he was in custody, the police did not confiscate it from him as was initially reported. They were just doing their job.'

Convenient. My next engagement with Inspector Omereji promises to be quite interesting.

'So, your meeting with Kevin was to do what exactly?' Chika throws in.

'We were going to confront Godwin about it.'

'Godwin?' Chika and I say almost at the same time, unable to hide our surprise.

At this point, Tamuno looks around as if checking if anyone is listening in on our conversation. His voice lowers conspiratorially. 'Kevin had it on good authority that Godwin was the one who reported Momoh to the police, claiming that there was gay porn on his phone.'

'Kevin told you this?' I ask.

'Yes.' Tamuno nods. 'He showed me his text exchange with Godwin. He had confronted Godwin about it and of course that one denied it.' Tamuno's derision towards Godwin is evident every time he mentions the name.

'So, you decided to go there to confront him in person …?' Chika prompts.

'When Kevin found out what my paper was about, he offered to help. We just planned to ask Godwin some questions that would either confirm or disprove his suspicions.'

'But why would Godwin do that to this Momoh boy?' I ask, genuinely perplexed.

Again, Tamuno looks around to be sure no one is within earshot. 'Because Momoh found out that he was selling drugs and was planning to expose him.'

'Godwin was selling drugs?' Chika asks, not giving any indication that this supported his earlier theory.

'Big time, sir. When Momoh found out, Godwin told him to keep quiet or else. Momoh said he was uncomfortable with the unsavoury people who were coming to the compound at all times of the night. They were rowdy and even violent. Momoh then gave Godwin an ultimatum to move out or he was going to report him to the police and the school authorities.'

'You're saying Godwin had a bone to pick with this Momoh?' I ask, also lowering my voice.

'Yes, sir. Kevin told me Momoh had asked his advice on how to deal with the situation, so he knew Godwin must have been the one who told the police about the pictures on Momoh's phone. The police said they acted on an anonymous tip, and the fact that Momoh's inhaler was somehow empty on the day of his arrest seemed to point to someone orchestrating everything.'

'But Kevin could not be sure it was Godwin?'

'As far as Kevin was concerned, no one else had a motive. The question was whether Godwin knew Momoh would die in custody and Kevin felt confronting Godwin would reveal the truth.'

'And he needed you to come with him?'

'No, sir, he didn't.' Tamuno's face falls again. 'I offered. Since my paper was about the burden of evidence in prosecuting cases like that, I was interested in knowing if Kevin's assumptions were true.'

'Did Kevin know Godwin was on drugs?' Chika asks.

'Everyone knows that,' he says dismissively. 'In fact, Kevin and I banked on Godwin being so high he'd admit to his role in Momoh's death. We even planned to record the interview.'

'Godwin claims he does not know how Kevin became part of the Okriki Three.' I hold Tamuno's gaze.

'He is lying!' Tamuno's voice rises, contempt mixed with outrage. 'He may not have known we were coming, but I reckon Bona and Winston came to buy drugs from him, a fight must have ensued, and that was when Kevin must have appeared on the scene.'

I shake my head. 'But if they came to buy drugs, why bring a gun? They're customers after all.'

Tamuno shrugs. 'Who knows with that boy? Some people say he was owing Winston money and they wanted drugs as payment and he refused. And if Kevin was there confronting him about his role in Momoh's death, I imagine Godwin was feeling threatened on all sides. Everything must have been too much for his drug-crazed mind. He cried for help and the townspeople rushed to the compound. The rest is …'

Tamuno shakes his head sadly, looking very near tears. There is a brief silence as I allow him to compose himself.

'You were supposed to meet Kevin. Why weren't you there? Where were you?'

Tamuno breathes in deeply and exhales. 'Maybe it's all my fault, sir.'

'Why do you say that?' I ask.

'Because that day I had a lot of classes that ran over and I called Kevin to postpone, but he said he was already on his way there. I begged him to wait, but he refused.'

I can believe this about Kevin Nwamadi, having met his father.

'So, you never saw what actually happened?' Chika asks before I can counsel the young man not to beat himself up over something he clearly had no control over.

Tamuno shakes his head, and exhales deeply.

'You never shared this information with the police?' Chika asks.

'I did, sir!' Tamuno insists as if we would contradict him. 'I swear I went there myself the very next day after the tragedy and asked to speak to the investigating officer. I told him what I knew, but he said it was all conjecture since I was not actually there. I went as far as telling him the reason he didn't want to take my testimony was because it proved that Godwin may have used the police to get rid of Momoh. He sent me away and told me to come back when I was ready to tell the truth.'

Even if Inspector Omereji was not around when this might have happened, it doesn't quell my anger every time I consider the role – or lack thereof – of the police in all this. Such compelling account from someone like Tamuno would have gone a long way to shed more light on what happened that October day.

'Thank you so much, Tamuno,' I say. 'You've really been a great help.'

Tamuno nods and his eyes brim with tears. 'I am just glad someone finally hears me. I know it can't bring Kevin or the other guys back, but it's the least I can do.'

I don't have much else to ask the young man because all I can think of is how badly I need to speak with Godwin again.

FINGER OF SUSPICION

I call Tom Ikime's office as soon as we drop Tamuno off at Harcourt Whyte Hall. The secretary says he's not available. I request the letter for the Dean of the Law Faculty, to which she responds that it is not ready yet. I hide my exasperation and ask her to relay my intention to interview Godwin again.

'I'll let him know, sir.' The secretary hangs up without saying goodbye.

I put the phone away, irritated.

'We can drive to his hall,' Chika says.

'You know it?' I am surprised, even though by now I know I shouldn't be.

'If we ask around, someone can tell us where he's staying.'

I'm sure Chika's right, but the registrar might not be as understanding if we speak to Godwin without his consent or prior knowledge.

'No,' I say. 'Let's go back to the hotel. Before we see Godwin again, I want us to be sure what we want him to clarify.'

'Like?'

'Tamuno's recollection of events aligns with Mercy's, but could it also be that Godwin does not recall the events as they happened because he was high?'

'Could be, but he has had a year and a half to re-evaluate his testimony and he didn't. He insists that he does not know how Kevin came to be at the compound. His story checks out and matches the timeline of events down to the Momoh incident. It finally makes sense why the police did not help out when they realised Kevin was involved.'

I agree. But it is all too easy. That three lives were lost because of Godwin's lies seems too convenient. Besides, I refuse to be arrogant enough to think I have found the answers in less than four days when even Emeka's months-long independent investigation could not uncover the truth of what led to the events of that day.

We are driving past the campus bus stop on the way out of the main gates when I'm struck by a thought.

'Is it always like this?' I ask, looking around at the rows of cars and motorbikes.

'Like what?'

'Not busy.'

'It *is* busy,' Chika answers and slows the car. 'Public transport is not allowed on campus. These are the accredited taxi drivers. This is as busy as it gets.'

'And the bikes? They also go off campus?'

'If you pay enough, but mostly they're for within-campus trips. There's no reason to take them for off-campus trips unless you're in a big hurry.'

I observe the orderly way the taxis move along and away as they get filled. Chika is right.

'If this is as busy as it gets here, there would have been no reason for Bona and Winston to take a bike.'

'I agree,' Chika says. 'And since it was a weekend and even less likely to be busier than this, they most likely got into a taxi as soon as they walked here from the hall.'

I press the stopwatch on my phone as we drive out of the campus. 'I reckon it should not take more than fifteen to twenty minutes to walk from Whyte Hall to the bus stop. Add that to the time they left, so they got in a taxi say at 4:20-ish?'

Chika nods. 'Makes sense ...'

I am still calculating how long it must have taken Bona and Winston to get to Okriki as we drive into town. When we drive past the police station towards Godwin's old compound, I check my stopwatch.

'Seventeen minutes from the taxi rank,' I say, frowning. 'Do the taxis drop passengers at their destinations or only at the bus stop?'

'It depends. Everyone could go as far as the last stop, but if your destination is on the route, you'll be dropped there.'

I look back at the police station, and again, the feeling that this is all too easy hits me. Even trying to match the timelines of the boys' arrival in Okriki seems unnecessary if, in fact, Godwin was lying about everything.

'Let's pay our friends at the police a quick visit.'

Chika does not argue as he turns the car round. Perhaps it's the time of day, but the station is relatively empty. The rude rookie is absent and we've never seen the bored-looking officer at the front desk, who doesn't keep us waiting after confirming that the Inspector can see us briefly.

'Are you sure about this?' Chika's tone is hushed as we walk past the holding cells towards Omereji's office.

'No.' I slow my steps but speak in a rush. 'He wasn't here when all this happened, but I want to get an idea what he knew and buried, and what he flat out refused to explore further.'

'That's a lot.'

'Let's just say after speaking with Tamuno, I'm feeling lucky.'

Minutes later, Inspector Mike Omereji's derisive laughter fills his office. 'Is that the best you can come up with?'

'That's not a denial,' I say, holding his gaze.

'Because there's nothing to deny,' he answers sharply.

'You have to admit it's not looking good for the police ...' Chika says from where he stands at the door of Omereji's office.

'I was not talking to you,' Omereji snaps at him.

'Don't talk to me like that,' Chika says very softly, and despite knowing he's not speaking to me, I feel a chill go down my spine.

'You're in my office,' Omereji says, matching his tone.

'And you're a public servant who has no reason to speak to me like that,' Chika shoots back.

'Gentlemen!' I raise my voice to cut the tension between them as they look like starving dogs about to tear each other apart.

Inspector Omereji hisses, 'This conversation is over. And for the record, so is any other conversation with you two in future. You may leave.'

'Inspector, we just want some answers,' I say.

'You're throwing accusations around.'

'We're telling you what we found out!' My voice rises despite my best efforts. 'This boy Momoh Kadiri was arrested by the police here. He was put in custody, he had an asthma attack and died.'

'The police gave him asthma?'

I ignore the sarcasm. 'He didn't get treatment –'

'And what has this got to do with the Okriki Three?' Omereji cuts in again.

'We know Kevin started a social media movement to make the police take responsibility for what happened to Momoh,' Chika says. 'The #justice4momoh campaign was gaining traction –'

'Where?' Omereji asks with derision. 'On campus? With his fellow troublemakers and cultists?'

'It doesn't matter whose attention it gained,' I snap, beside myself with irritation. 'It did gain attention and the police didn't like that.'

'So, we set him up? The police somehow managed to frame him for armed robbery, set the whole town on him to beat and burn him and his friends to death?'

I take a deep breath and try another tactic. 'You were not even here when it happened. All we're asking is that you look –'

'Dr Taiwo, you're accusing the police of murder and conspiracy. I am the highest-ranking officer in this station; pardon me if I take offence on behalf of the force.'

'Hear me out,' I say, reaching out my hand conciliatorily. 'We're not saying the police set up the boys. We're saying – no, suggesting, that perhaps they were not motivated to help them when they realised Kevin was one of them.'

'Dr Taiwo, it was a mob. An angry mob. Do you really think anyone had the presence of mind to be that calculating?'

'But you're not denying it,' I insist.

'Okay, amateurs,' the Inspector sits back on his chair, his smile now patronising. 'Let me ask you just two questions, and if you can answer them, I'll oblige you further. Ready?'

Chika and I are silent. Omereji forges on.

'One: this Momoh boy was arrested on a tip-off. I read the report. Has anybody ever wondered who tipped the police off?'

'The police said it was anonymous,' I answer.

The Inspector scoffs, 'An anonymous tip simply means there's someone who has something at stake in divulging a piece of information. Furthermore, the police tried to find out who called in this tip about this specific person, and the closest we got was a random prepaid number that was not even registered with the network provider.'

'That's convenient,' Chika says and I shoot him a warning glance.

Inspector Omereji doesn't acknowledge the interruption. 'Two: if the court had already ruled that Momoh's death was accidental, how damaging do you think the police would have considered Kevin's campaign on social media?'

'He's from a powerful family. He could have attracted more attention than someone from a less influential family,' I counter.

'Nonsense. Kevin Nwamadi's pedigree was not advertised on his Facebook page. He was just a student making noise about the death of another student. Simple. You think the police cared enough to have him killed him for that?'

'Look, Mike,' I pause. 'I can call you Mike, right?' I don't wait for his answer. 'All we're asking is for you to consider the options. A lot of unanswered questions are coming up in this case and I'm hoping that your sense of responsibility will make you want to find some answers. Just consider the possibility that there is a conspiracy within your team. Let me speak with the investigating officers, give me the contact information of the officer who was redeployed. Let me –'

'No.' His tone is flat and final.

'And you wonder why we would suspect the police of foul play?'

'When you first came here, I told you not to go opening old wounds. Now you're asking my help to do exactly what I told you not to do.'

I am suddenly tired of Omereji's stubbornness. Besides, I had come here on intuition without a clear strategy, so the futility of this conversation is becoming apparent. I stand.

'Just think about it. We're on the same side here.'

'Are we?' Omereji's gaze is hostile.

'Let's go, Chika.'

'Have you told him yet, Chika?' Omereji says, when we get to the door. 'Have you told the good doctor who you are?'

'Who am I?' There's a challenge in Chika's tone.

The Inspector gives a cruel smile and sits back in his chair watching us. 'A dropout playing at being a detective.'

I grab Chika's arm and shake my head at Inspector Omereji. 'That's uncalled for –'

Chika tries to shake off my hold but I press tighter.

'Please, Chika,' the Inspector says from his desk, 'as they say in the movies, make my day. There's a very friendly group of men in the holding cell willing to make your acquaintance.'

'Chika!' I pull harder and Chika relents, jerks his hand out of mine and walks out.

'What did you mean by all that?' I ask Omereji.

'You're the investigator,' he says. 'Go investigate. I am just suggesting you start in your own backyard.'

NA ME KILL THEM?

Too much has happened today and I am burning with curiosity, but I need to focus on my real task in Okriki, so I don't confront Chika to ask what Omereji meant. I get in the Land Cruiser and point in the direction of the compound.

'Let's get closer.'

Wordlessly, Chika drives there and parks across from the building, which looks as desolate as the first time we were here. I alight and Chika follows.

'It couldn't have taken them more than forty minutes to get here from Whyte Hall. Matches Godwin's report that they got to his house around five.'

'He remembered the exact time Bona and Winston got here even under such stressful circumstances,' Chika says pointedly.

'Not too much of a stretch actually,' I say, squinting at a sun so harsh even my sunshades can't protect me. 'For one thing, he's been asked that question so many times, one can conclude that he's had to become sure of his facts to support his claims. Besides, I think it's normal to recall to the last second when someone pulls a gun at you.'

'And not recall when a whole human being joined the party?'

'He said he doesn't *know*,' I point out. 'Not that he can't *remember* ...'

Chika snorts. 'I would love to put him and Tamuno in the same room.'

I am about to say that might not be a bad idea when I catch a glimpse of Madam Landlady coming from behind the house, a large wrapper tied around her bosom. She's holding a machete. She heads straight for us and her aggressive manner indicates that she now knows our real purpose in Okriki.

'You again!' she shouts, coming at us. 'Troublemakers!'

'Madam ...' I start placating.

'Madam your mama! Get out of my compound now – now!'

'Technically, we're outside your compound,' Chika says calmly.

The landlady's rage reaches a boiling point. 'You want to lawyer me on my own property?' She turns her head and raises her voice. 'Dem don come again oh! People come help me oh! Dem don come again!'

Chika and I run to the Land Cruiser and quickly get in.

'You dey run? Come back now! Troublemakers! People come help me oh!'

She's screaming at the top of her lungs, every part of her body shaking with anger as she waves the machete at our car. Three, then four people have come out, more curious than threatening, but none implore the landlady to calm down. Chika roughly reverses on to the road as Madam Landlady keeps yelling for the benefit of the onlookers.

'Troublemakers! Leave me alone! Na me kill them? Have I not paid enough?! Leave me alone! Wetin you want from

212

me again?' She's screaming so vigorously that I'm afraid her wrapper will fall off.

Even when Chika turns a corner and the landlady is out of sight, her shrill voice and angry face stay with me as we head back to Hotel Royale. Today confirms that her bravado on our first meeting was an act. If anyone was feeling the impact of the Okriki Three tragedy in the town, it's people like the landlady who have lost income, reputation and peace of mind.

As much as I try to dredge up some compassion for her, I can't help but be irritated at the rashness of her actions. The mindless rage on her face when she came towards us must be reminiscent of the anger several of her neighbours had at the first sound of gunshots and Godwin's screams.

This immediate violent reaction to almost everything in Nigeria is something I can't get used to. So much aggression and anger in the air. There are places where I feel this kind of agitation in the States. Visits to New York leave me in a perpetual state of anxiety and my twin brother who lives in Chicago can't get me to spend more than a night in his house. So, I understand how crime drives uneasiness in most large cities. I also know how recurring crimes can determine the emotional state of a community. But Okriki is not a large city. Yet, there's a rage here that seems directed at everything and everyone, all at once.

'Why are they so angry?' I muse aloud.

'Because there's no reason to be happy?' Chika answers drily. 'Look around you. There's no electricity, the schools are run-down, there's no running water, no security ...'

'Is that any reason to turn on each other?' I ask, pained by the all too real picture Chika is painting.

'Let's be clear, they are turning on strangers, or anyone who they don't consider part of their community. Perhaps it's because strangers represent oil companies with head offices in Europe and America. Or even the government and politicians far away in Abuja. When they run out of outsiders to take their anger out on, maybe then they'll turn on each other,' he hisses as he finishes.

I can't counter him and this makes me sad. 'Those boys never stood a chance.'

'Why do you say that?'

'You saw that landlady. Did you see how quickly people started gathering when she shouted? How can what happened to those boys be stopped from happening again if people won't learn from their mistakes?'

'They first have to admit that they made a mistake before they can learn from it.'

I fall silent remembering the Chief's justification of his community's actions and the townsfolk's defiance in the face of nationwide condemnation. The whole thing brings to mind a study I was part of years ago, where we looked at the history of restitution in different cultures through history. Nations that swept their injustices under the carpet with nothing more than a vigorous 'Never Again', tended to repeat the same mistakes. The ones that took collective action towards recognising the injustice, understanding why and how it happened, and then taking concrete measures to prevent it happening again, tended to succeed. The conclusion of the study did not bode well for the future of the US when it comes to slavery and its impact on race relations today or for South Africa's post-apartheid future. On the contrary, the prognosis for Germany's post-Nazi efforts was exceptionally high, proving that it might take several decades but collective wrongs can be righted.

We are now at the Hotel Royale. We get out and as soon as we enter the reception, I feel uneasy. The manager throws us a belligerent greeting while the waiter looks away, without the warm welcome we've enjoyed ever since Chika started doling out tips for every errand. A soccer match is playing on the two TV screens. Some local youths were watching it and, despite the volume, they now seem more interested in Chika and me as we climb the stairs.

Apprehension makes me tense.

'Play it cool,' Chika says as we walk to our rooms. 'Don't let them think they're getting to you.'

'They *are* getting to me.'

At my door, I slot in the key as Chika goes on along the hall to his room. I turn the key to the left to open but it doesn't yield. I turn the key rightward and it gives.

'Chika?'

He stops and turns.

'My room's open.'

He walks back to me and we stare at each other. 'Maybe the cleaner forgot to lock it when –'

I open the door and what confronts us stops him short.

A tornado might as well have moved through my room. The mattress is on the floor and torn; its innards violently exposed. The chairs and the desk are overturned. My clothes are all over with my toiletries scattered too. The woody smell of my Armani fragrance tells me the perfume bottle is broken somewhere under all the mess. The wall that held my Post-its is stripped bare, and all my notes are shredded into pieces littering the floor like confetti.

Replacing the Post-it notes is a crudely pasted copy of a newspaper article on the Okriki Three. Black-and-white pictures of Winston, Bona and Kevin underneath the bold headline: 'Gang of Thieves Burnt to Death'.

Next to the newspaper cut-out is a warning rendered in red paint:

'Leave or burn!'

FIGHT OR FLIGHT

I lift the mattress, and then find my laptop under the over-turned desk just as Chika rushes back from his room. The letters of my keyboard scatter on to the floor like Scrabble pieces and the shattered screen is separated from the base like a decapitated head. My suitcase looks like someone took an axe to it.

Mindless. Wicked. I pick up the two separate pieces of this expensive machine, trying to recall when last I backed it up.

'I think the hard drive can be retrieved,' Chika says as he looks around.

'Your room?'

'Not as bad as yours. Just the same message.' He points to the wall.

Atoka stands at the door, looking smug rather than sorry.

'Gentlemen,' he announces pompously, 'you must leave my establishment. Clearly, you are a risk to my person, property and staff.'

'You bastard,' Chika says and lunges for him but I grab hold of him.

'And abusive too,' Atoka goads him.

'You know who did this, don't you?' Chika is shaking with rage.

'Why would I allow anyone to do this to my property?'

With one violent pull, Chika shakes off my grip, grabs Atoka by the neck and slams him against the wall.

'Chika!' I shout, but his fiery gaze is fixated on the manager, who has lost considerable bluster as his feet search for the ground.

'Who. Did. This?'

'I don't know!'

Chika's hands tighten around Atoka's neck. I rush to pull at Chika's shoulders, but I might as well be kneading rock.

'Chika. Please. It's not worth –'

'Was it the Chief?' Chika is not looking at me; the manager is now gasping for breath. 'Did he order this?'

'I ... I don't kkknow ...' the manager sputters, seeking air.

His eyes are bulging, and I fear if Chika doesn't let go now, I might be forced to do a mouth to mouth on the vile creature.

'Chika, let him go!'

Perhaps it's the panic in my voice because he drops the manager suddenly. Atoka scrambles up almost immediately and backs away from us into the corridor.

'You must leave!' the manager croaks defiantly, rubbing his bruised neck. 'And I am not returning any deposit to you!'

Atoka scampers away. I'm breathing heavily from the ordeal. Chika, on the other hand, breathes as evenly as if he just had taken a leisurely stroll. Only his eyes give any indication of how close he had been to squeezing the life out of the manager with his bare hands.

'We need to leave here,' I state.

'The bank has a guest house in Port Harcourt, but it's too far from here.'

'We might not have a choice.'

'We can also try the university's guest house. It's always full, but we might be lucky.'

'Why not? That's a plan. In fact, I'm sure if we call the Registrar, he might be able to help.'

I reach for my phone and try to see whether any of my messages to the Registrar have been returned. None, but there's a text message from Salome Briggs. I see it was sent seventeen minutes earlier.

'Come to PH. It's not safe there. Trust me, Sal.'

I show Chika the message. He reads, frowns and looks at me.

'Who's this?'

'A friend in Port Harcourt. Well, sort of. We met on the flight. Her mom is from around here.'

'She seems to know a lot for someone far away in PH.'

'I know.' I look around the room, 'Someone must have told her.'

'You trust her?'

'I've no reason to distrust her.'

Chika nods and hands back my phone. 'Then we must hurry. The longer we stay here, the greater the danger of me doing something I'll regret.'

He starts picking the pieces of paper up off the floor while I call Salome. She answers on the first ring.

'Thank heavens, you're fine.'

'How did you know?' I ask.

'No time for questions. Just get over here. As soon as you get into PH, call me. I've already booked you both into a hotel.'

'Will you be there?'

'If you want me to –'

I decide quickly before the pause becomes an awkward silence.

'If it's not too much trouble, yes, I would like you to be there.' Despite my brisk tone, I see Chika slightly pause as he gathers shreds of paper off the floor.

'No problem.' Her tone is practical. 'Just hurry.'

She hangs up.

Chika has amassed a significant amount of torn paper and I join him in sorting through the debris.

'Did your lady say who her source is?' Chika asks drily.

'She's not my lady,' I snap, more abruptly than necessary. 'And I'm sure she'll tell me everything when she sees me later. She's booked us a hotel.'

'Hmm … she just happened to book us a hotel in anticipation of the vandalisation of our rooms?'

When Chika puts it like that, it does seem rather stupid to rush off to Port Harcourt on Salome's say-so. In truth, what do I really know about this woman?

'So, we don't go?' I ask.

'It's a more interesting option than the bank's guest house in PH. I think we, I mean, you should follow the trail. It'll be interesting to find out what she knows. Besides, you say you trust her.'

I can't tell him about my sudden doubt, so I remain silent as we hurriedly gather the salvageable items in my room into a bed sheet Chika has turned into a makeshift rucksack. My destroyed laptop is wiped clean of dirt and put back in its bag, and we look around to be sure we have everything that isn't beyond remedy.

The soccer game is still on when we come back downstairs, but the young men are all standing, their backs to the TVs, unmoved by the excited speech of the commentator. The manager is at the entrance door, arms akimbo, eyes belligerent.

As I walk past the men, the smell hits me. I stop and face them.

'Guys, I can smell my wife's Christmas present to me on some or all of you. So, I can assume some or all of you were responsible for vandalising my room.'

Silence, but their body language says they are raring for a fight. An overwhelming sense of violation shoots through me. These thugs tore through my personal things and now stand here, watching me leave the Hotel Royale, an image of defeat. The thought makes my blood boil, but I know not to make a volatile situation worse.

'Tell whoever sent you they've made a big mistake because I'll not stop until I find what you're trying to hide,' I say to the cluster.

We look like a scene from a Western; me staring down the recalcitrant youths while Chika blocks the manager from stepping into it.

I turn and start to walk away. What follows happens fast. Chika swings his fist and I duck out of the way just in time, turning just as his uppercut connects with the chin of one of the youths who I'm realising was going to tackle me from behind. He falls to the ground with an agonised yelp, gritting his bloodstained teeth in pain. The others start to advance threateningly on Chika who discards the 'ruck-sack' on the floor.

My voice is calm as I address the manager. 'Tell them to back down, or I promise you, the damage to your hotel will be more than anyone can pay.'

Atoka takes too long to respond and Chika drop-kicks a second man.

'Enough!' Atoka shouts. He glares at me, equal parts angry and afraid. 'Just go! Please.'

'Chika, let's go.'

Chika holds his combat-ready position, looking from the manager to the young men in a dare.

'Chika!' I raise my voice.

He reluctantly picks up his suitcase and the 'rucksack' of my stuff, turns and walks out. I follow him with my battered Samsonite and laptop bag, getting into the Land Cruiser just as he switches on the ignition.

I've barely closed the passenger door when he reverses so forcefully that I can smell burning rubber.

A LADY OF INFLUENCE

It is well past 9 p.m. when we stop for the military police
on our way into PH. There's no exchange of pleasantries as
Chika passes two hundred naira through the window and
my phone beeps. It's Salome sending her location. I click
on it and Google maps informs me we are about sixteen
minutes away.

I switch on the electronic voice of the navigator to guide
us through the city towards the Tropicana. The avenue leading up to the enormous gates of the hotel is lined by huge
palm trees and well-tended lawns. There are heavily armed
guards at the entrance who use flashlights to peer into the
Land Cruiser and ask if we are guests or just visiting.

'Guests,' Chika answers brusquely.

One of them uses his flashlight to flip through a list.

'Philip Taiwo?'

'That's me,' I respond.

'ID please.'

I reach in my pocket for my American passport and
stretch across Chika to hand it to the guard. He points the
light into the car again, checks and closes the passport and
hands it to Chika, who gives it back to me.

'Please proceed.'

'Your friend must be very connected,' Chika says as he drives through the gates. 'The Tropicana is one of the best hotels in town. It's where the expatriates stay.'

'Explains why it's heavily guarded.'

'The insurance on the lives of the guests here is the GDP of some countries.'

The hotel is huge and if there's any similarity with Hotel Royale, it's only in the humming sounds of generators. The whole compound is lit up like a Christmas tree, and it's hard to fathom any part hidden from the watchful eyes of the armed security guards parading the grounds.

A uniformed concierge rushes towards us as we disembark from the Land Cruiser.

'Welcome to the Tropicana.' He touches a hat that's more suited to the host of a circus show and bows. He is dressed in a double-breasted coat embroidered with the crest of the hotel on the left breast pocket. 'My name is George. Do you need help with your luggage?'

He sounds quite chirpy for this time of night. How he's not breaking out in sweat under so many clothes is beyond me. Chika opens the trunk and George doesn't bat an eyelid at what he sees inside. The makeshift rucksack from Hotel Royale is lifted out with the same reverence he would have given a Luis Vuitton bag.

Another concierge joins George with a trolley and we follow them into the grand hotel lobby where Salome is looking as glamorous as the last time I saw her nearly five days ago.

She walks over to us like she owns the place.

'Thank heavens, you made it.'

Should I shake her hand or hug her? She makes the decision for me with an embrace of such warmth that all my

224

inhibitions dissolve and I'm introducing her to Chika like she's an old friend.

'Thank you for all your help, madam,' Chika says the same way he used to address me. *This far, but no more.*

If Salome notices Chika's reservation, she gives no sign of it, as she laughs in that unfettered manner that had invited stares on the flight. 'First things first, drop the madam. Second, go to your rooms and freshen up. I asked the kitchen to prepare something light for you. Come down as soon as you're ready.'

One of the concierges approaches us with two key cards. Salome collects them and hands them to us.

'You're on the same floor. George will see you to your rooms.' She turns to him and speaks rapidly in Ikwerre.

'Thank you,' I say.

'Thank me after you look and sound human. I'll be here.' She points further into the lobby where I can see a smattering of patrons seated in what appears to be a bar.

'Go. I can't keep the kitchen open for much longer. They close at 10 p.m. sharp.'

My gratitude and relief at such kindness drives me to hug her again.

'Go!' She pushes me off with a laugh. 'Sentimental Americana.'

I chuckle, a bit embarrassed, and follow Chika towards the elevator that George and his colleague are holding for us.

My room is sheer luxury compared to the one at Hotel Royale and ranks well above average by any standard. A vast bed dominates the centre and all the amenities of a five-star hotel confront me. George drops my bags on one side of the room and places the 'rucksack' gently on the thickly carpeted floor. Like any well-trained concierge, he walks me through the amenities in the room. The minibar is fully stocked, the TV has more cable channels than anyone would need, and the bathroom is bigger than my entire room at Hotel Royale.

'Thank you, George.'

I'm rummaging through my pockets for my wallet when I realise I have no money save my emergency hundred-dollar bill.

'Don't worry, sir,' George says. 'Miss Salome has taken care of everything.'

Salome tipped the concierge in advance of my arrival? I smile to hide my sudden discomfort. 'But still, I promise to give you something before I leave.'

'No problem, sir. I shall tell Madam that you will be down in ten minutes?'

'Please do that. What room is my friend?'

He tells me and gives instructions how to call Chika's room.

As soon as George bows and leaves, I flop on to the bed and close my eyes for a brief moment. I can't help but feel like a pauper raised to the station of a prince. One moment I am in Okriki fighting off assailants, next I am in a five-star hotel in Port Harcourt. Only in Nigeria.

The phone rings and I jump. I reach for the receiver on my bedside table.

'Oga …'

'We've moved from sir to Oga?' I answer Chika wryly.

'Anyone who knows anyone who can find us accommodation in the Tropicana is an Oga. In fact, the person is *the* Big Oga.'

I laugh heartily, amused and relieved that we are both fine. 'I take it you like your room.'

'I like it so much that I'm not leaving here tonight. I've asked for my food to be brought up. Please give your friend my apologies.'

'Chika, I think she's expecting both of us –' I protest, worried that Chika thinks he would be intruding. I can't admit that I'm somewhat nervous about being alone with Salome.

'I'm sure she is. And believe me, I have many questions I would like to ask her, but tonight I think I'll stay in the room and pray this is not a dream. Don't stay up too late. You still have an investigation to finish.'

'How can I forget?' I sigh.

'And Philip, I don't know if it's my place to say this, but please be careful.'

I am quiet for a beat. I can pretend I don't know what he's talking about, but Chika and I are beyond that now. 'I will. Thanks.'

I hang up and walk to the bathroom.

Chika's admonition plays back in my head as I look at my face in the mirror above the sink. Am I that obvious? Sure, Salome is attractive, but I hope that's not what Chika meant when he asked me to be careful. Or was his admonition regarding the investigation?

Folake's face rises before me in the mirror. 'Be careful.' But she says it in a mocking tone.

'I saw you!' I want to shout at the image, but I don't. Why am I questioning my motives for having a drink with a helpful *friend* who has done nothing to warrant suspicion?

Folake's face in the mirror contorts and her lips form the words reminiscent of her goodbye to me: *Psychobabble nonsense.*

I hiss as I turn away. A drink is exactly what I need right now, I tell myself as I leave the room. Nothing more.

Salome is waiting. She rises from the bar and walks towards me with a smile.

'Well, you clean up good.'

I feel my face heat up. 'It's the best I can do with no change of clothes.'

'Who're you changing for?' She snorts. 'Come and eat.' She guides me towards one of the tables in the bar.

A place has been laid out, and I notice that some of the patrons, mostly white middle-aged men dressed in khaki and J. Crew shirts with short sleeves or sleeves rolled high up their arms, are looking at us.

'Your friend says he'll eat in his room. I sent it up,' Salome says as we settle into our seats.

'Thank you.'

'I'm sure you have many questions …'

The fare is roasted chicken and thickly cut potato wedges with steamed vegetables on the side. The chicken is the most flavourful I've tasted in a while, and I'm famished, causing me to shamelessly talk between mouthfuls.

'The first question is how you got us in here.'

'Easy. The owner's a client of our firm, an old friend who owes me a couple of favours. Besides, our law firm does a lot of conferences here, so we're good customers. I just made a call.'

'How did you know what was happening in Okriki?'

'I asked my cousin to check up on you. You know, just to be sure you're fine.'

'You were checking up on me?'

'Not the way you make it sound, Americana. I meant I was just making sure you're okay.'

'Well, thank you. So, who's this cousin of yours?'

'I believe you met him. He is the police inspector –'

A piece of drumstick pauses midway to my mouth.

'You're kidding, right?'

'Nope. Mike is my first cousin.'

'So, the Chief is …'

'My uncle. My late mother's eldest brother.'

I drop my fork.

'You know he ordered the attack on my room, right?'

She waves an elegant hand dismissively. 'He did no such thing. Eat your food. Trust me, if my uncle wanted you harmed in any way, he'd have done it the minute you set foot in that town.'

'He told me to my face that I was not welcome in Okriki.'

'The same thing I said to you when you told me why you were going to Okriki and here we are.'

'You're saying the Chief and Inspector Omereji didn't know about what happened today at the hotel?'

'Not before it happened. Certainly after it did, they knew, but what could they do?'

'Omereji could have arrested them!'

'Calm down. Or I'll stop talking.'

I take a deep breath. I look at her, then around me. In less than three hours, Salome had commandeered the whole hotel in my favour. It's close to 11 p.m., and she's here, welcoming me and being a most gracious hostess.

'Yes, Philip Taiwo, you can trust me.'

As before, it's like she can read my mind. I let out my breath and look at the food, then back at her. I start to eat again but my eyes are locked on her heavily kohled ones.

'Okay, I'm listening.'

'Wow. Aren't we bossy?'

'Salome …' My voice carries a light warning.

'Okay, okay. It's simple. As soon as you told me what you were going to Okriki to do, I asked Mike to look out for you –'

'More like spy on me.' I know I sound ungracious, but I can't help it.

'Whatever. I knew your paths would cross anyway, but I wanted him to know you're a friend.'

'He didn't treat me like one –'

'What did you expect? Anyway, he did keep an eye out for you on more occasions than you know.'

'My eternal gratitude to him.'

'Sarcasm is quite unbecoming with an American accent …'

'I need a drink.' I signal to the barman who walks over as I push my half-eaten plate away.

'A double Jack please.'

'Madam?'

'Courvoisier. Lots of ice.'

The barman walks away, and Salome continues. 'So, he was the one that found out what those boys did to you and your colleague's rooms.'

'And he didn't round them up as any law-abiding officer should have done?'

'You're misjudging him.'

'He's hiding something,' I insist. 'That whole town is in collusion, including your uncle,' I hiss, all my anger coming back as I recall the state of my hotel room just hours ago and how violated I felt.

Our drinks arrive. I grab my whiskey and down it in one go.

'Philip Taiwo, don't make me regret helping you.'

'Then tell me *why* you're helping me.'

'Because you're doing the right thing. The parents of those boys deserve to know what really happened.'

'Is that it?'

'What other reason could there be?'

'Perhaps the same reason the Inspector was transferred back to Okriki to keep an eye on the investigation, to make sure that nothing that will damage the town further is discovered.'

'So, I'm helping you just to influence your research?' She is derisive, but yet there's a curve to her lips that makes me think she is laughing at me. 'It *is* research, right?'

'What else can I think?' The lightness in my head is swift and sudden. I realise too late that I should have ordered a beer.

She drains her glass and reaches for her phone, tapping it and putting it to her ear.

'Come to the front.' She hangs up and looks at me. 'It's okay to be suspicious of me, Philip, but I suggest you pick your battles. I saved your ass today. Yours and your friend's. Why would I do that? Ask yourself that question before you start throwing accusations around.'

She stands and I am forced to look up at her beautiful face.

'My mother's people are not bad people,' she says, looking down at me. 'They're not good either. They are just humans. What they did is inexcusable in a world that makes sense. But you've been here long enough to see that very little makes sense in this part of the world. Not lately, at least. But I like the idea of knowing *why* what led us all here, happened. Perhaps if you can find some explanation for that madness, I can bear to look at my people again without shame. That's why I'm helping you.'

She walks away before I can say anything.

AN EXPECTED ACCIDENT

Chika opens the door at my frantic knocking, rubbing his eyes.

'What is it? Are you okay?'

My answer is to press the voice recording on my phone.

'Hello, Dr Taiwo. It's me. Tom Ikime. We found Godwin dead in his room yesterday. A really sad development. I'll call you again in the morning.'

'Shit,' Chika says, sleep wiped off his face.

'We have to go to the university.'

'What time is it?'

I check the cell phone. '8:17.'

'I'll get dressed right away.'

I rush back to my room and jump into the shower.

Godwin is dead and, given my interview with Tamuno yesterday, this is not just a sad development but a major setback. Coming after the vandalisation of our rooms, I am suddenly overwhelmed with all the dead ends this case is presenting. I hate feeling out of control, and events are happening around me that seem to have little relation to my purpose in Okriki, but are impacting on it anyway.

My feeling of despair stays with me as I dress in the previous day's clothes and head into the elevator to meet Chika at the lobby.

'What if it doesn't add up?' I ask, as soon as Chika and I are en route to Okriki.

'What?'

'All of it. Everything we know about this case, what if everything doesn't add up because it isn't supposed to?'

'Where's this coming from?'

'Don't mind me.' I look out of the window, reluctant to burden Chika with my insecurities.

'Is it because of Godwin's death? But you and I saw where the boy was headed …'

'Yes, I know, but that doesn't make it easier to accept. Perhaps it's a sign –'

'That everything won't add up?'

'A sign that the whole Okriki Three matter was just another example of the random violence that happens everywhere in this country.'

'Even after what that Tamuno boy told us?'

'Yes. Godwin might have lied about knowing Kevin, he might have called out for help if he felt attacked by Bona and Winston, but he did not instruct the people of Okriki to torture and kill those boys. That's on them.'

'That may be true, but isn't that what you're here to do? To make sense of what everybody considers senseless?'

'And I am saying I don't think I can.'

'Please don't let Godwin's death make you doubt the progress you're making. See how far we've come since you arrived. How much we now know …'

To what end? I want to ask but we are now at the military police checkpoint, so I say nothing. Chika slows, but we are waved past, and one of the heavily armed soldiers actually smiles at us.

'We've become regulars,' Chika says, as he picks up speed and waves back at the soldiers.

'It's a good thing?'

'You could say so. It just means the next time they won't need to ask before I give them something.'

Maybe everything's not so senseless, after all. On the one hand, proactively bribing armed soldiers to pass through a public road might come across as corrupt but on the other, the people who pay have accepted this as *the* modus operandi. There's clearly some kind of honour amongst thieves. The armed soldier acknowledges our past encounters by letting us through without fuss, and Chika will honour this by proactively offering a bribe the next time we drive through the checkpoint. There is a method to this madness.

We drive straight to the Registrar's office at TSU only to find he has left a message for us with his secretary that he's at the morgue of the teaching hospital. I'm about to ask for directions but Chika says he knows it and we are back in the car driving towards the North Campus.

'The hospital is not on campus?'

'It's in another town. TSU is made up of three big campuses. We're coming from the East Campus that has the Humanities and Arts department. The West Campus is Engineering, and the North is Medical Sciences.'

'Is the North Campus far?'

'No, it's in the middle of another town called Apamor, and we should be there in about thirty minutes if I take the short route.'

I nod and reach for my ringing phone. It's Ikime.

'We're on our way,' I say.

'The Senate has called an emergency meeting and I have to attend. I've asked Dr Okaro to assist you. She's the Chief Coroner and Head of Pathology.'

'You're sure you can't wait for us?' Even as I ask this, I feel relieved. Ikime's role as part of the spin machine of the university might impede some of the questions I plan to ask the coroner.

'I'm sorry, Dr Taiwo. But I assure you I've requested Dr Okaro to be as cooperative as possible. You can call my office if you still want to see me. I'll make time.'

I tell him I understand and thank him for letting me know about Godwin. But my mind is still on what all this means so I am silent for the rest of the trip.

The teaching hospital is a huge multi-storey complex. We stop by the entrance to Casualty and ask for directions to Pathology. When we enter, the first thing that strikes me is how similar morgues all over the world are: sterile, silent and sad.

'Dr Okaro's expecting you,' the uniformed receptionist says after we introduce ourselves. She reaches for the receiver of a telephone straight out of the eighties. 'Please, have a seat.'

We sit on a hard bench in front of her. She smiles at us as she drops the receiver back down. 'She'll be with you now.'

Some students in white overalls are coming in from outside, smiling and chatting amongst themselves in a manner that seems out of place with the sombreness of a morgue. They disappear through double doors, from where a crisp-looking woman emerges moments later. She's not wearing make-up, her hair is pulled back in corn rows. She is wearing a pair of bifocals and I can make out a simple print dress under her pristine white lab coat.

'Dr Taiwo?' she says when she reaches us.

Chika and I stand.

'I'm Dr Taiwo, and this is my colleague, Chika Makuochi.'

'I am Dr Ngozi Okaro. The Registrar informs me that you're interested in the body that was brought in yesterday.'

She speaks matter-of-factly and seems to demand the same. Just as I am about to give a rehearsed speech as to the nature of my interest, she gestures that we should follow her.

She continues to speak as she walks us through the double doors. 'I must say this is highly unusual. Normally, we only entertain this level of interest from family members and the police. Ikime told me you're none of these.'

'We're not,' I confirm.

'Nonetheless, I serve here at the behest of the university, and if the Registrar thinks I should answer your questions, I will.' She stops and faces us. 'Have either of you seen a dead body before?'

I'm as taken aback by her sudden stop as I am by the abruptness of her question.

'I have,' Chika answers flatly.

'You?' She's looking at me above the rim of her glasses.

'It's not a problem.'

'That doesn't answer my question.'

I don't bother to confirm that I'm one of those who find being around the dead disconcerting. Viewing dead bodies doesn't bother me as much as that they remind me of my own mortality. In that sense, it never gets easier.

Dr Okaro shrugs and opens a door, motioning for us to enter. The stench of chloroform hits us inside the small room where six bodies lie on metal stretchers, covered in threadbare white cloth, their bare feet poking out from under the sheets. There are no tags on their big toes, just numbers written with black markers on the soles of both feet.

Dr Okaro navigates around the dead and stops in front of one. Without ceremony, she lifts the white cloth off, revealing Godwin's still face. My mind races to the last time I saw him. Agitated. Manic even. The antithesis of this still form. There are no marks on his gaunt face, no sign of blunt trauma.

'Time of death?' I ask.

'We estimate between 7 and 8 p.m. yesterday. He was DOA when they took him to the hospital.'

I make a note to ask for the report to see if any resuscitation efforts could have tampered with an accurate diagnosis of the cause of death.

'Cause of death?'

'Smoke inhalation. Most likely accidental.'

'How do we know?' I ask.

Her answer is to pull the cloth down further and the sight of the massive burns on Godwin's right side is enough to make the uninitiated gag. I quickly look at Chika. His face is inscrutable.

'He was right-handed,' Dr Okaro says. 'From the intensity of the burn, we think he was smoking and must have fallen asleep. The cigarette must have fallen from his fingers on to the mattress. See his fingers? Third-degree burns led to charring. And the right side of his torso has the same degree of burn ...'

'There was a fire?'

'It was the smoke from his room that alerted the students. They broke down the door after banging for a long time.'

'So, no fire?'

'Slow burn,' Dr Okaro says. 'I suspect it's the type of mattress. All the burn is around the hand and his right side. See here.' She points to Godwin's hand, which is so badly burnt that you can see the blackened bone matter through the charred fingers.

'He slept through that kind of pain?' This is the first time Chika has spoken since we came in, his voice calm and neutral.

'We can assume he took a soporific whose effect was further exacerbated by alcohol intake.'

'Toxicology?' I ask.

'I sent samples to the lab as is routine, but the parents are coming to collect the body soon. We can't do more tests if they don't give their consent.'

'Even if we suspect foul play?' I am surprised, as an autopsy should be compulsory in such circumstances.

'Do *we*, Dr Taiwo?' Dr Okaro looks at me, her eyes daring me to tell her how to do her job.

I make my tone more conciliatory. 'It just seems to me that we must do everything to rule out foul play before concluding that it is an accidental death, especially given the victim's history.'

'It is the victim's history of drug use that corroborates the diagnosis of accidental death.'

'Without toxicology, we are just guessing.'

Dr Okaro points at the terrible burns on Godwin's body. 'The only explanation for anyone to die like that is accidental.'

'Toxicology will certainly give a more conclusive diagnosis as to how the accident happened,' I challenge further. 'At the very least, I think we should confirm if the victim died before inhaling smoke or after.'

She cocks a brow at this. 'I can't open him up without his parents' permission. That's the law.'

'I understand, but at least we can find out what kind of drugs would induce such deep slumber.'

Dr Okaro is silent as she looks from Godwin's body and back at me. I press on.

'Surely you would like to know, if only for academic interest?'

I suspect Dr Okaro is not one to walk away from a challenge. She reaches in her lab coat pocket and passes her cell phone to me across the body of Godwin Emefele.

'Your number,' she says. 'If I find anything of interest, I'll ask Ikime to let me know if it's all right to tell you.'

As soon as I enter my telephone number, Chika and I say our thanks and rush out.

'What now?' Chika asks as we jump into the Land Cruiser.

'I need to see Godwin's room.'

ACT THREE

*light waves change direction when they
pass from one medium to another*

SCHEMES AND SIGNS

John Paul is calm as he sits across from the flustered branch manager of one of the Port Harcourt branches of the National Bank.

'This is highly unusual.' *The manager shakes his head.*

'It's my money,' *John Paul says calmly, pushing my glasses up the bridge of his nose.*

'Yes, of course, it's your money, but we're a small branch.'

'I am not withdrawing the cash now; all I am doing is buying US dollars from you and transferring them to a domiciliary account.'

'Yes, but you are transferring the funds to another account in the name of this –' *He checks the papers on his desk,* 'John Paul Afini-Clark. That means you're closing your account. The regulations have changed a lot for FOREX. To buy that amount of USD, we have to apply for –'

'Spare me your process, please. We both have a choice, I either withdraw all my cash right now, all 28 million naira of it, and go buy dollars on the black market, or you do what I ask and make a hefty commission.'

The possibility of losing a customer and bonus is unacceptable. 'I'll see what I can do, sir.'

John Paul stands and is gathering the identification papers he brought to validate his request for meeting the branch manager.

'If you don't mind my asking, sir, what should I say is the purpose of such a transaction?'

John Paul does not miss a beat. 'A business transaction with Amaso Dabara. You want to look him up?'

The manager sputters and assures John Paul there would be no need for that. His hands are shaking when he returns John Paul's handshake.

The visits to the next two banks go the same way. The only difference is that he requests euros at one and British sterling at the last.

That evening, rather than go to a cybercafe to post messages from Alfurquran's Facebook page and @NoOtherGodbutJesus Twitter account, John Paul breaks routine. He posts instead from his room, using his laptop and a smartphone with a brand-new SIM card from a wireless hotspot.

He had paid a lot of money to the salesperson at the cell phone company to overlook his lack of identification as he registered his SIM card under the name Amaso Dabara, and I had taken the salesperson's inability to recognise the name as a good sign.

A very good sign indeed.

THE ORIGIN OF BURN

A call to Ikime was all it took to get into Godwin's room. Back in the States, I would have had to fill forms in quadruplicate to get access to a crime scene. The police, the lawyer for the suspect – if there is an indication of foul play – and the prosecution might insist on being present. The keys to the room would most likely be in some vault, encased in an evidence bag with a long list attached of all the people who have had access to it.

At TSU however, the police in Okriki have not even been notified of Godwin's death. Campus Security are still preparing the report, which will be finalised when Dr Okaro determines the cause of death, and this will then be sent to the police who may or may not request further investigation. Should Godwin's parents insist that there is foul play, the police will write a formal request to the university and only then will they be allowed on to the university campus to conduct investigations.

All this is explained to Chika and me as Johnny, the Campus Security official on duty, pulls out the key to Godwin's room from his pocket as casually as he would the keys to his own house. He is an amiable fellow who talked non-stop as he rode with us in the Land Cruiser because the university's transport division had no car to spare.

'We all saw it coming,' he says as he opens the door.

'That's what everyone keeps saying,' Chika mumbles drily.

'The boy was trouble from day one. We knew he was selling drugs even when he was a jambite, but no one had proof. Even before the Okriki thing happened, the boy was gone. High every day. Skipping classes. Causing trouble at parties. Everyone was quite happy when he moved off campus until the Okriki thing happened and then he had to come back here.'

I dare say Emeka and would not call the necklace killing of their sons a 'thing' but I remain quiet as Johnny opens the door. I've always disliked too much talk around me when entering a crime scene.

'The lock has not been fixed properly,' Johnny says, as he struggles to open the door. 'It's quite a mess in here. Our Oga said no one should touch anything until the report for the police is complete.'

Only sensible thing anyone has done so far, I think as Johnny finally gets the door open.

The stench hits us hard, but I try not to let it bother me as I stand at the doorway and look around.

Disorganised crime scene.

Cigarette butts in makeshift ashtrays, bottles of beer in the corner of the small room and lots of empty bottles of what looks like cough syrup. Codeine-based. An open bottle of locally produced gin is on the floor next to the single bed. The edge of the bed is charred from the burning.

Dirty clothes on the floor and what looks like dried vomit close to the side of the bed.

'It was a good thing people saw the smoke coming from his window,' Johnny says. 'If they had gone by the smell alone, everyone would have assumed he was smoking weed or something.'

'The students broke the door to get in?' I ask as I look around.

'Yes.'

'But you used a key ...'

'The hall supervisor fixed it himself. He said he didn't want the room burgled.'

Why students would steal from a room where another student just lost his life is beyond me. Chika and I walk outside and peer at the door. Indeed, there's a sign of breakage and the crooked lock shows crude straightening to allow the key to work.

I look down the corridor. The building is relatively quiet at this time of the day, since most of the students are in class or exam halls.

Chika is still bent over, examining the lock. 'We can't confirm if the door was tampered with before the students forced it open.'

'I know. We would've been able to guess if there were two sets of forced entry if the lock had not been fixed.' I keep my irritation in check as I don't want to set the amiable Johnny on his guard.

Chika straightens up from inspecting the door. 'The good news is that the place was sealed.'

'And the bad?'

'We have to go back in there.'

We both suck in our breaths and enter Godwin's room again.

Chika brings out some naira notes from his wallet and gives them to Johnny, who is looking around like he doesn't know what to do with himself.

'Don't worry about us, my brother. Try and eat something, then come back in about an hour or so.'

Johnny collects the money. 'Here's my number. Call me when you're done.'

Chika saves the number on his phone with a broad, fake smile of thanks.

As soon as Johnny disappears, we get to work.

The roof is covered in greyish ash. An indication that there was no burning flame or at least no large one that would have caused more and blacker smoke to fill the room. The wall facing the door has a window, also covered in grey soot. I turn to the door and look back at the window.

'There's a draft coming from the door,' I say aloud. 'It blew the smoke to this side, and the smoke that couldn't get out of this window gathered on the wall. See how dense the soot is on this side of the room?'

Chika nods and bends towards the bed with a frown. I join him to peer at the worn mattress. The midpoint of the soft foam is burnt right through and I can see the metal springs of the bed through the hole. If Godwin was holding a burning cigarette, his height and the length of his arms should confirm this point as the source of the burn. I lean closer to the mattress. Something is not quite right.

'What?' Chika asks, following my gaze.

'The mattress is made of synthetic foam.'

'And?'

'Look here,' I point to the most severely burned part. 'Can you see the intensity of how it burned here compared to the edges?'

'Yes.'

'You see the fire burned the mattress right through here but nowhere else?'

'So?'

'The intensity of the burn reduces as it spreads out … Look here and here …' I point to the edges of the burn. 'When a synthetic material is exposed to fire, it burns quickly and keeps spreading, but here that's not the case.'

'Maybe Godwin's body stopped the spread of the fire.'

'Ordinarily, that would make sense, but a cigarette tip is not a fire. It is combustible with synthetic fibre like foam, but it can't burn hot enough to drill a hole through the mattress before it spreads out.'

'I get you. It should first heat up the mattress and then start spreading to the sides and depth of the bed.'

'An even, steady rate, not a fast spread.'

Chika peers closer to where the burn hole reveals the steel springs in the mattress. 'Unless something made the heat burn fast …'

'Something was poured on this spot that accelerated the fire but was not strong enough to sustain an even spread.'

'Not petrol or kerosene?'

'No. The smell doesn't indicate that. Something milder.' I lean in till my nose is inches from the mattress and sniff, attempting to register a smell other than the stench in the room. That's when I spot the suitcase through the hole and the network of springs. It is stashed underneath the bed, towards the headboard, so it's not visible through the burn

hole, except at an angle. Unfortunately, this is the area closest to the dried vomit, and it takes enormous willpower and
covered noses to pull out the suitcase.

It is padlocked and untouched, and the dust on it shows
it's been a while since it's been disturbed. Its position under
the bed also saved it from the soot coating every surface in
the room.

Chika and I look at each other.

'Are you thinking what I'm thinking?' I ask.

'Let's do it.'

I look around for something to break the lock, but Chika
is ahead of me. He goes to the small reading table and finds
a paperclip. I've seen this done in movies and have even
asked my colleagues at the SFPD if it was possible. They
assured me it was mostly creative licence and few locks can
open with a straightened paperclip. 'It must be a terrible,
cheap lock to open that easily,' they told me.

Well, either Godwin has used a cheap lock, or Chika
really knows how to pick one because we are looking at the
contents of the suitcase in less than ninety seconds.

Some clothes, pornographic magazines, a bag of weed
and DVDs, which from the covers, I assume are the live-
action versions of the magazines. Since I don't have any
gloves, I use my middle finger in order to be as undisrup-
tive as possible. I see some papers and slide them out to
read quickly. Correspondence from the school authorities
over suspicion of dealing in narcotics and then handwritten
rebuttals of the allegations in different drafts. I hand these
over to Chika and go back to the suitcase.

When I've confirmed that my finger won't encounter anything slimy or liquid, I feel around beneath the

magazines, papers, et cetera. I pause when I touch something hard.

'What is it?' Chika asks, seeing my frown and the way my body goes still.

Slowly, I pull out what I immediately recognise as a .45 automatic.

SMOKE

The handgun is safely hidden in the Land Cruiser and we make our faces deadpan when Johnny returns, his own smile broad. It's clear from the strain on his lower shirt buttons that he has put Chika's largesse to good use.

We drop him off at the Campus Security office and high-tail it towards Okriki.

'We can't tell the Registrar, right?' Chika asks, driving faster than he should on university grounds.

'Tell Ikime we found a gun in Godwin's room? Heck, no! Not until we can confirm that it is Godwin's.'

'How will we do that?'

'There must be some kind of record of sale, or reports of it being stolen ...'

My voice trails off as Chika shakes his head in the way that has become all too familiar.

'Oga, I've told you to forget all those American protocols you're used to. Where does one start to trace a firearm around here? Could easily have been smuggled across the border, or stolen from the police. The police themselves might well have recovered it from armed robbers and sold it on the black market. That's a wild goose chase at best.'

I turn to him. 'Speaking of the police, am I the only one that finds it strange that Godwin dies immediately after we confront Omereji about their involvement in Momoh's death?'

'I don't know what you were looking for, but a lot of things didn't add up in that room.'

'The whole scene was staged; everything placed precisely to give the impression of an accident.'

'And you think the police might be responsible?'

'At this point, I'm open to all sorts of possibilities, but it's not adding up. Why now?'

'Because you're on to them? You linked their motivation to silence Kevin with their negligence in the Momoh case.'

'Tamuno said he went to the police with his statement, meaning the police knew from the outset that someone had made a connection between Momoh's death and the mob action. It just doesn't add up.' I let out an exasperated breath.

'You think Godwin might have been the one who fired the gun and not Winston as he claimed?' Chika asks, his eyes fixed on the road.

'That's a possibility. But it's also possible Godwin stole the gun after the crowd came down on the three boys.'

'What for?'

'There's no way of knowing for sure now, but if Godwin fired the gun and then screamed for help, it certainly points to premeditation. He'd have counted on the reaction of the townspeople to do just that.'

'You're saying he screamed knowing the crowd would come, round up the boys and kill them?'

'Well, maybe not kill them, but at least cause a distraction or do serious harm. Outsourced violence.'

Chika thinks on my words for a moment, then nods. 'Makes sense. With the string of robberies at Okriki and the town setting up its own vigilante group to protect itself, a foiled armed robbery attempt in the daytime would certainly not have gone unpunished.'

'Thing is, somehow I don't see Godwin coming up with an idea like that.'

'Me neither.'

I am glad someone else sees this. 'He seemed more like the sort of person who acted on a whim and the drugs wouldn't have helped him with the careful planning such a scheme would have required.'

We are now on the road that will take us past where the boys were killed, the police station and Madam Landlady's compound.

'I feel like we're missing something, like someone is pulling strings,' I muse aloud.

'Perhaps his drug supplier?'

'Maybe. And besides, what sort of supplier uses a drug dealer with a habit, unless the dependency is all part of the plan? Whatever the case, if Godwin only just became a liability that had to be eliminated, what changed in the last few days?'

'He spoke to us,' Chika replied, the picture starting to make sense to him.

'Yes, and if there's a murderer on the loose who killed Godwin because he spoke to us …'

'Then we are in danger.'

'Yes. Which is why we need the police on our side.'

'Assuming it's not the police themselves ...' Chika says wryly.

'Only one way to find out.' I whip out my cell phone and tap. 'Gimme a second.'

Salome picks up on the first ring. 'Are you okay?'

'I need your help.'

I quickly explain everything from the discovery of the gun in Godwin's apartment to our suspicion that it could be the same one that had alerted the people of Okriki to an alleged robbery on the day the three were executed.

'Now, as to why I'm calling ... I need to talk to the Inspector about this, but with the way we left things the last time –'

'You're sure this gun may be connected to the killing of those boys?' Salome asks.

'I have my suspicions.'

'Perhaps that would mean other parties are involved besides the current accused standing trial?'

I think quickly. Of course, Salome would be interested in anything that lessens the culpability of her towns-people in the killings. And by extension, so should the Inspector.

'I can't answer that if I don't know the role of the gun in the whole thing.'

There is silence on the other side. If it's true that she's being helpful because of her interest in knowing what pushed the people of Okriki over the edge, I am hoping she will get me the access I need.

'You want me to ask Mike to check it out for you?' Salome asks.

'Yes, but he said the case was closed.'

'Nonsense.' I picture her dismissive wave of bejewelled fingers. 'A case is only closed as long as there's no new discovery. You go on there. Leave Mike to me.'

'Who was that?' Chika asks when I hang up.

'Salome. I need her to speak with Omereji ahead of our arrival.' The Okriki Police Station looms into view in the distance.

'I am not sure you want to do that.'

'Why? She can get us access to Omereji, they are cousins.'

'Small world.' His sarcasm is evident but his face is unreadable.

'I am sure she can help us to get him –'

'To what? Help themselves?'

'Salome has not given me any reason to –'

'Oga, I think you're trusting this friend too much.'

'You keep saying that. Do you know something you're not telling me?' There's a challenge in my tone, and perhaps this is when I expect Chika to explain what the Inspector had meant at our last meeting. But, clearly not now because Chika keeps his face on the road and shrugs as if to say 'whatever'.

I would have pushed further, but we are now at the police station. I flick a quick glance at Chika and wonder if the heightening stakes in this case worry him more than he cares to show. Having a baby on the way and discovering that your life might be in danger do not make good bedfellows.

'Let me talk to Omereji. Get a feel for where his head's at with this new information. Then we'll know better what we're dealing with.' My reassuring tone does not seem to have much effect on Chika. He simply reaches under the driver's seat and hands me the black plastic bag.

I quickly check the .45 to be sure it's empty and the safety catch is on. I wrap it back in the bag and slide it into the waistband of my trousers, pulling my shirt over it as soon as I get out of the Land Cruiser.

The police station is full of noise and shouting when I walk in, a senior officer banging on his desk with a baton, shouting 'Order!' repeatedly, as if he's a judge or bailiff. I notice some of the Muslim men that Chika and I had seen at the community hall.

'If the police won't protect us, we will have to protect ourselves!'

'What is the danger to protect you from?' the officer sneers.

All the men raise their voices and speak at once. There's more banging of the baton on the desk and there's a measure of silence. The lead complainant amongst the men pushes a cell phone into the face of the Baton Banger.

'Have you seen this? This is what they're saying about us. Our lives are in danger!'

More ruckus erupts and I decide I've seen enough. Clearly, the meeting at the community hall didn't resolve the conflict between the Christians and Muslims. And from the look on the faces of the officers as they observe the aggrieved Muslim men, it won't be resolved here either.

I shake off my misgiving at the scene before me and head to the rookie's desk. He looks at me with as much animosity as at our first encounter.

'I would like to see Inspector Omereji,' I say without bothering to greet him.

My voice must have carried as silence descends on the room. All eyes look in my direction.

'The Inspector?' I prod, keeping my voice even. 'Is he in?'

'Do you have an appointment?'

'No.'

'Then, you will wait like everybody else.' He turns his face to some scribbles he is making in a logbook.

'Who else is waiting to see him?'

The rookie looks around.

'You? Aren't you here to see the Inspector?'

He's pointing at a youth who is sitting on the floor with a broken tooth and a bloody nose. His swollen eye is half closed and I can't tell whether he is reporting an assault or he has been dragged to the station for further punishment for a crime he must have committed at a bar or the marketplace.

'Me? Yes. I want to see the Inspector,' the youth responds with a slight slur. Definitely an altercation at a beer parlour.

As soon as he struggles to stand up, more people start to speak and all claim to want to see the Inspector. I look at the rookie who now has the face of one that has bitten off more than he can chew.

'I'll wait,' I say with a smile.

I go to a corner while people move in a swarm to the rookie, demanding to see the Inspector. The senior officer bangs his baton more loudly on the desk and calls for order.

'*I am here, but they won't let me see him,*' I text Salome.

I pretend to ignore the looks of the people who are not sure whether to pursue the possibility of seeing the Inspector to spite me, or take their chances with the officer who is shouting and looks like he wants to use his baton on their heads rather than on the long-suffering desk.

'*Wait. He will come.*' Salome's text pops up on my screen.

I try not to count the minutes but it doesn't take that long before Inspector Omereji appears at the doorway and, without looking in the direction of anyone in the crowd, waves me over. I follow him through the hall, sidestepping the furniture and piles of files to get to his office.

'Two visits in twenty-four hours, Dr Taiwo. It must be important or we're growing on you.'

I take the seat he offers. 'Let's go with important.'

Inspector Omereji sits back in his chair. 'My cousin says you need my help. How can that even be possible?'

'I have evidence that may shed more light on what happened that day.'

'We know what happened.'

I am tired of this cat-and-mouse game. 'Just hear me out. If you still don't want to help afterwards, I won't push.'

Omereji raises his hand in mock surrender. 'Okay. I'm listening.'

'On one condition.'

'You want my help on a condition?' he asks mockingly, but his eyes are not smiling.

'When I tell you what I know and show you what I have ... if you can't help, this conversation stays between us for now.'

'Dr Taiwo, you do remember that I am an officer of the law, right?'

'I know. And I promise you that I am not trying to compromise you in any way. I'm just saying that if you can't help me, you must give me the opportunity to look for someone who will.'

'I won't promise, but I'll give you the benefit of the doubt.'

It's the best I am going to get so I pull up my shirt, bring out the black plastic bag and place it on the desk between us.

'What's that?'

I pull out the .45 and leave it on the plastic bag. Omereji's expression does not change.

'Now, I'm glad I didn't promise anything …'

'You remember Godwin?' My eyes are fixed on him.

'The boy who died yesterday?'

Does he know because he was told or because –?

'We are the police, Dr Taiwo,' Omereji says drily, and I can see my face has betrayed me again. 'We are told these things and even if it's the university, we remain on standby to go in if our help is required.'

'Well, your help should have been sought because the campus security is messing up evidence big time in that place.'

'They said it's an accidental death.'

'Not from what I can see.'

Omereji sits up straighter. 'You think he was killed?'

His alertness and the note of surprise in his voice are not feigned. While Godwin's death might not be a surprise to Omereji, the possibility that he was murdered is. This makes me even more sure of the gamble I am taking by being here.

'I'm not sure,' I respond honestly. 'But I am sure I found that gun in his room.'

Omereji's eyes pop. 'They let you into his room?'

I shrug. 'They don't think it's a crime scene because they're assuming accidental death …'

'Even then …' Omereji shakes his head.

'You remember in the report,' I continue quickly before police procedure – or lack thereof – derails my purpose, 'fired bullets and their casings were found in the compound as evidence of the gunshots everyone heard?'

'Yes. The townspeople always maintained that it was the gunshots that convinced them that a crime was in progress.'

'You and I know automatics like this one will leave casings on discharge. I've got no proof but my gut tells me that if you do a ballistic check on this gun, you might find it's the one that fired those bullets in evidence.'

Omereji looks at the gun as if it's a hissing cobra. 'What are you saying?'

'Godwin said one of the boys, Winston to be precise, fired the gun several times. If it's the same weapon, then I'm sure you'd like to know how it came to be in Godwin's possession and why he never declared it in his testimony.'

Omereji looks from the gun to me. 'Maybe he fired it?'

'Or someone else who Godwin was protecting?'

'Someone who now wanted him dead …'

Omereji and I look at each other. There's nothing more to say.

'I'll have to send it to ballistics in PH.'

I pick up my laptop bag and stand while he packs away the gun.

'Where's your sidekick?'

'If you mean Chika, he's staying in the car.'

'He lies,' the Inspector announces.

I frown but can't ignore the slight fluttering in my gut. 'That's a strong allegation.'

'He never went to the TSU. His name is not on the graduating list of 2012.'

This throws me, but I recover quickly. 'Maybe it was a little lie to get you to bond with him.'

'So, what lies did he tell you to get *you* to bond with him?'

A SURPRISE DEFENCE

The drive back to the Tropicana is my formal introduction to the legendary Port Harcourt traffic. Previously, we've always managed to beat the rush hour but today, it is clear we miscalculated. Badly.

We spend hours on the road so that by the time we arrive back at the hotel, we are too exhausted to do more than confirm the next day's programme, eat and sleep.

I wake up quite refreshed, and eager to continue what I consider my lucky streak of discoveries from yesterday. My misgivings about the assignment are much less this morning and I am momentarily regretful yet hopeful that Godwin's death might lead to some of the answers I came to Okriki to find.

I am about to jump out of bed when the text message arrives, complete with visuals. Trouble by Boucheron; my wife's favourite perfume.

'*I would have preferred a call, but this is the best apology so far!*' Folake adds several kiss and heart emoticons to this message.

I'm still trying to wrap my head around it all when Tai's message appears: '*You owe us, Pops.*' I am adding two and two together, when Lara's message comes: '*Dad, got a long list of tinz u're gonna do to make it up 2 me 4 donating all my pocket money*', and it all makes four. I am moved and ashamed at the same time. I immediately call Lara.

'Safe to talk?' I say as soon as she answers.

'Wait, Dad, lemme go to the boys' room.'

I picture her padding upstairs to their bedroom.

'You're on speaker, Dad ...'

'Guys, I just want to say a big thank you –'

'Nah!' This is Kay. 'Not that easy, Pops. Guys, we can't let him off the hook just like that.'

'Kay, remember that basketball camp you want to go to in Montana?' I ask pointedly.

'*Er, Dad, I can assure you pitching in to buy Mom a present was the least we could do ...*'

I can mentally see Tai punching him for the about face while Lara rolls her eyes. I laugh and thank them again. I really have the best kids in the world.

I talk with them a little longer and let them off when they tell me their mom is ready to take them to school. I should be worried that this time they don't implore me to call her, but kids are sensitive. They feel things, and sometimes it's best to follow their lead, so I don't ask them to hand their mother the phone.

I go to the shower, dress in the express laundered clothes from yesterday and join Chika at breakfast.

'I could get used to this,' Chika says, as he looks around at the buffet. There's no sign of the tension between us from the previous day.

'Me too!' I order an omelette and help myself to some cereal.

264

We were supposed to visit the prisons and interview some of the accused today. The interviews had been set, but Chika received a message from his contact at the prisons that they were all scheduled to be in court. We agree it's a better idea to visit the court and observe the proceedings. It should allow me to see most of the players on one space. How they interact and play off each other might be revealing.

'What time do the courts start?' I ask Chika.

'Eight.'

Our omelettes arrive and we eat hurriedly to avoid the early-morning traffic that is typical of any major city but must be far worse in Port Harcourt given yesterday's experience.

The main road itself is a delight of colours, blaring horns and enterprise. Roadside hawkers run from one car to another, peddling everything from cell phone accessories to boiled corn. Several billboards celebrate the current governor's numerous achievements side by side with the ones for Coca-Cola and evangelists inviting everyone to crusades with their themes written in bad grammar. It's bustling and alive, and after the antagonism from the indigenes of Okriki, I feel anonymous and safe in this city. I like the feeling.

The Rivers State Judicial Service Commission is a legal estate of sorts. Before we park, Chika has to ask for directions that lead us past the magistrates' courts, lower courts, Federal High Court, and finally to the front of the State High Court.

As we exit the car, two men rush towards us.

'Photocopy?' one asks.

'Affidavit?' asks the other.

Chika says no to both, but asks for details of the court-room where the Okriki Three case is being heard.

When we get there, the clerk outside pompously informs us that the Honourable Justice Saronwiyo Dakolo-Jack doesn't tolerate disturbances when in session. However, on pocketing the money Chika discreetly hands over, the clerk opens the door and ushers us in.

The courtroom is jam-packed – standing room only – so our entrance is blocked by people facing the front of the room. We manoeuvre our way to a spot where we can see as much as possible.

On the left of the room is a bench where the accused – two women and five men – sit. They are dressed in green khakis, and are haggard and tired-looking. They stare straight ahead, their eyes dull, and their lack of anima-tion makes me wonder if they've been drugged. I've read enough journals on criminal reforms in Nigeria to know that Thorazine is the drug of choice for controlling pris-oners. The somewhat passive demeanour of the accused might also be a sad testimony of how long this case has been in the courts.

From where we are, I can only see the backs of the lawyers. There are quite a number on both sides, their wigged heads making them look like actors in costume. I assume the lawyers for the accused are the ones seated closest to them, while the prosecution sits to the right. At the moment, I don't know which side is cross-examining but I recognise Dr Ngozi Okaro sitting in the square wooden box.

'… you're saying your autopsy didn't reveal anything that can shed more light on the cause of death?' the counsel asks.

'As I've said numerous times, the bodies were burnt beyond recognition. Any conclusion beyond death from third-degree burns would be speculative.'

'Dr Okaro, you've made it clear that this is not your first time here. Can we skip this prefix to every one of your answers?'

This admonition is from the Honourable Justice, a man in his late fifties or early sixties who looks as tired as the accused. He takes his glasses off-and-on depending on whether he is reading from the sheaf of papers in front of him (on) or looking at the witness or lawyer (off). He was writing as the questioning progressed and I will later learn that lawyers prefer his courts because he writes faster than most. Apparently, judges here write all court proceedings by hand. I can guarantee Folake will never practise in Nigeria. Her impatience won't allow it.

'I apologise, My Lord,' Dr Okaro says unconvincingly. 'But I've been here numerous times on behalf of the state and have been cross-examined by every lawyer on both sides of this case. My Lord, when will it end?'

'It is not so simple, Dr Okaro,' the Honourable Justice says almost sympathetically. 'We have to ascertain that the accused were responsible for the beatings and the fire that caused the deaths of the victims.'

'That logic is lost on me, My Lord. They're here because they were identified as being at the scene of the crime, right?'

'Objection, My Lord. The witness is not here to give her verdict on the degree of guilt of the accused.'

My eyes widen. Even if I can't see the face, that voice is unmistakable. I look at Chika. His face is impassive but he is nodding towards the front as if asking me to confirm what he heard.

Salome is the lawyer objecting!

She is on the left side of the room. I look at Chika again, but even though I still can't read his face, I know he must have recognised her. He knew! He *always* knew. But how?

'... witness shall refrain from giving comments outside of the specific questions asked of her,' the Honourable Justice says. 'Understood?'

Dr Okaro throws a disdainful look Salome's way. The tension between both women is palpable even from where Chika and I are standing.

'Dr Okaro,' the prosecution continues after a bow to the judge, 'in your report, you stated that one of the victims died from blunt trauma to the head. Correct?'

'Correct,' Dr Okaro answers.

'Can you state which victim, for the record?'

'Kevin Nwamadi.'

'And the cause of death for the other two?'

'Excessive burns.'

'Doctor, in your professional opinion, for anyone to die like that, would we be right to assume that they were set ablaze with the deliberate intention of killing them?'

'Objection. Calls for speculation,' Salome and two other lawyers chorus with varying levels of intensity.

'I will rephrase,' the prosecutor continues, unfazed. 'Dr Okaro, do you think the victims could have been saved during the fire?'

'Tyres were placed over them. Petrol was poured on them. They were set ablaze. I'm no legal expert, but I do know that whoever did *all* of that meant for the victims to die.

Could they have been saved? Of course. Maybe before the fire caught someone could have pulled them free and doused the fire with water or something. But in my opinion, such burn intensity is sure to lead to death.'

'But no one tried to save the victims, right?'

'I wasn't there.' Dr Okaro answers before another round of objections come from various defence lawyers. 'But I *know* they were burnt to the point where we could only use dental records and the videos of their torture to identify them. So, yes, I can confirm that there's no evidence anyone tried to save the young men from burning to death.'

'Thank you, Dr Okaro. No further questions.'

'Defence, any questions for the witness?'

Salome stands. 'Salome Briggs representing accused number four.'

The Honourable Justice looks towards the bench where the accused sit. The loud voice of someone who must be the court clerk or bailiff barks out: 'Accused number four, stand up!'

One of the five men stands up. He appears to be in his early twenties but is so spent he looks much older.

The clerk/bailiff orders him to sit and the Judge turns to Salome. 'Please proceed.'

'Dr Okaro, you've confirmed that the cause of death is the burning of the victims?'

'With the exception of Kevin Nwamadi who suffered blunt trauma to the head, yes, the primary cause of death in the other two victims was extensive burns.'

'May I ask my client to stand again?'

It is quite sad the way the Accused Number 4 stands, so soon after sitting. Like a puppet on display. Almost definitely Thorazine.

'Defence presents Ezenwo Dikeh for the record.' Salome points at her client and then turns back. 'Dr Okaro, have you seen the videos of the killings?'

'Everyone has.'

'Have you?'

'Yes. Many times.'

'Did you see my client in any of the videos?'

'Definitely.'

The prosecutor stands up quickly. 'My Lord, Dr Okaro is a pathologist, not a video reviewer. Can Ms Briggs establish relevance, please?'

'I'm getting there, My Lord,' Salome answers, and I see her mocking smile in my mind's eye. 'Dr Okaro, so you can identify my client as one of the people in the mob?'

'In the videos, I have seen, yes.'

'Was there any time that you saw my client put tyres around the victims, pour petrol on them and set them alight?'

Even I can see where Salome is going. I feel like shouting at the prosecutor to object immediately. It's not relevance Salome wants to prove.

'Of course not,' Dr Okaro answers, bristling. I suspect she knows she's been set up.

'So, *if* the fire killed the victims, and *if* my client didn't put the tyres over them, or pour the petrol, or light the match, he shouldn't be standing trial for their murders?'

The whole courtroom seems to come alive. Outrage and shock at Salome's audacity fill the room. Surely she can't hope to get away with it.

'Ridiculous!' The lawyers on the prosecution side are standing, all speaking at the same time. The one who had been questioning Dr Okaro faces Salome. 'Your client was clearly there. He is in the video and we have proof that he laid several blows on more than one of the victims.'

Salome shrugs and points to Dr Okaro. 'But there's no proof that my client's blows were the direct cause of death.'

The prosecutor gasps for effect. 'Are you being serious?'

'Enough!' The Honourable Justice bangs his gavel repeatedly, causing a gradual hush in the courtroom. 'Ms Briggs, are you seeking an acquittal?'

'My Lord, my client never denied that he was present at the unfortunate incident that led to the deaths of the victims. All I'm saying is that the state's demand for the maximum charge is punitive unless *mens rea* and *actus rea* are proven.'

'That's what we're doing!' the prosecutor shouts, livid.

Salome doesn't miss a beat. 'If, as your expert witness states, the cause of death was burning, and your main proof of guilt is my client's presence at the scene of the crime, I am demanding that you show him putting tyres around the necks of the victims, lighting the fire and watching them burn without trying to save them. If you can't, drop the current charges and give him a lesser one.'

The whole court is in an uproar. The noise is so loud that the Honourable Justice's shout for order is lost on everyone.

If I were not still in shock from seeing Salome here, I'd be applauding.

CONFIRMATIONS AND REVELATIONS

From where we stand next to the Land Cruiser, Chika and I watch Salome walk towards us. The sun is on her face and I wonder how she manages to look like she just stepped out of an air-conditioned room while everyone else is sweating like they were in a sauna.

'Gentlemen,' she says.

'You're certainly full of surprises,' I try unsuccessfully to keep the resentment out of my voice.

'You knew I'm a lawyer –'

'You said oil and gas.'

'And that's true,' she answers calmly.

'Not the lawyer for the accused of a case I'm working on!' Her composure makes me raise my voice louder than I would've liked.

'Does it matter? You said you were here to find out why it happened, not apportion guilt,' she answers coolly.

'There's something called disclosure,' Chika interjects before I can respond.

'To an interested party, yes,' she says in a voice slightly colder than the one used towards me. Be careful, the tone says to Chika. Know your place.

There's an awkward silence as Chika glowers, his fists clenched. Just then, Dr Okaro walks over to us and the tension rises a thousand notches.

'Ms Briggs.'

'Dr Okaro.'

The two women eye each other like two harrier birds gauging the best angle for attack.

'I see you remain determined to ensure the guilty go unpunished,' Dr Okaro says with contempt.

'I assume that an academic such as yourself should know that without allowing for credible defence, the state would be guilty of the same jungle justice my clients are accused of.'

'Bending the truth is not a defence,' Dr Okaro says with a derisive snort.

'It's called proving a case. Something your side is doing a poor job of. Excuse me.'

Salome walks away, leaving a tense silence. I give Dr Okaro a tight smile, trying to quell the urge to apologise for Salome's comments.

'You did very well in there, madam,' Chika says, and I could have hugged him when Dr Okaro's stern demeanour dissolves as she looks at him with a somewhat sad smile.

'What good will it do? I've given my evidence numerous times, and each time, Ms Briggs still manages to get yet another accused off because the prosecutors didn't do their homework.'

'It must be frustrating,' Chika says sympathetically.

'You can't imagine. And it's going to get even worse now that Godwin Emefele is dead. Which is why I've come over.'

Dr Okaro looks at me with less warmth. 'I saw you come into court and I said to myself, what a coincidence. I was going to call you ...'

'You found something?' I'm unable to keep the excitement out of my tone.

'It's not conclusive, but there're strong indications of alkaloids in Godwin's blood.'

'Alkaloids?' Chika asks.

'Poison,' I say to him and turn back to Dr Okaro. 'Any chance it can be identified?'

'The boy had so many chemicals in his body it was a mission to separate one from the other. But given the manner of death, I'm now almost certain it wasn't deliberately ingested.'

'Are you going to change your report?' I ask, wondering how the university will spin this new piece of information.

'I'll discuss it with Ikime, but, yes, my report will change. The rest is left to the authorities.' Dr Okaro's tone is resigned, like one who has seen too many cases like this. 'Anyway, I hope it helps with whatever you two are doing. You have my number if you have more questions.'

Dr Okaro nods at us, says goodbye and walks away.

'He was murdered,' Chika states the obvious.

'Just as we suspected ...' My phone thrums. I click open the text message.

'*The bullets match*', the text reads and I guess it's from Omereji. I show the message to Chika.

'This is definitely a day of confirmations and revelations,' Chika says.

His tone when he says 'revelations' is dry and I suspect he is referring to Salome.

'If the bullets match,' he continues, 'that means Godwin either fired that gun himself and caused those boys to be attacked or he stole it off them.'

'Either way, we can't trust anything Godwin told us. But we do know two things.'

'What's that?'

'There is a murderer on the loose.'

'And?'

'Until we can be sure Godwin's death has nothing to do with this case, we are not safe.'

A CURIOUS EXCHANGE

I can't work. Without a laptop, I can't update the comprehensive report I've been putting together for Emeka, although the last draft is saved, safe in the cloud. If I can get a smart keyboard, I can sync it to my iPad and do some work. I still have no idea how to broach the subject of Godwin's murder in the report, and I am ill prepared to evade the pursuit of a killer.

A knock. When I open the door, I can't help feeling like my thoughts summoned him because it is Chika looking as inscrutable as ever.

'You wanted something?' I ask as calmly as I can.

'The boss is here,' he answers, his eyes giving away nothing.

'Emeka's here? Now? Did you tell him –?'

'Are you coming, sir?' he interrupts.

'Give me a moment to put something on.'

He turns and leaves. I can't shake the disconcerting feeling that I've been reported to the school principal. Emeka being here so soon after Chika questioned my judgement regarding Salome can't be a coincidence.

Emeka is nursing a cognac when I reach the corner of the huge lobby. His blazer is unbuttoned but his tie is perfectly knotted. Chika sits across him and from their silence, I suspect they were talking about me.

'Emeka, what a surprise,' I say with forced enthusiasm.

'Philip.' Emeka's voice is cold. 'Do have a seat, please.'

I sit and turn to Chika. 'Is something wrong?'

He stands immediately and looks at Emeka. 'I shall wait outside, sir.'

'A drink?' Emeka asks as soon as we are alone.

'No. I'm fine. You haven't answered my question.'

'It seems you may be in danger of compromising yourself on this assignment.'

'Is that what Chika told you?'

'My sources tell me you're staying here –' He waves his hand around the lobby, 'at the pleasure of the legal counsel for the people who murdered my son.'

If Emeka didn't look so serious, I would've derided his choice of words by telling him to expect the hotel bill as part of my expenses. Instead, I look at him, seeing how gaunt he is, and how his eyes are sunken and ringed with dark circles. Compassion moves me, so when I speak, my voice is soft and kind, but firm.

'Is that how you see everything? For or against you?'

'They killed my son ...'

'And I'm sorry about that, Emeka. But I'm an adult, not a schoolkid on a field trip. You can't talk to me like you're doing now.'

'You're losing sight of the goal here, Philip.'

'The goal is to find out how and why your son was killed and not once in the past week have I thought of, or done anything else.'

'That woman is defending the people who killed my son.'

'Is her crime doing her job or being my friend?'

'Both!' Emeka spits out so loudly that there is a slight lull in the noises around us. I steal a glance around, and I can see some of the patrons deftly pretending they are not looking at us.

'Look, Emeka,' I lower my voice to placatory level. 'I promise you I've done nothing to compromise this assignment. If Chika has been briefing you as accurately as he should have, he'll tell you that we've made significant progress –'

'Progress raising more questions than providing the answers I asked you to find,' he says more calmly.

'It takes time. In a case like this, the questions provide the leads.'

Emeka sips the cognac, places the glass on the table and leans forward. 'I don't have the time for more questions. If everything goes according to Ms Briggs' plan, another one of the accused will be let off by the next court hearing.'

'I'm not the police, Emeka. I told you what I do from the very beginning. I can't give you information to determine the guilt of –'

'Then perhaps I should just pull the plug on this whole thing.'

I check to see if he's bluffing but I can't read him. 'You want to end the investigation?'

Emeka shakes his head stubbornly. 'There's no point going on.'

I take a deep breath. 'Emeka, you and I both know I can't face my father without the answers he convinced me to look for.'

There is an uncomfortable pause. Emeka breaks our gaze by downing his cognac, and placing the glass on the table again.

'Dr Taiwo, I have always been grateful to your father and his friends for all their support ever since my father died.'

'So, you understand –'

'Please, let me finish. My gratitude does not mean I condone what their generation created in our university system many years ago.'

'You knew?'

'Not at first. I thought they were all just close friends. And until my son went away to the university and he was killed because people suspected he was a cultist, it didn't bother me.'

'And when you knew?'

'I cut them all off.'

'You cut them off?'

Emeka nods. 'I did. If there was even a chance that cultism was part of the reason my son was killed, I couldn't associate with my late father's friends.'

Now I understand why my father wanted me to take the case. He is trying to reconcile with Emeka.

'So, you didn't tell my father to convince me to take the case?'

Emeka shakes his head. 'Some time ago, at the country club, he approached me and told me you were back in the country and you might be able to help me with the investigation. I told him no thanks, but I did my own research, found out where you work, and the rest is where we are now.'

So, how did my dad know that I had been approached or that I was not inclined to take the case? He has been quite protective since I came back from the States; keeping tabs on me, and even passing on Abubakar's contacts to me when he thought it was taking me too long to find a job.

Abubakar! Did he call my father? I can't wait for a proper sit-down with my old man as soon as I get back to Lagos.

'You understand why it's important that I conclude this investigation.' I keep my gaze steady on Emeka, stopping short of pleading. 'My father is counting on me. Clearly, you and your family mean a lot to him. To them.'

Emeka waves his hand impatiently. 'How? You're getting nowhere.'

'I am sure Chika told you about Godwin –'

'Another distraction,' he cuts in sharply. 'My heart goes out to his parents, but the boy was a ticking bomb. Everyone knew he would self-destruct sooner rather than later.'

'That's the point. I know for sure it's not self-destruction.'

'Even if the young man was killed, who else would be responsible but the same people who killed my son?'

'What if you're wrong? What if –'

He cuts me off sharply. 'There's no what if and the only reason you're considering any other possibility is because your judgement is compromised.'

There is a tense silence as our gazes lock again. I know it's time.

'That's rich –' I sit back in the chair and speak casually, 'coming from someone who has been less than honest with me himself.'

'I don't follow …' he says with a frown.

'Chika is not a driver, is he?' I ask levelly.

Emeka bends slightly to reach for his glass, sees it's empty, leaves it on the table and leans back into the leather chair. When he looks at me, his face is impassive, but he says nothing.

'You're not going to deny it?'

'Deny what?'

'That you sent Chika to spy on me?'

Emeka crosses his legs. 'Now you're getting paranoid, Dr Taiwo. Chika was in the picture long before I thought of you for this assignment.'

'As a driver?'

'That folder Abubakar shared with you, who did you think put it together?'

It all makes sense. Chika's knowledge of so many aspects of the case. His quick thinking and proactive insights.

'Why didn't you just tell me from the beginning?'

'Because I didn't want you to be prejudiced. I wanted you to start afresh in case he missed anything.'

'So, what is he? Some kind of detective?'

Emeka uncrosses his legs, stands and looks down at me with a smile that is far from his eyes.

'Dr Taiwo, I've waited for five hundred and seventy-six days for answers I am paying you to find. You'll understand when I say my patience is wearing rather thin.'

'You're not answering *my* question,' I say, also standing up.

'A question that has no bearing on the matter at hand.'

'Who is Chika Makuochi?' I insist.

'That's one question I'm not paying you to ask. Keep your eye on the prize, Dr Taiwo. You have one week to give me something I can use.'

'Use for what?' I ask, but he is already walking away, elegant in what must be a bespoke suit

I sit back down and signal to the waiter. When my double shot of whiskey comes, I knock it back. I'm about to order another when the wooziness hits me. I ask for the check and sign my room number. I stand, steady myself, then walk towards the elevator. As I pass by the large glass doors of the hotel's impressive entrance, something catches my eye.

There, in the parking lot, Emeka is talking to Chika, more animated than I've ever seen him and gesturing wildly with his hands. Chika's back is towards me, but I see him shaking his head.

Just then, a uniformed man who I recognise as Emeka's driver approaches them. He is carrying a large bag, which he hands over to Emeka respectfully. Emeka hands it to Chika. A few words delivered more calmly elicit nods from Chika. Soon, the Range Rover is reversing and making its way out of the hotel's large gates while Chika heads towards the Land Cruiser.

I turn slightly to ensure he doesn't catch sight of me. When he gets to the car, he opens the trunk. I can't see much from where I stand, but when he closes the trunk and turns towards the hotel entrance, I walk as fast as I can to the elevators. Luckily, they open as soon as I press the up arrow.

As the doors close, I see Chika enter and make his way towards the bar in the lobby. Empty-handed.

LITTLE WHITE LIES

'I left my iPad in the car,' I say again in front of the bathroom mirror.

I know it's ridiculous that I am practising how to get the keys to the car from Chika, but I am quite aware of how bad at lying I am, and how good Chika is at reading people. I have to say I need the iPad to get some work done, unhurried but eager enough, with the right amount of casualness.

'I think I left my iPad in the car …' Yes, that's much better. Saying 'I think' sounds appropriately unsure. I down the last bit of the drink I ordered and head down the hall to his room.

I would have turned back straight away if he did not answer the door on my first tentative knock.

'I think …' The words are stuck in my throat. He looks tortured, so instead my planned deception becomes a sincere question. 'What's wrong?'

'Nothing.'

'Your wife?'

'She's fine. You want to come in?' He steps aside and I have no good reason to decline.

Inside the room, I am flustered, wondering whether to revert to my original intention or get him to tell me what is bothering him.

'I owe you an apology,' Chika says, still at the door.

I am caught off guard, but can't pretend I don't know what he is apologising for.

'You could have told me. It would have made my job a lot easier.'

Chika nods. 'I was planning to tell you … I am really sorry, Philip.'

The words are solemn, and I think if he had added 'sir' again, I would've waved off the apology. But the way he said my name carried both respect and regret, and it would have been ungracious not to respond in kind.

'It's all right. I am sure you and Emeka had your reasons,' I shrug.

'I should've told you what my real role was in all of this.'

'It wouldn't have hurt.'

'It wouldn't have helped either.'

If I think about the different ways I could have gone about this assignment if I knew who Chika really was, I would beg to differ. Most of all, I don't like being deceived. 'You're a detective?'

He shakes his head. 'Security expert. National Bank is one of my clients. I evaluate the risks to their systems, provide training support for the guards who carry cash around, and sometimes I'm called in for special assignments like this.'

'Are you really married?'

He smiles. 'Yes. And yes, my wife is really expecting our first baby.'

'Thank heavens. I would hate to think I wasted marital advice.'

He laughs. 'It was not wasted at all. I took it, and I'm happy to report that she's much calmer and more supportive.'

A series of images flash through my mind.

– Chika standing against the Land Cruiser waiting for me after my interview with Sobi

– the familiar way he approached the security guard at Whyte Hall, and their quick, easy laughter

– the way Sobi frowned when he saw Chika

'There was no Tochukwu was there?' I ask.

'What?' He seems taken aback.

'That day at Harcourt Whyte, you'd been there before. You didn't interview anyone. You were giving me information you already had.'

'Yes. But I swear I didn't know about Tamuno.'

'You never spoke to Mercy?'

He shakes his head. 'It was too risky in those early months. She was too fragile. It would have been cruel then.'

That was why he encouraged me to go to the hospital, and was so pushy when we were speaking to Mercy. It's all making sense now.

'The Registrar, you've met him before ...'

Chika looks away. I would like to think he's a tad ashamed.

'Yes. I interviewed him a number of times in the first weeks afterwards.'

'What about Godwin?' I ask, holding my breath.

Chika looks back at me sharply, shaking his head.

'No. It was the same situation as Mercy. I was not allowed to speak with him because he was considered too unstable, and I was neither an investigator nor the police. It was one of the conditions of Ikime helping us now, especially because the university was still doing its own investigations then. I listened to his audio interviews, gathered information from

285

other students and studied him from afar, but I swear I didn't speak with him directly.'

I want to believe him, but at this point, my trust level is abysmally low. Who else knows? Surely my dad cannot be part of this whole charade. Abubakar? Salome? The Inspector? My head is swimming with questions, but I am not convinced I will get the whole truth from Chika now, not with that exchange with Emeka at the parking lot fresh in my mind.

I play back the words that confirmed the unsettling feeling that Chika was not who he claimed to be.

A dropout playing at being a detective.

'And TSU?' I ask aloud. 'Did you really go there?'

Chika walks to the window and stares out. 'I did, I just never graduated.'

'What happened?'

'I was rusticated in my third year for being a cult member.'

I am ill prepared for this revelation. I take in a deep breath, trying to find the right response, but the words don't come.

'It's not something I am proud of,' he says into the silence.

I keep my tone as neutral as possible when I speak. 'Do you know for sure if the boys were in a cult or not?'

Chika turns towards me but says nothing, hesitant.

'Chika?'

He faces me slowly, but it's like his eyes are begging me not to ask more questions.

'I did find out that Winston and Bona were popular because they supplied drugs – ecstasy, poppers, even cocaine – at the parties.'

'Godwin was their supplier?'

He nods. 'It seems so. They bought from him and sold at the parties they went to, but they were not part of any cult.'

'And Kevin?'

Chika lets out a deep breath and looks away again.

'You must promise not to tell Mr Nwamadi that I knew this.'

I refuse to be part of this whole deception game, but I suspect Chika will not talk further if I don't make a commitment.

'I will try. I can promise that.'

He looks at me squarely, his eyes are sad. 'Kevin was a cultist. Took me weeks to find proof, but, yes, he was in a cult.'

I let out a deflated sigh and sit in the nearest chair. 'You never told Emeka?'

Chika shakes his head. 'I couldn't. Especially because I also found out that after Kevin started his relationship with Mercy, he tried to get out. He stopped going to meetings and took up causes like Justice for Momoh to prove he was reformed.'

'But you still couldn't explain how Kevin came to be with Winston and Bona?'

Chika shakes his head again. 'It all got confusing as soon as I knew Winston and Bona were not in a cult and there was no proof that Kevin was taking or selling drugs. And I couldn't push further without telling Emeka that his son was indeed a cult member.'

'That's why you agreed to help me to find out what you already knew, so I would be the one to tell him.'

Chika nods, and smiles ruefully. 'Guess that backfired because we now know cultism had nothing to do with why those boys were killed. We wouldn't have known that if Emeka hadn't brought you in.'

This is little consolation given the amount of deceit that went into getting me on board.

'You uncovered several critical aspects that would have made my job easier if I had known.'

He is dismissive. 'I'm a glorified muscleman without your insights and expertise.'

'You underestimate yourself.'

'You are kind, but I know my limitations.'

We're silent for a while.

'The rustication ...?'

He smiles, and I am not sure whether it's in resignation or regret.

'I deserved it. I was stupid. It set me back several years and made me ineligible for admission into any university in the country.'

'If you don't mind my asking, what made you join?' I ask, thinking of my father.

He gives his characteristic shrug. 'I wish I could say peer pressure, but it wasn't. I went to the university with good grades and to be honest, I felt sort of special. I come from a family of traders. I was the first to attend university but I might as well have been invisible. I was special at home, but just one of over tens of thousands of undergraduates. I wanted to stand out, to be someone to be reckon with, to have power. They didn't recruit me. I sought them out and I fit the bill: eager, reckless and stupid.'

There's no self-pity in his voice. These are no more than details of a past he'd made peace with. I wait for him to say more, and when he doesn't, I change direction.

'Does Emeka have a private jet?'

'Yes.' He briefly looks at me with a frown. 'Why?'

'That would explain how quickly he got here today.'

Chika doesn't respond, and I'm now learning that rather than lie, he tends to keep quiet. I can, therefore, deduce Emeka didn't arrive in Port Harcourt today but earlier. Perhaps even as early as when I arrived. I wouldn't put such close monitoring beyond a man as driven as Emeka.

Which brings me to my original intention for coming to Chika's room.

'I came because I can't find my iPad. I think I left it in the car,' I state with surprising ease.

Perhaps because the atmosphere is charged and Chika is feeling guilty about his own extensive deception, he appears grateful for the change of subject.

'I can go check for you.'

'No, no. It's fine. I'll do it.'

I catch sight of the car keys on the desk and pick them up. I pat his shoulder. 'You did a fine job, Chika. I wish you had told me all this from the beginning but I also understand why you didn't. It might have even coloured my perception of the whole thing, so maybe it was a good thing.'

My smile is sincere but his remains guarded.

'Be right back,' I say as casually as I can muster and leave.

I almost choose the stairs when the elevators take longer than usual to arrive, but will myself to be casual. I get in calmly when the elevator arrives, and at the lobby, I greet the doorman at the entrance and head towards the parking lot.

I look up at the windows of the hotel to be sure Chika is not looking out. I walk over to the car and quickly open the trunk.

The jack and wheel wrench are lying on top of the mat and not underneath. I gently move them aside and lift the carpet. There is the black bag. I turn back to look around me. Nothing. No one is watching.

I quickly unzip the bag, my heart thudding in my chest. On some level I have known all along what I would find, but confirmation only made me feel even more out of my depth.

I take out my phone, my hand shaking slightly as I capture what lies inside with its camera. I zip the bag back up and carefully cover it with the mat, close the trunk and press the car remote.

I hope I'm a picture of calm as I walk back into the hotel. Once inside my room, I rush to my iPad.

It takes some searching online, but I do find a match with what I saw in the bag.

Brügger & Thomet APR 338. A sniper rifle renowned for both its silence and long-range capabilities.

TURNING TABLES

I pretend I am on the phone with Folake when I knock on Chika's door. I wave the iPad in his face while mumbling a 'hold on' to the pretend caller.

'Thanks,' I say, as I hand the key back to Chika and indicate the phone. 'Home. Later.'

'You were saying, Sweets?' I ask as Chika's door closes behind me.

As soon as I enter my room, I head for the minibar and am quite tipsy when I do call my wife. It's either this or march straight back to Chika's room and demand answers.

'Hey,' she says groggily.

'Sorry I woke you.'

'No. It's okay. Are you all right?'

'Nope.'

'What's wrong?' I can picture her sitting up in our bed. 'What happened?'

I tell her everything, the past week pouring out in a torrent of words that slip into a ramble.

'Sweet, are you drunk?' she asks when I am done.

'Almost.'

'You want to sleep and call me back in the morning?'

'No. I'm coming home.'

'But you're not done.'

'Have you been listening to me? Everything is a mess. I don't know anything any more.'

'Because you found a sniper rifle in a bag that was given to this Chika by your client, suddenly everything doesn't make sense?'

'Why would Emeka give him a rifle, Folake? Explain that to me –'

'I can't. All I know is, I'm not sure you'll like yourself if you come back before finding the answers you went looking for.'

'No one's telling the truth –'

'That's generally the case when a crime is being concealed.' I can hear the dryness in her tone.

'Well, I'm not going to be part of it any more. I'm coming home.'

'As what?' I hear the challenge in her tone.

'What do you mean?'

'You heard me, Phil. Are you coming back as my husband or the angry man who left this house a week ago?'

I am silent. A part of my brain struggles to reconcile the events of the past days as having happened in a week.

'Phil?'

'I don't know,' I finally answer.

'I think you should before coming back. I had hoped this assignment would restore whatever you believe leaving the States has taken from us. Maybe it's prestige, or pride or whatever.'

'I lost you,' I say before I can catch myself. It clicks somewhere in my mind that I'm not tipsy but quite drunk. But it's too late.

'What do you mean?'

'I saw you, Folake,' I say, trying to stem the anger that is threatening to become a sob in my throat. 'I saw you.'

'You saw what?'

'You and that boy. Your graduate assistant!'

The words tumble out. I tell Folake how I came to her office to pick her up, hoping to regale her with my first impressions of Emeka Nwamadi while driving us to watch our sons at their school's basketball tournament. I tell her how I parked the car and called her on the phone to come down. When she didn't pick up the call, I looked up at the large windows that framed her office. And that was when I saw them.

She and the young man who had visited our house many times to drop off papers, grade assignments and pass on administrative tidbits that needed Folake's attention. I remember his name: Soji Bello. A nice enough young man who I never paid more than the most cursory mind, until the moment I saw my wife in his arms.

'You said you were caught in traffic,' Folake says when I pause for breath.

'I drove off. I had to think. To clear my head.'

There's silence. I want to scream at her to say something, anything to defend herself but –

'Let me let you sleep,' she says. 'I can't talk to you like this.'

'What would you say? I know what I saw!'

'Go to sleep, please. I'll call tomorrow.'

And with that, she hangs up with a finality that enrages me further. I redial her number. It just rings and takes me to voicemail. The operator informs me her phone is switched off on all my subsequent attempts. I throw the phone aside. In my mind, I had practised how I was going to confront her: to her face, calmly and coolly. The very opposite of what I just did.

The minibar is now empty, so I order more bourbon from room service and fall into a restless sleep.

Surprisingly, I don't have a headache when I wake up. My mouth is dry and my stomach is queasy, but, otherwise, I am fine. But I don't look fine. My eyes are bloodshot as I stare at the bathroom mirror after relieving myself and I hold on to the sides of the sink to steady myself. As the hungover tend to do, I try to recall everything that happened last night and the accuracy of my memory is not comforting.

I walk back to the room and check my phone. Nothing from Folake. I want to call her, but I stop myself. She should be the one calling me, pleading for forgiveness.

I toss the phone on the bed and go into the shower. When I return, it is to four missed calls from Salome. She didn't leave a message. I'm not in the mood to speak to her anyway. She's part of this whole mess. No, Ms Salome Briggs, I'm not going to be party to whatever game you're playing. Not today.

I have a murderer to find.

Chika seems to be in good spirits when we meet in the hotel restaurant.

'Rough night?' he asks.

'We really must get going. No time for chit-chat.' I wave the waiter away. No breakfast today.

'Someone is in a foul mood,' he says with a levity that irritates me even further, then chuckles. 'Well, let's hope this cheers you up.'

'What?' I'm desperate for some good news, so I pull out a chair and sit.

Smiling, Chika takes out his cell phone and waves it triumphantly 'Look what my hacker friend sent me.'

I squint at him. 'They got into Kevin's account?'

Chika nods and hands me his phone.

I swipe through screenshots of messages that confirm what Tamuno told us about Godwin. He *knew* Kevin very well. In the series of messages between them, Godwin appears to be denying the accusation of being the one who tipped off the police about the damning images found on Momoh's phone.

'*He was living next to u,*' Kevin wrote. '*U know it was a setup!*'

'*If any1 tip off d police, it wz not me!!!!!!*' Godwin replied, with a series of angry and confused emoji faces.

'*Some1 was sending those pix to Momoh. He told me.*'

'*Am going 2 blk u if u keep sending me diz messages. Am blocking u now!*'

'*U can block me, but you can't hide! I know u know sumtin abt this.*'

This was the last communication between Kevin and Godwin.

I look at Chika. 'So, it's all linked to #justice4momoh?'

Chika nods. 'You remember Tamuno said he was writing a paper that Kevin was helping him out with?'

'Yes?'

'I clicked a link on one of Kevin's #justice4momoh posts and it redirected me to the article in a journal on legal reform. I downloaded it.' Chika waves a flash drive.

'Remember, I don't have a laptop any more.' Without a keyboard, working off my iPad is a chore.

Chika rises. 'I'll just have it printed at the reception desk.'

'Thank you.'

As he walks away, I return to the exchanges between Kevin and Godwin on his phone. It occurs to me that if Chika's friend can hack into Kevin's Messenger account, he can do the same with Godwin's. Perhaps this would give us some insight into Godwin's killer and how all this is linked to the Okriki Three. I also think it would be quite useful to speak with Tamuno again, knowing what we now know.

When Chika returns it's in the company of three policemen, their guns pulled. My heart skips a beat when I recognise the rookie from the Okriki Police Station. Behind them are the armed guards who are supposed to protect the hotel from attack by militants, robbers and kidnappers, but not policemen.

It is the rookie who speaks. 'Philip Taiwo?'

'That's me.' I try to be calm, but I am remembering too much of what I know. It takes all my willpower to wear a mask of polite surprise, balanced with a slight embarrassment at the scene being caused.

'You are under arrest.'

'For what?' Chika asks insolently, no doubt for the umpteenth time.

The rookie puffs out his chest. 'For the attempted murder of Chief Kinikanwo Omereji, Paramount Chief of the Okriki Community.'

HIGHER POWERS

Three hours and thirty-six minutes. That's how long I've been left alone in this little room in the Okriki Police Station. My phone was confiscated by the rookie who looked very pleased with himself as he led me to the police car at the hotel, while I gave the unnerved Hotel Manager Abubakar's number and he took Emeka's from Chika. The manager had asked me if there was a significant other I wanted him to call. Considering how the conversation with Folake went last night, I told him informing Abubakar was adequate for now. If my suspicions are correct, the Commandant will call my father who, I am hoping, will use his discretion regarding what Folake should know.

All through the drive to Okriki, the rookie refused to answer any of my questions. Chika was transported in another vehicle, and I was without anyone to share my befuddlement at this sudden turn of events. How had I gone from the investigator to the investigated in a matter of hours?

The door opens and Inspector Omereji comes in. He looks like hell and I can see from the expression on his face that he will do whatever it takes to get the answers he wants.

'My father was shot yesterday night,' he announces, as he pulls up the chair across from me and sits down.

'Shot?' I ask tentatively. I must be careful. 'Is he all right?'

'ICU. He's in his seventies so the prognosis is not good.'

'I'm sorry to hear that,' I say sincerely.

'Are you?'

'Of course I am. And if you brought me here because you think I've got something to do with it, then you've made a mistake.'

'What about your friend Chika?'

I squash the image of the Brügger & Thomet rising in my mind. 'What about him?'

'Where was he last night?'

I shrug and tell the truth. 'We left here, got to the hotel and went to our separate rooms.'

'That's convenient.'

'Mike –' He glowers at me when I say his name, so I fall back on formality. 'Inspector, you've got to believe me, I know nothing about what happened to the Chief.'

'But I think you do, and you will tell me.' The threat in his voice is unmistakable. In the States, I would be asking for my lawyer and challenging my detention without being read my Miranda rights. But those rules don't apply in Okriki, and this scares me.

'Look –' I make my tone conciliatory, 'I know you must be terribly distressed right now, but I promise you, you're wasting your time talking to me when the real culprit is out there.'

'Let me be the judge of that. What time did you get to the hotel in PH?'

'Around 6:30.'

'And what did you do when you got to the hotel?'

'I told you … Chika and I went our separate ways. I had drinks in the lounge and decided to have an early night.'

'You don't know what he was up to yesterday?'

'No. Not last night at least.'

'That's strange, because he swears you and him were together –'

Chika can't be so stupid as to use me as an alibi, especially as we had not discussed it beforehand. So, I say nothing and just hold Omereji's steady gaze.

Omereji changes tactics. He smiles and moves closer to me. It is the you-can-help-me-get-the-bad-guy-and-be-a-hero look. Clearly, he doesn't know of my past life in the San Francisco Police Department.

'Look, Dr Taiwo, I'm sure you didn't pull the trigger. I know a killer when I see one.'

'So, what am I doing here?'

'Because you know who did.'

'Should you even be doing this? Are you not too close to the matter to be completely objective?'

His smile is patronising. 'You are not in America, Dr Taiwo.'

I return his smile with a dry one of my own. 'So everyone keeps reminding me.'

Omereji is about to speak again when his phone rings. He looks at it and frowns, stands and, without excusing himself, walks out.

I wait, burning with curiosity.

The sniper rifle.

Chika.

Emeka.

Chief Omereji shot.

What is going on? I try to stop myself thinking, to keep a cool facade when Omereji comes back. He stands at the door but I can't read his expression.

'You may go.'

'What?'

He smiles coldly. 'Your contacts have called higher contacts who insist without more evidence against you and your friend, I must let you go.'

'Abubakar called you?'

'Higher. You may go. But pray my father lives, because if he dies, I promise you none of your powerful contacts will be able to save you and your friend.'

'For what it's worth, I really hope your dad makes it.'

'Goodbye, Dr Taiwo. You can be sure this won't be our last meeting.'

I walk towards him and stop. 'Get some rest, Mike.'

He doesn't look at me, so I leave.

I walk past Omereji's office, the holding cells and into the reception area, which remains as crowded and noisy as ever. The rookie coldly hands back my phone in a plastic bag branded with a popular supermarket-chain's logo. I look at the people who have paused everything to point and whisper. One particularly angry man spits on the floor, his mouth curled in disdain as he eyes me.

I pretend not to notice all this as I walk through them. I am barely out of the station when I hear the eruption of voices in several dialects and I would bet my bottom dollar that I'm the topic of conversation.

I see Chika standing outside, his clothes rumpled, and it's obvious he has been roughened up quite a bit. But his eyes are fiery as I approach him.

'They bring us here in their vehicles and then refuse to take us back,' he says as soon as I reach him.

'We can take a taxi,' I attempt to placate him.

'Why should we? They brought us here!'

I am looking at him, looking for signs of guilt, but all I see is irritation.

'Were they hard on you?' I ask as we start to walk into the street.

He shrugs. 'No more than I expected.'

'You know why they would think we know something?'

'Is it not the police?' he hisses. 'Do they need any reason to bully law-abiding citizens? Instead of doing their jobs, they drove almost an hour to come and arrest us without any proof. Nonsense.'

'Chika! Hold on. You're walking too fast.'

'Sorry.' He slows his pace and we look out for taxis driving by. Some stop, take one look at us, exchange looks and a barrage of words in Ikwerre with their passengers, and they are gone. It's clear we will not get transport to Port Harcourt from here. At least not from a local taxi.

'Let me call the boss,' Chika says, bringing out his phone. 'He can send a car –'

'Emeka's still in Port Harcourt?'

'He never left,' Chika says brusquely and puts the phone to his ear.

I think of calling Salome. She must be devastated by the attempt on her uncle's life. Maybe that was why she was calling earlier, but I don't want to speak to her in front of Chika, so I send a text message.

'Sorry to hear about your uncle. Just leaving the station. Will call.'

Chika has finished the call. 'We should walk to the bus stop,' he says, pointing. 'There's shade there. The boss says he'll send a car, but it'll take a couple of hours depending on traffic.'

We head towards the section of the road where the Okriki Three were killed. A sense of déjà vu hits me as we walk along the road, looking for a taxi in the midst of the cars and the motorbikes – most carrying more than the mandated one passenger – that zip past us. There is also an uneasiness in the air that I can't shake off, as the town's now familiar antagonism towards our presence bubbles to the surface.

'You think everyone knows what we were being questioned for?'

'We can assume they do,' Chika answers, his stride quickening. 'Let's just get to the bus stop, and if we're lucky, we might get one that's not driven by a local.'

'And the car Emeka is sending?'

'I just want to get out of this place,' Chika says harshly. 'We can meet up with it in another town.'

Perhaps it is the way people are looking at us, or the fact that I am plain nervous, but I am walking as fast as Chika. We quicken our steps to get past Madam Landlady's compound as fast as possible.

I am sweating and almost out of breath by the time we reach the roundabout where the famous cannon stands. I really don't feel safe sitting amongst a hostile group of people waiting for a taxi, so I suggest we wait at the round-about rather than at the bus stop.

A car swings around the circle and stops next to us. The driver, who already has a passenger in the front seat, bends to look at us.

'You dey go campus?' the taxi driver asks.

I look at Chika and towards the crowded bus stop.

'Let's just get out of here,' I say.

ATTACK OF THE DAMNED

We get in the back seat and the taxi circles the round-about and heads towards the empty road that people have stopped using since the incident, proving the driver is new to these parts. We relax.

Chika continues texting and I bring out my phone to check if Salome has sent any more messages. None. The taxi driver makes a turn off the road.

'Hey, hey!' Chika protests. 'This is not the –' The passenger in front turns towards us with a gun. Instinctively, I drop my phone and raise my hands. Chika does not move.

'You should not have come back.' The passenger removes his dark shades and tilts the baseball cap back. I catch my breath as I recognise him as one of the young men who had vandalised our rooms at Hotel Royale.

'Where're you taking us?' Chika asks.

'Where you're not coming back from.' The taxi driver throws a dirty look at us through the rear-view mirror. 'You tried to kill our chief, and now you'll pay!'

'We've just been interviewed by the police,' I say with my hands still up. 'They can prove we didn't try to kill your chief.'

The passenger pointing the gun at us doesn't waver; his gaze is steady on me and burning with hatred. I steal a glance at Chika. He looks as relaxed as if he is being given a tour of the town. His hands are not up, and I can see that he is discreetly pressing something on his phone.

The car stops and I look around. We are at a clearing, off the beaten path. My heart starts to beat faster, and sweat pools under my armpits.

'Keep them talking,' Chika whispers urgently, as we are roughly pushed out of the car. 'The boss is listening.'

'Kneel down!' the passenger orders.

Now Chika's hands are also in the air, and slowly we kneel.

The taxi driver is on his phone, waving his own gun and speaking excitedly in rapid Ikwerre. I hope he is calling for reinforcements. We need the time.

'We said stay away!' The passenger kicks Chika.

'Hit me again without the gun pointed at me, and let's see who's a man.'

The passenger partially obeys Chika because he lands the butt of the gun in Chika's face.

'Stop it! Why are you doing this?' Panic makes my voice louder than usual. 'We told you we have nothing to do with –'

'You lie!' This is the driver. 'Someone saw this one last night.'

He joins the passenger in kicking Chika, who is now crouched on the ground, his face bloodied.

'Is that the best you can do?' Chika rises with a malevolent smile that looks eerie considering his lips are split and his teeth are all red. 'Is that how you kill people in this town? Kidnapping those who can't defend themselves and burning them?'

I do a quick calculation. If Emeka is still on the phone and perhaps calling for help, where will it come from? Who will he ask to come to our rescue all the way from Port Harcourt? Going by the beating Chika is getting, when the young men turn on me, I am not sure I will weather the blows as well as he seems to be doing.

'Those boys were thieves!'

'And your whole town are killers!' Chika taunts. 'That's what you want to do, right? Bringing us to the same place where you killed those poor boys in order to kill us.'

Is Chika giving our location to Emeka over the phone? Oh, Lord, I hope so.

The taxi driver kicks Chika further into the ground and now the passenger is pointing the gun at me. I hear the roar of motorcycles and a car coming closer. Reinforcements for the men or help for us?

'You! Our chief warned you to go back; he told you what would happen if you kept snooping around.'

Say something, Philip. Keep him talking. 'Yes. And I left. I told you we were arrested by the police.'

'Because you tried to kill our chief!'

'So why did they let us go if we did it?'

In the split second that he is searching for an answer, Chika has risen ever so slightly and spits into the face of the taxi driver. The passenger swears and the driver, enraged, kicks Chika so hard that he slides several metres in the muddy ground.

That's when the cell phone falls out of his pocket. The taxi driver picks it up, and looks even more enraged by what he sees.

'Who is listening?'

Chika laughs. 'The world. They will know you and every-one in this town for what you are!'

'Chika!' I shout a warning now. There is goading and there is downright dangerous.

'You can't save them!' the driver shouts into the phone and then proceeds to throw it on the ground and stamp on it repeatedly.

I see three motorcycles, each carrying two passengers, and the car come into view. The taxi driver and passenger speak excitedly, raising fists and waving at the newcomers.

Damn! Reinforcements.

Chika has moved slightly, forcing the assailants to back away from me, all their attention on him. I seize the chance, rising swiftly from my kneeling position and running into them with all the force I can muster. I know it is a useless move, but anything is better than just kneeling in the mud with my hands raised.

Chika is up like lightning, and as I swing my hand blindly, it meets with a cheekbone – or is it a jaw? I'm not sure because what must be a stick or something equally hard connects with my ribs and I double over.

More men join in. I hear bone crack and through my pain I see Chika drop-kicking the passenger and trying to get the gun off him.

Kicks and punches land on me from several more attack-ers, and I double over but it doesn't stop. I see Chika hit the ground, but my vision is becoming blurred. Then I hear a loud noise. Like a gunshot. I think. Another one goes off, and I see Chika on the ground. Everything starts to go black.

Has he been shot?

Or maybe, I'm the one who has been.

I can't seem to figure this out as I start falling into a blank, endless space.

THE OTHER SON

I gave John Paul the light so he could meet his mother.

I have been doing this a lot lately, especially as The Final Plan gets closer. Besides, it's time Mama met her son's two selves.

John Paul takes the lift all the way to the oncology ward, not bothered by the smell of medicine, puke and sickness. He flashes a smile at the nurse on duty who thinks she recognises him and waves him towards our mother's ward.

When he enters, he pulls a chair to sit close to her bed and whispers into her ears, 'I am taking you away from here.'

My mother's eyes glint with a smile. 'Don't speak nonsense. It's a good hospital.'

'I can take better care of you.'

'You're not a doctor.'

'I learnt many things at the monastery, Mama, and one of them is how to take care of the sick.'

'My sickness is not something you can take care of.'

'So why did you call for me?' John Paul says rather harshly.

My mother stares at him, frowning. The smile on her face disappears.

'You're not him,' she says flatly.

John Paul does not bother to deny it. 'How do you know?'

'Your eyes. They're dead. You're the devil that takes over him. The one that killed his father.'

309

'He was not his father.'

'He was a good man who took us in when your father abandoned us.'

'He was abusing your son.'

'You lie!'

Mama is getting agitated, and so am I, watching from the shadows. I want to scream at John Paul to stop this conversation, but his hold is too strong.

'You know I'm not lying.'

'He was a good man,' my mother insists.

'He was a rich man who used his money to blind you.'

'He loved you … He was just being affectionate.'

'He was raping me, Mama –'

I stop reaching for the light. Did John Paul just say he is me? He can't be. It happened to me! I was the one who needed saving, not him.

'It's the evil one in you that is saying these things. Call the nurse. You must leave. Don't come back until you have my son.'

Mama tries calling out for a nurse but her voice is too weak. John Paul stands and pulls the curtain, blocking her bed from the view of the nurses and other patients.

'I want the nurse,' Mama insists.

'I showed you the bruises, the bleeding, but you refused to believe me.' John Paul bends to her, his face twisted with anger. 'You sacrificed me to your husband because he gave you a roof over your head and bought you expensive gifts.'

'You had an active imagination. Always creating stories, drawing crazy things on every paper in the house. How was I to know it was not one of your stories?'

'Did you ask him? Confront him?'

'With what? I never saw him be anything other than a father to you and you killed him.'

'And even after he died, you abandoned your child –'

'You were with men of God!'

'You know nothing of God!' John Paul hisses. 'They know nothing of God.'

'And you do?'

'I am my only god.'

'You're the devil.' It's like Mama has become filled with strength drawn from an unknown source because she grabs John Paul's hand and lifts her head towards him. 'But, it's not too late. You can be saved.'

'Saved?'

'Look at me. I am dying of a disease that has no cure. This is my punishment. But it's not too late for you. If you go to the police –'

'No.' John Paul's answer is an echo of mine in the shadows.

'You killed a man!'

'He deserved to die, and if you were any kind of mother, you would have done it instead of me.'

'Just confess, my son. I'll call the police, and the priest, we will confess together –'

As she speaks, John Paul stands to his full height, jerks his hand out of her grip.

'We can even tell them it was self-defence,' Mama says, her voice pleading, urging. 'But we can't commit our souls to hell by not confessing this mortal sin.'

John Paul walks back to my mother. He checks the IV, looks at the machine monitoring her vitals, and then looks at her.

Mama is still talking. 'My son, please, even if we are punished on this earth, we will find peace in heaven. We have to con—'

John Paul leans towards Mama, kisses her forehead gently.

'That's from your son,' he whispers.

He then pulls the pillow from under her head and puts it over her face.

'This is from me.'

ACT FOUR

light waves change direction when passing through an opening or around a barrier

AIR

I try to breathe and it feels like a thousand knives are piercing my sides. The pain forces me to open my eyes.

To chaos.

People are speaking rapidly, but I can't make out what they are saying.

White is everywhere. Even the people are white, their faces blurring into their white clothes like a watercolour painting.

A blurry face gets very close to me, and a ray of light pierces my vision.

I flinch from the brightness, and the sharp, numbing pain in my sides threatens to pull me back under.

– He's with us. What's your name! Tell me your name! –

I want to say don't shout but instead –

Philip.

– What number follows one? –

Two.

My voice seems to be coming from a far-off place. But it is me, answering.

Breathing.

– Who's the President of Nigeria? –

It hurts to take in more air.

Who cares?
– Good. He's with us. Prep surgery –
I'm alive. But where's Chika?
I'm not sure I ask this before everything goes black again.

RUDE AWAKENING

The first time I open my eyes, it is to the blinding white ceiling. A fan rotates slowly, making it seem like the room is spinning. I close my eyes and everything stills. I decide to keep them like that for a while longer.

The second time, it is to a blinding headache that forces me to press my eyes shut again. Even with my eyes closed, the persistent thudding in my head stays. A piercing sound fills the room, and I want to cover my ears but for all the wires attached to me. The shrill sound gets louder. I keep my eyes closed until the sound becomes a series of beeps and the thudding in my head goes flat.

The next time I open my eyes, it's because I hear voices.

'He knows something –'

'You don't know that.'

I can't decide if I'm dreaming or if Omereji and Salome are really at the foot of my bed, facing each other and talking animatedly.

'They tried to kill my dad. Your uncle,' Omereji says in a rushed whisper.

Everything is coming back. The police station. The kidnap. Chika!

'You can't prove that –' Salome is saying.

'Guys,' I call out weakly.

Omereji and Salome turn towards me at the same time, but it's Salome who comes to my side.

'You're awake!'

'Who can sleep with all the noise?' I attempt to joke while trying to lift myself to a sitting position.

'Don't move. You have a cracked rib and a concussion.'

I touch my head and feel the bandage. That explains the headaches. And the tightness in my chest is not from lack of air, it's because I am wrapped up like a mummy.

'How long have I been here?'

Salome looks at Mike, who has not taken his eyes off me since I spoke, then back at me.

'Three days. They induced a coma because they were worried about a brain bleed.'

'Three?' I try to sit up sharply and regret it immediately. 'Where is Chika?'

'Your friend is fine,' Omereji answers flatly. 'He sustained minor injuries after inflicting quite a few more on your attackers.'

I settle back down.

'They didn't shoot him?'

'No, Philip,' Salome answers. 'He's fine.'

'But I heard gunshots –'

'I think you should rest for now,' Salome says. 'Mike and I came by the hospital to see my uncle, so we thought we'd drop in on you.'

'Your uncle, how is he?'

'Out of ICU, he's stable now.'

'Thank God.'

Omereji has a look on his face, and I sense what's coming next. I suddenly feel bone-weary.

'Do you suppose you can answer a few questions?' he asks, coming closer. He still looks like he hasn't slept in days.

'Philip, you don't have to do this –' Salome protests.

'What do you want to know that you didn't ask when you wrongfully arrested me?'

'Look, about that, you can understand my situation ...'

My attempt at a smile becomes a grimace because I feel a return of the headache with greater force.

'That's not an apology,' I say to buy time and compose my mind.

'An apology?'

I would have laughed at the consternation on Inspector Omereji's face if I wouldn't hurt in every part of my body.

'You arrested me on assumptions and personal –'

'I had good reason!' Omereji hisses.

'You want to tell that to his lawyer?' Salome retorts, a challenge on her face as she looks at her cousin.

There's a tense silence for quite a while. My head is now pounding and my heart is beating rather fast, but I know I have to stay calm.

'Dr Taiwo, I would be lying to you if I said I am sorry for bringing you in. But I am sorry for not following protocol, for not providing you with protection in a town that I knew was antagonistic towards you, and well, I –'

'It's okay ... really.' It is painful to watch the proud officer admit fault and it would be ungracious of me to let him go on, knowing what I know. 'I understand.'

I plaster a proper smile on my face, while Salome beams like a kindergarten teacher who just averted a playground conflict.

'What do you want to know?' I ask.

Salome jumps in. 'Philip, you really don't have to –'

Omereji speaks over her protests. 'We've done a ballistics test on the bullet that hit my dad. It's from a sniper rifle. It's not standard. It's expensive and quite rare to find in these parts. I believe it was an assassination attempt.'

'And you still think I know something about it?' I ask calmly, even as my headache worsens and my heart beats fast.

Salome sighs. 'Mike has no proof, but he suspects Chika was the one who shot my uncle.'

'Why?' I ask.

Omereji answers. 'Because he was in town right after those boys were killed. Snooping around, asking questions and trailing people. Including my father.'

'Why didn't you pick him up then?' I ask with a wince. I see Salome touch Mike, as if asking him to go easy.

'I would have, if I was here then, but even so, on what grounds?' Omereji answers. 'At first, people thought he was a journalist, then when he didn't leave, some thought he was writing a book. After some time, he just disappeared, and everyone forgot about him and they barely recognised him when he came back with you.'

'That was when we found out that you were hired by Emeka Nwamadi,' Salome says.

'Which means,' Omereji adds, 'Nwamadi hired your Chika too.'

I look from Salome to him. She'll know I'm lying, so I tell the truth. 'I guarantee you, if Chika shot the Chief, he wouldn't miss.'

Salome and Omereji look at each other. He gives a resigned shrug. Salome looks down at me. Her make-up is smudged around her eyes, and I suspect, like her cousin, she's been having difficulty sleeping.

'We'll go and see my uncle,' she says. 'You're on the same floor, but he is in the West Wing with 24-hour care because of his age. But I'll see if I can check in on you again.' She pats my hand and turns to Omereji who's fixed me with an unblinking gaze.

'Mike, let's go.'

'It was a Brügger & Thomet.'

'Pardon?' My voice wavers.

'The rifle used to shoot my father. A Brügger & Thomet. Let me know if you come across one.'

'Let me know when you arrest the people who attacked Chika and me.'

'He has,' Salome says. 'Mike rounded them up the same day you were brought here.'

'You'll have to make some identification and do an interview before we lay formal charges, but, yes, we have ten local youths in custody.'

'Thank you,' I say to Omereji, a bit ashamed.

'Let me know if you come across that assault rifle, Dr Taiwo. Get well soon.'

He turns and leaves. Salome sighs, waves at me and follows him.

AN UNFORESEEN KINDNESS

Knowing what I know, I'm not sure who I'd rather see first: Chika or Emeka. But the decision is made for me when Emeka walks into my hospital room in the company of the man I recognise from my disastrous visit to the State Psychiatric Hospital.

'Dr Taiwo.'

'Emeka,' I answer guardedly, my eyes on Mercy's father.

'I brought you a visitor. Elechi Opara, meet Dr Philip Taiwo.'

Elechi Opara steps to the foot of my bed, his smile bright and warm. I feel ashamed anew.

'I'm really sorry about –' I begin but he holds up a hand.

'It's okay, Dr Taiwo,' he says kindly. 'I hold no grudge. Emeka explained the pressure he was putting on you.'

'Nevertheless, sir, I'm very sorry. How is Mercy?'

'She's better and back at home. We're hoping she'll stay like this for a long time.'

Emeka steps forward. 'I brought Elechi here so we can both formally thank him –'

I frown at the two men, confused. Emeka is smiling broadly, and even puts his arms around Elechi Opara's shoulders.

'Thank him?'

'They've not told you?'

'Told me what?'

'Elechi was the one who saved you from those hooligans.'

This is totally unexpected.

'How ... did you –?' I stutter, unsure what to say or ask.

'It was pure luck that I found myself not too far from where you were being attacked when Emeka called me –'

'You called him?'

Emeka nods. 'I could hear the danger you were in when Chika called. I had to act fast and there was no one in the area I could call but Elechi.'

'It was not hard to find you. When I saw the direction some of the youths were going, already making noises, I knew they must be headed towards you, so I hailed a motorbike and followed them.'

'Even after what I did,' I shake my head in wonder, 'you still helped us –'

'What else could I do?' Elechi Opara says.

'I apologised on our behalf to Elechi and explained how I was pushing you to finish the report,' Emeka explains. 'He was really the only one I could think of, because there was no way I could have gotten there in time, before those boys did real damage.'

I look towards Elechi. 'You were the one who shot at them?'

'In the air, not at them. It was the only way to get their attention.'

'Lucky you were armed.' It is both a question and statement. Even in the States, I could never understand how people carry guns around like an accessory. I have seen more guns here in less than two weeks than during a whole year of working in the San Francisco Police Department.

'My townspeople killed my daughter's friend and even attacked her when she tried to save Kevin. I've been carrying a gun around ever since.'

'And even luckier for us you were carrying it with you when Dr Taiwo was attacked,' Emeka says, thumping Elechi on the shoulder, in an overly jolly manner that I sense is to mask his pain every time Kevin's name comes up.

'And Chika,' I say quietly.

Emeka's face becomes implacable. 'Of course. And Chika.'

'Where is he?' I ask, disappointed that he has not come to see me, if indeed he is fine.

'He's sorting out some things for me in Port Harcourt. He'll come by soon. For now, regain your strength. We need you on your feet asap.' He looks at Elechi. 'Let's allow him to rest.'

'Thank you, Mr Opara,' I say sincerely.

'I couldn't have done less, Dr Taiwo.'

We exchange a feeble handshake because every slight movement causes me pain.

'I don't know how I can repay you, sir,' I say.

Elechi looks to Emeka, and the latter nods.

'Emeka told me you're a psychologist,' Elechi starts awkwardly. 'I don't want to take advantage and I know the doctors at the psychiatric hospital are doing their best for Mercy ...'

His voice trails away as I am trying to grasp what he is saying. When the penny drops, I immediately start to shake my head and Emeka jumps in.

'I explained to Elechi that you're not that kind of psychologist, but all he is asking for is a second opinion.'

'Yes. Nothing more than that. I am hoping you may see something our Nigerian doctors can't see ...' Elechi smiles at me, but there is a sadness in his eyes that reminds me of Emeka's own when he speaks of Kevin.

'But, sir, I am not that kind of psychologist. I am not a clinician.'

Elechi's face falls and I look towards Emeka for help, but he just shrugs as if to say I am on my own.

'I am a researcher at best, sir.'

'But a psychologist ...' Elechi insists.

'Yes, but not the kind that can diagnose or prescribe medicine.'

'But you can give an opinion? Maybe even advise where we can go for help?'

'I specialise in crime and –'

I stop my well-rehearsed speech because I can see Elechi will not understand my reluctance. As far as he is concerned, I am a psychologist. Any explanation about my expertise will come off as an excuse or, worse, a refusal. Besides, I owe the man my life.

'I can only say what I think, and maybe give you some names of clinicians ...' I say.

'That's all I want.' Elechi Opara smiles widely. 'As soon as you're better, I can come and pick you up in Port Harcourt –'

I want to say Elechi is moving too fast, but I can't dampen the relief on his face.

'In fact,' Elechi turns to Emeka, 'what about the thanksgiving?'

'Thanksgiving?' I ask. The thudding in my head is a clear indication that this is not something that I would like to attend but which I might be unable to refuse.

'Elechi is having a thanksgiving lunch at his house for Mercy's return home,' Emeka says.

'Mercy's godparents are organising a small service at their church on that day and we'll eat at our place afterwards. If you can join us, you can observe Mercy and talk to her –'

I stare at Emeka but I can't read his expression. Does he want me to go? Is he going?

'All of this is if you're feeling better, of course …?' Elechi says, and this caveat allows me to smile sincerely and promise to consider the invitation.

Emeka steps forward. 'We should let you rest.'

I ignore the discomfort and hold on to the hand he placed in mine, indicating with my eyes that he should stay.

He turns to Mercy's father. 'I'll join you, Elechi –'

Opara nods but stops his exit at the door. 'You'll let me know if you can make it?'

I'm still grasping Emeka's hand, but I manage a smile of gratitude.

'I'd be honoured, sir,' I respond. The die is cast.

'I'll send the details to Mr Nwamadi.'

Opara smiles at me again, and as soon as he leaves, I ask Emeka point-blank: 'Did you order Chika to kill Chief Omereji?'

Emeka snatches his hand out of mine. 'What're you talking about?'

'I saw you give him the bag with the gun, Emeka. Tell me the truth.'

'You took a bad knock to your head, Philip.'

'Don't patronise me, Emeka.'

He looks around as though someone might be listening. When he looks back at me, his face is contorted to mime outrage.

'You're accusing me of something terrible ...'

'You're a grieving father. An angry man. I would understand ...'

'No one can understand,' he says coldly and makes towards the door.

'Did you at least speak with my father? Did you tell him what happened to me?'

Emeka's face becomes shuttered. 'For what it's worth, Philip, I did speak to him. And thanked him for convincing you to take the case. I also gave him updates on your well-being. I think he has been speaking to the doctors here.'

I nod. Perhaps my dad and his friends will use this as a way of getting Emeka back into the fold.

'I want to see Chika,' I say.

Emeka nods with a fake smile. 'I'll let him know.'

'You know he must have missed deliberately, right?'

'I don't know what you're talking about. You must rest now.'

'He missed, to save you from a terrible mistake,' I insist, agitated.

'Rest, Dr Taiwo.' Emeka's tone says the discussion is over, and the door closing behind him makes sure I get the message.

For the second time today, I am left alone to wonder who the real villains are in the Okriki Three tragedy.

REUNIONS

I dream that Folake is seated at the foot of my bed. I smile at her and she smiles back.

'Hey, Sweets,' I say.

When she stands and rushes to my side, I realise she really is here. My heart is beating with joy. I feel a perverse sense of gratitude for the Okriki youths that attacked Chika and me. The look of concern on my wife's face makes the pain from the cracked and sore ribs and pounding headache almost worth it.

'Thank God,' she says.

'I'm not dreaming …'

'I'm here, Sweets.'

'The kids?' I look behind her.

'They're fine. They're with your mom.'

'But how did you –?'

'Your dad. Told me there's been an accident and connected me with Emeka, who organised for me to come down here.'

'In his private plane?'

She grins. 'You bet.'

'Ha. Star treatment.'

I can't help but laugh even though it hurts my ribs. Folake is laughing too and squeezing my hand, but, without warning, her laughter turns to sobs.

'Please don't cry ...'

'I was so afraid,' she says through sobs. 'I couldn't reach you. Your phone was off.' She goes to her handbag on the chair for a handkerchief and blows her nose. 'And ... because, I thought, well, the things you said when we spoke –'

The tears start again. At that moment, I know that no matter what I saw, whatever she has done, she loves me. And I love her. But it stands between us, the things I said. What I saw. I wave to her to come closer. She does, blowing her nose noisily.

Slowly, wincing slightly, I move my body to one side of the bed, and she climbs in. She can't rest on my chest, so she shifts slightly so that her head is on my shoulder. I close my eyes and inhale the smell of coconut oil and shea butter in her locks. I lean in and kiss her forehead.

We just lie there. Silent. Together.

She doesn't leave my side and the nurses don't seem to mind. Since no harm is being done, they let her be and we spend the night together for the first time in almost two weeks.

I am tired and drowsy, but I've missed my wife so much. I stay awake to hear her regale me with stories of the children, her work and everything but our last phone call.

Less than forty-eight hours after Folake arrived, my CT scan confirms that my head is fine. I should take things easy for a couple of days and use the painkillers for my aching ribs, but otherwise, I am in good enough health to leave the private ward of the State University Teaching Hospital.

I am ready to call a taxi to take Folake and me back to PH, but I get a text from Emeka that Chika is on his way to me. So, I wait.

'You really haven't seen him since the attack?' Folake asks as she helps me to dress in the change of clothes she had brought for me from Lagos.

'Not once. I think he's ashamed,' I answer, wincing as I raise my hand to put on a shirt.

'Why would he be?'

I try to shrug and fail. 'I've only been honest with him and he has been less than that with me.'

'The assault rifle Emeka gave him, right?' Folake buttons my shirt for me.

I want to share my suspicion regarding the attempt on Chief Omereji's life, but it's best to wait until we get to the hotel. I want to get out of here.

Just then, the door opens, and Salome enters. She stops when she sees Folake. It is brief, almost imperceptible, but the smile on her face wavers and then becomes extra-wide as she walks towards us.

'You must be Professor Taiwo. Hi, I am Salome Briggs.'

If Folake is taken aback, she doesn't show it. She offers her hand.

'Pleased to meet you.'

'Americana,' Salome turns to me. 'You look much better.'

'I feel like I've been gift-wrapped in these bandages.'

Salome laughs gaily. 'And now you have madam here to unwrap the gift.' Her wink is not as salacious as it is teasing, and she's not waiting for our reaction because she is already heading back towards the door. 'I'm visiting my uncle, so I thought I should check on you before I go to him and get stuck there with the whole family.'

'How is he?' I ask.

'Much better. Nice to meet you, Prof.'

And just like that, she's gone.

'Americana?' Folake says into the brief silence.

I don't say anything to explain Salome's moniker for me.

'That was a quick visit,' Folake continues, without looking at me.

'She's quite busy. I'm surprised she finds time to visit her uncle as regularly as she does.'

'Who is she?'

Then it hits me. In the past two days, I've told Folake almost everything about my experience in Okriki and PH, but never mentioned Salome. By name, at least. Freud's having a field day.

'Remember the friend I told you organised our accommodation in PH?'

'That's the *friend*?'

I ignore Folake's emphasis on 'friend'. 'She's a lawyer for some of the accused in the Okriki case.'

Folake's eyes widen. 'And she's your friend?'

'Yes.' I turn and slowly pick up my watch from the bedside table, but I feel the heat of her gaze on my back.

'And her uncle's here?'

The glass covering is cracked in several places, but it's still working.

'Her uncle is Chief Omereji.' I keep my voice neutral.

'Wow, Sweet. You sure know how to pick friends.'

I'm spared coming up with a response because just then Chika walks in.

He looks tired and the plaster on his forehead makes him look ill. I'm happy to see him but happier for the conversation his presence halted.

'Hello, stranger,' I say.

The smile doesn't reach his eyes. 'Hello, sir,' he answers.

I breathe in deeply. Back to square one.

CONFESSIONS OF AN ASSASSIN

After the uncomfortable nights Folake spent with me at the hospital, the Tropicana is paradise. As soon as we checked back into my old room, she runs a bath for herself, selects a playlist on her phone and basically moves into the luxurious bathroom.

Maybe it's the pain medicine, or the fact that I've been sleeping for almost six days straight, but I am restless, with my mind playing back all the events of the past two weeks.

I am aware that the attempt on Chief Kinikanwo's life has triggered a series of events in Okriki. The news of the unrest in the community is everywhere. It's funny that a month ago, even the deaths of three undergraduates had not stirred my curiosity about Okriki. Today, the town and its people are all I can think about.

High doses of tramadol, a Band-Aid as large as a planet on my forehead and thick bandages around my ribs all combine to remind me how close I came to losing my life. On reflection, I must admit that being attacked didn't come as a surprise. After the vandalisation of my hotel room and the antagonism that greeted Chika and me at different times, it was really only a matter of time before things got violent.

I have spoken to my mom and the kids, who are being spoilt rotten by their grandparents. I have reassured them all of my well-being, but I have not been able to do more than send a brief text message of thanks to my dad. When all this is over, I know we are going to have very serious talks that will extend well past dawn.

I can hear Folake humming Nina Simone's 'Feeling Good', and I can't help but reflect on her brief meeting with Salome earlier today. My wife is no fool and she certainly sensed the undercurrents between myself and Salome. My not mentioning her by name when I related the events that brought me to the Tropicana is damning, and although I have never been unfaithful in seventeen years of marriage, I can't say for sure if I would have remained immune from Salome's charms were the circumstances different.

Then, there's Chika.

The music coming from the bathroom changes to a selection of Anita Baker's greatest hits and recognising that particular playlist, I know it will be a while before my wife comes out. I check the time and get up from the bed a bit too quickly. I steady myself and walk over to the desk to write a quick note to Folake. I pause.

On the desk is a manila envelope with my name and room number written across it. I open it and see that it's the printout of the article and its extract from the *Nigerian Journal of Law Reform*: 'Legal Implications of the Anti-Gay Bill in Nigeria. A case study of Momoh Kadiri vs Rivers State Police' by Tamuno Princewill, Faculty of Law, The State University.

Ah. Yes, the files Chika went to print right before our arrest. He must have given my name for delivery. I see the study was supervised by Professor Esohe, and marvel how quickly things have changed since I never did get to meet the Dean of the Faculty of Law at TSU.

I don't put the print-outs back in the envelope. That'll remind me to make it my night-time reading.

I head to Chika's room.

'You're supposed to be resting,' he says as soon as he opens the door.

'I could say the same for you.'

He shrugs as usual.

'Won't you let me in?' I ask and he hesitates before stepping out of the way.

I follow him inside. While my room looks like I now live there, with Folake's things and mine strewn around, Chika's room is tidy, his suitcase open.

'Going somewhere?'

'Home.'

'Without telling me?'

Chika looks everywhere but at me. 'The boss says he'll tell you himself.'

'Why?' Chika still won't look at me, walks to the suitcase and starts rearranging well-packed clothes.

'Why?' I ask again. 'Why are you leaving?'

'The boss will inform you when he's ready.'

'But I'm asking *you*.'

'I was fired, Philip,' Chika announces tersely. 'He told me I couldn't deliver and to go home. He only called me to come back yesterday because he needed to keep up the pretence with you.'

'What? But why pretend at all?'

Chika locks his gaze with mine. 'You know why.'

Emeka must have told him my suspicions, perhaps even thinking Chika had confided in me.

'You missed deliberately.'

Chika laughs sardonically. 'I was incompetent.'

'That's what you wanted Emeka to think. Why?'

He turns his attention back to the suitcase.

'Chika, please be honest with me. Who are you? What do you do?'

He stops fiddling with his clothes and starts pacing. I can see him considering the wisdom of talking to me. I walk over to the large bed and sit. And wait.

As if spurred by something he can't control, Chika looks at me.

'You remember what I told you about being in a cult.'

I nod. I'm afraid if I speak too soon, he might lose his nerve.

'What I didn't tell you was what I did after I was rusticated.'

I say nothing.

Chika sighs. 'I joined a security firm. They train young men and women in private security. Some of us who are good, get sent to be personal bodyguards to very important people. Those of us who are the best, become part of an elite group of fighters. And we get contracted to go to war zones. Most times we still end up being bodyguards of ambassadors and travelling dignitaries, but sometimes, some of us are hired out as fighters.'

'Mercenaries?'

'Yes.'

It's like a tale straight out of the movies, or a Le Carré novel. But the look on Chika's face tells me this is not a story fabricated to intrigue or entertain. I remember the scars on his back.

'You were one of those sent to fight?'

Chika shrugs matter-of-factly. 'It gave me purpose. I was a drop-out, no school would have me, my family was disappointed in me, and well, I needed the money.'

'You don't have to explain. It was a job.'

'I hated it, but I was good at it. And I would have continued doing it until I got captured in Say'un. In Yemen. Me and two of my mates. One was from the US, and immediately got a deal and was repatriated. The other one was from South Africa. It took a while, but he also got a deal and was released. Me? Well, Nigeria didn't even want to acknowledge that there was such a thing as mercenaries. I spent two years and three months in that jail, until the company I worked for raised enough money to get me released.'

'That's where the scars come from –'

He smiles ruefully. 'Those are the ones you can see. But, yes, it happened there. Regular beatings and starvation are standard torture techniques in a country at war.'

'But it wasn't your war –'

'Which made it worse. I belonged to no side, so I was fair game. Being black didn't help.'

'So, you were released ...' I say to get him to continue.

His trademark shrug now comes across as one shaking off a history that can't be rewritten. 'I took a desk job at the security firm, worked off my ransom and became a free man.'

'But Emeka knew about you?'

Chika nods. 'When I started my security firm, supplying bodyguards and providing cyberware advice for the bank, I had to tell him my background.'

'So, when Kevin was killed, he called you in?'

'Actually, I offered. I was so angry about what happened, I went to him and offered my support. I told him I would come to Okriki and find out how Kevin got involved in it all.'

'That was when you put the file together –'

'Yes. But I couldn't find out anything beyond what you read in there. And Emeka was getting impatient.'

'Who suggested assassinating the Chief?'

There's silence for a beat, then Chika looks at me with a cold smile on his face. 'The Chief was not the only target.'

It takes me a moment to find my voice.

'You can't mean … He wanted you to go after the killers?'

Chika's silence is a confirmation.

'If that was the plan,' I choke out, 'why did he hire me?'

'I started doubting everything when I found out Kevin was part of a cult. It threw me and made me wonder if there were more things I could be wrong about. I don't have the expertise to confirm what I found out and I told Emeka this. He didn't agree and I couldn't tell him what I knew about Kevin. I told him I'm not a detective and if I'm going to be asked to kill anyone, I needed to be sure they deserved to die. That's when he told me about your dad saying that you were back in the country.'

'I was a verification exercise?'

That shrug again. 'You can call it that –'

There will be enough time to reflect on this blow to my ego. For now, I need to know. 'You say it's not only the Chief …'

Chika walks to the desk, opens his laptop, and there is a sheet of paper lying on the keyboard. He seems to consider for a brief second, then he hands me the paper.

It is a list of names, all fitting onto the A4 paper, typed, double spaced. Many of them I recognise from the list of the suspects initially arraigned in the Okriki murder trial. I look back at Chika, who is now shaking his head like someone who needs to wake up from a bad dream.

'I couldn't do it, Philip. I just couldn't. Especially when we found out there might be a real killer out there. I couldn't pull that trigger knowing what we were uncovering.'

'That's why you missed.'

'But he won't stop. I know Emeka. He'll either find someone else or do it himself.'

I look back down at the paper in my hands. Below Chief Kinikanwo's name are about a dozen others, which all become a blur as soon as my eyes rest on one.

Salome Briggs.

PILLOW TALK

It's late when I get back to my room. Folake is still awake, reading in bed. When I close the door, she takes off her reading glasses and lifts some papers.

'You've read this? I saw it on your desk.'

I start taking my night dose of painkillers and antibiotics. 'Not yet.' I am still reeling from what Chika told me and the list.

'Did you speak to the student who wrote this?'

'Yes, why?'

'Do you know there's mention of Godwin as a witness for the police because he had first-hand knowledge of this Momoh's alleged homosexual activities?'

'I would imagine that's the whole point of the paper,' I say as I get into bed.

I give her a quick rundown of Kevin's #justice4momoh campaign.

Folake frowns and shakes her head. 'I've read tons of case notes, but this one reads like a witness report, at least in the background section. The legal arguments are brilliant, but the notes, impressions and insights, they are too – how shall I say? – first-hand.'

'The boy knows his stuff. A lot of what he told Chika and me led to the breakthroughs we've made so far.'

Folake looks at the papers in her hand again. 'Professor Esohe. I know of him …'

'He's the Dean of the Law Faculty.'

'You spoke to him?'

'Not yet.' And perhaps never, I think inwardly. Knowing the real reason for being hired has shaken me, and for now, I have no plan whatsoever beyond looking for a way to convince Emeka to forget his plans for the people on that hit list. But I can't tell Folake this, so I try to distract her – and my turbulent thoughts – by ignoring the pain to my side and pulling her close.

'Do you think you can put that article away for a moment?' I ask suggestively.

But there's a stiffness to her, and an unwillingness to melt into my arms as she did in the past. I look at her, frowning, and search for a clue as to what she is thinking. She looks back at me, as if doing the same, but her body arches away from my embrace.

'I assure you I'm healing very nicely if that's what's worrying you.' My attempt at a joke, but it seems to fall flat, because she pulls herself out of my arms decisively and turns to place the papers on the bedside table next to her.

I hold her from the back and when I simulate a spooning positioning, she doesn't move away, but I can feel her body tense, as if she wants to bolt.

'Sweet?' I say to the back of her head, tentatively.

She doesn't answer me but I can feel she's alert, coiled like a cat ready to spring. I tighten my hold.

We stay like that for a while, and then her body heaves and I sense she's crying. I stay still and wait. Perhaps talking about it will give me the opportunity to tell her that I've forgiven her. Maybe it's my brief brush with mortality or the simple, undeniable fact that I do love my wife, but from the moment I saw Folake at the foot of my hospital bed, I knew I had moved on. All I want to know is what I may have done to push her into the arms of another man.

'I blamed myself,' Folake cuts into my thoughts.

'Pardon?' I'm not sure I heard correctly. I pull her closer, ignoring the pain in my side and hoping she'll turn around and let me see her face.

She doesn't but rather manoeuvres out of my arms and climbs out of the bed. I watch as she pulls the hotel's bathrobe around herself and walks to the window. She's silent as she looks out at the night sky and I steel myself and wait.

'What happened with Soji, my GA, I blamed myself,' she says to the window, 'that's why I said nothing.'

I swear I can hear my heart beat in the silence that follows her words.

'I liked him, and maybe I was too open with him,' she continues, and I strain to hear because she is turned away from me and her voice is low. 'He's a sharp boy, quick thinking and has a legal mind well above his experience. I took him under my wing. I think I saw him as a friend of sorts. I confided in him and encouraged him to do the same. In the States, it would have been okay. But here –' She looks at me then, her eyes filled regret, 'I guess I crossed a line.'

She turns back to the window and sighs very deeply. She wipes her face with a hand and as much as it breaks my heart to see her in distress, I know her well enough to stay on the bed and let her speak.

'He made a pass at me, Phil. He thought all my attention meant I was attracted to him and he made a pass. He confessed his apparent love for me. Even when I told him that he was being inappropriate, he didn't listen. He got … quite physical.' She turns to face me and smiles bitterly. 'You must have walked away before I pushed him off and told him to find another PhD supervisor.'

'The bastard!' The young man is lucky not to be in my vicinity.

'I felt dirty, cheap, available.'

I get up and walk to her as she is turning back to the window. I try to pull her into my arms but she resists.

'You are reporting him –' I say indignantly.

She turns to face me, wiping tears away. 'What good will it do? I am a female lecturer in a university system riddled with sexual assault cases from lecturers to students. Can you picture how I would be painted? Returnee American lecturer who doesn't know where to draw the line?' She shakes her head and rushes on as she sees I don't agree with her summation. 'He was misguided. Young. Definitely stupid. I was the one who should've known better and kept the lines unblurred. I was the older, wiser one and I felt there was something about me, about my behaviour that made it seem okay for him to *think* he could do that. And, yes,' she looks down and away from me, 'I also thought maybe I should've seen something, suspected something. And that if I didn't see or suspect something, it was because a part of me was flattered. That was when I started feeling ashamed.'

I want to tell her she has done nothing to be ashamed of and that it is I who should be ashamed for not trusting her. Not being there to protect her.

She lets out a deep breath into the brief silence. 'In the States, I wouldn't have thought twice about bringing a

disciplinary action against him. But here, well, it's new territory. Who would believe me? He's young, good looking and
smart. I am middle-aged –'

'Hardly!' I protest. 'Besides, you're a brilliant lawyer –'

'A woman first. Of course, I can argue my case very
convincingly. The point is, do I want to? Do I need to?'

'Yes!' I am emphatic, but I see where she is going and a
part of me is sad. In less than a year after coming back to
this country, my wife, whose nickname at the University
of San Francisco was 'Black Pantheress' may have lost her
fighting spirit. A part of me wonders what caused this. What
made us leave the States or come back to Nigeria?

'You can't let him get away with it. I won't let him –'

'You will,' she says firmly. 'You have to. Besides, think of
the children. What will reporting him do to them? They're
only just finding their way in that school. What would I
have achieved but just draw attention to myself and distract
from my career?'

'So, he'll get away with it?' I spit out bitterly.

'I told you, I am not sure I didn't encourage him. I can't
honestly say I never wondered what if I wasn't married,
with kids –'

The image of Salome flashes through my mind. That list
of names. But this conversation is too important. This, right
here in this room, is *my* life.

'That's why you never said anything?' I ask gently. 'Even
to me?'

'I'm sorry, Philip. I really am. If I had known that was the
reason you were so cold, I would've spoken.'

'But when I did speak, you said nothing.'

'I was angry.' Her voice rises, and a trace of my strong wife emerges. 'I felt you believed the worst of me too quickly and it hurt.'

'I'm sorry,' I say quietly. 'I'm an idiot.'

'As much as I'd like to contradict you ...' Folake shrugs but she's smiling.

'I still want to beat him to a pulp.'

'Not worth it,' she scoffs.

I pull her close. 'I disagree.'

She doesn't move away. 'What?'

'That you're not worth it.'

'I mean he's not –'

I cover her lips with mine, stemming words that no longer have any bearing on now, or the future.

When she finally gives up her lips to mine, her shoulders relax, and she puts her arms around me. I pause, look into her eyes and search for any doubt about me, her and us. I see none.

When I gently pull her towards the bed, she follows me.

TMI

I am waiting for Chika at breakfast the next morning. I stop myself from tapping on the sheaf of stapled papers where I have highlighted several portions of text. I can't afford to be impatient. Care must be taken from this point on, especially with Folake being here. Less than two weeks ago, working with several unknowns, I could never have thought that I was in any kind of danger. But Godwin's murder, the attack on Chika and me and now, the possibility of Emeka planning a series of assassinations, all combine to make me decidedly on edge.

I can't endanger Folake's life, yet how can I avert the disaster that I feel is imminent ever since Chika showed me the hit list? If I was hired simply to confirm who truly deserved to be punished, with death no less, for the killing of the Okriki Three, would it not be irresponsible to walk away? Especially now that I know most, if not all of the people on that list did not deserve the fate Emeka has in store for them?

Chika comes into the restaurant and I wave at him. When he gets closer I can see he hardly slept. His eyes are bloodshot and because he has not shaven, he looks unkempt.

He barely settles down before I push the document at him. He looks at me quizzically.

'Philip, I told you I was fired –'

'Yes, but I wasn't. And I am on the clock here. Emeka gave me a week to get the job done, so I effectively have three days to give him enough information to stop him from doing what you told me he is hell-bent on doing.'

'What are you saying?'

I take a sheet of paper from under my coffee mug and hand it over.

'That's your booking here at the Tropicana on my account for those three days. All paid for.'

'Philip, I can't –'

'I know you have a pregnant wife and you have a life in Lagos.' I lower my voice and lean closer to him. 'And after what you did to Chief Omereji, you really shouldn't be around here. But we can't walk away now, knowing what we know and what Emeka is planning.'

Chika looks at me and then at the paper in his hand. 'I'm not sure anything can change Emeka's mind.'

'We can try, and the only way I can think of doing that is presenting him with the facts.'

'We don't have that.'

'Which is why you should read this.'

'All that?' Chika wrinkles his nose as he takes in the cover page. 'I am not fond of academic papers.'

I chuckle. 'You don't have to read the whole thing. Lucky for you, I have highlighted key areas that should be of interest.'

Chika drops his hotel booking form, picks up the document and flips through. I wait for him to get to the sections I marked. If I am correct, his expression should prove that I am on the right track.

347

He frowns slightly, sits up a bit more and reads: '"With the anti-gay bill, using an archaic indecency act, the government of the Federal Republic of Nigeria has effectively weaponised its citizenry, turning neighbours, families and communities on each other ..."'

'That word: "weaponised". It got me thinking about our conversation last week. Remember I said "Outsourced violence"?'

Chika frowns slightly, then he nods as recollection comes to him.

'Continue.'

Chika flicks through more pages and stops to read. '"Was Momoh Kadiri handed over to the police for contravening the indecency act or was he a victim of inter-cult rivalry within a university that has yet to find ways to ..."' Chika looks at me, his eyes round. 'You think Tamuno knew Kevin was in a cult?'

'I don't know, but if you read all the highlighted areas, you will see that Tamuno knew a lot. Folake calls it pre-knowledge.'

'How's madam? Is she not coming down for breakfast?'

'Folake would gag if she saw all this.' I wave my hand towards the buffet. 'She is definitely not a breakfast person.'

'Did you tell her what I told you –'

'No, no. Besides, I was still nursing a bruised ego from what you told me last night.' I smile wryly.

Chika goes back to the document. 'To be fair, Tamuno did say he knew a lot about the case, but the police were not willing to listen.'

'Yes, but go to page eight, in the conclusion section.'

Chika flips through and pauses on the last page. '"Without clear protocols for presenting evidence of homosexual activities, the anti-gay bill places every citizen in danger. In the case of Momoh Kadiri, the police never questioned the source of a tip-off from a prepaid telephone number that was not even registered with the network provider."'

His head snaps up, his eyes wide. It was the reaction I had hoped for.

'Exactly,' I say, nodding. 'He used Omereji's words. So, my question is, if Tamuno said he got no joy in getting the police to listen to what he had to say about the Okriki Three, how did he have access to information that suggests he has contacts with at least one member of the police force there or he knows something only the police know?'

'I see what you mean. The boy knows a lot more than he told us.'

'He gave answers to the questions we asked. It will be interesting to speak to him now that we know so much more. Are you in?'

Chika gives me a wide smile. 'An all-expense-paid stay at the Tropicana and a chance to get to the bottom of all this? You bet I am.'

SAME, NOT SAME

Back in my hotel room, I explain to Folake why I need to go to the State University. She is not convinced, but I think I must have conveyed a sense of urgency, because soon she is making me promise to take it easy. I ask her if she wants to go with me and she flat out refuses to come anywhere near Okriki, except for Mercy's father's invitation to the thanksgiving service and lunch.

'And that's because I am grateful for what he did for you,' Folake says emphatically.

I am happy about this, to be honest. The less exposure to Okriki, the better for all of us. As if on cue, my phone beeps, and I check the message.

'*I hope you're feeling better. Please let me know when we can speak, I want to run something by you.*' I frown.

'Who is it?' Folake asks.

'It's from Inspector Omereji ...'

'The one whose father was shot? Did they find the shooter?'

I hope not, but what does the Inspector want from me? 'I don't know, Sweet, but Chika and I are going to TSU anyway, so I will drop in. You're sure you'll be okay?'

Folake settles further into the bed. 'I promise you I will be fine.'

I kiss her and rush off to join Chika, promising to contact Elechi Opara for his address and that of the church where the thanksgiving service will take place.

When Chika and I get to TSU, we drive straight to Harcourt Whyte Hall.

There is haste in our steps as we alight from the car and climb the many stairs to Room 481, but since my morning dose of tramadol is still in effect, I can almost keep up with Chika. But still –

'Slow down!' I cry out.

'Sorry.' But he does reduce his pace.

We are now on the fourth floor and by the time we get to 481, I've regained my breath. Some of it.

Chika knocks on the door. No answer. Another knock and the door is yanked open, by a dishevelled-looking Tamuno.

'What?!' he barks out so loudly Chika and I take a step back.

I notice he is not wearing his glasses, but his eyes are sharp and alert, even when he squints in sudden recognition. I see him try to arrange his face into something close to what we saw at our first meeting more than a week ago.

'Hello? Dr Taiwo, right?'

'Yes, and you remember my colleague, Chika.'

Tamuno seems impatient. 'Yes, yes. Can I help you?'

'We just have some more questions regar—'

'I'm busy now,' Tamuno interrupts rudely.

Chika leans forward slightly. 'We just want to clarify –'

'I'm busy. Visitor –' His eyes dart into the room and come back to us in a suggestive wink. 'Guys, don't come in and spoil my show.' He lowers his voice to a conspiratorial whisper. 'Come back another time!'

Tamuno closes the door on us firmly.

Chika and I look at each other.

'Is that the same guy –?' Chika says, shaking his head in wonder.

Even the cadence of Tamuno's speech was different. Compared to our first visit when he spoke in measured tones, giving the impression of private schooling and impeccable manners, today he sounded like a rap artist trying to find a rhyme.

I consider banging on the door again until Tamuno is forced to open it, just to be sure of what we just witnessed. Yet I get a strong sense that the young man I just saw is prone to aggression. After what I know of Chika, such aggression will certainly lead to a violence that will be counterproductive. I must find another way to speak to Tamuno. Urgently.

We walk back to the Land Cruiser and explore our options. One of them is forcing another interview via the Dean of the Law Faculty.

'Folake says she knows of him,' I say, trying to be careful of my bandaged chest as I get in the car. 'We can't keep waiting for the approval letter from Ikime's office.'

'I guess it's true,' Chika muses as he starts the car. 'These kids are one thing in front of elders and another when they're alone.'

'That's the point, Chika,' I say, replaying the scene at Room 481. 'We were the same elders he was respectful to when we met before. What changed today?'

Chika considers, 'Maybe he's on drugs or something. Drugs do that, right? Make you one thing this moment, and another in the next?'

I'm not sure I agree, even if in theory this is true. I remember the look on this Tamuno's face. Sharp. Alert. He didn't look spaced out. It was his demeanour, the way he carried himself and the aura that was different.

I turn to Chika. 'You know I have twin boys.' Chika nods, and I continue. 'They're monozygotic –'

'Identical.'

I nod. 'Spitting image. But I've never mistaken them for each other. Even when they were babies, their personalities were distinct. I can tell who is who from the walk, the gestures and even their speech patterns. Folake's even better than me. She can *feel* them. She's never, ever mixed them up.'

'You're saying maybe Tamuno has a twin?'

'I don't know, but I was really taken with him when we met him, so I studied him.'

'And?' Chika prompts.

'That guy back there is not the same Tamuno we met at the Students' Village.'

A SOURCE OF MISCHIEF

It would have been insensitive to ask Chika to join me for my meeting with Inspector Omereji.

'I'll be quick. I am just curious about what he wants to share ...'

Chika nods, clearly uncomfortable around the town from the way his face is set like he is expecting the worst, eyes darting around.

'Perhaps you could call Ikime's secretary to check on that clearance to speak with Professor Esohe. If it's going to take longer, I can ask Folake to talk to him ...'

'On it,' Chika says as he brings out his cell phone.

I enter the police station and, without acknowledging anyone, head straight to Inspector Omereji's office. I am a bit surprised that no one tries to stop me, although their tense gazes are trained on me. I suspect the Inspector must have told them of his invitation.

When I get to his office, his demeanour is different from the last time we saw, even if he still looks a lot worse for wear.

'You came,' he says, standing to greet me. 'I said at your convenience.'

'I know. But we were in the neighbourhood.' I weigh the wisdom of telling him about our meeting with Tamuno and decide against it. No relevance. Yet.

'Okay.' He motions me to sit, but I don't move.

'Mike, your message. Does it have anything to do with the boys who attacked Chika and me?'

'Not really. But it has a lot to do with the tension in this whole town.'

I am curious and a bit confused. 'And you wanted to see me?'

'I spoke to my cousin and googled you. I saw your area of expertise. Quite impressive.'

I suspect this is the highest praise I'm ever going to get from the Inspector but if it prompted his asking for a meeting, I'll take what I can get.

'So, please, I'd like your thoughts on something here, Philip,' he says, waving me to come closer.

Philip. Must be serious. I walk quickly to stand behind him and bend towards his laptop screen.

The Inspector opens some files, and I immediately see that they are screenshots of Twitter and Facebook messages.

'What's this?' I ask after reading some of the posts; incredulous and revolted at such a level of vitriol in the name of religion.

'About four, maybe six months ago, no one is sure, a slew of social media messages about Okriki started flooding the Internet. No one paid any mind. The town had been the subject of such a storm before, so we ignored it. After a few weeks, they became more specific –' Omereji points at the Facebook page. 'This guy, Alfurquran, is a Muslim and seems to be fomenting a lot of anti-Christian sentiments on social media.'

'Anti-Christians in Okriki specifically?'

'Yes. This is not some random person anywhere in the world; this person is right here amongst us. And he seems to have made a counterpart …'

Inspector Omereji clicks and screenshots of several messages from another Twitter handle fill the screen. If Alfurquran is reminiscent of extreme jihadists all over the world, then @NoOtherGodbutJesus takes the prize for unbridled hatred backed up by specific quotes from the Bible. And his following is huge. It saddens me that such fanatics can attract so many admirers.

'You think this is where all the tension is coming from?' I ask Omereji.

He nods. 'We *know* this is where it's coming from. Look at this one from this Christian guy – he calls for the burning of the only mosque in Okriki. Look at how many likes he got ...'

I peer closer to the screen. 'Seven thousand two hundred and three. Wow. What're you going to do about it?'

'Well, here's the thing. I managed to use my contacts with Interpol and the cybercrime unit of the police force –' Omereji must have seen my expression. 'Yes, Dr Taiwo, the Nigerian Police does have a cybercrime unit.'

I raise my hands and respond in my best American accent, 'I didn't say nuttin.'

He turns back to the laptop. 'We were trying to trace the IP addresses where the messages are coming from.'

He clicks again, and a row of IP addresses scroll up the screen –

'There are a lot.' I peer closer at the screen, frowning at the random addresses. 'That means it's not one person –'

'Or it's not one computer. But they all have one thing in common. All these addresses are from cybercafes operating in TSU.'

I am taken aback. 'TSU? Are you sure?'

'I am. And before you think it's a bunch of kids causing mischief, look here.'

He points to the latest set of IP addresses with more recent dates.

'Notice anything?'

'They're all the same.'

'Exactly. One, all the messages now seem to be coming from one IP address. Two –'

I finish it for him. 'Alfurquran and Christian are using the same computer and/or IP address.' I look at him. 'Why're you telling me this?'

'Because you understand human nature. And you have a visitor's eyes. What happened to those three boys, was that normal to you?'

'But it happened, Mike,' I say gently. 'You may wish it hadn't because you love your people, but it did.'

'But *why* did it happen?' He sounds pained, so I let him speak. 'Were the people not pawns then as they are being made pawns now in the hands of this Alfurquran and/or Christian?'

I think about this for a beat, and perhaps doubt shows on my face because Inspector Omereji continues.

'Look, I know it sounds crazy, but I have seen it happen before. A couple of years ago, there were a number of violent clashes between religious groups in Jos. You know the place?'

I nod.

'Up there in the middle belt. A normally peaceful city that has had Muslims and Christians living in harmony for years and years. The violence was so sudden, so surprising, no one could explain it. The police deployed extra men to investigate the source. It started just like this. Social media posts fomenting intolerance. I was part of the investigating team. For months we tried to trace where the posts and bulk messages originated from. When we finally made a breakthrough, with Interpol's help, you know where they were coming from?'

I shake head.

'A flat in Brixton, all the way in London.'

'But why?'

'No one knows.' The Inspector shrugs. 'When UK police stormed the place, they saw all the computers but could not find anyone. They are still searching. Point is, someone or some people were manipulating people, using them.'

I nod. Hyper-targeting. Using data to manipulate public opinion and perception. It's been used in advertising and even changed the outcome of elections. I can believe it being done by a group of people in Europe and the US, but that required expertise and a lot of resources. I try to explain this to the Inspector.

'What happened in Jos was some years back, Philip. Today, more people have smartphones than ever, and you don't need that much data to create messages like these. Especially when it's about religion in a small town like ours.'

Since I started my investigation, I've been working on the assumption that the disorganised socio-political system, environment and culture of chaos combined to create the tragedy of the Okriki Three. I wanted to believe that the failure of systems in the country had forced people to become self-reliant; creating solutions that were not sustainable in themselves but which served immediate needs. Lack of water? Dig your own well. Lack of electricity? Get a generator. Lack of security? Create vigilantes.

This was easier to understand because it made sense. The people of Okriki killed three young men because they had been robbed before. Because they got scared when they heard gunshots. Because, because –

But what Omereji is now suggesting is even more chilling. That some mischief maker is weaponising the chaos and rage within people to foment unrest.

Outsourced violence.

'I'm not done yet.'

I look from the computer screen to Mike Omereji. 'There's more?'

'That IP address –' He points to the screen, 'has been traced to Harcourt Whyte Hall specifically.'

GUN GONE

Folake is in good spirits when I get back to the hotel. She shows off the hamper of gifts she has put together for Elechi Opara and his family from a supermarket not far from the hotel. I tell her she shouldn't have, but she insists again that it's the least we could do for someone who saved my life. I let it go, not wanting to explain the misgivings I have about being asked to do a psych evaluation of Mercy. Better we view it as a social meeting. Less pressure.

We exchange tidbits about the day, with my impressions of Tamuno being the highlight of mine.

'You think drugs?'

I shake my head. 'No. He was too alert, too present. His pupils were not dilated, his speech was measured, at least after he recognised us.'

Her expression becomes sceptical when I speculate about the possibility of the young man having a dissociative disorder or even a split personality.

'And don't say psychobabble nonsense,' I say, trying to tease, but not quite succeeding.

Folake looks at me with regret. 'I said I was sorry.'

I love it when my feisty wife admits being wrong. It's a rare event so when it happens, I tend to milk it for all it's worth.

'No, you didn't.'

'I did!' She insists and we go back and forth like this for a while, teasing, making up and rediscovering each other. Then, we call our children.

Lara immediately starts complaining about her laptop and how it is beyond ancient even though it's less than a year old.

'That laptop's got selective reasoning, Mom,' Lara says.

'What does that mean?' Folake asks, rolling her eyes.

'It selects when and where it suits it to pick Internet service.'

I butt in quickly because I know where this is headed. 'Lara, you're not getting a new –'

Just then, there's a knock on the door. Folake keeps talking to Lara while I answer it.

Chika's face is cryptic. 'May I see you in private?'

'What's wrong?'

He jerks his head towards where Folake is still talking on speakerphone to Lara. I nod and pop my head into the room to indicate to Folake that I'll be back, close the door and follow Chika to his room.

Inside, he turns to me and speaks in a rush. 'I don't want you to panic, but it's missing, Philip. Someone came into my room and took it –'

'Took what?'

'The rifle!'

'You had it with you all this time? Here? In this room?'

'I couldn't leave it in the Land Cruiser in case the police searched it. I planned to return it to Emeka when he told us what to do next, but he never came –'

'Maybe the room service …?' My voice trails off, unconvincing.

Chika shakes his head. 'I went downstairs and asked around. Emeka's driver was here.'

'How?'

'I don't know!' He waves his key card. 'These things are not hard to clone.'

Someone could have also claimed to have lost their card, and asked for another one. I imagine if someone of Emeka's stature did this, no one would question his right to a new key card. Heck, the man could book a whole suite in the hotel just to get a card.

'So, okay. Emeka took back his gun.' I try to stay calm for Chika's sake. 'That means he got the message that you won't be killing anyone –'

Chika cuts me off with quiet confidence. 'Philip, he's going to use it.'

Chika goes to his desk and picks up a familiar sheet of paper. The targets. 'Each person on this list was carefully researched: their routines, where they are at any given time of day. The Chief, for example, takes a walk between 9 and 10 every night except when he has a community meeting of elders. That happens on Tuesdays from 4 p.m. to 9 p.m. He drinks one small Guinness stout –'

'And Salome?' I interrupt, my voice slightly shaky.

Chika's look is steady on me. 'She goes to the Bar Association's monthly meeting the last Wednesday of the month at 8:30 p.m.'

'Today is … Oh, God!'

'She's the secretary of the State Bar Association. With the exception of when she travels, she *has* to be at the meeting,'

Chika says, in a rush. 'The meeting happens only once a month, Philip. If a sniper misses today, it's another month before another opportunity presents itself at that location.'

I look at my watch. 7:18.

'We have to hurry,' I say as Chika grabs the keys for the Land Cruiser.

RUSH

Chika is driving very fast.

'You know where they'll be?' I ask, after texting Folake a deliberately vague message that Chika and I are following a lead.

'When I was preparing for this hit, I scoped the area around the NBA Secretariat and selected two buildings to shoot from,' Chika says, without taking his eyes off the road. 'You'll see when we get there.'

See how? I want to ask. Because there's been a power failure, and without street lights, it's hard to make out anything. I check the time. 7:59. My sides start to throb and I realise I had not taken tonight's dose of painkillers and antibiotics.

'Are we close?'

'Yes.' He's slowing down the car now, peering into the darkness. 'I think we should park and walk.'

'Why?'

'Because if Emeka is in either of the buildings I selected, he might see us coming.'

Ah. Makes sense.

Chika parks and we race towards the Secretariat.

'See, that's it over there –' Chika points, and despite the darkness, I can see the Secretariat is almost in front of the Judicial Service Commission where the Okriki Three case is being heard. There's a lot of activity inside. The building is situated in the business district, but it stands out tonight as the only building that has electricity.

8:03.

I look around. 'Which buildings did you select?'

'It's either this one,' Chika points at a building about ten storeys high, which the illuminated wall signs proclaim as housing mostly legal and accounting firms. It squarely faces the Secretariat. But apart from the signage, which must be running on rechargeables, it's all dark. Even the entrance is manned by a security guard who is using his cell phone to read a rumpled newspaper.

'– or that one.' Chika points at another building.

Of course. While not quite in front of the Bar Association, the building is a taller one that has a National Bank branch in it. The ATM section has downlights, and we can hear the rumble of a generator in the distance.

'It's this one,' Chika says confidently, looking up. 'He would've been able to scope out the place because his bank has offices here.'

'But I can't see any light –' I strain to see any kind of movement through the windows.

'The rifle has night vision. Come, I think I know where he'll be –'

He runs into the building, but the pain does not allow me to run as fast. I get to him just as a flashlight shines on us.

'Where you dey go?' a voice thunders.

Chika smiles as if he's not blinded by the light. He waves the keys to the Land Cruiser and his hotel key card. 'I work here o, my brother. I forget something –'

'You get ID?' the security guard barks out.

'I get my key now … if I no work here, I go get key?'

There's a pause, then –

'And ya friend?' the guard asks, his tone suspicion laden.

'I no wan leave am for car. We no go take long,' Chika answers smoothly.

We wait for a beat; the light on our faces must make us look like clowns frozen in perpetual fake smiles.

'Watch ya step,' the guard says, using the flashlight to wave us in.

Chika whispers, 'We have to take the stairs.'

I check the time on my phone: 8:21. We have to hurry.

I follow Chika, who is now using his phone as a flashlight. After what seems like one million painful steps, we get to the floor Chika believes Emeka will be on just as his phone dies.

'Shit.' I hear him curse in the dark.

I bring out my phone, switch on the iFlashlight –

8:28.

– we are standing in front of a door labelled 'Meeting Room'.

'He's not aiming from his bank?' I ask in an urgent whisper.

'Wrong angle,' Chika whispers back. 'This is the common room for all tenants in the building and faces the Secretariat.'

We enter. It's a big room and pitch dark.

'Call him,' Chika whispers.

'Emeka!' I shout.

'Who's that?'

I walk towards the voice. Chika makes a movement with his hand. I think it means he doesn't want Emeka to know he is with me.

'It's me. Philip.' Our voices are carrying.

'Philip!' A flashlight comes on in my face. I direct my phone in Emeka's face. He squints.

'What are you doing, Emeka?'

'If you're here, you know very well what I'm doing.'

'Emeka, please listen to me. We've made a lot of progress. We know a lot of things about how Kevin died.'

The flashlight moves off my face briefly. I catch a glimpse of Chika crouching on the far-right side of the huge room.

Emeka's voice is ragged with pain. 'I know how he died!'

'Did you know Kevin was running a campaign for his friend who died in police custody? Did you know that he discovered that his friend may have been framed? Did you know that?'

Emeka's tone is at once bitter and pained. 'What does it matter?'

'Oga, the woman has come out o.' Emeka's driver's voice comes from right about the centre of the room, somewhere behind his boss.

I move my light from Emeka's face towards a space behind him to spot the driver's position and perhaps help Chika see better. I don't know if it works because I can barely make out a figure. It's that dark and clearly, Emeka has come prepared because his driver must be dressed in the same dark clothing that he is.

'You're getting your driver to pull the trigger?' I deliberately put a jeer in my tone. Where is Chika? Has he figured out the driver's location and therefore the rifle's exact position? If he has, what he is waiting for?

'I can pull it myself.' Emeka's defensive tone shows my goading worked.

'Oga,' the driver whispers urgently, 'she dey come down step oh.'

'Shoot her,' Emeka orders abruptly.

'You go and pull the trigger, Emeka,' I also whisper urgently. 'If you think Salome Briggs should die, then you pull it. It's not your driver's son who died. It's *your* son.'

'Shoot her!'

The gunshot sounds like a whistle, and in that same instant, I see a body slams into the driver. I rush past Emeka, knocking him over on my way to the window. There is a commotion down at the Bar Association's Secretariat and alarmed noises rise. I see people pointing up, towards where we are.

I turn to the three men on the floor. 'Run!'

LETTING GO

I practically pull Emeka down the stairs until we get to the National Bank branch entrance. We can already hear voices from downstairs demanding to come in. Emeka's driver has keys, and he hurriedly opens the office door. We enter just as the steps and voices pass, climbing higher towards the meeting room from where the shot was fired.

All four of us are breathing heavily and trying to stay quiet. It is still dark, but we can make out each other's faces.

'What took you so long?' I whisper to Chika.

'I couldn't see in the dark!' Chika responds in the same urgent whisper. 'I had to follow his voice to be sure where he was.'

The driver is breathing harshly, shaken.

'They must all die,' Emeka mumbles.

I crawl to him. This powerful man, broken by the loss of his child. Many things scare me in the world, but none paralyse me like the fear of losing any of my children.

'Emeka …'

'Why did you stop me?' Emeka hisses at me.

'You were going to turn your driver into a killer.'

'I would have pulled the trigger myself!'

'And become no better than the people who took your son from you.'

I make out Chika at the water dispenser in a corner. He brings a plastic cup to Emeka. The older man swings his hand like an angry child, and the cup, with its contents, falls.

'They don't deserve to live! All of them! Animals!'

'I have observed that town. There is no peace there, Emeka. Trust me, they're paying for what they did to Kevin and those other boys. But if you had succeeded tonight and if Chika had killed the Chief, how would you live with yourself?'

'I don't want to live,' Emeka answers in a flat voice. 'I want my son back.'

There's a time to console a grieving person. There's also a time to be quiet and let him express his pain. Tonight is neither of those times.

'Emeka,' I say softly, 'Kevin's not coming back.'

Emeka shakes his head, refusing to let my words sink in. 'I want my son. I want to hold my son.'

'Kevin is gone. And you'll always want to hold him, and you'll miss him every day, every second, but the only way you can honour your love for him is through love. Only love.'

'He was such a good boy,' Emeka says, his voice breaking.

'He was raised by a good father,' I say softly.

There, in the darkness, on the floor of one of the branches of the third largest bank in Nigeria, Emeka Nwamadi lets me pull him, shaking, towards me. His head moves from side to side, refusing to accept the irrefutable. My one hand rests firmly on his shoulder while the other gently turns his face towards me. He doesn't stop shaking his head as he looks at me, his eyes large and lost.

'He's gone,' I say gently, nodding. Slowly. My gaze fixed on Emeka. And gradually, the shaking of his head becomes a mirror of my nod.

'He's gone,' Emeka says, as though he's just discovered a painful secret.

I nod. He nods. And then he collapses into my arms. A man who has been strong much longer than he should have.

I hold him like this for a while, mourning the young man who I never met.

It is close to half past eleven when Chika and I leave a somewhat calmer Emeka at the National Bank guest house, where I suspect he has been staying ever since I myself arrived in PH. It was not an easy exit given the man's emotional state, but I am confident that for now at least, his vengeful rage has abated. The presence of the very shaken driver seems to have had a sobering effect on Emeka. By the time Chika and I get into the Land Cruiser, we are relatively sure that the two men will be fine. For now.

We are silent as we drive through the gates of the Tropicana. For some reason, I am only just feeling the pain in my ribs now. The power of adrenaline. I rub the bandages through my shirt. Everything seems intact, but I can feel the inflammation. I need my pain meds.

While waiting for the elevator in the quiet lobby, Chika looks at me and speaks for the first time since we drove away from the National Bank guest house.

'Thank you for not telling him about Kevin ... you know, about him being in a cult.'

'What good would it do?' I exhale. 'What would it add? Besides, we are now fairly sure that the cult is not the reason why he was killed.'

'But thank you all the same. Emeka wouldn't have believed that I didn't know.'

'No, thank you for trusting me. For telling me.'

He nods and we are silent again when the elevator arrives. When the doors open on our floor, we step out and say goodnight.

'Philip?' Chika calls when I'm at my door.

I turn to face him.

'This isn't over, is it?'

I hold his gaze for a moment. 'No. We still have work to do.'

He nods. 'Goodnight.'

'Night.'

Folake is sitting up in bed when I let myself in, waiting.

'You just disappeared,' she says.

'We had an emergency. I sent you a text.'

'I saw it and tried to call –'

Using my cell phone as a flashlight for so long ran down the battery, but if I say that, then I'll have to tell her why and what happened. And who I was saving from Emeka's vengeful quest. I keep quiet.

She looks at me coolly. 'This emergency, does it have anything to do with that woman? The woman at the hospital. Salome?'

I stay silent.

'She called the room. Said she saw your missed call and wanted to ask if you're all right.'

'She's been very kind.'

'That's all you're going to say? "She's been very kind"?'

We're looking at each other like two people afraid to start a conversation for fear where it will go.

'Nothing happened, Folake.'

'Today or before?'

'Both.'

'Did you want something to happen?'

I walk to my side of the bed and reach for my medicines.

'You won't answer my question?'

I look at her squarely, 'Because there's nothing to say. We're friends. Nothing more.'

For a tense moment, I think she's going to insist.

'I think I'll have a bath,' she announces in a flat tone. She goes into the bathroom and closes the door with a finality that lets me know not to follow her.

LIGHT AND DARK

You won't get away with it.

John Paul's head snaps up from the laptop. He looks around wildly. When he sees that he is indeed alone, he smiles. He shakes his head slightly, and sniggers.

You killed her! I scream from the shadows.

He turns back to the laptop and speaks under his breath, like one would to a child who refuses to sit still.

'She was talking of going to the police. We can't have that.'

You didn't have to kill her.

He doesn't look up from the laptop. 'She was dead anyway. Stage 4 cancer. Did her a favour. Now the plan must go on.'

He is now typing furiously; the clatter of the keyboard is loud in the small room.

I don't want to do this any more.

I can hear myself, and I am sure I sound petulant. Weak, even.

But I am scared. Too much is happening too fast. Too many unknowns. Too many questions being asked. I also know that ever since John Paul placed that pillow over Mama's head, I have become more afraid of him than of the risk of The Final Plan going awry.

We can stop, I say, in case he did not hear me from the shadows.

John Paul stops typing, looks around, his eyes wildly looking for me. 'You don't mean that.'

You killed Mama.

My pain and anger must have come through in my accusation, because John Paul stands and raises his voice so loud I am sure he can be heard across the hall.

'For you! For us!' John Paul's eyes seem to become steady and it's almost like he can see me, standing there in front of him. He lowers his voice. 'She was weak. Just like you. She had to go.'

She had no choice.

John Paul clenches his fist, and if I was really standing in front of him, I know he would hit me. He lets out a sharp laugh, mocking and goading me, all at once.

'Everyone has a choice,' he says flatly, and suddenly, his face becomes twisted with anger like I have never seen. 'You ingrate! I saved you from that monster. You were dying, too weak to fight him until I came to your rescue. Where was your dear mother then?'

With this, John Paul gives a long, drawn out hiss and walks back to the laptop. He starts to type again.

I don't want more people to die.

'Everyone dies,' he says to the screen.

MERCY, MERCY

Chika pretends not to notice the coolness between Folake and me. As we drive into Okriki, towards the Oparas' home, he points out places of interest to Folake and she ramps up her enthusiasm as a way of avoiding talking to me.

To say I'm perplexed would be an understatement. Women are strange. Here I am, ready to forgive and forget when I suspected she had cheated on me, and she is determined to punish me for a crime I only *thought* of committing.

My phone rings.

'Hi, Philip. I just wanted to give you feedback. The IP address,' Inspector Omereji says.

'Yes!' I exclaim, causing Chika and Folake to pause their exchange. I lower my voice. 'What happened?'

'There's been an increase in activity from Harcourt Whyte Hall, the messages are coming almost every half hour –'

'From both of them? Alfurquran and Christian?'

'Yes. And they're getting worse. More personal in some cases. Alfurquran sent one about an hour ago claiming to know who is causing hatred in Okriki and that he'll send proof in a couple of hours. He's asking all his Muslim brothers to be on standby –'

'That can't be good.' I can sense Chika and Folake listening intently to my side of the conversation.

'No, it's not. We've asked the local government to support our appeal for a curfew, but they're refusing because they say there's no danger. My father is not well enough to call a meeting of the Council of Chiefs.'

'What will you do now?'

'I made an urgent application to the TSU to come on campus with my team and look around, but the Registrar just says he'll get back to me within the hour. That was three hours ago.'

'I'm also around now. I can drop in at the station later.'

'Good. Let's compare notes. I'll keep you posted.'

Then there's a pause on the other end, and I just know he's going to ask. I have my answer ready.

'Philip, something happened yesterday. To Salome, well not to her directly but –'

'Is she okay?' I cut in.

'Yes. Yes. But I want to know. Were you with your friend Chika all yesterday?'

My 'yes' rings true and confident. There's an awkward silence in the car when I hang up.

'What was that about?' she asks, curious in spite of her annoyance with me.

I hide a relieved smile and quickly share the essentials of the Inspector's side of the conversation.

'You think it's all connected to the Okriki Three?' Folake asks from the back seat.

'I don't know,' I answer honestly. 'It doesn't fit, but there's something there.'

We're now in the neighbourhood where the GPS says Elechi Opara lives. It is quite genteel and comprised of the more white-collar indigenes of Okriki. I call Opara and he picks up almost instantly and confirms we are on the right street and that he'll be standing outside his house, so we don't miss it.

As soon as we enter the Oparas' house, we are introduced to his three daughters, including Mercy, who is looking much better than when I saw her at the hospital. According to Elechi, she's been home now for almost a week, and so far there's been no indication of a possible breakdown.

'She's been sleeping through the night. No bad dreams or crying,' he says when the girls go off to tell their mom of our presence.

Amaka, Elechi's wife, comes in and she quickly puts us at ease with a wide smile, asking us to sit and offering us drinks.

'Food is after the church service but we have prepared something to hold the stomach until then,' Amaka says after she is reassured of our comfort.

We say we'd rather wait until after the service and hand over our thank-you gifts. Chika sits with Folake, as Amaka continues to fuss over them, still insisting that they eat something.

I pull Elechi aside to talk about Mercy. While I am not ready to give an opinion of her condition yet, I want to be sure he is aware of the danger of her being in a large crowd.

'You're right,' he nods in appreciation. 'We discussed the thanksgiving with her doctor, and he says as long as she takes her medication, she'll be fine. The other day, he asked us to do a test run of sorts. I drove Mercy and her sisters to the market and she seemed fine. I told the doctor this.'

This feedback pleases me. It might be that if Mercy is with family members, she can handle the challenges of being in open spaces with people. This is consistent with the responses of people that have experienced trauma in a public space or had it brought on by the actions of strangers, like Mercy's witnessing the killing of her boyfriend.

I discuss the medication she is on and share my concern regarding the high dosage of clonazepam for a condition I think may be better addressed by psychotherapy and counselling. I pass on the name of a psychiatrist friend at the University of Lagos and ask Elechi to consult with him before Mercy's next visit to her doctor in PH. He thanks me and calls Mercy to come join us.

'Dr Taiwo has been giving advice about your condition. Thank him for us,' Elechi instructs her, and despite my protests, she obeys her father.

'Did you write your report?' she asks.

It takes me a second to remember the cover story Chika and I had given her at the hospital. 'We're still working on it.'

'Why is it taking so long?'

I consider telling a version of the truth and look around to gauge our semi-privacy. The other daughters have joined in the conversation with their mother, Chika and Folake. I look back at Mercy and decide to risk telling the truth.

'Mercy, we have too many questions. And the most important is not knowing what Kevin was doing at Godwin's compound that day –'

She frowns. 'But sir, I told you. He went to see Tamuno.'

'Yes, you did. And we spoke to Tamuno.'

'Is he saying it's not true?'

'On the contrary, he said he was late for his meeting with Kevin and blames himself –'

'Meeting?'

379

'Tamuno says he and Kevin were working on a paper regarding Momoh's death.'

Mercy gives a dry laugh. 'There's no way Kevin and Tamuno Princewill were doing anything together.'

The back of my head starts tingling. 'Why?'

'Sir, they couldn't stand each other. Also, Kevin found out that Godwin knew that Momoh was set-up and Godwin told him Tamuno was the one who did it.'

'Chika?' I try to keep my voice level, but the urgency carries. 'Come, please.'

Chika leaves Mercy's sisters and comes over, while Elechi hovers like a guard dog. Folake and Amaka stop talking when they see the attention Mercy is getting.

'Mercy,' I ask gently, 'are you saying Kevin thought Tamuno had something to do with Momoh's death?'

'No, sir. I'm saying Godwin told Kevin that Tamuno was the one that planted those pictures on Momoh's phone.'

I can hear Folake gasp behind me, but my eyes are on the young woman.

'But if Kevin knew this, why did he go to Tamuno?' I ask.

'Kevin didn't believe Godwin. Everyone knows he's on drugs and tells stories. Kevin wanted to confront Tamuno and they planned to meet at Godwin's place.'

Chika moves to my side. 'Are you sure?'

Mercy takes a deep breath. I can see she's trying to stay calm. 'I'm sure, sir. I told him not to go. That Momoh was dead anyway. But Kevin is stubborn. I never liked that Tamuno guy. That's why I rushed there when I didn't hear from Kevin.'

To be sure, I ask, 'Tamuno was the one who invited Kevin to come to him?'

'Yes,' Mercy answers with a confident nod.

ARROW OF WRATH

It takes an enormous amount of control for Chika and me not to rush out of the Oparas' house and go looking for Tamuno. But it will be rude to leave when the thanksgiving service we came for is yet to start.

'I'm sure Elechi would understand, given the circumstances,' Folake is saying, as Chika drives behind Elechi towards the church where the service is to take place.

'Yes, but if I am right, then I think it's prudent to have Inspector Omereji there when we question Tamuno.'

'Is that not premature?' Folake frowns.

'He invited Kevin to Godwin's compound,' Chika says. 'Which means he most likely pointed him out to the mob.'

'He didn't tell us he saw Kevin that day, or that he was even at the compound the day the boys were killed,' I say, struggling with the idea that this Tamuno could have orchestrated the death of three of his schoolmates.

'That's weird ...' Folake says from behind. I turn to follow her gaze.

We're driving past the cannon at the roundabout. Normally, cars and people zip past with hawkers making desperate attempts to sell their wares. But today, the traffic is slower, and the pedestrians are gathered in little groups, talking animatedly, some looking at their cell phones and gesturing angrily. I try to shake off a sense of foreboding.

I share Omereji's fears with Chika and Folake, and suggest that it's possible this might be the reason why the townspeople seem tense and agitated.

'Surely people can't believe so much nonsense without at least trying to know where it's coming from?' Folake asks with exasperation.

'People are generally more likely to go with popular opinion than dissent. It's not unique to Okriki,' I answer drily.

Chika kisses his teeth with irritation. 'But this town takes the cake. Everyone's on edge. Always ready to believe the worst of each other.'

We've now left the town centre and are on a less crowded street. Elechi's car slows and turns into a large compound with several vehicles already parked in front of a warehouse-like structure with a huge banner proclaiming it as the premises of 'Light of the World Ministries'.

Elechi drives to a less crowded space at the side of the building. Chika follows and parks the Land Cruiser next to Elechi's car.

Elechi walks over. 'We're parking here because we're guests of honour. Mercy's godparents are deacons here. Follow me, and we will enter through the side.'

He waves at an elderly usher, who is smiling broadly and urging us to come his way.

'Let's just show our faces at the service and let Elechi know we can't go back to his house for lunch,' I say to Chika, as we follow the Opara family into the church.

There's singing already coming from inside. The entrance brings us in at the front of the church, right by the pulpit.

We can see the whole congregation as they join the choir in a rousing rendition of a popular praise and worship song translated into Ikwerre. When the congregation of well-wishers see the Oparas, there are loud cheers, yodelling, and hugs. The music rises and changes tempo and Amaka even starts to dance towards the seats the whole family and we ourselves are now being guided to.

We sing praises to the Lord
He reigns!

The singing and dancing go on for quite a while, but, enthralling as it all is, my mind is on Tamuno. Who is he? What is he hiding? Is he working for someone? The personality change the last time Chika and I saw him at Whyte Hall was startling. Could he, like Godwin, be on drugs? Is that what he's hiding? Or was there a sexual relationship between him and Momoh? Otherwise, how could he have conceived of planting lewd pictures on Momoh's phone? Which would more likely drive one to kill: the possibility of being outed or one's drug addiction?

'We serve a God who reigns!' The Pastor's booming voice jolts me to real time.

Elechi leans back and whispers, 'He's the Senior Pastor. Jeremiah Oriakpu. Very charismatic. My wife and I come to evening services here when there's no mass.'

'Our God reigns over everything and every condition,' Pastor Oriakpu declares again.

The congregation shout their agreement with him in Hallelujahs and Amens. I catch Folake's eyes. We are both uncomfortable with extreme displays of faith, being very conservative, lapsed Anglicans ourselves. She nods towards the back of Elechi's head and I understand she's enjoining me to remember why we are here. I'll wait for the right opening.

Several exhortations later, punctuated by more singing, standing, sitting, dancing to the altar, giving of offerings, waving of handkerchiefs and then comes a rather long sermon about the wisdom of thanksgiving. Pastor Oriakpu seems to be taking his time to get to the reason why we are here.

I check my broken but functional watch. We've been here for fifty-two minutes and there's yet no end in sight. I surreptitiously bring out my phone and check if Omereji has sent a message. Folake kicks my foot and I put it away, but not before confirming that there's nothing from him.

'Today, we've come for this special service to thank God for the life of our daughter, Mercy Opara –'

Finally! I almost jump up in my own hallelujah chorus and dance.

The Pastor points at us where we stand with the Opara family. He waves his hand, beckoning the family to the altar.

The Pastor turns to the choir. 'Let's sing a good song of praise as this blessed family comes forward.'

The choir raises another loud song of praise and Elechi motions for us to come forward with his family, I look at Chika who is shaking his head. I point to indicate that it would be rude if we don't join the Oparas at the –

The screams start a nanosecond after my eyes see the arrow shoot over Elechi's head straight into the Pastor's chest. I look back and there are several men in white robes wading into the congregation carrying machetes and bows and arrows.

People are running and screaming. I pull at Folake, while Chika rushes towards the Oparas. He gets to the shocked family just as several of the men in white robes jump up to the pulpit. I am searching for the quickest escape; the entrance we came through is now blocked by men in white robes and skullcaps.

I see Chika pulling the Opara girls into his arms and shielding Mercy by burying her head in his chest. Folake is calling the names of our children in rapid succession like an urgent prayer against my chest, although I can see she is also searching for an escape. But there is none. Every exit is blocked by the men in kaftans and kufis.

My eyes shoot towards the altar and I see two of the men bend as if to check the Pastor's pulse. A pool of blood is spreading from where the arrow pierced his chest. Amidst the screaming and panic, the men by the altar appear supremely calm as they rise up over the Pastor. One of them spits on the still body that I can guess is lifeless, going by the satisfied nods the men exchange.

Then, one of them raises a gun and shoots into the roof. Folake stiffens in my arms but the men standing at the altar appear unfazed, even as debris rains down over their heads.

'Listen and listen carefully!' one of the men shouts and I recognise him as the spokesperson for the Muslims who had brought their grievances before the Chief at the community hall.

Another gun is fired into the side of the altar, away from the choir, and this time there's semi-silence.

'We came for the Pastor!' the man from the community hall shouts. 'A godless man who has blood on his hands. And now, you must leave this place and go to your homes because we are about to do to it what was done to our own place of worship! Now!'

As if on cue, the men blocking the doors move aside and people stampede out of every exit. Chika is ushering the Oparas out by the side entrance and I follow with Folake.

We run towards our cars. I make sure Folake is safely in the back seat of the Land Cruiser and turn back towards the Oparas' car where Chika is helping them. I rush to the side where Mercy is already in the back seat of the car.

'Mercy! Are you okay?'

The girl doesn't speak, but she nods. I look at her and while there's fear in her eyes, there's not enough panic for me to suspect an imminent breakdown. Elechi climbs into the driver's side and starts the car.

'Follow me. I know a way to get home quickly!'

Chika and I run to the Land Cruiser where Folake appears to have calmed down. I jump in the back seat with her and hold her tight, both our hearts pounding.

'Watch out!' Folake exclaims, as Chika steps on the accelerator and tries to avoid people running in different directions. I look behind us at the church building being engulfed by fire.

'What's happening?' Folake asks no one in particular. Chika's focus is determinedly on the road, following Elechi and several other cars.

'It's okay. It's okay. We'll be fine,' I say repeatedly to her, until Chika starts slowing down.

'Why are we stopping? What's goi—?' I stop abruptly as I see the pandemonium ahead of us. People are shouting and pointing. There are some bloodied people on the side of the road. Wounded people are being guided out of a compound.

'The mosque,' Chika says, horrified. 'I think the mosque has been bombed.'

In front of us, I see the smoke rising from the roof of the mosque where the crescent moon and the star are blackened by soot but remain strangely intact.

'... *we are about to do to it what was done to our own place of worship!*' That's what the attackers meant. Someone had attacked the mosque and they believed it was on the order of Pastor Oriakpu.

'Turn around! Turn around! Elechi's turning around, follow him!' There's a tinge of hysteria in Folake's voice, and I'm suddenly overwhelmed with guilt. She wouldn't be here if it were not for me. I think of our children, and my heart pauses and then pumps faster than before. We have to make it out of this.

Chika turns the car wildly around and we are behind Elechi again, driving away from people covered in soot, dust and blood, with black smoke rising high from the roof of the mosque behind us.

RAGING FIRE

'OhmyGodOhmyGod!' Folake is saying over and over, as Chika speeds behind the Oparas' car towards the latter's house.

I hurriedly dial Omereji.

'Alfurquran sent one about an hour ago claiming to know who is causing hatred –'

The rage on the faces of the men running into the church will be with me for a long time. It was not a random rage. It was specifically targeted at that pulpit, and the man standing on it.

The Inspector's phone alternates between going straight to voicemail and giving the engaged tone.

'Send a text,' Folake says.

I start typing, but before I finish, a text comes from the Inspector. I read out: *'Can't talk. Stakeout at Whyte Hall.'*

Chika nods as he drives faster. 'That means he got permission to go on campus –'

The traffic has slowed. We look around, and we can hear the noise coming from the distance. Elechi's car makes another detour on to a gravel road and Chika follows swiftly. I look back and can make out people running and carrying children into the houses that line the road.

Chika steps on the gas till we get to the Oparas' house right behind the distraught Opara family.

Elechi is speaking Ikwerre into his phone, and helping Amaka to guide a shell-shocked Mercy out. I run towards them.

'I'm fine,' Mercy is saying, but I can see she's not. I can only thank heavens that the whole family was facing the congregation, which meant Mercy didn't see the arrow diving over their heads straight into the Pastor's chest.

'I'll take her in,' Amaka says, as the women cooking at the back of the house run to her. They all burst into rapid Ikwerre almost carrying Mercy off her feet into the house.

Elechi gets off the phone just as Chika and Folake reach us.

'They say there's videos of Pastor Oriakpu calling for the Muslims to be removed all over the Internet,' Elechi speaks hurriedly. 'The people who saw the video threw petrol bombs into the mosque and the Muslims got angry. That's why they attacked him at the church. Now, Christians want to retaliate again. You must stay here –'

The Pastor was *killed*, not attacked. But, I don't say this. I look at Chika. 'We can't stay.'

'What?' Folake almost screeches.

I face her. 'We have to go to the campus.'

'Through that mayhem?' She shakes her head. 'Heck, no!'

'Sweet, we have to go. This is all related. The Okriki Three, Momoh, this riot in town, and I think Tamuno is at the centre of it all. We have to get to the university.'

Folake is shaking her head in protest. 'To do what?'

'Find him!' I turn to Chika but see that he's already heading back to the car.

'I'm coming with you,' Folake says as if it's a done deal.

'*No.*' There's no way I am taking her back through what we just escaped.

'You gotta be kidding me. There's no way I'm staying here while you go back out there –'

I cradle her face in my hands. 'They need you here. Your calm, your logic. Mercy might break down and Elechi and her mom won't know what to do. I can't stay, but you can. Please, baby.'

I kiss her before she can form an argument. 'I'll be right back. I promise.'

'You better,' she sobs, tears streaming down her face.

I run to the Land Cruiser and have barely climbed in when Chika reverses at top speed. I catch one last look at Folake, her face stained with tears, and I'm determined that this won't be the last image I'll have of my wife.

MAYHEM

It's madness in the town centre.

Chika manoeuvres through the crowds of people brandishing leaves and chanting war songs. Many young men pound on the hoods of the cars struggling to drive through town. I knew Okriki was larger than the average town, but I never imagined so many people lived here. All of them angry.

I turn to Chika. 'You think the police station route will be lighter?'

'Let's try it.'

I redial Inspector Omereji but he's doesn't answer. Chika veers off the road that is teeming with angry crowds and starts to drive through farmlands, and the backyards of houses. I hold on for dear life as the Land Cruiser bounds unsteadily over uneven ground and we near the police station.

We get out of the car and run in.

'There's no one here!' I almost scream in frustration.

Chika is about to say something when my phone rings.

'We have them!' Inspector Omereji says as soon as I pick up and put him on speaker.

'Them?' I ask, not pausing our race out of the station.

'All of them in one place. They did it, Philip! They planned it all.'

'Who?'

'Amaso Dabara and some kids from campus. We have them. The laptop, the drugs. Everything! We got them!'

My brain is going in many directions, but I try to calm it. There is a noisy crowd coming towards the police station from the direction of Madam Landlady's compound, meaning they are coming from the bus stop at the roundabout. The same direction that the mob that attacked the Okriki Three came from. I stem my panic and try to focus, ignoring the pain that's coming from my bandaged ribs.

'Listen to me, Mike, do you have a guy called Tamuno there?'

'Hey, which of you is Tamuno?! You! Answer me!' He comes back to me. 'There's no Tamuno here –'

'Where are you?'

'At Harcourt Whyte.'

'Which room?'

'481.'

Realisation hits me and I grab on to Chika's arm as my legs almost give way. 'It's a diversion, Mike! You have to come back here. The town needs police more than ever. Whatever Tamuno was planning is here. Off campus. Come back quickly!'

A petrol bomb flies through the air and lands on the rusty roof of the police station. The fire is immediate, spreading as another petrol bomb hits it from another side.

We run into the Land Cruiser and Chika throws it into gear and hightails it.

Inspector Omereji is still on the phone. 'Philip!' he yells. 'Who's Tamuno? What's going on?!'

'Come now! There's –'

The rear windshield of the Land Cruiser shatters.

'Oh, shit!' Chika cries out just as I also see it. A petrol bomb inside the car. There's no time for me to climb into the back, pick it up and throw it out, but I'll try all the same.

Chika makes to grab me. 'You won't make it! We have to jump!'

A searing pain tears through my ribs as I reach as far as I can towards the petrol bomb. Chika is driving fast, and his sudden swerve throws me to the side, stopping my progress.

'Jump!' Chika shouts.

He opens his door, not stopping the car as we speed through the very section of road where Winston, Bona and Kevin were beaten and led to their deaths. The same place we almost lost our lives. This thought spurs me. I open the door on my side, the road spinning beneath me, and the crowd receding behind us.

'Jump!' Chika shouts again.

I close my eyes and roll on to the hard earth, the pain in my sides making me see a bright hot light. I yell and open them in time to see the Land Cruiser explode in front of us.

LAST SUPPER

'I have a surprise for you. From all of us,' Father Ambrose whispers in the kitchen.

John Paul smiles and asks what it could be.

Father Ambrose grins. 'It's a secret,' he says. 'We've been planning it for some time.'

John Paul waits until Father Ambrose carries the bucket of bread loaves to the dining hall and then he gets to work. From under his cassock, he brings out pouches filled with tablets. He goes to the door of the kitchen and peeks into the dining hall. The priests are trickling in, chatting amongst themselves while Father Ambrose places bread on the eight tables.

John Paul walks back into the kitchen and goes to the pot and empties the pouches of neurotoxins into it. He'd tested the same composition on Godwin, so he is sure of its potency.

He takes two old towels and wraps them around his hands to allow him to carry the hot pot. It is heavy, but he carries it as easily as he has done the past eleven years. Some of the monks wave at him and he smiles back at them.

Do they know Mama is dead? Is that why they are being so nice?

Clearly, no one is aware of the chaos in town. It's safe to assume it won't be long before the injured and fatally wounded from the riots in town rush to the monastery, looking for help.

John Paul walks back into the kitchen briskly. He works fast, putting the last of the poison in the drinking water, properly measured so as not to overtly affect the taste.

John Paul uses the kitchen knife to deftly create a hole in the rubber pipe behind the ancient cooker that supplies the gas burners. He pours water in a large pot and puts it on the naked flame. In case Father Ambrose comes in, he must think the boiling water is for drinking and not switch off the gas.

John Paul checks the gas pipe again. It's leaking fast. Too fast. The flame beneath the pot is flickering; not getting enough fuel to keep burning. He should have thought of this.

He walks to the pantry and retrieves the Sellotape. Working quickly, he seals a significant portion of the hole he had opened. The flame beneath the pot of water steadies.

Satisfied, John Paul then turns the control of the gas cylinder anti-clockwise, causing the gas to leak from there. Now, he needs to guess how long it will take for the gas to fill the kitchen, since all his earlier calculations had been based on a leak from the pipe rather than from the faster control switch. He must hurry.

He places the poisoned jugs of water on the old trolley that Father Ambrose had used for years to wheel food into the dining room. Eight jugs. Eight tables. He pushes the trolley into the dining room and stops when he sees where Father Olayiwola and another monk place a cake on the largest of the tables.

Suddenly, the room bursts into cheers and there is a lot of clapping. The monks come one by one to hug him, patting *his back, congratulating him. They pull him towards the cake and he makes out the writing on the icing.*

'Congratulations to our lawyer!' they cheer.

No! Don't be nice, I shout from the shadows. Not today!

They pray over John Paul, thinking he is me. They clap, and sing, while John Paul smiles, desperate for them to start eating. He sees Father Ambrose taking over the water trolley and his eyes follow the old monk as he places a jug on each of the tables.

The monks insist John Paul makes a speech but he pretends to be self-conscious and stumbles through a smattering of thank yous to the monks. As his expression assumes that of humble appreciation, I see his eyes counting the monks in the dining hall. The celebration means all of them are accounted for. All forty-seven. There is no one in the prayer room, dispensary or running errands in the chapel. They are all here.

I watch them all from the shadows as the eating and drinking begin, and the monks are trading stories about some of my escapades in the past years. They make fun of me and when John Paul feigns laughter, they think it is me and laugh too.

I want this. This joy. Redemption. Love. I've wanted these for so long.

Even in the shadows, I swear I can hear the hissing of air from the gas cylinder in the kitchen. I look at the monks drinking poisoned water and eating poisoned food. Soon, there will be vomit and then the inevitable paralysis that will make them unable to run from the fire.

Suddenly, it hits me that this is the only home I know. That I will ever know.

I think of Mama. Gone forever. A part of me wanted more time with her. Hearing her laugh and call me her gift from God. Her Tamunotonye.

My mother.

And John Paul killed her.

I killed my mother.

John Paul is in me. I am John Paul.

There it is. The truth that must be faced.

I close my eyes in the shadows and let the laughter of the monks usher me towards the light.

John Paul pauses as he cuts a piece of cake. He sees me coming. But he can't stop me. The happiness of the priests makes everything brighter until I can touch the light. I see John Paul's hand tremble as he holds the cake to his mouth.

But I am the one who reaches for the water.

AFTERMATH

With the smouldering hulk of the Land Cruiser behind us, Chika and I ran into the bush and beat a path back to the Oparas' house, avoiding the chaos on the main roads.

There, we waited, listening to the sounds of violence, huddled in the living room with the women, subdued and scared, my aches abated by my medicines which Folake had brought in her handbag. Mercy was sedated, asleep in her room and thankfully unaware of the fear and agitation that had the whole town in its grip.

The explosion in the distance, far away from where we were, we would later learn to be from the Monastery of the Anargyroi Order of St Cosmas and Damian. This added to the confusion. Did the Muslims go there too?

When helicopters had flown over the roof and we had heard several sirens in the distance, I called Omereji and he confirmed that the state had appealed to the federal government for support, and the result was an invasion of heavily armed military police in Okriki. But it was still some time before anyone knew where the explosion came from and for any kind of help to be rendered to the monks.

There were no survivors. The place was razed to the ground and Omereji's eyes were red with exhaustion and a deep sadness as he relayed what the police, firemen and other volunteers had seen at the monastery.

'You think the boy did it?' I asked as Omereji drove Chika, Folake and me back to PH.

'We have to assume he did.'

'So, instigating the riot was some kind of diversion to prevent help from getting to the monastery?' Folake asked from the back seat where she sat next to a quiet and uncomfortable Chika.

'Again, we don't know; we can only assume that the boy planned everything all along. Why he did it?' Omereji sighed. 'Unless we can find him to explain, we can only guess.'

I could already see he wouldn't stop until he found Tamuno Princewill and made him answer for his heinous crimes, or at least proved his innocence.

We would have asked more questions on that drive back to PH, but Omereji was both distraught and distracted. It was in contemplative silence that we arrived back at our hotel.

It's been two days now, and as much as Folake and I are eager to get back to our lives in Lagos, she understands why I need to see this through. I know that while she has chosen not to come with Chika and me to the police headquarters in PH, she won't be lying in the comfortable bed at the Tropicana but pacing the room. Worried and restless. This is perhaps the most horrible legacy of exposure to unexpected unrest and violent mob actions: a morbid sense of dread that it will happen again. Anytime, anywhere.

The police station in Okriki couldn't contain the number of arrests made during the violent unrest in the town, so almost all – both Christians and Muslims – who were suspected of being involved were transported to the police headquarters in PH. It is also where Amaso Dabara, his henchmen and four undergraduate students of the State University are being held. Which is why Chika and I are now being ushered into a room to observe what we are told is the fifth interrogation of the drug lord in the two days since he was arrested in Room 481 at the Harcourt Whyte Hall.

'I was played! We were all played,' the skinny man in handcuffs says.

'That's what you keep saying but the evidence says otherwise,' Inspector Mike Omereji bears down on Amaso, his disdain evident.

'What evidence?' Amaso asks.

'What we found when we searched your house in Havana. Everything that proves you are the mastermind behind all the violence in Okriki.'

'That's a lie! Ask everyone – even your fellow police – Amaso only sells drugs. I don't do politics. I don't do religion.'

'The list of your transactions, the telephone calls you made to your suppliers are not making things look good for you.'

Amaso looks at Inspector Omereji with bloodshot eyes and I can see his hands are shaking and his nose is dripping. Forty-eight hours in jail cannot be good for a drug addict. I've no doubt Amaso will crack soon, but I'm not sure he'll say anything that can shed light on how Tamuno Princewill played everyone and disappeared. Like all of us, I suspect Amaso Dabara doesn't know.

'I've told you. It's that boy, Tamuno. He planned it all.'

And Amaso tells it again: how he approached Tamuno when the boy was a freshman and recruited him.

'That boy is the devil! He set me up. Gave me the hard drive and the phones. He told me it contained the names of the distributors. Then he set up a meeting with his buyers and made me come, then disappeared …'

'It's not adding up, Amaso,' Omereji says. 'Why would this Tamuno go to this extent to set you up? The laptop in Room 481 was the one used to post the messages that caused the fighting in Okriki. One of the phones in that room belonged to that boy who was one of the Okriki Three. Yet you say you don't know how all of this got into a room that you clearly had access to. Can't you see how ridiculous you sound?'

'I'm telling the truth! I wanted to deal with that Godwin boy when we found out he was blabbing his mouth around, but Tamuno told me he would do it. I told you this before!'

I turn away from the one-way mirror towards Chika.

'He doesn't know any more.'

'You reckon?'

'He's an addict who's desperate for a fix,' I explain. 'Very soon he'll start crying and will say anything to get to his drugs. Whatever he says after that point will be virtually useless because it will be whatever Omereji wants to hear.'

'So, there was no point in our coming here then?'

'Oh, there is. Let Omereji finish and we can ask for access to those files on the hard drive Amaso claims Tamuno gave him.'

'Did you hear what he said?' Chika says, his face turned towards the one-way mirror, 'about the cell phone that belongs to one of the boys?'

'If it's true and it belongs to one of them, then that, my friend, is when we can officially say we've solved the mystery of the Okriki Three.'

GETTING TO WHY

Emeka won't set foot in Okriki, so I'm grateful to Mike Omereji for agreeing to meet with him at the National Bank guest house in PH.

'It's the least I can do,' the Inspector had said when I called to inform him that I was preparing to give my final report to Emeka and would appreciate his presence.

Chika and I arrive at the guest house and I'm impressed to see Omereji already there, waiting next to his car and dressed in his full police uniform. We exchange pleasantries and my respect for the officer soars when he shakes Chika's hand as if there was never any animosity between them.

We walk into the house and are ushered into the living room by Emeka's driver.

Emeka is unshaven, but looks better than the last time I saw him. He welcomes us and asks us to sit.

'Before we start, sir,' Omereji begins, 'I want to formally, on behalf of the people of Okriki, offer my sincerest condolences for the loss of your son.'

Emeka looks at him, unsure how to react to the unexpected opening.

'I assure you, sir, that in light of some of what Dr Taiwo and his colleague have been able to uncover, I will do everything in my power to reopen the investigation and bring the people involved to justice.'

'Your father will never let you do that,' Emeka says bitterly.

'My father is old and at times misguided in his beliefs. The events of the past few days have shown him that the only way to protect his people is by making sure there are consequences for actions that threaten the peace and prosperity of Okriki. I promise you sir, justice shall be served.'

Emeka looks away. The bitterness and anger he has harboured for close to two years can't be easily erased but he is gracious enough to respect Omereji's sincerity.

An awkward silence follows and I look at Omereji, my brow arched in a silent question. He nods at me to proceed and I clear my throat. There is no easy way to do this.

'Emeka, we can confirm that Kevin was neither part of a cult nor any gang intent on robbing Godwin Emefele.'

Emeka's face becomes alert, and my heart breaks for the hope I see in his tired eyes.

'The Police were recently able to recover Kevin's phone and when we looked through his messages, it became clear that he somehow stumbled on a fellow student's drug-trafficking ring.'

'How?'

'Sir,' Inspector Omereji says, 'it seems Kevin's friend Momoh Kadiri was the one who discovered that Tamuno Princewill was selling drugs on campus. To silence Momoh, we believe this Tamuno set him up by sending him pornographic images that suggested Momoh was a homo-sexual. He then tipped off the police who arrested Momoh based on what they saw on his phone. When Momoh died in custody, Kevin suspected foul play and started a campaign to investigate his death.'

Emeka's face is reminiscent of Folake's expression when we were combing through the numerous files on what we now know to be Tamuno's laptop, and the messages on Kevin's phone.

'A lot is still not clear, especially because we can't find this Tamuno boy anywhere,' I quickly add. 'But from what we have gathered so far, it seems Kevin did some digging of his own and somehow traced Momoh's arrest to Godwin Emefele, who was buying drugs from this Tamuno to sell and use. We cannot say for sure whether Momoh's inhaler was stolen at the time of his arrest, but we know he had an asthma attack in custody and that's how Kevin managed to link his death to the people selling drugs on campus.'

'And that is it? Kevin was killed because he discovered drug pushers on campus?'

'He was threatening to expose Godwin and Tamuno if they didn't come clean about Momoh,' I say, nodding.

'Why didn't he come to me?' Emeka says, agonised. 'I would have told him to let it go.'

'Maybe because he knew you would say that,' I say as gently as I can.

Emeka squares his shoulders, and I'm worried he'll break down again, but after some time, he raises his head and looks at Chika, Omereji and myself with determined eyes.

'How did he do it? This Tamuno. How did he get my son killed?'

Chika and the Inspector look at me and I take that as the cue for me to be the one to answer. 'We think he convinced

Godwin to invite two of his buyers who had not been paying off their debts over to his room off campus ...'

'Bona and Winston?'

'Yes,' I nod. 'Godwin somehow convinced them to come to his room and get new supplies and discuss a payment plan for their outstanding debts. From the detailed messages between him and Tamuno on the laptop we recovered from the latter's room, it seems Godwin was told to demand his money from Bona and Winston at gunpoint.'

'The gunshots people heard?' Emeka asks, looking at Chika.

'We believe Godwin was the one who shot at Bona and Winston,' Chika answers with a nod.

'But why did Kevin go there?' Emeka asks, still shaking his head in disbelief.

'Tamuno asked him to come,' I answer. 'From Kevin's messages we could deduce that Tamuno invited him to come for a discussion so they could clear the air.'

'And this Tamuno was so calculating that he was able to predict what would happen if the neighbours heard that a robbery was in progress?' Emeka asks in understandable wonder.

'I've seen how easy it is for people to be manipulated, Emeka,' I say sadly. 'All it takes is careful observation of trends and behavioural patterns and it can be pretty easy to make people do what you want them to do. Especially in a group.'

'I'm ashamed to admit it, sir,' Inspector Omereji says solemnly, 'but Dr Taiwo is right. Okriki people have been victims of several robberies blamed on the university students in the past. The unemployed youths who couldn't get admission into that university also harbour a lot of resentment against the students. This Tamuno boy certainly knew this and used it for his diabolical plans. My towns-people fell for it.' His voice trails off as he shakes his head sadly.

'So, Kevin was the real target and Bona and Winston were what? Collateral damage?'

It was not the time to tell the older man about the disturbing video we had found on the hard drive from Room 481. The gruesome images of Kevin's last moments are only matched in horror by the ones of Godwin Emefele gasping for air and finding death. It's also not pertinent to share our suspicions about Tamuno's role in the recent violent unrest in Okriki. We are all still grappling with the enormity of his machinations and for now, it's best to stick to why Emeka had hired me in the first place.

'This boy, Tamuno, you say ...' Emeka sounds as perplexed as we all are. 'Where is he? Where is this monster?'

None of us has an answer.

HOME

Folake has boarded Emeka Nwamadi's private jet. I am now alone with Omereji on the part of airstrip where the rich and powerful are spared the ordeal of ordinary citizens travelling through the Port Harcourt International Airport. The events of the past few days have taken a toll and we both look like what we have been through has marked us.

'You think he got away with it?' I ask Omereji.

'We can't trace him. They are still identifying the bodies at the monastery but we can't know for sure if he was there.'

'It doesn't matter. There will always be a Tamuno around us. You see it everywhere. Politicians. Businessmen. People who prey on our fear of each other for their selfish gains.'

'It scares me,' Omereji says sadly. 'And it's true what you say. But what scares me the most is seeing how easily people can be manipulated.' He shakes his head as if to banish a terrible vision. 'And we still can't figure out why he started the social media thing –'

I shrug. 'Who knows with someone like that? When they succeed at first, they try again and again, getting bolder, thinking bigger. He was definitely a narcissist, who wanted us to know what he did and got away with. You can see it in the evidence he left behind in his room. He probably saw the whole world as some kind of a social experiment, a lab full of rats, with him as the mastermind. I'm sure the social media campaign was his final show of power, to prove to himself what he's capable of.'

Inspector Omereji shakes his head at this. 'I'm ashamed of my people –'

'They're human, first and foremost. Easy to manipulate. Quick to act and without thinking. You'd be amazed how common that is.'

Omereji sighs and I see the captain of the plane waving at us. It is time.

'We must keep in touch,' Omereji says as he shakes my hand.

I agree and turn towards the plane's short flight of steps. My phone beeps, and before I climb in, I open it.

'Emeka called me. Told me everything you did. I am very proud of you, my son. Thank you and come home safe.'

I breathe in deeply, revelling in the simple joy of my father's approval. Yes, indeed, I did it.

I head on to the plane. Chika is sitting at the back. I wave at him and sit next to Folake.

'Well, Dr Taiwo, remind me to say no next time you get an assignment to write –' She holds her fingers in air quotes, 'a report.'

I laugh, not wanting to remind her that she did say 'no'. I fasten my seat belt. Then, I see Salome through the window. She is standing with Omereji and both of them are waving.

Lady and gentlemen, welcome to this private flight to Lagos –

I smile. She did come to say goodbye after all but perhaps respects Folake enough to do it from a distance. Or she came late, and used her cousin as her 'queue boy' to keep me talking until she got here. Classic Salome.

I wave back as the plane starts to move.

– the flight duration will be approximately fifty-five minutes –

The air shifts when Folake sees who I am waving at. She makes a production of her interest in the safety instructions being played on the screen.

We have been airborne for about fifteen minutes when I nudge her with my elbow. She turns her gaze to me.

'I liked her. She has a sharp mind and a kind heart.'

'And gorgeous as hell,' Folake says.

'Not like you.'

Folake snorts and looks away. I reach out and run a finger across her jawline till she turns to me.

'Not. Like. You. There's no one like you. And believe me when I say, nothing happened with Salome.'

'I know,' she says rather haughtily.

'How?'

'Because I'm here, with you. Even after all you thought you knew, you're here with me. Must be love.'

I burst out laughing and she joins me. We quickly turn to look behind us and see Chika is asleep, oblivious to us. We lean closer to each other.

'You're right,' I say. 'Must be love.'

She giggles, her laugh light and gay. I catch my breath and pull her into my arms.

We are like this, all the way to Lagos.

Home.

NOW READ ON FOR BONUS
MATERIAL EXCLUSIVE
TO THIS WATERSTONES
SPECIAL EDITION

YOU'RE WHAT YOU WRITE

BY FEMI KAYODE

Did you write in English? The email from the journalist arrived after an extensive one-on-one interview prior to the publication of my debut novel in Italy. I was a bit surprised. Our entire conversation was conducted in English, my bio gave very detailed evidence of my education in English speaking schools. Why would this nice journalist ask me that particular question?

I pondered this mystery as only a Black writer would. It is part of the baggage we've carried around ever since those of us from former colonies of England were required to write (and pay for) English proficiency tests to study, live or work in the UK, USA and Canada. The fact that 99% of these former colonies' educational systems are based on the English system – and that most, if not all, studies are done in English – appears to be lost on those who made this exploitative rule. This 'burden of proof' must be carried along with us every time we are told — very nicely too – that we 'speak English very well'. (Sick of this patronizing compliment, a friend once responded, 'Not by choice.') This 'baggage' and the carryover effect of my journey to writing *Lightseekers* influenced how I processed the interviewer's question.

During my MA at one of the most respected Creative Writing Programmes in Europe, I was taken aback by the dearth of texts by Writers of Colour. There was a *suggestion* we read Mosley's 'Devil in a Blue Dress', but we were *mandated* to read almost every classic crime novel written by a Caucasian, English-speaking male writer. At first, I thought this was because I was on a Crime Writing course, and this genre is still in its infancy in Africa. But on speaking to writers (of Colour) in other creative writing programmes, in other institutions across the UK, it seemed their experience was virtually the same as mine.

I got bored with the readings. This is not to cast aspersions on the very brilliant (Western) writers on the reading list. The fault was all mine. I could not identify with a lot of the stories, characters and plot. There was a similarity across most of these texts that unsettled me. Setting had no distinctive factor, context was missing and characters operated within an island of individual choices, which had hardly any ripple effect on the larger world they inhabit. You could literally transplant the whole story to another locale without changing a character or word of dialogue, and you'd miss nothing.

My angst about this admittedly subjective observation inspired my approach to writing *Lightseekers*. I was convinced that for readers to appreciate my world, they needed to have context, and for them to appreciate the story, they needed to experience the characters' lives through the lens of context. Context in crime fiction is a complex mix of culture, history, environment, weather, politics, sociology and more, which enable the crime under investigation and contribute to the unique challenges that will face those trying to solve it. If a reader cannot understand the impact of traffic on the average Nigerian, how can they appreciate the challenges an investigator will encounter while zipping from one state to another to solve a crime? If the writer does not give background on how the most populous nation in Africa gets less than two hours of electricity a week, it's hard for international readers to appreciate the levels of crime and corruption that the perennial lack of power enables and sustains.

Writing *Lightseekers* was an experiment of sorts. I wanted to know if it was possible to tell a different kind of crime story – one that is rich in the history and culture that shape the contemporary experiences of Nigerians – that reveal a world hitherto unknown and, therefore, misunderstood. I wanted to counter the existing rhetoric that's reinforced by mainstream media about my country in particular and Africa in general.

Writing the novel was not as difficult as pitching it though. Every time I had to tell the story to a panel, I found myself having to justify the complexity. I was encouraged to *simplify, compress* and *delineate*. Remove anything that did not drive the plot forward. It was hard to explain that this would be the most inauthentic approach for me. To fit my story into the narrow confines of existing models of crime writing would be a disservice to centuries of oppression, freedom fighters, civil wars and more. It would mean ignoring a time when my ancestors were masters of their own fate, blessed with immense creativity and a shrewdness in trade that would make Google's board meetings look like kindergarten. To streamline my story to the needful, to focus only on what is immediately important to the plot, would not acknowledge history, or effectively challenge the present.

Write a love letter to Nigeria. My tutor advised when this dilemma got too much for my mind to unravel. Suddenly, I was free. I let the characters tell me *their* stories, unrestrained by the demands of *my* plot. I allowed the story to expand, embracing the environment, the sights and sounds of the setting, the history, the food, and the culture. It was becoming a love letter indeed, albeit one with a heinous crime at its centre. But it was not the solving of the crime that was the sole purpose of the story – it was about how the crime revealed character(s), and unpeeled layers of myths that made it possible for the crime to happen.

Writing this way led to a discovery: I love my country. And because love is a complex emotion, I was able to embrace my angst about all that is wrong in Nigeria, while celebrating all that is good. I learnt to find connections and parallels with other parts of the world. Not just the conflict ridden or 'developing' ones, but parts that are deemed evolved, developed and 'civilized'. For instance, the impact of social media is relatively universal; the vulnerability to misinformation is not the preserve of the uneducated African, and while corruption has a cultural nuance, it does exist everywhere.

Did you write in English? Back to the Italian journalist. Upon reflection — my baggage notwithstanding — this is perhaps the most respectful question I have been asked since *Lightseekers* was published. The journalist did not take it for granted that I wrote the novel in English. He did not assume I pandered to an established model of storytelling that is proven to work, albeit not for every story or writer. He paid homage to my heritage by acknowledging that while I might be English-*speaking*, it does not mean I *am* English. In that moment of consideration, I almost wished I could write in my native Yoruba language. How wonderfully relevant and local my novel might have been if it was written in one of the over 200 indigenous Nigerian languages! But alas, I had a decidedly British-modelled education, and although I might still be required to take English proficiency examinations, I write in English. Apparently, well enough to be published. For now, that must be good enough.

ACKNOWLEDGEMENTS

The viral video of four young undergraduates of the University of Port Harcourt, being lynched and burnt alive, haunts me till today. The murders of Ugonna Obuzor, Toku Lloyd, Chiadika Biringa, and Tekena Elkanah inspired this book. I honor them and the victims of vigilantes across the world. It is my hope that this novel can contribute to any serious discourse about the prevalence and prevention of such violent crimes committed by mobs.

Writing this novel was an exorcism of sorts. I thank my tutor, William Ryan for seeing this desperate purpose and guiding me towards telling the story in my heart and in the process, restoring my love for my homeland.

Thank you Sodienye Kurubo, for late night chats, legal advice, well written research, a memorable tour of Port Harcourt and startling insights. I will be back.

My classmates at UEA were an invaluable source of support and guidance. Thank you to Dimitris Akrivos, Nicole Valentine, Peter Selby, Roe Lane, Louise Sharland, Mark Wightman, Denise Beardon, Freya Fowles, Amanda Rigali, Natalie Marlow and Niamh O'Connor. Bob Jones made my sporadic trips to the UK a treasure trove of friendship and guidance. Matthew Willis, through his frank feedback, committed editing, and late-night conversations, became a brother. My immense gratitude to Henry Sutton, Laura Joyce and Tom Benn, who were more than teachers, but a support system that I cherish to this day. Thank you, Ed Wood and Lucy Dauman of the Little, Brown/UEA Crime Fiction Award committee. Harriet Tyce opened her heart and home to me, and in her I found a champion long before I knew I needed one. I am grateful.

Harry Illingworth is my knight, guide, friend and agent. Many thanks to you and the team at DHH Literary Agency for believing in me and this book. Shout out to the dynamic duo of Jemma McDonagh and Camilla Ferrier at the Marsh Agency. Where my representation is concerned, indeed; *non, je ne regrette rien.*

Alison Hennessey is the *kapellmeister* of this book. She heard notes I didn't know were there, saw connections that eluded me, and pursued a nuanced performance, relentlessly. She gave this book lots of love and a home at Raven Books. I learnt so much, kicking and screaming all the way, but infinitely pleased with what she has helped me and this book become. Big thank you to Sara Helen Binney, Lilidh Kendrick, Emilie Chambeyron, Amy Donegan, Amy Wong and Jonathan Leech for holding my hands through this. Thank you, Emma Ewbank for the gorgeous cover design, Lin Vasey, whose brilliant copyediting smoothened out the edges, Sarah Bance, my eagle-eyed proofreader and the whole Bloomsbury UK and International sales team for having my back.

On dark days, I still retrieve the letter Josh Kendall wrote me just before acquiring the US rights to this book. His words inspired me, then and now. I am honored to call him my editor and privileged to have the passion of Alexandra Hoopes, Sareena Kamath, Pamela Brown, Alyssa Persons,

Bruce Nichols, Judy Clain and the entire sales team of Little, Brown/Mulholland Books behind me. Thank you.

Ade Fakoya, Femi Olawoyin, Anita Verna Crofts, Kehinde Bademosi, Pearl Osibu, Fabian Lojede, Unoma Azuah, Leye Adenle, Tsitsi Dangarembga, Jessica Ann Wheeler, Yinka Adeleke, Idiare Atimomo, Chika Olejeme, Tom Alweendo, Berlindi Van Eck, Bosede Ogunlana, Selma Neumbo and the inimitable Esosa Omo-Usoh were the early readers who said 'don't stop' when I needed to hear it most. Abius Akwaake pushed and challenged me while taking care of the things I didn't have the time or mind to do. Matthias Langheld gave time, space and friendship. My team at Adforce Advertising cheered on and forgave my long absences. I appreciate you all.

Chiedozie Dike. You deserve your own paragraph. Thanks for coming through every step of the way. I promise to retaliate.

Thank you to my parents, who encouraged my love for words and gave me my sister, Bose; my prayer warrior, cheerleader and number one fan, from day one.

My eternal gratitude to my best friend and wife, Nneka and the two wonderful humans we have been blessed to call our sons, Simi and Tomi. Thank you for making the home front free of the nightmare that inspired this book.

Above all, to God, who gave me this and more, thank you.